# THE RED ROVER

# THE RED ROVER

## JAMES FENIMORE COOPER

*Edited with an introduction by*

Warren S. Walker

UNIVERSITY OF NEBRASKA PRESS · Lincoln · 1963

813.2
C18r
71093
august 1970

# INTRODUCTION

IF James Fenimore Cooper had written nothing but his eleven tales of the sea, he still would have been a major figure in American literature, for with these works he shaped a special genre. From his time to our own the nautical novel has been a staple of prose fiction, produced alike by a host of popular writers—the Nordhoffs, the McFees, the Foresters—and by such masters as Melville and Conrad, both of whom acknowledged indebtedness to Cooper. Carl Van Doren was voicing the collective judgment of literary historians to his time when he declared in 1921 that Cooper had "created a new literary type."

Cooper's first sea story, *The Pilot,* was his fourth novel and his third consecutive best-seller. *Precaution* (1820), a society novel set in England and written in the manner of Jane Austen, had been a failure, but one which proved to be tonic: challenged by his critics to produce an American novel, Cooper responded with our country's first significant contribution to prose fiction, *The Spy* (1821). This historical romance of the American Revolution was indeed a native work, the first of its kind in many ways; none of its predecessors had employed so much indigenous material or evoked so much national pride. On both sides of the Atlantic, Cooper was seen as the long-heralded writer who would put America into literary works of epic proportion. That such acclaim was fully justified became apparent in 1823 when the "American Scott," as he was then called, published *The Pioneers,* the first Leatherstocking Tale in his five-volume saga of the American wilderness, which sold

3,500 copies on the first day. And then, in January of 1824, came *The Pilot*.

Just as Cooper had written his first novel after a challenge from his wife and the next two in answer to the exhortation of reviewers, so he began writing sea fiction on a dare. At a dinner party in New York City, he listened with growing irritation to the praise heaped on Sir Walter Scott's latest novel, *The Pirate*—annoyed not so much because he was jealous of Scott as because his friends attributed *vraisemblance*, or verisimilitude, to Scott's lubberly treatment of the nautical scenes. When he could forbear no longer, Cooper dissented in such sharp terms as to provoke an invitation to try and do better himself. Poor Scott, the unwitting competitor in this contest, never had a chance; he had neither love for the sea nor knowledge of its ways, while Cooper had both in abundance.

Cooper's knowledge of the sea had been gained at firsthand. In 1806, after his expulsion from Yale College for misconduct, he had been sent to sea before the mast. His father, long a champion in Congress of a large navy, saw a future for his son in the service; and in a day when there was no naval academy, a stint aboard a merchantman provided the basic nautical training for an officer. Young Cooper shipped out of New York on the *Stirling* to London, to Spain, back to London, and finally to the States—a voyage marked by such adventures as storms, impressment of crew members by a British man-of-war, and a hot chase by pirates off the coast of Portugal. In this year of hardship and rigorous duty, Cooper learned the ropes thoroughly, and on January 1, 1808, was issued a midshipman's warrant. His romantic dreams of a life on the rolling deep were, however, doomed to disappointment for, much to his chagrin, he was repeatedly assigned to shore duty. Other obstacles—

family responsibilities resulting from the death of his father in 1809, and his courtship of Susan DeLancey, whom he married on New Year's Day, 1811—blocked his sea-going career. He took what he thought would be no more than a year's leave to put his house in order, but he never returned to active duty.

Yet Cooper had fallen in love with the sea, and for the rest of his life returned to it at every opportunity. He accepted invitations from former naval colleagues, now ranking officers, to take cruises on American warships. One such junket occurred in 1842 when Commodore William Shubrick (to whom Cooper dedicated *The Pilot*) treated him to a twelve-day voyage aboard the *U.S.S. Macedonian*. Both at home and during his seven-year sojourn abroad, Cooper always chose to live within sight of navigable water. During a summer in Switzerland he rented a small sailboat on Lake Geneva, and back on Lake Otsego he kept afloat a yawl of his own. He was probably indulging his enthusiasm for sailing when he purchased a two-thirds interest in the whaleship *Union* in 1819. Whenever she was in her home port of Sag Harbor, Cooper personally took charge of the ship, outfitting her for the next voyage and testing her sea-worthiness in the coastal waters off Long Island. Although the venture was economically unprofitable, he allowed himself to lose money in it for three years before reluctantly selling his share in the *Union*.

In addition to his firsthand maritime experience, Cooper researched his subject so carefully that he became an authority on nautical matters. In 1839 he published a two-volume *History of the Navy of the United States,* devoted largely to the nascent navy of the early Republic, a study so thorough that it remained the definitive work until the twentieth century. The *History* went through several printings in the first decade after it appeared, and was soon translated into French and German. Subsequently, Cooper wrote ten biographical sketches of naval heroes for *Graham's Magazine,* collected in 1846 under the title *Lives of Distinguished American Naval Officers.* Of the two settings most frequently used in his novels, the forest and the sea, Cooper was far better acquainted with the latter. It is ironic that so many people today read his Leatherstocking Tales while so few read even the best of his nautical novels.

## II

Whether Cooper added more to the romance or to the realism of sea fiction has often been a point at issue among students of his novels. On whichever side the balance lies, the more important fact, confirmed by the debate, is the dual nature of his contribution to the genre. With his sublime and picturesque seascapes, his highly individualistic and often swashbuckling heroes, and his melodramatic plots, he added new dimensions to its romanticism; with his detailed descriptions of the operation of sailing ships, his sympathetic sketches of common deck hands, and his accurate portrayal of day-to-day shipboard life he set the nautical novel on a firm foundation of factual data.

Until Cooper appeared, the most "realistic" spinner of yarns had been the Scottish novelist Tobias Smollett, whose *Roderick Random* (1748) and *Peregrine Pickle* (1751) had included a number of nautical scenes, some of which provided new insights into the sailor's way of life. But Smollett had confined his maritime world to the Royal Navy, in which he had served as a surgeon, and he had projected the sea as the pathway *to* adventure rather than the pathway *of* adventure. Most of the action in his novels occurs ashore. The reader has only to compare Smollett's most seaborne novels with those of Cooper to measure the relative "saltiness" of their fiction. Only 17 per cent of *Roderick Random*, for example, takes place at sea, as opposed to 72 per cent of the action in *The Red Rover* and 99 per cent in Cooper's *Homeward Bound*.

Cooper's crews spend long hours hoisting anchors, furling sails, and manning the pumps, while his captains and mates supervise the men and attend to the details of navigation. It is by dint of hard work and not by any magic that ships alter course or change position at sea, and Cooper takes into account all the details of each maneuver. Thus, it requires a whole chapter (XII) for the *Royal Caroline* to move the very short distance from the wharf at Newport to the anchorage of the Rover's *Dolphin* at the mouth of the harbor. To appreciate Cooper's attempt at verisimilitude one has but to contrast such a full description with the brief paragraphs in which his predecessors often summarized voyages of a thousand miles. In a typical passage of *Roderick Random* (Chap. LXV), Smollett dismissed a trip of forty-odd days from West Africa to Uruguay with the barest possible log entry: "Our complement being made up, we took our departure from Cape Negro, and arrived in the Rio de la Plata in six weeks, having met with nothing remarkable in our voyage except an epidemic fever...." And then in the very next chapter the same short shrift is accorded the voyage from Uruguay to the West Indies: "...Coming on board of my uncle's ship, with the first favorable wind we sailed from the Rio de Plata, and in two months came safe to an anchor in the harbour of Kingston, in the island of Jamaica."

In an era when the novel was just evolving as a democratic form, Cooper's fiction focused sharply on the common man. His most memorable character creations are uneducated men, without fortune or social position. Often they are folk types as well as individuals; for example, Natty Bumppo serves as the *beau ideal* of the frontiersman, and Harvey Birch as that of the Yankee pack peddler (turned espionage agent for *The Spy*). In the nautical novels their folk counterpart is the "old salt," the deck hand who has lived so much at sea that he is awkward and uncertain ashore. Long Tom Coffin of *The Pilot* speaks for this type:

> "Give me plenty of sea-room and good canvas, where there is no occasion for pilots at all, sir. For my part, I was born on board a chebacco-man [a special type of fishing vessel used on the Grand Bank], and never could see the use of more land than now and then a small island to raise a few vegetables, and to dry your fish. I'm sure the sight of it always makes me feel uncomfortable, unless we have the wind dead offshore."

Similar figures had appeared in Smollett's works in the persons of Bos'n Pipes and Commodore Trunnion, but the Scottish satirist had made caricatures of them. With a character like Dick Fid in *The Red Rover,* Cooper went a long way toward humanizing the type, suggesting some of its rich oral tradition and reproducing accurately its briny dialect.

His ear for seaman's cant is but one indication of Cooper's general interest in language. His novels are filled with words and expressions peculiar to specific locales and social groups. The Glossary of Nautical Terms (see pages 523–529) attests to Cooper's extensive marine vocabulary, as well as to his fund of proverbs, colorful similes, and vigorous metaphors used by seamen in the age of sail.

Launching his sea tales at the height of Sir Walter Scott's popularity, Cooper worked at first in the romance tradition of the *Waverley* novels. His first three yarns are packed with high adventure, all of them taking to sea the pursuit-and-escape theme that he had exploited so successfully in *The Spy* and the Leatherstocking Tales. *The Pilot* draws upon the legend of John Paul Jones's hit-and-run tactics during the Revolutionary War; in *The Red Rover* the theme takes the form of piracy in the mid-eighteenth century, and in *The Water-Witch* (1830), smuggling in and around the harbor of colonial New York, 1710–1720. The laws of probability are frequently held in abeyance for the coincidence required by such plot-centered tales, although Cooper himself did not consider this unrealistic. He felt that mathematical chance, and the divine providence which man often interprets as chance, control human destiny:

> The foundations of great events are often remotely laid in very capricious and uncalculated passions, motives, or impulses. Chance has usually as much to do with the fortune of states, as with those of individuals; or, if there be calculations connected with them at all, they are the calculations of a power superior to any that exists in man.
>
> [Preface to *Satanstoe*]

But for many modern readers he pushes chance too far when he rigs his plots (as he does unnecessarily in *The Red Rover*) with such an age-old device of melodrama as the discovery of long-lost relatives.

The hunted (and sometimes haunted) titular heroes of novels like *The Pilot* and *The Red Rover* are romantic figures—noble, strong, individualistic, lonely, and, generally speaking, Byronic. In his Prefaces—as critically informative as those of Henry James—Cooper frequently claims the right of the novelist to draw his buskined figures larger than life-size: "A leading character in a work of fiction has a fair right to the aid which can be obtained from a poetical view of his subject." (Preface to the 1849 collected edition of the Leatherstocking Tales.)

Or, again: "All that is necessary is, that the pictures should be true to nature, if not absolutely drawn from living sitters. The knowledge we gain by our looser reading often becomes serviceable in modes and manners little anticipated in the moments when it is acquired." (Preface to *Afloat and Ashore*.)

Descendants of the traditionally aristocratic leads in literature, these upstage actors are, for modern readers, less believable than the earthy folk types Cooper was developing.

The love of Nature that infused the whole Romantic movement first found adequate expression in America in the landscape painting of the Hudson River School, in the poetry of William Cullen Bryant, and in the prose of Cooper. A close working relationship between the landscapists and the literati has been amply demonstrated by James Beard and others. The founders of American literature in the early nineteenth century were, in fact, often landscapists with pen instead of brush. Balzac found Cooper's rendering of the natural scene so picturesque that it "would drive to despair any novelist who felt the desire to follow in the footsteps of the American writer," and no one has praised Cooper's pictorial effects more fulsomely than did this contemporary French admirer:

> The art of writing never encroached more upon the art of painting. This is the school in which literary landscapists should study, for all the secrets of the art are there. This magic prose not only sets forth the peculiar characteristics of a river and its banks, a forest and its trees, but in achieving this it gives simultaneously both the details and the whole scene. The vast solitudes into which you penetrate become very complex and interesting. . . . When the spirit of solitude has spoken to you, when the tranquillity of the endless shad-

ows has charmed you, when you gaze down on the lush vegetation, your soul is thrilled. . . . You identify yourself with the
region; it becomes part of you and you part of it, without
being aware—because of his genius—just how the change is
effected; but it is impossible for you to separate the ground,
the vegetation, the waters, their extent and their shape from
the feelings which excite you.

[*Revue Parisienne,* 25 July, 1840. Author's translation.]

Cooper's seascapes were no less exciting than his forest
scenes in the judgment of Melville and Conrad, among
many others. In 1849 Melville reviewed for *The Literary
World* Cooper's last nautical tale, *The Sea Lions.* After
placing much of the action of the novel in Antarctic seas,
Cooper recreated the appropriate setting as it had been
reported by explorers and whalemen. Melville was moved
by the effects achieved: "Few descriptions of the lonely and
terrible, I imagine, can surpass the grandeur of many of
the scenes here depicted." And in the twentieth century
Conrad paid similar tribute to Cooper's treatment of the
sea:

For James Fenimore Cooper nature was not the framework,
it was an essential part of existence. He could hear its voice,
he could understand its silence, and he could interpret both
for us in his prose with all that felicity and sureness of effect
that belong to a poetical conception alone. . . . [He] loved
the sea and he looked at it with consummate understanding.
. . . His descriptions have the magistral ampleness of a gesture
indicating the sweep of a vast horizon. They embrace the
colours of sunset, the peace of starlight, the aspects of calm
and storm, the great loneliness of the waters, the stillness of
watchful coasts, and the alert readiness which marks men
who live face to face with the promise and the menace of
the sea.

[*Life and Letters*]

## III

Cooper wrote *The Red Rover* in the summer of 1827 while he was living at the little village of St. Ouen, on the Seine, near Paris. It sold better than any of his previous novels, and it won him many new readers in both this country and Europe, especially in Spain and France. Back home an anonymous critic for the *North American Review* argued at length that in writing *The Red Rover* Cooper had returned to his better self, the sea being a more suitable setting for his genius than the forest. He ended his condemnation of the Leatherstocking Tales by welcoming Cooper back aboard his proper vehicle:

> We are consequently disposed to greet him the more heartily on his own element. We are always well inclined to take a sea-breeze, after toiling for long days in tangled wilderness and heated towns. To no one, moreover, are we better inclined to submit ourselves on ship-board, surely with no one are we more ready to pass away the time, either above or below, in calm or tempest, than with our author. The quarter-deck is his home.
>
> [*North American Review,* XXVII, 1828]

In France the book became more closely associated with Cooper's name than any of his other works, except the Leatherstocking Tales. During the winter of 1851–1852, almost a quarter of a century after the publication of the novel, Berlioz renamed one of his more popular overtures *Le corsaire rouge* as a memorial to Cooper, who had died the autumn before.

Cooper probably touched more romantic chords in *The Red Rover* than in any of his other nautical tales. The maiden disguised as a man in order to be with her lover in his male world had long been a theme of ballads—"Jackie Munro" was one of the most popular—and "Roderick" fits the pattern perfectly. Equally legendary is the lore of the supernatural that Cooper includes in the novel. The *Dolphin* is made to appear a ghost ship as it gracefully glides, bare-masted and seemingly unmanned, past the sinking *Royal Caroline* at the height of the tempest. And Wilder, suspected of necromancy from the beginning of the voyage, now seems to his crew to be an agent of the phantom world sent to lead them all to their destruction. The resulting mutiny illustrates Cooper's ability to use folklore functionally. There is no need for even a momentary suspension of disbelief in the occult, for Cooper never suggests that the reader give it credence, but by motivating his characters with superstitions then popular among seamen, he invests the action of the whole story with overtones of the supernatural. For many modern readers his will be a more acceptable treatment of the "Flying Dutchman" motif than that rendered either by Coleridge in "The Rime of the Ancient Mariner" or by Poe in "MS. Found in a Bottle."

The use of piracy to provide the action of a novel presented both advantages and disadvantages to Cooper. It provided melodramatic materials for his pursuit-and-escape theme, of course, and it gave greater depth to the texture of romance in the book. American readers responded readily to tales of buccaneering, for the subject had become entwined with the history and legend of the new nation. America's first significant naval action had been the much-celebrated "war" with the Barbary Pirates between 1801 and 1805, and the exploits (and buried treasure) of Captain Kidd and Jean Lafitte had added new chapters to the annals of American folklore. Cooper found the pirate motif so appealing that he returned to it in the later novels—even in one of the Leatherstocking Tales. In *The Deerslayer* (1841) old Tom Hutter, the fresh-water sailor on Lake

Otsego, is finally identified as an ex-pirate in hiding. And one of the motives for the ill-starred voyage of the twin *Sea Lions* (1849) was an island cache of pirate gold. The chief difficulty with the subject was its moral liability. Could piracy sometimes be treated sympathetically, or must it always be viewed as totally criminal?

With the hero-villain of *The Red Rover*, Cooper came as close to resolving this dilemma as the mores of his time and his own sense of justice would permit. Although the hero-villain must die in the end for his offenses against society, both the extenuating circumstances involved in his becoming a freebooter and the ultimate sacrifice of his life for the cause of good finally bring him very close to redemption. The Rover is an American revolutionary born several decades too soon. An American in the Royal Navy, he fights a duel with an officer who has insulted his native land and, after killing his British opponent, has to flee the law. He then proceeds to carry on a one-man war against the Empire by preying on British shipping until the Declaration of Independence is enunciated, when he promptly joins the Patriot forces. He rationalizes his outlawry as an irony of history, and (for the American reader, at least) it does seem as if the time was out of joint and the Rover's life was part of the human price paid to set it right.

The Rover (hero-villain and antagonist to the main action) defends his way of life to the young protagonist, Wilder, who has been assigned the dangerous mission of capturing him:

> "You have seen my flags [the most striking of them the blood-red ensign from which he got his name], Mr. Wilder; but there was one wanting among them all; ay, and one which, had it existed, it would have been my pride, my glory to have upheld with my heart's best blood." . . .

"I will not affect to misunderstand your meaning [Wilder finally admitted], for I have known others as visionary as yourself in fancying that such an event may arrive."

"May!—As certain as that star will set in the ocean, or that day is to succeed night, it *must*. Had that flag been abroad, Mr. Wilder, no man would ever have heard the name of the Red Rover."

After the battle of Yorktown the fatally wounded Rover finds his long-sought flag at last, and he dies happily:

With supernatural effort, his form rose on the litter; and, with both hands elevated above his head, he let fall before him that blazonry of intermingled stripes, with its blue field of rising stars, a glow of high exultation illumining every feature of his face, as in his day of pride.

"Wilder!" he repeated, laughing hysterically, "we have triumphed!"—He fell backward, without motion, the exulting lineaments settling in the gloom of death, as shadows obscure the smiling brightness of the sun.

Through his genteel behavior and chivalry the Rover appeals further to both the protagonist and the reader. Although Wilder is sent to befriend the Rover and subsequently betray him to a British cruiser, he discovers in his quarry a most engaging personality. At the critical moment, when the Rover is in imminent danger of capture and possible execution, Wilder first delays identifying him and then persuades the British commander to offer him honorable terms of surrender (which are refused). The Rover, in turn, is equally magnanimous. When he discovers that Wilder and his two assistants are agents of the Crown aboard his ship, he returns them unharmed to the cruiser *Dart*. He has the essential nobility of character for a tragic hero. Wrong-headed and obsessive as old Ahab was later to be, the Rover also has many of the great whaler's more admirable qualities.

WARREN S. WALKER

# BIBLIOGRAPHY

THE earliest full-length life of Cooper was that of Thomas R. Lounsbury (Boston: Houghton Mifflin, 1882). More reliable are several recent biographies by Robert E. Spiller (New York: Minton Balch, 1931), Marcel Clavel (Aix-en-Provence: Universitaire de Provence, 1938), James Grossman (New York: Sloane, 1949), and Donald A. Ringe (New York: Twayne, 1962). James F. Beard has been working for years on what promises to be the definitive biography.

*The Correspondence of James Fenimore Cooper* (New Haven: Yale University Press, 1929), edited by his grandson, a useful reference, is in the process of being superseded by the more thorough *Letters and Journals of James Fenimore Cooper* (Cambridge: Harvard University Press, 1960), edited by James F. Beard. The first two volumes of Beard's work carry the letters through 1833.

Students of Cooper's nautical novels will find an excellent guide in Thomas Philbrick's *James Fenimore Cooper and the Development of American Sea Fiction* (Cambridge: Harvard University Press, 1961). Shorter studies of special merit are Louis Bolander's "The Naval Career of James Fenimore Cooper," *U.S. Naval Institute Proceedings,* LXVI (1940), 541–550; William H. Bonner's "Cooper and Captain Kidd," *Modern Language Notes,* LXI (1946), 21–27; Harold H. Scudder's "Cooper and the Barbary Coast," *Publications of the Modern Language Association,* LXII (1947), 184–192; Walter Muir Whitehill's "Cooper as a Naval Historian," *New York History,* XXXV (1954), 468–479; and Warren S. Walker's "The Gull's Way," in his *James Fenimore Cooper:*

xix

*An Introduction and Interpretation* (New York: Barnes & Noble, 1962). Background material for the "Flying Dutchman" motif in American literature can be found in Ralph des Childs' "Phantom Ships off the Northeast Coast of North America," *New York Folklore Quarterly,* V (1949), 146–165.

# THE RED ROVER

# CONTENTS

Introduction by Warren S. Walker     v

Bibliography     xix

A Note on the Text     5

Title page of the 1859
   "Darley Edition"     6

Preface     9

The Red Rover     13

Glossary of Nautical Terms     523

# A NOTE ON THE TEXT

The first edition of *The Red Rover* was published, in two volumes, by Carey, Lea & Carey of Philadelphia in 1828. It soon went through several editions and was translated into all of the major European languages. Until now there has been no text of the novel available to twentieth-century readers except those in the collected editions, the last of which was published by Putnam between 1895 and 1900. The definitive edition of Cooper's fiction is generally acknowledged to be the thirty-two-volume set published by W. A. Townsend of New York in the years 1859–1861, often called the "Darley Edition" out of respect for its noted illustrator, F. O. C. Darley. The text and prints of this edition are reproduced for the present volume.

# THE RED ROVER.

"The limb stiffened and fell, though the eyes still continued
their affectionate and glaring gaze on that countenance he had
so long loved, and which, in the midst of all his long endured wrongs,
had never refused to meet his look of love in kindness."

*Chap. XXXI. Page 505.*

NEW YORK, W. A. TOWNSEND & C<sup>o</sup>

*Title page of the 1859 "Darley Edition"*

# PREFACE.

Smollett had obtained so much success as a writer of nautical tales, that it probably required a new course should be steered in order to enable the succeeding adventurer in this branch of literature to meet with any favor. This difficulty was fully felt when this book was originally written, and probably has as much force to-day as it had then, though nearly a quarter of a century has intervened.

The history of this country has very little to aid the writer of fiction, whether the scene be laid on the land or on the water. With the exception of the well-known, though meagre incidents connected with the career of Kidd, indeed, it would be very difficult to turn to a single nautical occurrence on this part of the continent in the hope of conferring on a work of the imagination any portion of that peculiar charm which is derived from facts clouded a little by time. The annals of America are surprisingly poor in such events; a circumstance that is doubtless owing to the staid charac-

ter of the people, and especially to that portion of them
which is most addicted to navigation.

These difficulties were duly appreciated by the writer
of this book, who found it necessary to invent his legend
without looking for the smallest aid from traditions or
facts.    There is no authority whatever for any incident,
character, or scene, of the book now offered to the
reader, unless nature may be thought to furnish origi-
nals, in a greater or less degree, to some of the pictures.

A good deal of speculation has been resorted to by
different writers, in order to discover the history and
uses of the little stone ruin in which one of our incidents is laid.    Those who are not content to accept of
a simple solution of this antiquarian problem, have assailed the irreverent manner in which we have termed
it a mill, and have claimed for the little structure an
original as remote as the times of the Northmen who
are supposed to have preceded Columbus in his voyage
to this western hemisphere.    We pretend to no exclusive knowledge on the subject, never having seen this
much-talked of ruin but once, and then only in a hurried visit of a single half-hour.    It must be confessed
that it struck the writer as the very obvious remains of
a wind-mill, and as nothing else; though there may be
better reasons than any he can give to the contrary for
supposing it to have been erected as a fortress several
centuries ago.    We can imagine the use in placing a
mill on arches, as it is a very simple process, and one
often had recourse to, in order to prevent the ravages
of the mice; but it is not so easy to see why the extra
labour of forming arches, the loss of room, and the ad-

ditional risk from fire, should all be voluntarily incurred to raise up a fortress against savages. Under no circumstances, it would seem, could such a tower be less expensive, less difficult to construct, and less secure, by building it up as a solid structure from the ground, than by raising it in the air, on senseless because useless pillars, as must have been the case, if we are to suppose the building to have been erected for purposes of defence. The lower apartment, which, on this antiquarian theory, would be thrown away, might have been of great daily utility, as it certainly would have added to the strength of the tower; thus reducing these poor Northmen to the dilemma of having it inferred that their intelligence was of so low a stamp as to lead them to expend their time and labour in raising an elaborate structure that would be less likely to effect all their objects than one much more simple.

We trust this denial of the accuracy of what may be a favourite local theory, will not draw down upon us any new evidence of the high displeasure of the Rhode Island Historical Society, an institution which displayed such a magnanimous sense of the right, so much impartiality, and so profound an understanding of the laws of nature and of the facts of the day, on a former occasion when we incurred its displeasure, that we really dread a second encounter with its philosophy, its historical knowledge, its wit, and its signal love of justice. Little institutions, like little men, very naturally have a desire to get on stilts; a circumstance that may possibly explain the theory of this extraordinary and very useless fortification.

We prefer the truth and common sense to any other mode of reasoning, not having the honour to be an Historical Society at all. That which we have elsewhere written, and in a graver capacity, we think has been triumphantly vindicated; and we have given our reasons here for disbelieving the theory of the citadel of the Northmen. If others prefer to tilt with a windmill, we commend them to their own gallantry and the sympathy of Sancho Panza. Thank Heaven! we have never published any thing which involves the necessity of believing that four vessels, with their topsails aback, drifted round the whole earth in two hours and a half, in straight lines, regardless of islands and continents; which creates the necessity of supposing that a crippled craft will drift to windward; or have asserted that any particular battle, the property of the whole nation, belongs to "the naval annals of New York." They who have maintained these historical and philosophical *tours de force*, are quite right to top off their mental labours by maintaining that the "Newport Ruin" was a dwelling of the Cæsars!

Cooperstown, January 1, 1850.

# THE RED ROVER.

## CHAPTER I.

PAR. Mars dote on you for his novices.
*All 's Well that ends Well.*

No one who is familiar with the bustle and activity of an American commercial town, would recognise, in the repose which now reigns in the ancient mart of Rhode Island, a place that, in its day, has been ranked amongst the most important ports along the whole line of our extended coast. It would seem, at the first glance, that nature had expressly fashioned the spot to anticipate the wants and to realize the wishes of the mariner. Enjoying the four great requisites of a safe and commodious haven, a placid basin, an outer harbour, and a convenient road-stead, with a clear offing, Newport appeared to the eyes of our European ancestors designed to shelter fleets, and to nurse a race of hardy and expert seamen. Though the latter anticipation has not been entirely disappointed, how little has reality answered to expectation in respect to the former! A successful rival has arisen, even in the immediate vicinity of this seeming favourite of nature, to defeat all the calculations of mercantile sagacity, and to add another to the thousand existing evidences "that the wisdom of man is foolishness."

There are few towns of any magnitude within our broad
territories, in which so little change has been effected in half a
century as in Newport.   Until the vast resources of the interior
were developed, the beautiful island on which it stands was a
chosen retreat for the affluent planters of the south, from the
heats and diseases of their burning climate.   Here they resorted
in crowds to inhale the invigorating breezes of the sea.
Subjects of the same government, the inhabitants of the Carolinas and of Jamaica met here in amity, to compare their
respective habits and policies, and to strengthen each other in a
common delusion, which the descendants of both, in the third
generation, are beginning to perceive and to regret.

The communion left on the simple and unpractised offspring
of the Puritans its impression both of good and evil.   The inhabitants of the country, while they derived from the intercourse
a portion of that bland and graceful courtesy for which the gentry
of the southern British colonies were so distinguished, did not
fail to imbibe some of those peculiar notions concerning the
distinctions in the races of men for which they are no less remarkable.   Rhode Island was the foremost among the New-
England provinces to recede from the manners and opinions of
their simple ancestors.   The first shock was given through her,
to that rigid and ungracious deportment which was once believed
a necessary concomitant of true religion, a sort of outward pledge
of the healthful condition of the inward man; and it was also
through her that the first palpable departure was made from those
purifying principles which might serve as an apology for even
more repulsive exteriors.   By a singular combination of circumstances and qualities, which is however no less true than perplexing, the merchants of Newport were becoming, at the same
time, both slave-dealers and gentlemen.

Whatever might have been the moral condition of its proprietors at the precise period of 1759, the island itself was

never more enticing and lovely. Its swelling crests were still crowned with the wood of centuries; its little vales were then covered with the living verdure of the north; and its unpretend-ing, but neat and comfortable villas, lay sheltered in groves, and embedded in flowers. The beauty and fertility of the place gained for it a name which probably expressed far more than was properly understood at that early day. The inhabitants of the country styled their possessions the "Garden of America." Neither were their guests from the scorching plains of the south reluctant to concede this imposing title. The appellation de-scended even to our own time; nor was it entirely abandoned until the traveller had the means of contemplating the thousand broad and lovely valleys which fifty years ago lay buried in the dense shadows of the forest.*

The date we have just named was a period fraught with the deepest interest to the British possessions on this continent. A bloody and vindictive war, which had been commenced in defeat and disgrace, was about to end in triumph. France was deprived of the last of her possessions on the main, while the immense region which lies between the Bay of Hudson and the territories of Spain submitted to the power of England. The colonists had shared largely in contributing to the success of the mother-country. Losses and contumely, that had been incurred by the besotting prejudices of European commanders, were beginning to be forgotten in the pride of success. The blunders of Brad-dock, the indolence of Loudon, and the impotency of Aber-crombie, were repaired by the vigour of Amherst, and the genius of Wolfe. In every quarter of the globe, the arms of Britain were triumphant. The loyal provincials were among the loudest

---

* There is both a state and an island which bears the same name. Rhode Island (the state) is the smallest of the twenty-four sisters which compose the American Union. It is not so large as many English counties, has to-day a population not much exceeding one hundred thousand souls, and is well known for its manufacturing industry.

in their exultations and rejoicings; wilfully shutting their eyes to the scanty meed of applause that a powerful people ever reluctantly bestows on its dependants, as if love of glory, like avarice, increases by its means of indulgence.

The system of oppression and misrule, which hastened a separation that sooner or later must have occurred in the natural order of events, had not yet commenced. The mother-country, if not just, was still complaisant. Like all old and great nations, she was indulging in the pleasing but dangerous enjoyment of self-contemplation. The qualities and services of a race who were believed to be inferior were, however, soon forgotten; or, if remembered, it was in order to be misrepresented and vituperated. As this feeling increased with the discontent of the civil dissensions, it led to still more striking injustice and greater folly. Men who, from their observations, should have known better, were not ashamed to proclaim, even in the highest council of the nation, their ignorance of the character of a people with whom they had mingled their blood. Self-esteem gave value to the opinions of fools. It was under this soothing infatuation that veterans were heard to disgrace their noble profession by boastings that should have been hushed in the mouth of a soldier of the carpet: it was under this infatuation that Burgoyne gave, in the Commons of England, that memorable promise of marching from Quebec to Boston with a force he saw fit to name — a pledge that he afterwards redeemed by going over the same ground, with twice the number of followers as captives; and it was under this infatuation that England subsequently threw away her hundred thousand lives, and lavished her hundred millions of treasure.

The history of that memorable struggle is familiar to every American. Content with the knowledge that his country triumphed, he is willing to let the glorious result take its proper place in the pages of history. He sees that her empire rests on a broad and natural foundation, which needs no support from venal pens; and, happily for his peace of mind, no less than for his character, he feels that the prosperity of the republic is not to be sought in the degradation of surrounding nations.

Our present purpose leads us back to the period of calm which preceded the storm of the Revolution. In the early days of the month of October, 1759, Newport, like every other town in America, was filled with the mingled sentiments of grief and joy. The inhabitants mourned the fall of Wolfe, while they triumphed in his victory. Quebec, the stronghold of the Canadas, and the last place of any importance held by a people whom they had been educated to believe were their natural enemies, had just changed its masters. That loyalty to the crown of England, which endured so much before the strange principle became extinct, was then at its height; and probably the colonist was not to be found who did not, in some measure, identify his own honour with the fancied glory of the house of Brunswick. The day on which the action of our tale commences had been expressly set apart to manifest the sympathy of the good people of the town and its vicinity in the success of the royal arms. It had opened, as thousands of days have opened since, with the ringing of bells and the firing of cannon; and the population, at an early hour, had poured into the streets of the place, with that determined zeal in the cause of merriment, which ordinarily makes preconcerted joy so dull an amusement. The chosen orator of the day had exhibited his eloquence in a sort of prosaic monody in praise of the dead hero, and had sufficiently manifested his loyalty by laying the glory, not only of that sacrifice, but all that had been reaped by so many thousand of his brave companions also, most humbly, at the foot of the throne.

Content with these demonstrations of their allegiance, the inhabitants began to retire to their dwellings, as the sun settled towards those immense regions which then lay an endless and unexplored wilderness, but which now are teeming with the fruits and enjoyments of civilised life. The countrymen from the environs, and even from the adjoining main, were beginning to turn their face towards their distant homes, with that frugal care which still distinguishes the inhabitants of this portion of our country even in the midst of their greatest abandonment to pleasures, in order that the approaching evening might not lead them into expenditures which were not deemed germane to the proper feelings of the occasion. In short, the excess of the hour was past, and each individual was returning into the sober channels of his ordinary avocations, with an earnestness and discretion which proved he was not altogether unmindful of the time that had been squandered in the display of a spirit that he already appeared half disposed to consider as supererogatory.

The sounds of the hammer, the axe, and the saw were again heard in the place; the windows of more than one shop were half opened, as if its owner had made a sort of compromise between his interests and his conscience, and the masters of the only three inns in the town were to be seen standing before their doors, regarding the retiring countrymen with eyes which plainly betrayed that they were seeking customers among a people who were always much more ready to sell than to buy. A few noisy and thoughtless seamen, belonging to the vessels in the haven, together with some half dozen notorious tavern-hunters, were, however, the sole fruits of all their nods of recognition, enquiries into the welfare of wives and children, and, in some instances, of open invitations to alight and drink.

Worldly care, with a constant though sometimes an oblique look at the future state, formed the great characteristic of all that people who then dwelt in what were called the provinces of New England. Still the business of the day was not forgotten, though it was deemed unnecessary to digest its proceedings in idleness, or over the bottle. The travellers along the different roads that led into the interior of the island formed themselves into little knots, in which the policy of the great national events they had just been commemorating, and the manner they had been treated by the different individuals selected to take the lead in the offices of the day, were freely handled, though with great deference to the established reputations of the distinguished parties most concerned. It was every where conceded, that the prayers, which had been in truth a little conversational and historical, were faultless and searching exercises; and, on the whole, (though to this opinion there were some clients of an advocate adverse to the orator, who were moderate dissenters,) it was established, that a more eloquent oration had never issued from the mouth of man, than had that day been delivered in their presence. Precisely in the same temper was the subject discussed by the workmen on a ship which was then building in the harbour, and which, in the same spirit of provincial admiration that has since immortalised so many edifices, bridges, and even individuals within their several precincts, was confidently affirmed to be the rarest specimen then extant of the nice proportions of naval architecture!

Of the orator himself it may be necessary to say a word, in order that so remarkable an intellectual prodigy should fill his proper place in our frail and short-lived catalogue of the worthies of that day. He was the usual oracle of his neighbourhood, when a condensation of its ideas on any great event, like the one just mentioned, became necessary. His learning was justly computed, by comparison, to be of the most profound and erudite character; and it was very truly affirmed to have astonished more than one European scholar, who had been tempted by a fame which, like heat, was only the more intense from its being so confined, to grapple with him on the arena of ancient literature. He was a man who knew how to improve these high gifts to his exclusive advantage. In but one instance had he ever been thrown enough off his guard to commit an act that had a tendency to depress the reputation he had thus gained; and that was, in permitting one of his laboured flights of eloquence to be printed; or, as his more witty though less successful rival, the only other lawyer in the place, expressed it, in suffering one of his *fugitive* essays to be *caught.* But even this experiment, whatever might have been its effects abroad, served to confirm his renown at home. He now stood before his admirers in the dignity of types; and it was in vain for that miserable tribe of "animalculæ, who live by feeding on the body of genius," to attempt to undermine a reputation that was embalmed in the faith of so many parishes. The brochure was diligently scattered through the provinces, lauded around the teapot, openly extolled in the prints — by some kindred spirit, as was manifest in the similarity of style — and, by one believer, more zealous or perhaps more interested than the rest, it was actually put on board the next ship which sailed for "home," as England was then affectionately termed, enclosed in an envelope which bore an address no less imposing than that of the Majesty of Britain. Its effects on the straight-going mind of the dogmatic German who then filled the throne of the Conqueror were never accurately known, though they, who were in the secret of the transmission, long looked in vain for the signal reward that was to follow so favourable an exhibition of human intellect.

Notwithstanding these high and beneficent gifts, their possessor was now as unconsciously engaged in that portion of his professional labours which bore the strongest resemblance to the occupation of a scrivener, as if nature, in bestowing such rare endowments, had denied him the phrenological quality of self-esteem. A critical observer might, however, have seen, or fancied that he saw, in the forced humility of his countenance, certain gleamings of a triumph that might not be traced to the fall of Quebec. The habit of appearing meek had, however, united with a frugal regard for the precious and irreclaimable minutes, in producing

this extraordinary diligence in a pursuit of a character that was
so humble when compared with his recent mental efforts.

Leaving this gifted favourite of fortune and nature, we shall
now pass to an entirely different individual, and to another quarter of the place.   The spot to which we wish to transport the
reader, was neither more nor less than the shop of a tailor, who
did not disdain to perform the most minute offices of his vocation
in his own heedful person.   The humble edifice stood at no great
distance from the water, in the skirts of the town, and in such a
situation as to enable its occupant to look out upon the loveliness
of the inner basin, and, through a vista cut by the element between islands, even upon the lake-like scenery of the outer harbour.   A small, though little frequented wharf, lay before its
door; while a certain air of negligence, and the absence of bustle,
sufficiently manifested that the place itself was not the immediate
site of the much boasted commercial prosperity of the port.

The afternoon was like a morning in spring, the breeze which
occasionally rippled the basin possessing that peculiarly bland
influence which is so often felt in the American autumn; and
the worthy mechanic laboured at his calling, seated on his shop-
board at an open window, far better satisfied with himself than
many of those whose fortune it is to be placed in state, beneath
canopies of velvet and gold.   On the outer side of the little
building, a tall, awkward, but vigorous and well-formed countryman was lounging, with one shoulder placed against the side of
the shop, as if his legs found the task of supporting his heavy
frame too grievous to be endured without assistance, seemingly
in waiting for the completion of the garment at which the other
toiled, and with which he intended to adorn his person, in an
adjoining parish, on the succeeding sabbath.

In order to render the minutes shorter, and possibly in the indulgence of a very ungovernable propensity to talk, of which he
who wielded the needle was somewhat the subject, but few of the

passing moments were suffered to escape without a word from one or the other of the parties. As the subject of their discourse had a direct reference to the principal matter of our tale, we shall take leave to give such portions of it to the reader as we deem most relevant to a clear exposition of that which is to follow. The latter will always bear in mind, that he who worked was a man drawing into the wane of life; that he bore about him the appearance of one who, either from incompetency or from some fatality of fortune, had been doomed to struggle through the world, keeping poverty from his residence only by the aid of great industry and rigid frugality; and that the idler was a youth of that age and condition that the acquisition of an entire set of habiliments formed a sort of era in his adventures.

"Yes," exclaimed the indefatigable shaper of cloth, a species of sigh which might have been equally construed into an evidence of the fulness of his mental enjoyment, or of the excess of his bodily labours struggling from his lips; "yes, smarter sayings may have fallen from the lips of man, than such as the squire poured out to day, but we in the provinces have never heard them. When he spoke of the plains of Father Abraham, and of the smoke and thunder of the battle, Pardon, it stirred up such stomachy feelings in my bosom, that I verily believe I could have had the heart to throw aside the thimble, and go forth myself, to seek glory in battling in the cause of the king."

The youth, whose christian or "given" name, as it is even now generally termed in New England, had been intended, by his pious sponsors, humbly to express his future hopes, turned his head towards the heroic tailor, with an expression of drollery about the eye that proved nature had not been niggardly in the gift of humour, however the quality was suppressed by the restraints of a very peculiar manner, and no less peculiar education.

"There's an opening now, neighbour Homespun, for an ambitious man," he said, "sin' his majesty has lost his stoutest general."

"Yes, yes," returned the individual who, either in his youth, or in his age, had made so capital a blunder in the choice of a profession, "a fine and promising chance it is for one who counts only five-and-twenty; but most of my day has gone by, and I must spend the rest of it here, where you see me, between buckram and osnaburghs—who put the dye into this cloth, Pardy?—it is the best laid in bark I've fingered this fall."

"Let the old woman alone for giving the lasting colour to her web; I'll engage, neighbour Homespun, provided you furnish the proper fit, there'll not be a better dressed lad on the island than my own mother's son! But, sin' you cannot be a general, good-man, you'll have the comfort of knowing there'll be no more fighting without you. Every body agrees the French won't hold out much longer, and then we must have a peace for want of enemies."

"So best, so best, boy; for one who has seen as much of the horrors of war as I, knows how to put a rational value on the blessings of tranquillity!"

"Then you ar'n't altogether unacquainted, good-man, with the new trade you thought of setting up?"

"I!—I have been through five long and bloody wars, and I've reason to thank God that I've gone through them all without a scratch as big as one this needle would make. Five long and bloody, ay, and I may say glorious wars, have I liv'd through in safety!"

"A perilous time it must have been for you, neighbour. But I don't remember to have heard of more than two quarrels with the Frenchmen in my day."

You are but a boy compared to one who has seen the end of his third score of years. Here is this war, that is now so likely to be soon ended. Heaven, which rules all things in wisdom, be

praised for the same! Then there was the business of '45, when
the bold Warren sailed up and down our coasts; a scourge to his
majesty's enemies, and a safeguard to all loyal subjects.    Then,
there was a business in Garmany, concerning which we had awful
accounts of battles fou't, in which men were mowed down like
grass falling before the scythe of a strong arm.    That makes
three;" cocking his spectacles, and counting with his thimble
on the fingers of the other hand.    "The fourth was the rebellion
of '15, of which I pretend not to have seen much, being but a
youth at the time; and the fifth was a dreadful rumour that was
spread through the provinces, of a general rising among the
blacks and Indians, which was to sweep all us Christians into
eternity at a minute's warning!"

   "Well, I had always reckoned you for a home-staying and a
peaceable man, neighbour," returned the admiring countryman;
"nor did I ever dream that you had seen these serious movings."

   "I have not boasted, Pardon, or I might have added other
heavy matters to the list.    There was a great struggle in the
East, no longer than the year '32, for the Persian throne.    You
have read of the laws of the Medes and the Persians: well, for
the very throne that gave forth those unalterable laws was there
a frightful struggle, in which blood ran like water; but, as it
was not in Christendom, I do not account it among my own
experiences; though I might have spoken of the Porteous mob
with great reason, as it took place in another portion of the very
kingdom in which I lived."

   "You must have journeyed much, and have been stirring
late and early, good-man, to have seen all these things, and to
have got no harm?"

   "I've been something of a traveller too, Pardy.    Twice have
I been over land to Boston, and once have I sailed through the
Great Sound of Long Island, down to the town of York.    It is
an awful undertaking, the latter, as it respects the distance, and

more espècially because it is needful to pass a place that is likened, by its name, to the entrance of Tophet."

"I have often heard the spot called ' Hell Gate' spoken of; and I may say, too, that I know a man *well* who has been through it twice; once in going to York, and once in coming homeward."

" He had enough of it, as I'll engage! Did he tell you of the pot which tosses and roars as if the biggest of Beelzebub's fires was burning beneath, and of the hog's back over which the water pitches, as it may tumble over the Great Falls of the West? Owing to reasonable skill in our seamen, and uncommon resolution in the passengers, we happily had a good time of it through ourselves; though, I care not who knows it, I will own it is a severe trial to the courage to enter that dreadful strait. We cast out our anchors at certain islands, which lie a few furlongs this side the place, and sent the pinnace, with the captain and two stout seamen, to reconnoitre the spot, in order to see if it were in a peaceful state or not. The report being favourable, the passengers were landed, and the vessel was got through, by the blessing of Heaven, in safety. We had all reason to rejoice that the prayers of the congregation were asked before we departed from the peace and security of our own homes!"

"You journeyed round the ' Gate' on foot?" demanded the attentive boor.

" Certain! It would have been a sinful and a blasphemous tempting of Providence to have done otherwise, seeing that our duty called us to no such sacrifice. But all that danger is gone by, and so, I trust, will that of this bloody war, in which we have both been actors; and then I humbly hope his sacred majesty will have leisure to turn his royal mind to the pirates who infest the coast, and to order some of his stout naval captains to mete out to the rogues thè treatment they are so fond of giving to others. It would be a joyful sight to my old eyes to see the famous and long-hunted Red Rover brought into this very port, towing at the poop of a king's cruiser."

"And is it a desperate villain, he of whom you now make mention?"

"He! There are many hes in that one lawless ship, and bloody-minded and nefarious thieves are they, to the smallest boy. It is heart-searching and grievous, Pardy, to hear of their evil-doings on the high seas of the king!"

"I have often heard mention made of the Rover," returned the countryman; "but never to enter into any of the intricate particulars of his knavery."

"How should you, boy, who live up in the country, know so much of what is passing on the great deep, as we who dwell in a port that is resorted to by mariners? I am fearful you'll be making it late home, Pardon," he added, glancing his eye at certain lines drawn on his shop-board, by the aid of which he was enabled to note the progress of the setting sun. "It is drawing towards the hour of five, and you have twice that number of miles to go, before you can, by any manner of means, reach the nearest boundary of your father's farm."

"The road is plain, and the people honest," returned the countryman, who cared not if it were midnight, provided he could be the bearer of the particulars of some dreadful sea robbery to the ears of those he well knew would flock around him, at his return, to hear the tidings from the port. "And is he, in truth, so much feared and sought for, as people say?"

"Is he sought for! Is Tophet sought by a praying Christian? Few there are on the mighty deep, let them even be as stout for battle as was Joshua the great Jewish captain, that would not rather behold the land than see the top-gallants of that wicked pirate! Men fight for glory, Pardon, as I may say I have seen, after living through so many wars; but none love to meet an enemy who hoists a bloody flag at the first blow, and who is ready to cast both parties into the air, when he finds the hand of Satan has no longer the mind to help him."

"If the rogue is so desperate," returned the youth, straightening his powerful limbs, with a look of rising pride, "why do not the island and plantations fit out a coaster in order to bring him in, that he might get a sight of a wholesome gibbet? Let the drum beat on such a message through our neighbourhood, and I'll engage that it don't leave it without one volunteer at least."

"So much for not having seen war! Of what use would flails and pitchforks prove against men who have sold themselves to the devil? Often has the Rover been seen at night, or just as the sun has been going down, by the king's cruisers, who, having fairly surrounded the thieves, had good reason to believe that they had them already in the bilboes; but, when the morning has come, the prize was vanished, by fair means or by foul!"

"And are the villains so bloody-minded that they are called 'Red?'"

"Such is the title of their leader," returned the worthy tailor, who by this time was swelling with the importance of possessing so interesting a legend to communicate; "and such is also the name they give to his vessel; because no man, who has put foot on board her has ever come back to say that she has a better or a worse; that is, no honest mariner or lucky voyager. The ship is of the size of a king's sloop, they say, and of like equipments and form: but she has miraculously escaped from the hands of many a gallant frigate; and once, it is whispered, for no loyal subject would like to say so scandalous a thing openly, Pardon, that she lay under the guns of a fifty for an hour, and seemingly, to all eyes, she sunk like hammered lead to the bottom. But just as every body was shaking hands, and wishing his neighbour joy at so happy a punishment coming over the knaves, a West-Indiaman came into port, that had been robbed by the Rover on the morning after the night in which it was thought they had all gone into eternity together. And what makes the matter worse, boy, while the king's ship was careening with her keel out to stop the holes of cannon-balls, the pirate was sailing up and down the coast, as sound as the day that the wrights first turned her from their hands!"

"Well, this is unheard of!" returned the countryman, on whom the tale was beginning to make a sensible impression. "Is she a well-turned and comely ship to the eye? or is it by any means certain that she is an actual living vessel at all?"

"Opinions differ. Some say, yes; some say, no. But I am well acquainted with a man who travelled a week in company with a mariner, who passed within a hundred fathoms of her, in a gale of wind. Lucky it was for them that the hand of the Lord was felt so powerfully on the deep, and that the Rover had enough to do to keep his own ship from foundering. The acquaintance of my friend had a good view of both vessel and captain, therefore, in perfect safety. He said that the pirate was a man may-be half as big again as the tall preacher over on the main, with hair of the colour of the sun in a fog, and eyes that no man would like to look upon a second time. He saw him as plainly as I see you; for the knave stood in the rigging of his ship, beckoning, with a hand as big as a coat-flap, for the honest trader to keep off, in order that the two vessels might not do one another damage by coming foul."

"He was a bold mariner, that trader, to go so nigh such a merciless rogue."

"I warrant you, Pardon, it was desperately against his will! But it was on a night so dark——"

"Dark!" interrupted the other, who had the inquisitive shrewdness of a New Englander, notwithstanding his disposition to credulity; "by what contrivance, then, did he manage to see so well?"

"No man can say!" answered the tailor, "but see he did, just

in the manner and the very things I have named to you. More
than that, he took good note of the vessel, that he might know
her, if chance or Providence should ever happen to throw her
again into his way. She was a long black ship, lying low in the
water, like a snake in the grass, with a desperate wicked look,
and altogether of dishonest dimensions. Then, every body says
that she appears to sail faster than the clouds above, seeming to
care little which way the wind blows, and that no one is a jot
safer from her speed than her honesty. According to all that I
have heard, she is something such a craft as yonder slaver that
has been lying the week past, the Lord knows why, in our outer
harbour."

As the gossiping tailor had necessarily lost many precious moments in relating the preceding history, he now set about redeem-
ing them with the utmost diligence, keeping time to the rapid
movement of his needle-hand, by corresponding jerks of his head
and shoulders. In the meanwhile the bumpkin, whose wondering mind was by this time charged nearly to bursting with what
he had heard, turned his look towards the vessel the other had
pointed out, in order to get the only image that was now required,
to enable him to do credit to so moving a tale, suitably engraved
on his imagination. There was necessarily a pause, while the
respective parties were thus severally occupied. It was suddenly
broken by the tailor, who clipped the thread with which he had
just finished the garment, cast every thing from his hands, threw
his spectacles upon his forehead, and, leaning his arms on his
knees in such a manner as to form a perfect labyrinth with the
limbs, he stretched his body forward so far as to lean out of the
window, riveting his eyes also on the ship which still attracted
the gaze of his companion.

"Do you know, Pardy," he said, "that strange thoughts and
cruel misgivings have come over me concerning that very vessel?
They say she is a slaver come in for wood and water, and there

she has been a week, and not a stick bigger than an oar has gone up her side; and I 'll engage that ten drops from Jamaica have gone on board her, to one from the spring. Then, you may see, she is anchored in such a way that but one of the guns from the battery can touch her; whereas, had she been a real timid trader, she would naturally have got into a place where, if a straggling picaroon should come into the port, he would have found her in the very hottest of the fire."

"You have an ingenious turn with you, good-man," returned the wondering countryman; "now, a ship might have lain on the battery-island itself, and I would have hardly noticed the thing."

"'T is use and experience, Pardon, that makes men of us all. I should know something of batteries, having seen so many wars, and I served a campaign of a week in that very fort, when the rumour came that the French were sending cruisers from Louisburg down the coast. For that matter, my duty was to stand sentinel over that very cannon; and, if I have done the thing once, I have twenty times squinted along the piece to see in what quarter it would send its shot, provided such a calamity should arrive as that it might become necessary to fire it, loaded with real warlike balls."

"And who are these?" demanded Pardon, with that species of sluggish curiosity which had been awakened by the wonders related by the other: "are these mariners of the slaver, or are they idle Newporters?"

"They!" exclaimed the tailor: "sure enough they are newcomers; it may be well to have a closer look at them in these troublesome times! Here, Nab, take the garment and press down the seams, you idle hussy; for neighbour Hopkins is straitened for time, while your tongue is going like a young lawyer's in a justice's court. Don't be sparing of your elbow, girl; for it's no Indian muslin that you 'll have under the iron, but cloth that would do to side a house with. Ah! your mother's loom, Pardy, robs the seamster of many an honest job."

Having thus transferred the remainder of the job from his own hands to those of an awkward pouting girl, who was compelled to abandon her gossip with a neighbour, in order to obey his injunctions, he quickly removed his own person, notwithstanding a miserable limp with which he had come into the world, from the shop-board to the open air. As more important characters are. however, about to be introduced to the reader, we shall defer the ceremony to the opening of another chapter.

# CHAPTER II.

Sir Toby! Excellent! I smell a device.
*Twelfth Night.*

THE strangers were three in number; for strangers the good-man Homespun, who knew not only the names but most of the private histories of every man and woman within ten miles of his own residence, immediately proclaimed them to be in a whisper to his companion; and strangers, too, of a mysterious and threatening aspect. In order that others may have an opportunity of judging of the probability of the latter conjecture, it becomes necessary that a more minute account should be given of the respective appearances of these individuals, who, unhappily for their reputations, temporarily at least, had the misfortune to be unknown to the gossiping tailor of Newport.

The one by far the most imposing in his general mien, was a youth who had apparently seen some six or seven and twenty seasons. That those seasons had not been entirely made of sunny days and nights of repose, was betrayed by the tinges of brown which had been laid on his features, layer after layer, in such constant succession, as to have changed to a deep olive a complexion which had once been fair, and through which the rich blood was still mantling with the finest glow of vigorous health. His features were rather noble and manly than distinguished for their exactness and symmetry; his nose being far more bold and prominent than regular in its form, with his brows projecting, and sufficiently marked to give to the whole of the superior parts of his face that decided intellectual expression which is already becoming so common to American physiognomy. The mouth was firm and manly; and, while he muttered to himself and smiled, as the curious tailor drew slowly nigher, it discovered a set of glittering teeth that shone the brighter from being cased in so dark a setting. The hair was a jet black, in thick and confused ringlets; and the eyes were very little larger than common, grey, and, though evidently of a changing expression, rather leaning to mildness than severity. The form of this young man was of that happy size which unites activity with strength. It seemed to be well knit, while it was justly proportioned, and graceful. Though these several personal qualifications were exhibited under the disadvantages of the perfectly simple, though neat and rather tastefully disposed attire of a common mariner, they were sufficiently imposing to cause the suspicious dealer in buckram to hesitate before he would venture to address the stranger, whose eye appeared fastened, by a species of fascination, on the reputed slaver in the outer harbour. A curl of the upper lip, and another inexplicable smile, in which some strong feeling was mingled with his mutterings, decided the vacillating mind of the good-man. Without venturing to disturb a reverie that seemed so profound, he left the youth leaning against the head of the pile where he had long been standing perfectly unconscious of the presence of any intruder, and turned a little hastily, to examine the rest of the party.

One of the remaining two was a white man, and the other a negro. Both had passed the middle age; and both, in their appearances, furnished the strongest proofs of long exposure to the severity of many climates, and to numberless tempests. They were dressed in the plain, weather-soiled, and tarred habiliments of common seamen, bearing about their persons the other unerring evidences of their peculiar profession. The former was of a short, thickset, powerful frame, in which, by a happy ordering of nature, a little confirmed perhaps by long habit, the strength was principally seated about the broad and brawny shoulders and sinewy arms; as if, in the construction of the man, the inferior members had been considered of little other use than to transfer the superior to the different situations in which the former were to display their energies. His head was in proportion to the more immediate members; the forehead low, and nearly covered with hair; the eyes small, obstinate, sometimes fierce, and often dull; the nose snub, coarse, and vulgar; the mouth large and voracious; the teeth short, clean, and perfectly sound; and the chin broad, manly, and even expressive. This singularly constructed personage had taken his seat on an empty barrel, and, with folded arms, he sat examining the often-mentioned slaver, occasionally favouring his companion, the black, with such remarks as were suggested by his observation and experience.

The negro occupied a more humble post; one better suited to his subdued habits and inclinations. In stature, and the peculiar division of animal force, there was a great resemblance between the two, with the exception that the latter enjoyed the advantage in height, and even in proportions. While nature had stamped on his lineaments those distinguishing marks which characterise the race from which he sprang, she had not done it to that revolting degree to which her displeasure against that stricken people is sometimes carried. His features were more elevated than common; his eye was mild, easily excited to joy, and, like that of his companion, sometimes humorous. His head was beginning to be sprinkled with grey, his skin had lost the shining jet colour which had distinguished it in his youth, and all his limbs and movements bespoke a man whose frame had been equally indurated and stiffened by toil. He sat on a low stone, and seemed intently employed in tossing pebbles into the air, showing his dexterity by catching them in the hand from which they had just been cast; an amusement which betrayed alike the natural tendency of his mind to seek pleasure in trifles, and the absence of the more elevating feelings which are the fruits of education. The process, however, furnished a striking exhibition of the physical force of the negro. In order to conduct this trivial pursuit without encumbrance, he had rolled the sleeve of his light canvass jacket to the elbow, laying bare, by the act an arm that might have served as a model for the limb of Hercules.

There was certainly nothing sufficiently imposing about the persons of either of these individuals to repel the investigations of one as much influenced by curiosity as was our tailor. Instead, however, of yielding directly to the strong impulse, the honest shaper of cloth chose to direct his advance in a manner that should give the bumpkin a striking proof of his sagacity. After making a sign of caution and intelligence to the latter, he approached slowly from behind, with a light step, that might give him an opportunity of hearing any secret that should unwittingly fall from either of the seamen. His forethought was followed by no very important results, though it served to supply his suspicions with all the additional testimony of the treachery of their characters that could be furnished by evidence so simple as the mere sound of their voices. As to the words themselves, though the good-man believed they might possibly contain treason, he was compelled to acknowledge to himself that it was so artfully concealed as to escape even his acuteness. We leave the reader himself to judge of the correctness of both opinions.

"This is a pretty bight of a basin, Guinea," observed the white, rolling his tobacco in his mouth, and turning his eyes, for the first time in many minutes, from the vessel; "and a spot is it that a man, who lay on a lee-shore without sticks, might be glad to see his craft in. Now do I call myself something of a seaman, and yet I cannot weather upon the philosophy of that fellow in keeping his ship in the outer harbour, when he might warp her into this mill-pond in half an hour. It gives his boats hard duty, dusky S'ip; and that I call making foul weather of fair!"

The negro had been christened Scipio Africanus, by a species of witticism which was much more common to the Provinces than it is to the States of America, and which filled so many of the meaner employments of the country, in name at least, with the counterparts of the philosophers, heroes, poets, and princes of Rome. To him it was a matter of small moment, whether the vessel lay in the offing or in the port; and without discontinuing his childish amusement, he manifested the same, by replying, with great indifference, —

"I s'pose he t'ink all the water inside lie on a top."

"I tell you, Guinea," returned the other, in a harsh, positive tone, "the fellow is a know-nothing! Would any man, who understands the behaviour of a ship, keep his craft in a roadstead, when he might tie her, head and heels, in a basin like this?"

"What he call roadstead?" interrupted the negro, seizing at once, with the avidity of ignorance, on the little oversight of his adversary, in confounding the outer harbour of Newport with the wilder anchorage below, and with the usual indifference of all similar people to the more material matter of whether the objection was at all germane to the point at issue; "I never hear 'em call anchoring ground, with land around it, roadstead afore!"

"Hark ye, Mister Gold-coast," muttered the white, bending his head aside in a threatening manner, though he still disdained to turn his eyes on his humble adversary, "if you've no wish to wear your shins parcelled for the next month, gather in the slack of your wit, and have an eye to the manner in which you let it run again. Just tell me this; isn't a port a port? — and isn't an offing an offing?"

As these were two propositions to which even the ingenuity of Scipio could raise no plausible objection, he wisely declined touching on either, contenting himself with shaking his head in self-complacency, and laughing as heartily at his imaginary triumph over his companion, as if he had never known care, nor been the subject of wrong and humiliation, so long and so patiently endured.

" Ay, ay," grumbled the white, re-adjusting his person in its former composed attitude, and again crossing the arms, which had been a little separated, to give force to the menace against the tender member of the black, " now you are piping the wind out of your throat like a flock of long-shore crows, you think you 've got the best of the matter. The Lord made a nigger an unrational animal ; and an experienced seaman, who has doubled both Capes, and made all the head-lands atween Fundy and Horn, has no right to waste his breath in teaching common sense to any of the breed ! I tell you, Scipio, since Scipio is your name on the ship's books—though I 'll wager a month's pay against a wooden boat-hook, that your father was known at home as Quashee, and your mother as Quasheeba — therefore do I tell you, Scipio Africa — which is a name for all your colour, I believe — that yonder chap, in the outer harbour of this here seaport, is no judge of an anchorage, or he would drop a kedge, mayhap hereaway, in a line with the southern end of that there small matter of an island, and hauling his ship up to it, fasten her to the spot with good hempen cables and iron mud-hooks. Now, look you here, S'ip, at the reason of the matter," he continued, in a manner which showed that the little skirmish that had just passed was like one of those sudden squalls of which they had both seen so many, and which were usually so soon succeeded by corresponding seasons of calm, — " look you at the rationality of what I say. He has come into this anchorage either for something or for nothing. I suppose you are ready to admit that. If for nothing, he might have found that much outside, and I 'll say no more about it ; but if for something, he could get it off easier, provided the ship lay hereaway, just where I told you, boy, not a fathom ahead or astern, than where she is now riding, though the article was no heavier than a fresh handful of feathers for the captain's pillow. Now, if you have any thing to gainsay the reason of this, why, I'm ready to hear it as a reasonable man, and one who has not forgotten his manners in picking up his learning."

" S'pose a wind come out fresh here at nor-west," answered the other, stretching his brawny arm towards the point of the compass he named, "and a vessel want to get to sea in a hurry, how you t'ink he get her far enough up to lay through the weather reach ? Ha! you answer me dat; you great scholar, Misser Dick, but you never see ship go in wind's teeth, or hear a monkey talk."

" The black is right!" exclaimed the youth, who, it would seem, had overheard the dispute, while he appeared otherwise engaged; " the slaver has left his vessel in the outer harbour, knowing that the wind holds so much to the westward at this season of the year; and then you see he keeps his light spars aloft, although it is plain enough, by the manner in which his sails are furled, that he is strong-handed. Can you make out, boys, whether he has an anchor under foot, or is he merely riding by a single cable ?"

" The man must be a driveller, to lie in such a tides-way without dropping his stream, or at least a kedge, to steady the ship by," returned the white, without appearing to think any thing more than the received practice of seamen necessary to decide the point. " That he is no great judge of an anchorage, I am ready to allow; but no man who can keep things so snug aloft, would think of fastening his ship, for any length of time, by a single cable, to sheer starboard and port, like that kicking colt, tied to the tree by a long halter that we fell in with in our passage overland from Boston."

" 'Em got a stream down, and all he rest of he anchor stowed," said the black, whose dark eye was glancing understandingly at the vessel, while he still continued to cast his pebbles into the air. "S'pose he jam he helm hard a-port, Misser Harry, and take a tide on he larboard bow, what you t'ink make him kick and gallop about! Golly! I like to see Dick, without a foot-rope, ride a colt tied to he tree!"

Again the negro enjoyed his humour, by shaking his head as if his whole soul was amused by the whimsical image his rude fancy had conjured, indulging in a hearty laugh till the tears came, and again his white companion muttered heavy and sententious denunciations. The young man, who seemed to enter very little into the quarrels and witticisms of his singular associates, still kept his gaze intently fastened on the vessel, which to him appeared, for the moment, to be the subject of some extraordinary interest. Shaking his own head, though in a far graver manner, as if his doubts were drawing to a close, he added, when the boisterous merriment of the negro had ceased,—

"Scipio, you are right: he rides altogether by his stream, and he keeps every thing in readiness for a sudden move. In ten minutes he could carry his ship beyond the fire of the battery, provided he had but a capful of wind."

"You appear to be a capital judge in these matters." said a voice behind him.

The youth turned suddenly on his heel, and then, for the first time, was he apprised of the presence of intruders. The surprise, however, was not confined to himself; for, as there was another new comer to be added to the company, the gossipping tailor was quite as much, or even more, the subject of astonishment than any of that party which he had been so intently watching as to have prevented him from observing the approach of another utter stranger.

The new comer was a man between thirty and forty, and of a mien and an attire not a little adapted to quicken the active curiosity of the good-man Homespun. His person was slight, but it afforded the promise of exceeding agility, and even of vigour, especially when contrasted with his stature, which was scarcely equal to the medium height of man. His skin had been dazzling as that of woman, though a deep red, which had taken possession of the lower lineaments of his face, and which was particularly conspicuous on the outline of a fine aquiline nose, served to destroy all appearance of effeminacy. His hair was, like his com- plexion, fair, and fell about his temples in rich, glossy, and exu· berant curls. His mouth and chin were beautiful in their forma- tion; but the former was a little scornful, and the two together bore a decided character of voluptuousness. The eye was blue, full without being prominent, and, though in common placid and even soft, there were moments when it seemed a little unsettled and wild. He wore a high conical hat, placed a little on one side, so as to give a slightly rakish expression to his physiognomy, a riding-frock of light green, breeches of buckskin, high boots, and spurs. In one of his hands he carried a small whip, with which, when first seen, he was cutting the air with an appearance of the utmost indifference to the surprise occasioned by his sud- den interruption.

" I say, sir, you seem to me to be an excellent judge in these matters," he repeated, when he had endured the frowning exami- nation of the young seaman quite as long as comported with his own patience; "you speak like a man who at least feels that he has a right to give an opinion."

" Do you find it remarkable that one should not be ignorant of a profession that he has diligently pursued for a whole life?"

" Hum! I find it a little remarkable that one, whose business is that of a handicraft, should dignify his trade with such a sound- ing name as *profession*. We of the science of the law, and who enjoy the particular smiles of the learned universities, cannot say much more!"

"Then call it trade; for nothing in common with gentlemen of your craft is acceptable to a seaman," retorted the young mariner, turning away from the intruder with a disgust that he did not affect to conceal.

" A lad of some mettle !" muttered the other, with a rapid utterance and a meaning smile. " Let not such a trifle as a word part us, friend. I confess my ignorance of all maritime matters, and would gladly learn a little from one as skilful as yourself in the noble — *profession*. I think you said something concerning the manner in which yonder ship has anchored, and of the condition in which they keep things alow and aloft?"

" *Alow* and aloft !" exclaimed the young sailor, facing his interrogator with a stare that was quite as expressive as his recent disgust.

" Alow and aloft !" calmly repeated the other.

" I spoke of her neatness aloft, but do not affect to judge of things below at this distance."

" Then it was my error; but you will have pity on the ignorance of one who is so new to the *profession*. As I have intimated, I am no more than an unworthy barrister in the service of his majesty, expressly sent from home on a particular errand. If it were not a pitiful pun, I might add, I am not yet a judge."

" No doubt you will soon arrive at that distinction," returned the other, " if his majesty's ministers have any just conceptions of modest merit; unless, indeed, you should happen to be prematurely——"

The youth bit his lip, made a quick inclination of the head, and walked leisurely up the wharf, followed with the same appearance of deliberation by the two seamen who had accompanied him in his visit to the place. The stranger in green watched the whole movement with a calm and apparently an amused eye, tapping his boot with his whip, and seeming to reflect like one who would willingly find means to continue the discourse.

" Hanged !" he at length uttered, as if to complete the sentence the other had left unfinished. " It is droll enough that such a fellow should dare to foretell so elevated a fate for *me* !"

He was evidently preparing to follow the retiring party, when he felt a hand laid a little unceremoniously on his arm, and his step was arrested.

" One word in your ear, sir," said the attentive tailor, making a significant sign that he had matters of importance to communicate : " a single word, sir, since you are in the particular service of his majesty. Neighbour Pardon," he continued, with a patronising air, " the sun is getting low, and you will make it late home, I fear. The girl will give you the garment, and — God speed you! Say nothing of what you have heard and seen, until you have had word from me to that effect ; for it is seemly that two men, who have had so much experience in a war like this, should not lack in discretion. Fare ye well, lad ! — pass the good word to the worthy farmer, your father, not forgetting a refreshing hint of friendship to the thrifty housewife, your mother. Fare ye well, honest youth, fare ye well !"

Homespun, having thus disposed of his admiring companion, waited, with much elevation of mien, until the gaping bumpkin had left the wharf, before he again turned his look on the stranger in green. The latter had continued in his tracks, with an air of undisturbed composure, until he was once more addressed by the tailor, whose character and dimensions he seemed to have taken in, at a single glance of his rapid eye.

" You say, sir, you are a servant of his majesty?" demanded the latter, determined to solve all doubts as to the other's claims on his confidence, before he committed himself by any precipitate disclosure.

" I may say more ; — his familiar confidant !"

" It is an honour to converse with such a man, that I feel in every bone of my body," returned the cripple, smoothing his scanty hairs, and bowing nearly to the earth; "a high and loyal honour do I feel this gracious privilege to be."

"Such as it is, my friend, I take on myself, in his majesty's name, to bid you welcome."

"Such munificent condescension would open my whole heart, though treason, and all other unrighteousness, were locked up in it. I am happy, honoured, and I doubt not, honourable sir, to have this opportunity of proving my zeal to the king, before one who will not fail to report my humble efforts to his royal ears."

"Speak freely," interrupted the stranger in green, with an air of princely condescension; though one, less simple and less occupied with his own budding honours than the tailor, might have easily discovered that he began to grow weary of the other's prolix loyalty. "Speak without reserve, friend; it is what we always do at court." Then, switching his boot with his riding-whip, he muttered to himself as he swung his light frame on his heel, with an indolent, indifferent air, "If the fellow swallows that, he is as heavy as his own goose!"

"I shall, sir, I shall; and a great proof of charity is it in one like your noble self to listen. You see yonder tall ship, sir, in the outer harbour of this loyal seaport?"

"I do; she seems to be an object of general attention among the worthy lieges of the place."

"Therein I conceive, sir, you have over-rated the sagacity of my townsmen. She has been lying where you now see her for many days, and not a syllable have I heard whispered against her character, from mortal man, except myself."

"Indeed!" muttered the stranger, biting the handle of his whip, and fastening his glittering eyes intently on the features of the good-man, which were literally swelling with the import-ance of his discovery; "and what may be the nature of *your* suspicions?"

"Why, sir, I may be wrong—and God forgive me if I am—

but this is no more nor less than what has arisen in my mind on the subject.    Yonder ship, and her crew, bear the reputation of being innocent and harmless slavers, among the good people of Newport; and as such are they received and welcomed in the place; the one to a safe and easy anchorage, and the others among the taverners and shop-dealers.    I would not have you imagine that a single garment has ever gone from my fingers for one of all her crew; no, let it be for ever remembered that the whole of their dealings have been with the young tradesman named Tape, who entices customers to barter by backbiting and otherwise defiling the fair names of his betters in the business; not a garment has been made by my hands for even the smallest boy."

"You are lucky," returned the stranger in green, "in being so well quit of the knaves; and yet have you forgotten to name the particular offence with which I am to charge them before the face of the king."

"I am coming as fast as possible to the weighty matter.    You must know, worthy and commendable sir, that I am a man that has seen much, and suffered much, in his majesty's service. Five bloody and cruel wars have I gone through, besides other adventures and experiences, such as become a humble subject to suffer meekly and in silence."

"All of which shall be directly communicated to the royal ear.    And now, worthy friend, relieve your mind by a frank communication of your suspicions."

"Thanks, honourable sir; your goodness in my behalf cannot be forgotten, though it shall never be said that impatience to seek the relief you mention hurried me into a light and improper manner of unburthening my mind.    You must know, honoured gentleman, that yesterday, as I sat alone, at this very hour, on my board, reflecting in my thoughts — for the plain reason that my envious neighbour had enticed all the newly-arrived customers to his own shop—well, sir, the head will be busy when the hands are idle; there I sat, as I have briefly told you, reflecting in my thoughts, like any other accountable being, on the calamities of life, and on the great experiences that I have had in the wars : for you must know, valiant gentleman, besides the affair in the land of the Medes and Persians, and the Porteous mob in Edinbro', five cruel and bloody——"

"There is that in your air which sufficiently proclaims the soldier," interrupted his listener, who struggled to keep down his rising impatience ; "but as my time is so precious, I would now more especially hear what you have to say concerning yonder ship."

"Yes, sir, one gets a military look after seeing numberless wars; and so, happily for the need of both, I have now come to the part of my secret which touches more particularly on the character of that vessel. There sat I, reflecting on the manner in which the strange seamen had been deluded by my tonguey neighbour — for, as you should know, sir, a desperate talker is that Tape, and a younker who has seen but one war at the utmost — therefore, was I thinking of the manner in which he had enticed my lawful customers from my shop, when, as one thought is the father of another, the following concluding reasoning, as our pious priest has it weekly in his reviving and searching discourses, came uppermost in my mind : if these mariners were honest and conscientious slavers, would they overlook a labouring man with a large family, to pour their well-earned gold into the lap of a common babbler ? I proclaimed to myself at once, sir, that they would not. I was bold to say the same in my own mind; and, thereupon, I openly put the question to all in hearing, if they are not slavers, what are they ? A question which the king himself would, in his royal wisdom, allow to be a question easier asked than answered; upon which I replied, if the vessel be no fair-trading slaver, nor a common cruiser of his majesty, it is as tangible as the best man's reasoning that she may be neither more nor less than the ship of that nefarious pirate the Red Rover."

"The Red Rover!" exclaimed the stranger in green, with a start so natural as to evidence that his dying interest in the tailor's narrative was suddenly and powerfully revived. "That, indeed, would be a secret worth having!—but why do you suppose this?"

"For sundry reasons, which I am now about to name in their respective order. In the first place, she is an armed ship, sir. In the second, she is no lawful cruiser, or the same would be publicly known, and by no one sooner than myself, inasmuch as it is seldom that I do not finger a penny from the king's ships. In the third place, the burglarious and unfeeling conduct of the few seamen who have landed from her, go to prove it; and, lastly, what is well proved may be considered as substantially established. These are what, sir, I should call the opening premises of my inferences, all of which I hope you will properly lay before the royal mind of his majesty."

The barrister in green listened to the somewhat wire-drawn deductions of Homespun with great attention, notwithstanding the confused and obscure manner in which they were delivered by the aspiring tradesman. His keen eye rolled quickly and often, from the vessel to the countenance of his companion; but several moments elapsed before he saw fit to make any reply The reckless gaiety with which he had introduced himself, and which he had hitherto maintained in the discourse, was entirely superseded by a musing and abstracted air, which sufficiently proved that, whatever levity he might betray in common, he was far from being a stranger on proper occasions to deep and becoming thought. Suddenly throwing off his air of gravity, however, he assumed one in which irony and sincerity were singularly blended, and laying his hand familiarly on the shoulder of the expecting tailor, he replied,—

" You have communicated such matter as becometh a faithful and loyal servant of the king. It is well known that a heavy price is set on the head of the meanest follower of the Rover; and that a rich, ay, a splendid reward will be the fortune of him who is the instrument of delivering the whole knot of miscreants into the hands of the executioner. Indeed, I know not but some marked evidence of the royal pleasure might follow such a service. There was Phipps, a man of humble origin, who received knighthood——"

" Knighthood !" echoed the tailor, in awful admiration.

" Knighthood," cooly repeated the stranger; " honourable and chivalric knighthood. What may have been the appellation you received from your sponsors in baptism ?"

" My given name, gracious and grateful sir, is Hector."

" And the house itself?—the distinctive appellation of the family ?"

" We have *always* been called Homespun."

" Sir Hector Homespun will sound as well as another ! But to secure these rewards, my friend, it is necessary to be discreet. I admire your ingenuity, and am a perfect convert to your logic. You have so entirely demonstrated the truth of your own suspicions, that I have no more doubt of yonder vessel being the pirate, than I have of your wearing spurs, and being called Sir Hector. The two things are equally established in my mind; but it is needful that we proceed in the matter with caution. I understand you to say that no one else has been enlightened by your erudition in this affair ?"

" Not a soul. Tape would swear that the crew were conscientious slavers."

" So best. We must first render conclusions certain; then to our reward. Meet me at the hour of eleven this night, at yonder low point, where the land juts into the outer harbour. From that stand will we make our observations; and having removed every doubt, let the morning produce a discovery that shall ring from the Colony of the Bay to the settlements of Oglethorpe until then we part; for it is not wise that we be longer seen in conference.     Remember silence, punctuality, and the favour of the king.     These are our watchwords."

"Adieu, honourable gentleman," said his companion, making a reverence nearly to the earth, as the other slightly touched his hat in passing.

"Adieu, Sir Hector," returned the stranger in green, with an affable smile, and a gracious wave of the hand.  He then walked slowly up the wharf, and disappeared behind the mansion of the Homespuns, leaving the head of that ancient family, like many a predecessor and many a successor, so rapt in the admiration of his own good fortune, and so blinded by his folly, that, while physically he saw to the right and to the left as well as ever, his mental vision was completely obscured in the clouds of ambition

# CHAPTER III.

ALONZO. — Good boatswain, have care.

*Tempest.*

THE instant the stranger had separated from the credulous tailor, he lost his assumed air in one more natural and sedate. Still it would seem that thought was an unwonted or an unwelcome tenant of his mind, for, switching his boot with his little riding-whip, he entered the principal street of the place with a light step and a wandering eye. Though his look was unsettled, few of the individuals whom he passed escaped his quick glances; and it was quite apparent, from the hurried manner in which he began to regard objects, that his mind was not less active than his body A stranger thus accoutred, and one bearing about his person so many evidences of his recent acquaintance with the road, did not fail to attract the attention of the provident publicans we have had occasion to mention in our opening chapter. Declining the civilities of the most favoured of the innkeepers, he suffered his steps to be oddly enough arrested by the one whose house was the usual haunt of the hangers-on of the port.

On entering the bar-room of this tavern, as it was called, but which in another country would probably have aspired to be termed no more than a pot-house, he found the hospitable apartment thronged with its customary revellers. A slight interruption was produced by the appearance of a guest who was altogether superior in mien and attire to the ordinary customers of the house, but it ceased the moment the stranger had thrown

**3**

himself on a bench, and intimated to the host the nature of his wants. As the latter furnished the required draught, he made a sort of apology, which was intended for the ears of all his customers nigh the stranger, for the manner in which an individual, in the farther end of the long narrow room, not only monopolised the discourse, but appeared to extort the attention of all within hearing to some portentous legend he was recounting.

"It is the boatswain of the slaver in the outer harbour, squire," the worthy minister of Bacchus concluded; "a man who has followed the water many a day, and who has seen sights and prodigies enough to fill a smart volume. Old Bor'us the people call him, though his lawful name is Jack Nightingale. Is the toddy to the squire's relish?"

The stranger assented to the latter query by smacking his lips and bowing, as he put down the nearly untouched draught. He then turned his head to examine the individual who might, by the manner in which he declaimed, have been termed, in the language of the country, another "orator of the day."

A stature which greatly exceeded six feet, enormous whiskers, that quite concealed a moiety of his grim countenance; a scar, which was the memorial of a badly-healed gash, that had once threatened to divide that moiety in quarters; limbs in proportion; the whole rendered striking by the dress of a seaman; a long, tarnished silver chain, and a little whistle of the same metal, served to render the individual in question sufficiently remarkable. Without appearing to be in the smallest degree aware of the entrance of one, altogether so superior to the class of his usual auditors, this son of the ocean continued his narrative as follows, and in a voice that seemed given to him by nature in very mockery of his musical name; indeed, so very near did his tones approach to the low murmurings of a bull, that some little practice was necessary to accustom the ear to the strangely-uttered words.

" Well," he continued, thrusting his brawny arm forth, with the fist clenched, indicating the necessary point of the compass by the thumb: " the coast of Guinea might have lain hereaway, and the wind, you see, was dead off shore, blowing in squalls, as a cat spits, all the same as if the old fellow who keeps it bagged for the use of us seamen, sometimes let the stopper slip through his fingers, and was sometimes fetching it up again with a double turn round the end of his sack. — You know what a sack is, brother?"

This abrupt question was put to the gaping bumpkin already known to the reader, who, with the nether garment just received from the tailor under his arm, had lingered to add the incidents of the present legend to the stock of lore that he had already obtained for the ears of his kinsfolk in the country. A general laugh at the expense of the admiring Pardon, succeeded. Nightingale bestowed a knowing wink on one or two of his familiars, and profiting by the occasion " to freshen his nip," as he quaintly styled swallowing a pint of rum and water, he continued his narrative, by saying in a sort of admonitory tone,—

"And the time may come when you will know what a round-turn is, too, if you let go your hold of honesty. A man's neck was made brother, to keep his head above water, and not to be stretched out of shape like a pair of badly fitted dead-eyes. Therefore, have your reckoning worked up in season, and the lead of conscience going, when you find yourself drifting on the shoals of temptation." Then rolling his tobacco in his mouth, he looked boldly about him, like one who had acquitted himself of a moral obligation, and continued : — " Well, there lay the land, and, as I was saying, the wind was here, at east-and-by-south, or mayhap at east-and-by-south-half-south, sometimes blowing like a fin-back in a flurry, and sometimes leaving all the canvass chafing ag'in the rigging and spars, as if a bolt of duck cost no more than a rich man's blessing. I didn't like the looks

of the weather, seeing that there was altogether too much un-
sartainty for a quiet watch, so I walked aft, in order to put
myself in the way of giving an opinion, if-so-be such a thing
should be asked. You must know, brothers, that, according to
my notions of religion and behaviour, a man is not good for much
unless he has a full share of manners; therefore I am never
known to put my spoon in the captain's mess unless I am invited,
for the plain reason that my berth is for'ard and his'n aft. I do
not say in which end of a ship the better man is to be found;
that is a matter concerning which there are different opinions,
though most good judges in the business are agreed. But aft I
walked, to put myself in the way of giving an opinion, if one
should be asked; nor was it long before the thing came to pass
just as I had foreseen. 'Mister Nightingale,' says he; for our
captain is a gentleman, and never forgets his behaviour on deck,
or when any of the ship's company are at hand; '*Mister* Nightingale,' says he, 'what do you think of that rag of a cloud, hereaway at the north-west?' says he. 'Why, sir,' says I, boldly,
for I am never backward in speaking when properly spoken to—
so, 'why, sir,' says I, 'saving your honour's better judgment,'
—which was all a flam, for he was but a chicken to me in years
and experience; but then I never throw hot ashes to windward,
or any thing else that is warm—so, 'sir,' says I, 'it is my advice
to hand the three topsails and to stow the jib. We are in no
hurry; for the plain reason, that Guinea will be to-morrow just
where Guinea is to-night. As for keeping the ship steady in
these matters of squalls, we have the mainsail on her——' "

"You should have furl'd your mainsail too," exclaimed a voice
from behind, that was quite as dogmatical, though a little less
grum than that of the loquacious boatswain.

"What know-nothing says that?" demanded Nightingale,
fiercely, all his latent ire being excited by so rude and daring an
interruption.

"A man who has run Africa down, from Bon to Good Hope, more than once, and who knows a white squall from a rainbow," returned Dick Fid, edging his short person stoutly towards his furious adversary, and making his way through the crowd by which the important boatswain was environed, by dint of his massive shoulders. "Ay, brother, and a man, know-much or know-nothing, who would never advise his officer to keep so much after-sail on a ship, when there was the likelihood of the wind taking her aback."

To this bold vindication of an opinion which all present deemed to be so audacious, there succeeded a general and loud murmur. Encouraged by this evidence of his popularity, Nightingale was not slow, nor very meek with his retort; and then followed a clamorous concert, in which the voices of the company in general served for the higher and shriller notes, and through which the bold and vigorous assertions, contradictions, and opinions of the two principal disputants were heard running in a sort of thorough-bass.

For some time no part of the discussion was very distinct, so great was the confusion of tongues; and there were certain symptoms of an intention, on the part of Fid and the boatswain, to settle their controversy by the last appeal. During this moment of suspense, the former squared his firm-built frame in front of his gigantic opponent, and there were very vehement passings and counterpassings, in the way of gestures from four athletic arms, each of which was knobbed, like a fashionable rattan, with a lump of bones, knuckles, and sinews, that threatened annihilation to any thing that should oppose it. As the general clamour, however, gradually abated, the chief reasoners began to be heard; and, as if content to rely on their respective powers of eloquence, each gradually relinquished his hostile attitude, and appeared disposed to maintain his ground by a member scarcely less terrible than his brawny arm.

"You are a bold seaman, brother," said Nightingale, resuming his seat, "and, if saying was doing, no doubt you would make a ship talk. But I, who have seen fleets of two and three deckers —and that of all nations, except your Mohawks, mayhap, whose cruisers I will confess never to have fallen in with—lying as snug as so many white gulls, under reefed mainsails, know how to take the strain off a ship, and to keep my bulk-heads in their places."

"I deny the judgment of heaving-to a boat under her after square-sails," retorted Dick. "Give her the stay-sails, if you will, and no harm done; but a true seaman will never get a bagful of wind between his mainmast and his lee-swifter, if-so-be he knows his business. But words are like thunder, which only rumbles aloft without ever striking, as I have yet seen; let us therefore put the question to some one who has been on the water, and who knows a little of life and of ships as well as ourselves."

"If the oldest admiral in his majesty's fleet was here, he would n't be backward in saying who is right and who is wrong. I say, brothers, if there is a man among you all who has had the advantage of a sea education, let him speak, in order that the truth of this matter may not be hid like a marlingspike jammed between a brace-block and a yard."

"Here, then, is the man," returned Fid; and, stretching out his arm, he seized Scipio by the collar, and drew him without ceremony into the centre of the circle that had opened around the two disputants. "There is a man for you, who has made one more voyage between this and Africa than myself, for the reason that he was born there. Now, answer as if you were hallooing from a lee-earing, S'ip: under what sail would you heave-to a ship on the coast of your native country, with the danger of a white-squall at hand?"

"I no heave 'em to," said the black, "I make 'em scud."

"Ay, boy; but to be in readiness for the puff, would you jam her up under a mainsail, or let her lie a little off under a fore course?"

"Any fool know dat," returned Scipio, grumly, and evidently tired already of being thus catechised. "If you want 'em to fall off, how you'm expect, in reason, he do it under a main course? You answer me dat, Misser Dick."

"Gentlemen," said Nightingale, looking about him with an air of offended dignity, "I put it to your honours, is it genteel behaviour to bring a nigger, in this out-of-the-way fashion, to give an opinion in the teeth of a white man?"

This appeal to the prejudices of the company was answered by a common murmur. Scipio, who was prepared to maintain, and would have maintained, his professional opinion, after his positive and peculiar manner, against any disputant, had not the heart to resist so general an evidence of the impropriety of his presence. Without uttering a word in vindication or apology, he folded his arms and walked out of the house, with the submission and meekness of one who had been too long trained in humility to rebel. This desertion on the part of his companion was not, however, so quietly acquiesced in by Fid, who found himself thus unexpectedly deprived of the testimony of the black. He loudly remonstrated against his retreat; but finding it in vain, he crammed the end of several inches of tobacco into his mouth, swearing, as he followed the African, and keeping his eye at the same time firmly fastened on his adversary, that, in his opinion, "the lad, if he was fairly skinned, would be found to be the whiter man of the two."

The triumph of the boatswain was now complete; nor was he at all sparing of his exultation.

"Gentlemen," he said, addressing himself, with increased confidence, to the motley audience who surrounded him, "you see that reason is like a ship bearing down with studding-sails on both sides, leaving a straight wake and no favours. Now, I scorn boasting, nor do I know who the fellow is that has just sheered off in time to save his character; but this I will say, that the man is not to be found, between Boston and the West Indies, who knows better than myself how to make a ship walk, or how to make her stand still, provided I——"

The deep voice of Nightingale became suddenly hushed, and his eye was riveted, by a sort of enchantment, on the keen glance of the stranger in green, whose countenance was now seen blended among the more vulgar faces of the crowd.

"Mayhap," continued the boatswain, swallowing his words, in the surprise of seeing himself unexpectedly confronted by so imposing an eye,—"mayhap this gentleman has some knowledge of the sea, and can decide the matter in dispute."

"We do not study naval tactics at the universities," returned the other, briskly; "though I will confess, from the little I have heard, I am altogether in favour of *scudding*."

He pronounced the latter word with an emphasis which rendered it questionable if he did not mean to pun; the more especially as he threw down his reckoning, and instantly left the field to the quiet possession of Nightingale. The latter, after a short pause, resumed his narrative, though, either from weariness or some other cause, it was observed that his voice was far less positive than before, and that his tale was cut prematurely short. After completing his narrative and his grog, he staggered to the beach, whither a boat was shortly after despatched to convey him on board the ship, which, during all this time, had not ceased to be the constant subject of the suspicious examination of the good-man Homespun.

In the meanwhile, the stranger in green had pursued his walk along the main street of the town. Fid had given chase to the disconcerted Scipio, grumbling as he went, and uttering no very delicate remarks on the knowledge and seamanship of the boatswain. They soon joined company again, the former changing his attack to the negro, whom he liberally abused for abandoning a point which he maintained was as simple and as true as "that yonder bit of a schooner would make more way, going wing-and-wing, than jammed up on a wind."

Probably diverted with the touches of peculiar character he had detected in this singular pair of confederates, or possibly led by his own wayward humour, the stranger followed their footsteps. After turning from the water, they mounted a hill, the latter a little in the rear of his pilots, until he lost sight of them in a bend of the street, or rather road; for, by this time, they were past even the little suburbs of the town. Quickening his steps, the barrister, as he had announced himself to be, was glad to catch a glimpse of the two worthies seated under a fence, several minutes after he had believed them lost. They were making a frugal meal from the contents of a little bag, which the white had borne under his arm, portions from which he now dispensed liberally to his companion, who had taken his post sufficiently nigh to proclaim that perfect amity was restored, though still a little in the back ground, in deference to the superior condition which the other enjoyed in favour of his colour. Approaching the spot, the stranger observed,—

" If you make so free with the bag, my lads, your third man may have to go supperless to bed."

" Who hails?" said Dick, looking up from his bone, with an expression much like that of a mastiff when engaged at a similar employment.

" I merely wished to remind you that you had another messmate," cavalierly returned the other.

" Will you take a cut, brother?" said the seaman, offering the bag with the liberality of a sailor, the moment he fancied there was an indirect demand made on its contents.

" You still mistake my meaning; on the wharf you had another companion."

3 *

"Ay, ay,; he is in the offing there, overhauling that bit of a light-house, which is badly enough moored, unless they mean it to show the channel to your ox-teams and inland traders; hereaway, gentleman, where you see that pile of stones, which seems likely to be coming down shortly by-the-run."

The stranger looked in the direction indicated by the other, and saw the young mariner to whom he had alluded, standing at the foot of a ruined tower, which was crumbling under the slow operations of time, at no great distance from the place where he stood. Throwing a handful of small change to the seamen, he wished them a better meal, and crossed the fence, with an apparent intention of examining the ruin also.

" The lad is free with his coppers," said Dick, suspending the movements of his teeth, to give the stranger another and a better look; " but, as they will not grow where he has planted them, S'ip, you may turn them over to my pocket. An off-handed and a free-handed chap that, Africa; but then these law-dealers get all their pence from the devil, and they are sure of more when the shot begins to run low in the locker."

Leaving the negro to collect the money, and to transfer it, as in duty bound, to the hands of him who, if not his master, was at all times ready and willing to exercise the authority of one, we shall follow the stranger in his walk toward the tottering edifice. There was little about the ruin itself to attract the attention of one who, from his assertions, had probably often enjoyed the opportunities of examining far more imposing remains of former ages, on the other side of the Atlantic. It was a small circular tower, which stood on rude pillars, connected by arches, and might have been constructed, in the infancy of the country, as a place of defence, though it is far more probable that it was a work of a less warlike nature. More than half a century after the period of which we are writing, this little edifice, peculiar in its form, its ruinous condition, and its materials, has suddenly become the study and the theme of that very learned sort of individual, the American antiquarian. It is not surprising that a ruin thus honoured should have become the object of divers hot and erudite discussions. While the chivalrous in the arts and in the antiquities of the country have been gallantly breaking their lances around the mouldering walls, the less instructed and the less zealous have regarded the combatants with the same species of wonder as they would have manifested had they been present when the renowned knight of La Mancha tilted against those other windmills, so ingeniously described by the immortal Cervantes.

On reaching the place, the stranger in green gave his boot a smart blow with the riding-whip, as if to attract the attention of the abstracted young sailor, freely commencing a conversation at the same time, like one who was a regular companion, rather than an intruder on the other's time.

"A very pretty object this would be, if covered with ivy, to be seen peeping through an opening in a wood," he said. "But I beg pardon; gentlemen of your *profession* have little to do with woods and crumbling stones. Yonder is the tower," pointing to the masts of the ship in the outer harbour, "you love to look on; and your only ruin is a wreck!"

"You seem familiar with our tastes, sir," coldly returned the seaman.

"It is by instinct, then; for it is certain I have had but little opportunity of acquiring my knowledge by actual communion with any of the — cloth; nor do I perceive that I am likely to be more fortunate at present. Let us be frank, my friend, and talk in amity. What do you see about this pile of stones, that can keep you so long from your study of yonder noble and gallant ship?"

"Did it then surprise you that a seaman out of employment should examine a vessel that he finds to his mind, perhaps with an intention to ask for service?"

"Her commander must be a dull fellow, if he refuse it to so proper a lad! But you seem to be too well instructed for any of the meaner berths."

"Berths!" repeated the other, again fastening his eyes, with a singular expression, on the stranger in green.

"Berths! It is your nautical word for 'situation,' or 'station,' is it not? We know but little of the marine vocabulary, we barristers; but I think I may venture on that as the true Doric. Am I justified by your authority?"

"The word is certainly not yet obsolete; and, by a figure, I may venture to say, it is as certainly correct in the sense you used it."

"Obsolete!" repeated the stranger in green, returning the meaning look he had just received. "Is that the name of any part of a ship? Perhaps, by *figure*, you mean figure-head; and, by *obsolete*, the long-boat?"

The young seaman laughed; and, as if this sally had broken through the barrier of his reserve, his manner lost some of its restraint during the remainder of their conference.

"It is just as plain," he said, "that you have been at sea, as it is that I have been at school. Since we have both been so fortunate, we may afford to be generous, and cease speaking in parables. For instance, what do you think has been the object and use of this ruin, when it was in better condition than it is at present?"

"In order to judge of that," returned the stranger in green, "it may be necessary to examine it more closely. Let us ascend."

As he spoke, the barrister mounted, by a crazy ladder, to the floor which lay just above the crown of the arches, through which he passed by an open trap-door. His companion hesitated to follow; but, observing that the other expected him at the summit of the ladder, and that he very kindly pointed out a defective round, he sprang forward, and went up the ascent with the agility and steadiness peculiar to his calling.

"Here we are," exclaimed the stranger in green, looking about at the naked walls, which were formed of such small and irregular stones as to give the building the appearance of dangerous frailty, "with good oaken plank for our deck, as you would say, and the sky for our roof, as we call the upper part of a house at the universities. Now let us speak of things on the lower world. A—a—; I forget what you said was your usual appellation."

"That might depend on circumstances. I have been known by different names in different situations. However, if you call me Wilder, I shall not fail to answer."

"Wilder! a good name: though, I dare say, it would have been as true were it Wild-one. You young ship-boys have the character of being a little erratic in your humours. How many tender hearts have you left to sigh for your errors, amid shady bowers, while you have been ploughing—that is the word, I believe—ploughing the salt-sea ocean?"

"Few sigh for me," returned Wilder, thoughtfully, who began to chafe under this free sort of catechism. "Let us return to our study of the tower. What think you has been its object?"

"Its present use is plain, and its former use can be no great mystery. It holds at this moment two light hearts; and, if I am not mistaken, as many light heads, not over-stocked with the stores of wisdom. Formerly it had its granaries of corn, at least, and, I doubt not, certain little quadrupeds who were quite as light of fingers as we are of head and heart. In plain English, it has been a mill."

"There are those who think it has been a fortress."

"Hum! The place might do, at need," returned he in green, casting a rapid and peculiar glance around him. "But mill it has been, notwithstanding one might wish it a nobler origin. The windy situation, the pillars to keep off the invading vermin,

the shape, the air, the very complexion, prove it.    Whir-r-r,
whir-r-r; there has been clatter enough here in time past, I warrant you.    Hist!  It is not done yet!"

Stepping lightly to one of the little perforations which had
once served as windows to the tower, he cautiously thrust his
head through the opening; and, after gazing there half a minute,
he withdrew it again, making a gesture to the attentive Wilder
to be silent.  The latter complied; nor was it long before the
nature of the interruption was sufficiently explained.

The silvery voice of woman was first heard at a little distance;
and then, as the speakers drew nigher, the sounds arose directly
from beneath, within the very shadow of the tower.  By a sort
of tacit consent, Wilder and the barrister chose spots favourable
to the execution of such a purpose, and each continued, during
the time the visiters remained near the ruin, examining their
persons, unseen themselves, and — we are sorry we must do so
much violence to the breeding of two such important characters
in our legend — amused and attentive listeners to their conversation.

## CHAPTER IV.

They fool me to the top of my bent.
*Hamlet.*

THE party below consisted of four individuals, all of whom were females. One was a lady in the decline of her years; another was past the middle age; the third was on the very threshold of what is called "life," as it is applied to intercourse with the world; and the fourth was a negress, who might have seen some five-and-twenty revolutions of the seasons. The latter, at that time and in that country, of course appeared only in the character of a humble, though perhaps favoured, domestic.

"And now, my child, that I have given you all the advice which circumstances and your own excellent heart need," said the elderly lady, among the first words that were distinctly intelligible to the listeners, "I will change the ungracious office to one more agreeable. You will tell your father of my continued affection, and of the promise he has given, that you are to return once again, before we separate for the last time."

This speech was addressed to the younger female, and was apparently received with as much tenderness and sincerity as it was uttered. The one who was addressed raised her eyes, which were glittering with tears she evidently struggled to conceal, and answered in a voice that sounded in the ears of the two youthful listeners like the notes of the siren, so very sweet and musical were its tones.

"It is useless to remind me of a promise, my beloved aunt, which I have so much interest in remembering," she said. "I hope for even more than you have perhaps dared to wish ; if my father does not return with me in the spring, it shall not be for want of urging on my part."

"Our good Wyllys will lend her aid," returned the aunt, smiling and bowing to the third female, with that mixture of suavity and form which was peculiar to the stately manners of the time, and which was rarely neglected when a superior addressed an inferior. "She is entitled to command some interest with General Grayson, from her fidelity and services."

"She is entitled to every thing that love and heart can give !" exclaimed the niece, with a haste and an earnestness that proclaimed how willingly she would temper the formal politeness of the other by the warmth of her own affectionate manner; "my father will scarcely refuse *her* any thing."

"And have we the assurance of Mrs. Wyllys that she will be in our interests ?" demanded the aunt, without permitting her own sense of propriety to be overcome by the stronger feelings of her niece; "with so powerful an ally, our league will be invincible."

"I am so entirely of opinion that the salubrious air of this healthful island is of great importance to my young charge, madam, that, were all other considerations wanting, the little I can do to aid your wishes shall be sure to be done."

Wyllys spoke with dignity, and perhaps with some portion of that reserve which distinguished all the communications between the wealthy and high-born aunt and the salaried and dependent governess of her brother's heiress. Still her manner was gentle, and the voice, like that of her pupil, soft and feminine.

"We may then consider the victory as achieved, as my late husband the rear-admiral was accustomed to say. Admiral de Lacey, my dear Mrs. Wyllys, adopted it in early life as a maxim, by which all his future conduct was governed, and by adhering to which he acquired no small share of his professional reputation, that, in order to be successful, it was only necessary to be determined one would be so; — a noble and inspiriting rule, and one that could not fail to lead to those signal results which, as we all know them, I need not mention."

Wyllys bowed her head, in acknowledgment of the truth of the opinion, and in testimony of the renown of the deceased admiral; but did not think it necessary to make any reply. Instead of allowing the subject to occupy her mind any longer, she turned to her young pupil, and observed, speaking in a voice and with a manner from which every appearance of restraint was banished,—

" Gertrude, my love, you will have pleasure in returning to this charming island, and to these cheering sea-breezes."

" And to my aunt !" exclaimed Gertrude. " I wish my father could be persuaded to dispose of his estates in Carolina, and come northward to reside the whole year."

" It is not quite as easy for an affluent proprietor to remove as you may imagine, my child," returned Mrs. de Lacey. " Much as I wish that some such plan could be adopted, I never press my brother on the subject. Besides, I am not certain, that if we were ever to make another change in the family, it would not be to return *home* altogether. It is now more than a century, Mrs. Wyllys, since the Graysons came into the colonies, in a moment of dissatisfaction with the government in England. My great-grandfather, Sir Everard, was displeased with his second son, and the dissension led my grandfather to the province of Carolina. But, as the breach has long since been healed, I often think my brother and myself may yet return to the halls of our ancestors. Much will, however, depend on the manner in which we dispose of our treasure on this side of the Atlantic."

As the really well-meaning, though, perhaps, a little too much self-satisfied, lady concluded her remark, she glanced her eye at the perfectly unconscious subject of the close of her speech. Gertrude had, as usual, when her aunt chose to favour her governess with any of the family reminiscences, turned her head aside, and was now offering her cheek, burning with health, and perhaps a little with shame, to the cooling influence of the evening breeze. The instant the voice of Mrs. de Lacey ceased, she turned hastily to her companions; and pointing to a noble-looking ship, whose masts, as it lay in the inner harbour, were seen rising above the roofs of the town, she exclaimed, glad to change the subject in any manner,—

"And yonder gloomy prison is to be our home, dear Mrs. Wyllys, for the next month!"

"I hope your dislike to the sea has magnified the time," mildly returned her governess; "the passage between this place and Carolina has often been made in a much shorter period."

"That it has been so done, I can testify," resumed the admiral's widow, adhering a little pertinaciously to a train of thoughts which, once thoroughly awakened in her bosom, was not easily diverted into another channel, "since my late estimable and (I feel certain all who hear me will acquiesce when I add) gallant husband once conducted a squadron of his royal master, from one extremity of his majesty's American dominions to the other, in a time less than that named by my niece. It may have made some difference in his speed that he was in pursuit of the enemies of his king and country; but still the fact proves that the voyage can be made within the month."

"There is that dreadful Henlopen, with its sandy shoals and shipwrecks on one hand, and that stream they call the Gulf, on the other!" exclaimed Gertrude, with a shudder and a burst of natural terror, which makes timidity sometimes attractive, when exhibited in the person of youth and beauty. "If it were not for Henlopen, and its gales, and its shoals, and its gulfs, I could think only of the pleasure of meeting my father."

Mrs. Wyllys, who never encouraged her pupil in these natural weaknesses, however pretty and becoming they might appear to other eyes, turned with a steady mien to the young lady, and remarked, with a brevity and decision that were intended to put the question of fear at rest for ever, —

"If all the dangers you appear to apprehend existed in reality, the passage would not be made daily, or even hourly in safety. You have often, madam, come from the Carolinas by sea, in company with Admiral de Lacey?"

"Never," the widow promptly and a little drily answered. "The water never agreed with my constitution, and I have always made the journey by land. But then, you know, Wyllys, as the consort and relict of a flag-officer, it was not seemly that I should be ignorant of naval science. I believe there are few ladies in the British empire who are more familiar with ships, either singly or in squadron, particularly the latter, than myself. This information I have naturally acquired, as the companion of an officer whose fortune it was to lead fleets. I presume these are matters of which you are profoundly ignorant."

The calm dignified countenance of Wyllys, on which it would seem long cherished and painful recollections had left a settled but mild expression of sorrow, that rather tempered than destroyed the traces of character which were still remarkable in her eye, became clouded for a moment with a shade of melancholy. After hesitating, as if willing to change the subject, she replied,—

"I have not been altogether a stranger to the sea. It has been my lot to have made many long, and some perilous, voyages."

"As a mere passenger. But we wives of sailors, only, among our sex, can lay claim to any real knowledge of the noble profession! What natural object is there, or can there be," exclaimed the nautical dowager, in a burst of professional enthusiasm, "finer than a stately ship breasting the billows, as I have heard the admiral say a thousand times, its taffrail ploughing the main, and its cut-water gliding after, like a sinuous serpent pursuing its shining wake, as a living creature choosing its path on the land,

and leaving the bone under its fore-foot, a beacon for those that follow? I know not, my dear Wyllys, if I make myself intelligible to you, but to my instructed eye, this charming description conveys a picture of all that is grand and beautiful!"

The latent smile of the governess might have betrayed that she was imagining the deceased admiral had not been altogether devoid of the waggery of his vocation, had not a slight noise, which sounded like the rustling of the wind, but which in truth was suppressed laughter, proceeded from the upper room of the tower. The words, "It is lovely!" were still on the lips of the youthful Gertrude, who saw all the beauty of the picture her aunt had essayed to describe, without descending to the humble employment of verbal criticism. But her voice became hushed, and her attitude that of startled attention :—

"Did you hear nothing?" she said.

"The rats have not yet altogether deserted the mill," was the calm reply of Wyllys.

"Mill! my dear Mrs. Wyllys, will you persist in calling this picturesque ruin *a mill?*"

"However fatal it may be to its charms, in the eyes of eighteen, I must call it *a mill.*"

"Ruins are not so plenty in this country, my dear goveaness," returned her pupil, laughing, while the ardour of her eye denoted how serious she was in defending her favourite opinion, "as to justify us in robbing them of any little claims to interest they may happen to possess."

"Then, happier is the country! Ruins in a land are, like most of the signs of decay in the human form, sad evidences of abuses and passions which have hastened the inroads of time. These provinces are like yourself, my Gertrude, in their freshness and their youth, and comparatively, in their innocence also. Let us hope for both a long, an useful, and a happy existence."

"Thank you for myself and for my country; but still I can never admit this picturesque ruin has been *a mill*."

" Whatever it may have been, it has long occupied its present place, and has the appearance of continuing where it is much longer, which is more than can be said of our prison, as you call yonder stately ship, in which we are so soon to embark. Unless my eyes deceive me, madam, those masts are moving slowly past the chimneys of the town."

" You are very right, Wyllys. The seamen are towing the vessel into the outer harbour, where they will warp her fast to the anchors, and thus secure her until they shall be ready to un-make their sails, in order to put to sea in the morning. This is a manœuvre often performed, and one which the admiral has so clearly explained, that I should find little difficulty in superintending it in my own person, were it suitable to my sex."

"This is, then, a hint that all our own preparations are not completed. However lovely this spot may seem, Gertrude, we must now leave it, for some months at least."

" Yes," continued Mrs. de Lacey, slowly following the footsteps of the governess, who had already moved from beneath the ruin; " whole fleets have often been towed to their anchors, and there warped, waiting for wind and tide to serve. None of our sex know the dangers of the ocean, but we who have been bound in the closest of all ties to officers of rank and great service; and none others can ever truly enjoy the real grandeur of the ennobling profession. A charming object is a vessel cutting the waves with her taffrail, and chasing her wake on the trackless waters, like a courser that ever keeps in his path, though dashing madly on at the very top of his speed!"

The reply of Mrs. Wyllys was not audible to the covert listeners. Gertrude had followed her companions; but, when at some little distance from the tower, she paused to take a parting look at its mouldering walls. A profound stillness succeeded for more than a minute.

"There is something in that pile of stones, Cassandra," she said, to the jet-black maiden at her elbow, "that could make me wish it had been something more than a mill."

"There rat in 'em," returned the literal and simple-minded black; "you hear what Misse Wyllys say?"

Gertrude turned, laughed, and patted the dark cheek of her attendant, with fingers that looked like snow by the contrast, as if to chide her for wishing to destroy the pleasing illusion she would so gladly harbour, and then bounded down the hill after her aunt and governess, like a joyous and youthful Atalanta.

The two singularly consorted listeners in the tower stood gazing at their respective look-outs, so long as the smallest glimpse of the flowing robe of her light form was to be seen; and then they turned to each other, and stood confronted, the eyes of each endeavouring to read the expression of his neighbour's countenance.

"I am ready to make an affidavit before my Lord High Chancellor," suddenly exclaimed the barrister, "that this has never been a mill!"

"Your opinion has undergone a sudden change!"

"I am open to conviction, as I hope to be a judge. The case has been argued by a powerful advocate, and I have lived to see my error."

"And yet there are rats in the place."

"Land rats, or water rats?" quickly demanded the other, giving his companion one of those startling and searching glances, which his keen eye had so freely at command.

"Both, I believe," was the caustic reply; "certainly the former, or the gentlemen of the long robe are much injured by report."

The barrister laughed: nor did his temper appear in the

slightest degree ruffled at so free a hit at his learned and honourable profession.

"You gentlemen of the ocean have such an honest and amusing frankness about you," he said, "that I vow to God you are overwhelming. I am a downright admirer of your noble calling, and something skilled in its terms. What spectacle, for instance, can be finer than a noble ship ' stemming the waves with her taffrail,' and chasing her wake, like a racer on the course?"

"Leaving the ' bone in her mouth' under her stern, as a light-house for all that come after!"

Then, as if they found singular satisfaction in dwelling on these images of the worthy relict of the admiral, they broke out simultaneously into a fit of clamorous merriment, which caused the old ruin to ring, as in its best days of windy power. The barrister was the first to regain his self-command, for the mirth of the young mariner was joyous, and without the least restraint.

"But this is dangerous ground for any but a seaman's widow to touch," the former observed, as suddenly causing his laughter to cease as he had admitted of its indulgence. "The younger, she who is no lover of a mill, is a rare and lovely creature! it would seem that she is the niece of the nautical critic."

The young mariner ceased laughing in his turn, as if he were suddenly convinced of the glaring impropriety of making so near a relative of the fair vision he had seen, the subject of his merriment. Whatever might have been his secret thoughts, he was content with replying,—

"She so declared herself."

"Tell me," said the barrister, walking close to the other, like one who communicated an important secret in the question, "was there not something remarkable, searching, extraordinary, heart-touching, in the voice of her they called Wyllys?

"Did you note it?"

"It sounded to me like the tones of an oracle — the whisper-ings of fancy — the very words of truth! It was a strange and persuasive voice!"

"I confess I felt its influence, and in a way for which I cannot account!"

"It amounts to infatuation!" returned the barrister, pacing up and down the little apartment, every trace of humour and irony having disappeared in a look of settled and abstracted care. His companion appeared little disposed to interrupt his meditations, but stood leaning against the naked walls, himself the subject of reflection. At length the former shook off his air of thought, with that startling quickness which seemed common to his manner; he approached a window, and directing the attention of Wilder to the ship in the outer harbour, abruptly demanded —

"Has all your interest in yonder vessel ceased?"

"Far from it; it is just such a boat as a seaman's eye loves to study!"

"Will you venture to board her?"

"At this hour? — alone? — I know not her commander, or her people."

"There are other hours beside this, and a sailor is certain of a frank reception from his messmates."

"These slavers are not always willing to be boarded; they carry arms, and know how to keep strangers at a distance."

"Are there no watchwords in the masonry of your trade, by which a brother is known? Such terms as 'stemming the waves with the taffrail,' for instance, or some of those knowing phrases we have lately heard?"

Wilder kept his own keen look on the countenance of the other, as he thus questioned him, and seemed to ponder on what he heard before he ventured a reply.

"Why do you demand this of me?" he coldly asked.

"Because, as I believe that 'faint heart never won fair lady,' so do I believe that indecision never won a ship. You wish a situation, you say; and, if I were an admiral, I would make you my flag-captain. At the assizes, when we wish a brief, we throw out the proper feelers. But perhaps I am talking too much at random for an utter stranger. You will, however, remember, that though it is the advice of a lawyer, it is given gratuitously."

"Is it the more to be relied on for so extraordinary liberality?"

"Of that you must judge for yourself," said the stranger in green, very deliberately putting his foot on the ladder, and descending, until no part of his person but his head was seen. "Here I go, literally cutting the waves with my taffrail," he added, descending backwards, and seeming to take great pleasure in laying particular emphasis on the words. "Adieu, my friend; if we do not meet again, I enjoin you never to forget the rats in the Newport ruin."

He disappeared as he concluded, and in another instant his light form was on the ground. Turning with the most admirable coolness, he gave the bottom of the ladder a trip with one of his feet, and laid the only means of descent prostrate on the earth. Then, looking up at the wondering Wilder, he nodded his head familiarly, repeated his adieu, and passed with a swift step from beneath the arches.

"This is extraordinary, not to say insolent, conduct," muttered Wilder, who by the process was left a prisoner in the ruin. After ascertaining that a fall from the trap might endanger his legs, the young sailor ran to one of the windows of the place, in order to reproach his treacherous comrade, or indeed to assure himself that he was serious in thus deserting him. The barrister was already out of hailing distance, and, before Wilder had time to decide on what course to take, his active footsteps had led him into the skirts of the town, among the buildings of which his person became immediately lost to the eye.

During all the time occupied by the foregoing scenes and dia-

4

logue, Fid and the negro were diligently discussing the contents of the bag, under the fence where they were last seen. As the appetite of the former became appeased, his didactic disposition returned, and at the precise moment when Wilder was left alone in the tower, he was intently engaged in admonishing the black on the delicate subject of behaviour in mixed society.

"And so you see, Guinea," he concluded, "in order to keep a weather-helm in company, you are never to throw all aback, and go stern foremost out of a dispute, as you have this day seen fit to do. According to my l'arning, that Master Nightingale is better in a bar-room than in a squall; and if you had just luffed-up on his quarter, when you saw me laying myself athwart his hawse in the argument, we should have given him a regular jam in the discourse, and then the fellow would have been shamed in the eyes of the bystanders. Who hails? what cook is sticking his neighbour's pig now?"

"Lor'! Misser Fid," cried the black; "here Masser Harry, wid a head out of port-hole, up dereaway in a lighthouse, singin' out like a marine in a boat wid a plug out!"

"Ay, ay, let him alone for hailing a top-gallant yard, or a flying-jib-boom! The lad has a voice like a French horn, when he has a mind to tune it! And what the devil is he manning the guns of that weather-beaten wreck for? At all events, if he has to fight his craft alone, there is no one to blame but himself, since he has gone to quarters without beat of drum, or without in any other manner seeing fit to muster his people."

As Dick and the negro had both been making the best of their way towards the ruin, from the moment they discovered the situation of their friend, by this time they were within speaking distance of the spot itself. Wilder, in those brief, pithy tones that distinguish the manner in which a sea-officer issues his orders, directed him to raise the ladder. When he was liberated, he demanded, with a sufficiently significant air, if they had observed the direction in which the stranger in green had made his retreat?

"Do you mean the chap in boots, who was for shoving his oar into another man's rullock, a bit ago, on the wharf?"

"The very same."

"He made a slant on the wind until he had weathered yonder bit of a barn, and then he tacked and stretched away off here to the east-and-by-south, going large, with studding-sails alow and aloft, as I think, for he made a devil of a head-way."

"Follow," cried Wilder, starting forward in the direction indicated by Fid, without waiting to hear any more of the other's explanations.

The search was vain. Although they continued their enquiries until long after the sun had set, no one could give them the smallest tidings of what had become of the stranger in green. Some had seen him and marvelled at his singular costume, and bold and wandering look; but, by all accounts, he had disappeared from the town as strangely and as mysteriously as he had entered it.

## CHAPTER V.

Are you so brave? I'll have you talked with anon.
*Coriolanus.*

THE good people of the town of Newport sought their rest at an early hour. They were remarkable for that temperance and discretion which, even to this day, distinguish the manners of the inhabitants of New England. By ten, the door of every house in the place was closed for the night; and it is quite probable, that, before another hour had passed, scarcely an eye was open, among all those which had been sufficiently alert, throughout the day, not only in superintending the interests of their proper owners, but in bestowing wholesome glances at the concerns of the rest of the neighbourhood.

The landlord of the "Foul Anchor," as the inn, where Fid and Nightingale had so nearly come to blows, was called, scrupulously closed his doors at eight; a sort of expiation, by which he endeavoured to atone, while he slept, for any moral peccadilloes that he might have committed during the day. Indeed, it was to be observed as a rule, that those who had the most difficulty in maintaining their good name, on the score of temperance and moderation, were the most rigid in withdrawing, in season, from the daily cares of the world. The admiral's widow had given no little scandal, in her time, because lights were so often seen burning in her house long after the hour prescribed by custom for their extinction. There were several other little particulars in which this good lady had also rendered herself obı oxious to the whispered remarks of some of her female visitants. An episcopalian herself, she was always observed to be employed with her needle on the evenings of Saturdays, though by no means distinguished for her ordinary industry. It was, however, a sort of manner the good lady had of exhibiting her adherence to the belief that the night of Sunday was the orthodox evening of the Sabbath. On this subject there was, in truth, a species of silent warfare between her and the wife of the principal clergyman of the town. It resulted, happily, in no very striking marks of hostility. The latter was content to retaliate, by bringing her work on the evenings of Sundays, to the house of the dowager, and occasionally interrupting their discourse, by a diligent application of the needle for some five or six minutes at a time. Against this contamination Mrs. de Lacey took no other precaution than to play with the leaves of a prayer-book, precisely on the principle that one uses holy water to keep the devil at that distance which the church has considered safest for its proselytes.*

Let these matters be as they would, by ten o'clock on the night of the day our tale commences, the town of Newport was as still as if it did not contain a living soul. Watchmen there were none; for roguery had not yet begun to thrive openly in the provinces. When, therefore, Wilder and his two companions

---

* The puritans believed that the Sabbath commenced with the setting of the sun on Saturday, and ended at the same hour on Sunday. Thus the latter evening throughout all New England was, and in some measure is still, more observed as a fête, than as a time of worship, while the preceding evening is respected with the most rigid observances. The writer once had a discussion on this point with a New England divine. The latter had no very high biblical authority for the usage; but he very justly remarked, that there was something consolatory and grand in the idea that the whole of Christendom was keeping holy the Sabbath at precisely the same moment! It is scarcely necessary to add, that this opinion, besides the fact that the usage was confined to a sect or sects was met by the objection, that as we proceed east or west, there is a known difference in time to defeat the calculation.

issued at that hour, from their place of retirement into the empty
streets, they found them as still as if man had never trod there.
Not a candle was to be seen, nor the smallest evidence of human
life to be heard. It would seem our adventurers knew their
errand well; for instead of knocking up any of the drowsy
publicans to demand admission, they held their way steadily to
the water's side; Wilder leading, Fid coming next, and Scipio,
in conformity to all usage, bringing up the rear, in his ordinary,
quiet, submissive manner.

At the margin of the water they found several small boats,
moored under the shelter of a neighbouring wharf. Wilder
gave his companions their directions, and walked to a place convenient for embarking. After waiting the necessary time, the
bows of two boats came to the land at the same moment, one of
which was governed by the hands of the negro, and the other by
those of Fid.

"How's this?" demanded Wilder; "is not one enough?
There is some mistake between you."

"No mistake at all," responded Dick, suffering his oar to float
on its blade, and running his fingers into his hair, content with
his achievement; "no more mistake than there is in taking the
sun on a clear day and in smooth water. Guinea is in the boat
you hired; but a bad bargain you made of it, as I thought at
the time: and so, as 'better late than never' is my rule, I have
just been casting an eye over all the craft; if this is not the
tightest and fastest rowing clipper of them all, then am I no
judge; and yet the parish priest would tell you, if he were here,
that my father was a boat-builder, ay, and swear it too; that is to
say, if you paid him well for the same."

"Fellow," returned Wilder, angrily, "you will one day induce
me to turn you adrift. Take the boat to the place where you
found it, and see it secured as before."

"Turn me adrift!" deliberately repeated Fid, "that would be

cutting all your weather lanyards at one blow, Master Harry. Little good would come of Scipio Africa and you, after I should part company. Have you ever fairly logg'd the time we have sailed together?"

"Ay, have I; but it is possible to break even a friendship of twenty years."

"Saving your presence, master Harry, I'll be d——d if I believe any such thing. Here is Guinea, who is no better than a nigger, and therein far from being a fitting messmate to a white man; but, being used to look at his black face for four-and-twenty years, d'ye see, the colour has got into my eye, and now it suits as well as another. Then, at sea, in a dark night, it is not so easy a matter to tell the difference. I am not tired of you yet, Master Harry, and it is no trifle that shall part us."

"Then, abandon your habit of making free with the property of others."

"I abandon nothing. No man can say he ever know'd me to quit a deck while a plank stuck to the beams; and shall I abandon, as you call it, my rights? What is the mighty matter, that all hands must be called to see an old sailor punished? You gave a lubberly fisherman, a fellow who has never been in deeper water than his own line will sound, you gave him, I say, a glittering spaniard, just for the use of a bit of a skiff for the night, or, mayhap, for a small reach into the morning. Well, what does Dick do? He says to himself — for d——e if he's any blab to run round a ship grumbling at his officer — so he just says to himself, 'That's too much,' says he; and he looks about to find the worth of it in some of the fishermen's neighbours. Money can be eaten; and, what is better, it may be drunk; therefore, it is not to be pitch'd overboard with the cook's ashes. I'll warrant me, if the truth could be fairly come by, it would be found that, as to the owners of this here yawl and that there skiff, their mothers are cousins, and that the dollar will go in snuff and strong drink among the whole family — so, no great harm done after all."

Wilder made an impatient gesture to the other to obey, and walked up the bank, to give him time to comply. Fid never disputed a positive and distinct order, though he often took so much discretionary latitude in executing those which were less precise. He did not hesitate, therefore, to return the boat; but he did not carry his subordination so far as to do it without complaint. When this act of justice was performed, Wilder entered the skiff; and, seeing that his companions were seated at their oars, he bade them pull down the harbour, admonishing them, at the same time, to make as little noise as possible.

"The night I rowed you into Louisburg, a-reconnoitring," said Fid, thrusting his left hand into his bosom, while, with his right, he applied sufficient force to the light oar to make the skiff glide swiftly over the water — "that night we muffled every thing, even to our tongues. When there is occasion to put stoppers on the mouths of a boat's crew, why, I'm not the man to gainsay it; but, as I am one of them that thinks tongues were just as much made to talk with, as the sea was made to live on, I uphold rational conversation in sober society. S'ip, thou Guinea, where the devil are you shoving the skiff to? — here-away lies the island, and you are for going into yonder bit of a church."

"Lay on your oars," interrupted Wilder; "let the boat drift by this vessel."

They were now in the act of passing the ship which had been warping from the wharfs to an anchorage, and in which the young sailor had so clandestinely heard that Mrs. Wyllys and the fascinating Gertrude were to embark, on the following morning, for the distant province of Carolina. As the skiff floated past, Wilder examined the vessel, by the dim light of the stars, with a seaman's eye. No part of her hull, her spars, or her rigging, escaped his notice; and, when the whole became confounded, by the distance, in one dark mass of shapeless matter, he leaned his head over the side of his little bark, and mused. To this abstraction Fid presumed to offer no interruption. It had the appearance of professional duty; a subject that, in his eyes, was endowed with a species of character that might be called sacred. Scipio was habitually silent. After losing many minutes in this manner, Wilder suddenly regained his recollection. and abruptly observed—

"It is a tall ship, and one that should make a long chase!"

"That's as may be," returned the ready Fid. "Should that fellow get a free wind, and his canvass all abroad, it might worry a king's cruiser to get nigh enough to throw the iron on his decks; but jamm'd up close hauled, why, I'd engage to lay on his weather-quarter with the saucy He——"

"Boys," interrupted Wilder, "it is now proper that you should know something of my future movements. We have been shipmates, I might almost say messmates, for more than twenty years. I was no better than an infant, Fid, when you brought me to the commander of your ship, and not only was instrumental in saving my life, but in putting me into a situation to make an officer."

"Ay, ay, you were no great matter, master Harry, as to bulk; and a short hammock served your turn as well as the captain's berth."

"I owe you a heavy debt, Fid, for that one generous act, and something, I may add, for your steady adherence to me since."

"Why, yes, I've been pretty steady in my conduct, Master Harry, in this here business, more particularly seeing that I have never let go my grapplings, though you've so often sworn to turn me adrift. As for Guinea, here, the chap makes fair weather with you, blow high or blow low, whereas it is no hard matter to get up a squall between us, as might be seen in that small affair about the boat——"

4 *

" Say no more of it," interrupted Wilder, whose feelings appeared sensibly touched, as his recollection ran over long-past and bitterly-remembered scenes; " you know that little else than death can part us, unless indeed you choose to quit me now. It is right you should know that I am engaged in a desperate pursuit, and one that may easily end in ruin to myself and all who accompany me. I feel reluctant to separate from you, my friends, for it may be a final parting, but, at the same time, you should know all the danger."

" Is there much more travelling by land?" bluntly demanded Fid.

" No; the duty, such as it is, will be done entirely on the water."

" Then bring forth your ship's books, and find room for such a mark as a pair of crossed anchors, which stand for all the same as so many letters reading ' Richard Fid.' "

" But perhaps when you know——"

" I want to know nothing about it, Master Harry. Haven't I sailed with you often enough under sealed orders, to trust my old body once more in your company, without forgetting my duty? What say you, Guinea? will you ship? or shall we land you at once, on yonder bit of a low point, and leave you to scrape acquaintance with the clams?"

" 'Em berry well off here," muttered the perfectly contented negro.

" Ay, ay, Guinea is like the launch of one of the coasters, always towing in your wake, Master Harry; whereas, I am often luffing athwart your hawse, or getting foul, in some fashion or other, on one of your quarters. Howsomever, we are both shipped, as you see, in this here cruise, with the particulars of which we are both well satisfied. So pass the word among us what is to be done next, and no more parley."

" Remember the cautions you have already received," returned

Wilder, who saw that the devotion of his followers was too infinite to need quickening, and who knew, from long and perilous experience, how implicitly he might rely on their fidelity, notwithstanding certain failings, that were perhaps peculiar to their condition; "remember what I have already given in charge; and now pull directly for the ship in the outer harbour."

Fid and the black promptly complied; and the boat was soon skimming the water between the little island, and what might, by comparison, be called the main. As they approached the vessel, the strokes of the oars were moderated, and finally abandoned altogether: Wilder preferring to let the skiff drop down with the tide upon the object he wished well to examine before venturing to board.

"Has not that ship her nettings triced to the rigging?" he demanded, in a voice that was lowered to the tones necessary to escape observation, and which betrayed, at the same time, the interest he took in the reply.

"According to my sight, she has," returned Fid; "your slavers are a little pricked by conscience, and are never over-bold, unless when they are chasing a young nigger on the coast of Congo. Now, there is about as much danger of a Frenchman's looking in here to-night, with this land breeze and clear sky, as there is of my being made Lord High Admiral of England; a thing not likely to come to pass soon, seeing that the king don't know a great deal of my merit."

"They are, to a certainty, ready to give a warm reception to any boarders!" continued Wilder, who rarely paid much attention to the amplifications with which Fid so often saw fit to embellish the discourse. "It would be no easy matter to carry a ship thus prepared, if her people were true to themselves."

"I warrant ye there is a full quarter-watch at least sleeping among her guns, at this very moment, with a bright look-out from her cat-heads and taffrail. I was once on the weather fore yard-arm of the Hebe, when I made, hereaway to the south-west, a sail coming large upon us——"

" Hist ! they are stirring on her decks !"

" To be sure they are. The cook is splitting a log; the captain has most likely sung out for his night-cap."

The voice of Fid was lost in a summons from the ship, that sounded like the roaring of some sea-monster, which had unex-pectedly raised its head above the water. The practised ears of our adventurers instantly comprehended it to be, what it truly was, the manner in which it was not unusual to hail a boat. With-out taking time to ascertain that the plashing of oars was to be heard in the distance, Wilder raised his form in the skiff, and answered.

" How now ?" exclaimed the same strange voice ; " there is no one victualled aboard here that speaks thus. Whereaway is he that answers ?"

" A little on your larboard bow; here, in the shadow of the ship."

" And what are ye about, within the sweep of my hawse ?"

" Cutting the waves with my taffrail," returned Wilder after a moment's hesitation.

" What fool has broke adrift here ?" muttered his interrogator. " Pass a blunderbuss forward, and let us see if a civil answer can be drawn from the fellow."

" Hold !" said a calm authoritative voice, from the most distant part of the ship; " it is as it should be; let them approach."

The man in the bows of the vessel bade them come alongside, and the conversation ceased. Wilder had now an opportunity to discover that, as the hail had been intended for another boat, which was still at a distance, he had answered prematurely. But, perceiving that it was too late to retreat with safety, or perhaps only acting in conformity to his original determination, he directed his companions to obey.

" 'Cutting the waves with the taffrail' is, of a surety, not the civilest answer a man can give to a hail," muttered Fid, dropping the blade of his oar into the water; "nor is it matter to be logged, that they have taken offence at the same. Howsomever, Master Harry, if they are so minded as to make a quarrel about the thing, give them as good as they send, and count on manly backers."

No reply was made to this encouraging assurance; for, by this time, the skiff was within a few feet of the ship. Wilder ascended the side of the vessel amid a deep, and, as he felt it to be, an ominous silence. The night was dark, though enough light fell from the stars, that were here and there visible, to render objects sufficiently distinct to the eyes of a seaman. When our young adventurer touched the deck, he cast a hurried and scrutinising look about him, as if doubts and impressions, which had long been harboured, were all to be resolved by that first view.

An ignorant landsman would have been struck with the order and symmetry with which the tall spars rose towards the heavens, from the black mass of the hull, and with the rigging that hung in the air, one dark line crossing another, until all design seemed confounded in the confusion and intricacy of the studied maze. But to Wilder these familiar objects furnished no immediate attraction. His first rapid glance had, like that of all seamen it is true, been thrown upward, but it was instantly succeeded by the brief, though keen, examination to which we have just alluded. With the exception of one who, though his form was muffled in a large sea-cloak, seemed to be an officer, not a living creature was visible on the decks. On each side was a dark, frowning battery, arranged in the beautiful and imposing order of marine architecture; but nowhere could he find a trace of the crowd of human beings which usually throng the deck of an armed ship, or that was necessary to render the engines effective. It was quite in rule that most of her people should be in their hammocks at that hour; but still it was customary to leave a sufficient number on the watch, to look to the safety of the vessel. Finding himself so unexpectedly confronted with a single individual, our adventurer began to be sensible of the awkwardness of his situation, and of the necessity of some explanation.

"You are no doubt surprised, sir," he said, "at the lateness of the hour that I have chosen for my visit."

"You were certainly expected earlier," was the laconic answer.

"Expected!"

"Ay, expected. Have I not seen you and your two companions who are in the boat, reconnoitring us half the day from the wharfs of the town, and even from the old tower on the hill? What did all this curiosity foretell, but an intention to come on board?"

"This is odd, I will acknowledge!" exclaimed Wilder in some alarm. "And, then, you had notice of my intentions?"

"Hark ye, friend," interrupted the other, indulging in a low laugh; "from your outfit and appearance, I think I am right in calling you a seaman. Do you imagine that glasses were forgotten in the inventory of this ship? or, do you fancy that we don't know how to use them?"

"You must have strong reasons for looking so deeply into the movements of strangers on the land?"

"Hum! Perhaps we expect our cargo from the country. But I suppose you have not come so far in the dark to look at our manifest. You would see the captain?"

"Do I not see him?"

"Where?" demanded the other, with a start that proved he stood in salutary awe of his superior.

"In yourself."

"I! I have not got so high in the books, though my time may yet come some fair day. Hark ye, friend; you passed under the stern of yonder ship, which has been hauling into the stream, in coming out to us?"

"Certainly; she lies, as you see, directly in my course."

"A wholesome-looking craft that! and one well found, I warrant you. She is quite ready to be off, they tell me."

"It would so seem: her sails are bent, and she floats like a ship that is full."

"Of what?" abruptly demanded the other.

"Of articles mentioned in her manifest, no doubt. But you seem light yourself: if you are to load at this port, it will be some days before you put to sea."

"Hum! I don't think we shall be long after our neighbour," the other remarked, a little drily. Then, as if he might have said too much, he added hastily, "We slavers carry little else, you know, than our shackles and a few extra tierces of rice; the rest of our ballast is made up of these guns, and the stuff to put into them."

"And is it usual for ships in the trade to carry so heavy an armament?"

"Perhaps it is — perhaps not. To own the truth, there is not much law on the coast, and the strong arm often does as much as the right. Our owners, therefore, I believe, think it quite as well there should be no lack of guns and amunition on board."

"They should also give you people to work them."

"They have forgotten that part of their wisdom, certainly."

His words were nearly drowned by the same gruff voice that had brought-to the skiff of Wilder, which sent another hoarse summons across the water, rolling out sounds that were intended to say,—

"Boat ahoy!"

The answer was quick, short, and nautical; but it was render-ed in a low and cautious tone. The individual, with whom Wil-der had been holding such equivocating parlance, seemed embar-

rassed by the sudden interruption, and a little at a loss to know
how to conduct himself. He had already made a motion towards
leading his visiter to the cabin, when the sounds of oars were
heard clattering in a boat alongside of the ship, announcing that
he was too late. Bidding the other remain where he was, he
sprang to the gangway, in order to receive those who had just
arrived.

By this sudden desertion, Wilder found himself in entire possession of the part of the vessel where he stood. It gave him a
better opportunity to renew his examination, and to cast a scrutinising eye over the new comers.

Some five or six athletic-looking seamen ascended from the
boat, in profound silence. A short and whispered conference
took place between them and their officer, who appeared both to
receive a report, and to communicate an order. When these preliminary matters were ended, a line was lowered from a whip on
the main-yard, the end evidently dropping into the boat. In a
moment, the burden it was intended to transfer to the ship was
seen swinging in the air, midway between the water and the spar.
It then slowly descended, inclining in-board, until it was safely,
and somewhat carefully, landed on the decks of the vessel.

During the whole of this process, which in itself had nothing
extraordinary, or out of the daily practice of large vessels in port,
Wilder had strained his eyes, until they appeared nearly ready
to start from their sockets. The black mass, which had been
lifted from the boat, seemed, while it lay against the back-ground
of sky, to possess the proportions of the human form. The seamen gathered about this object. After much bustle, and a good
deal of low conversation, the burden or body, whichever it might
be called, was raised by the men, and the whole disappeared
together, behind the masts, boats, and guns, which crowded the
forward part of the vessel.

The whole event was of a character to attract the attention

of Wilder. His eye was not, however, so intently riveted on the group in the gangway, as to prevent his detecting a dozen black objects, that were suddenly thrust forward, from behind the spars and other dark masses of the vessel. They might be blocks swinging in the air, but they bore also a strong resemblance to human heads. The simultaneous manner in which they appeared and disappeared served to confirm this impression; nor, to confess the truth, had our adventurer any doubt that curiosity had drawn so many enquiring countenances from their respective places of concealment. He had not much leisure, however, to reflect on all these little accompaniments of his situation, before he was rejoined by his former companion, who, to all appearance, was again left to himself in entire possession of the deck.

"You know the trouble of getting off the people from the shore," the officer observed, "when a ship is ready to sail."

"You seem to have a summary method of hoisting them in," returned Wilder.

"Ah! you speak of the fellow on the whip? Your eyes are good, friend, to tell a jack-knife from a marling-spike, at this distance. But the lad was mutinous; that is, not absolutely mutinous—but drunk. As mutinous as a man can well be, who can neither speak, sit, nor stand."

Then, as if as well content with his humour as with this simple explanation, the other laughed and chuckled in a manner that showed he was in perfect good humour with himself.

"But all this time you are left on deck," he quickly added, "and the captain is waiting your appearance in the cabin. Follow; I will be your pilot."

"Hold," said Wilder; "will it not be as well to announce my visit?"

"He knows it already: little takes place aboard here that does not reach his ears before it gets into the log-book."

Wilder made no further objection, but indicated his readiness to proceed. The other led the way to the bulk-head which separated the principal cabin from the quarter-deck of the ship; pointing to a door, he then whispered,—

"Tap twice; if he answer, go in."

Wilder did as directed. His first summons was either unheard or disregarded. On repeating it, he was commanded to enter. The young seaman opened the door, with a crowd of sensations, that will find their solution in the succeeding parts of our narrative, and instantly stood, under the light of a powerful lamp, in the presence of the stranger in green.

## CHAPTER VI.

——— The good old plan,
That they should get, who have the power,
And they should keep, who can.
*Wordsworth.*

THE apartment in which our adventurer now found himself, afforded no bad illustration of the character of its occupant. In its form and proportions, it was a cabin of the usual size and arrangements; but in its furniture and equipments, it exhibited a singular admixture of luxury and martial preparation. The lamp, which swung from the upper deck, was of solid silver; and though adapted to its present situation by mechanical ingenuity, there was that in its shape and ornaments which betrayed it had once been used before some shrine of a more sacred character. Massive candlesticks, of the same precious metal, and which partook of the same ecclesiastical formation, were on a venerable table, whose mahogany was glittering with the polish of half a century, and whose gilded claws and carved supporters bespoke an original destination very different from the ordinary service of a ship. A couch, covered with cut velvet, stood along the transom; while a divan, of blue silk, lay against the bulk-head opposite, manifesting, by its fashion, its materials, and its piles of pillows, that even Asia had been made to contribute to the ease of its luxurious owner. In addition to these prominent articles, there were cut-glass mirrors, plate, and even hangings; each of which, by something peculiar in its fashion or materials, bespoke an origin different from that of its neighbour. In short, splendour and elegance seemed to have been much more consulted than propriety or taste, in the selection of most of those articles which had been oddly enough made to contribute to the caprice or to tue comfort of their singular possessor.

In the midst of this medley of wealth and luxury appeared the frowning appendages of war. The cabin included four of those dark cannon whose weight and number had been first to catch the attention of Wilder. Notwithstanding they were placed in such close proximity to the articles of ease just enumerated, it only needed a seaman's eye to perceive that they stood ready for immediate service, and that five minutes of preparation would strip the place of all its tinsel, and leave it a warm and well-protected battery. Pistols, sabres, half-pikes, boarding-axes, and all the minor implements of marine warfare, were arranged about the cabin in such a manner as to aid in giving it an appearance of wild embellishment while, at the same time, each was convenient to the hand.

Around the mast was placed a stand of muskets; and strong wooden bars, that were evidently made to fit in brackets on each side of the door, sufficiently showed that the bulkhead might easily be converted into a barrier. The entire arrangement proclaimed that the cabin was considered the citadel of the ship. In support of this latter opinion there was also a hatch, communicating with the apartments of the inferior officers, and which opened a direct passage into the magazine. These dispositions, a little different from what he had been accustomed to see, instantly struck the eye of Wilder, though leisure was not then given to reflect on their usages and objects.

There was a latent expression of satisfaction, something modified perhaps by irony, on the countenance of the stranger in green (for he was still clad as when first introduced to the reader), as he arose, on the entrance of his visiter. The two stood several moments without speaking, when the pretended barrister saw fit to break the awkward silence.

"To what happy circumstance is this ship indebted for the honour of such a visit?" he demanded.

"I believe I may answer, to the invitation of her captain," Wilder answered, with a steadiness and calmness equal to that displayed by the other.

"Did he show you his commission, in assuming that office? They say at sea, I believe, that no cruiser should be found without a commission."

"And what say they at the universities on this material point?"

"I see I may as well lay aside my gown, and own the marling-spike!" returned the other, smiling. "There is something about the trade — *profession*, though, I believe, is your favourite word — there is something about the profession which betrays us to each other. Yes, Mr. Wilder," he added, with dignity, motioning to his guest to imitate his example, and take a seat, "I am, like yourself, a seaman bred; and happy am I to add, the commander of this gallant vessel."

"Then must you admit that I have not intruded without a sufficient warrant."

"I confess the same. My ship has filled your eye agreeably; nor shall I be slow to acknowledge, that I have seen enough about your air and person to make me wish to be an older acquaintance. You want service?"

"One should be ashamed of idleness in these stirring times."

"It is well. This is an oddly-constructed world in which we live, Mr. Wilder. Some think themselves in danger with a foundation beneath them no less solid than *terra firma*, while others are content to trust their fortunes on the sea. So, again, some there are who believe praying is the business of man; and then come others who are sparing of their breath, and take those favours for themselves which they have not always the leisure or the inclination to ask for.   No doubt you thought it prudent to enquire into the nature of our trade, before you came hither in quest of employment?"

"You are said to be a slaver, among the townsmen of New-port."

"They are never wrong, your village gossips!  If witchcraft ever truly existed on earth, the first of the cunning tribe has been a village innkeeper; the second, its doctor; and the third, its priest.   The right to the fourth honour may be disputed between the barber and the tailor. — Roderick!"

The captain accompanied the word with which he so unceremoniously interrupted himself, by striking a light blow on a Chinese gong, which, among other curiosities, was suspended from one of the beams of the upper deck, within reach of his hand.

"I say, Roderick, dost sleep?"

A light and active boy darted out of one of the two little state-rooms which were constructed on the quarters of the ship, and answered to the summons by announcing his presence.

"Has the boat returned?"

The reply was in the affirmative.

"Has she been successful?"

"The general is in his room, sir, and can give you an answer better than I."

"Then, let the general appear, and report the result of his campaign.

Wilder was by far too deeply interested to break the sudden reverie into which his companion had fallen, even by breathing as loud as usual.   The boy descended through the hatch like a serpent gliding into his hole, or, rather, a fox darting into his burrow, and then a profound stillness reigned in the cabin.   The commander of the ship leaned his head on his hand, appearing unconscious of the presence of a stranger.   The silence might have been of much longer duration, had it not been interrupted by the appearance of a third person. A straight, rigid form, slowly elevated itself through the little hatchway, very much in the manner that theatrical spectres are seen to make their appearance on the stage, until about half of the person was visible, when it ceased to rise, and turned its disciplined countenance on the captain.

" I wait for orders," said a mumbling voice, which issued from lips that were hardly perceived to move.

Wilder, started at this unexpected vision, nor was the stranger wanting in an aspect sufficiently remarkable to produce surprise in any spectator. The face was that of a man of fifty, with the lineaments thoroughly indurated by service. Its colour was an uniform red, with the exception of one of those expressive little fibrous tell-tales on each cheek, which bear so striking a resemblance to the mazes of the vine, and which would seem to be the true origin of the proverb which says that " Good wine needs no bush." The crown of the head was bald; but around each ear was a mass of grizzled hair, pomatumed and combed into military bristles. The neck was long, and supported by a black stock; the shoulders, arms, and body, were those of a tall man; and the whole were enveloped in an over-coat, which, though it had something methodical in its fashion, was evidently intended as a sort of domino. The captain raised his head as the other spoke, exclaiming, as if taken by surprise,—

"Ah! general, are you at your post? Did you find the land?"

" Yes."

"And the point? — and the man?"

" Both."

" What did you?"

" Obey orders."

" That was right.—You are a jewel for an executive officer,

general; as such, I wear you near my heart. Did the fellow complain?"

"He was gagged."

"A summary method of closing remonstrance. It is as it should be, general; as usual, you have merited my approbation."

"Then reward me for it."

"In what manner? You are already as high in rank as I can elevate you. The next step must be knighthood."

"Pshaw! my men are no better than militia. They want coats."

"They shall have them. His majesty's guards shall not be half so well equipped. General, I wish you a good night."

The figure descended in the same rigid spectral manner as it had risen on the sight, leaving Wilder again alone with the captain of the ship. The latter seemed suddenly struck with the fact that this odd interview had occurred in the presence of one who was nearly a stranger, and that, in his eyes at least, it might appear to require some explanation.

"My friend," he said, with an air something explanatory, while it was at the same time not a little haughty, "commands what, in a more regular cruiser, would be called the 'marine guard.' He has gradually risen, by service, from the rank of a subaltern, to the high station which he now fills. You perceive he smells of the camp?"

"More than of the ship. Is it usual for slavers to be so well provided with military equipments? I find you armed at all points."

"You would know more of us, before we proceed to drive our bargain," the captain answered with a smile. He then opened a little casket that stood on the table, and drew from it a parchment, which he coolly handed to Wilder, saying, as he did so, with one of the quick searching glances of his restless eye, "You will see by that we have 'letters of marque,' and are duly

authorised to fight the battles of the king, while we are conducting our own more peaceable affairs."

"This is the commission of a brig!

"True, true. I have given you the wrong paper. I believe
you will find this more accurate."

"This is truly a commission for the 'good ship Seven Sisters;'
but you surely carry more than ten guns; and then, these in
your cabin throw nine instead of four pound shot."

"You are as precise as if you had been the barrister, and I
the blundering seaman. I dare say you have heard of such a
thing as stretching a commission?" continued the captain, carelessly throwing the parchment back among a pile of similar
documents. Then rising from his seat, he began to pace the
cabin with quick steps, as he continued, "I need not tell you,
Mr. Wilder, that ours is a hazardous pursuit. Some call it lawless. But, as I am little addicted to theological disputes, we will
waive the question. You have not come here without knowing
your errand?"

"I am in search of a berth."

"Doubtless you have reflected well on the matter, and know
your own mind as to the trade in which you would sail. In
order that no time may be wasted, and that our dealings may be
frank, as becomes two honest seamen, I will confess to you, at
once, that I have need of you. A brave and skilful man, one
older, though I dare say not better than yourself, occupied that
larboard state-room, within the month; poor fellow, he is food
for fishes ere this."

"He was drowned?"

"Not he! He died in open battle with a king's ship!"

"A king's ship! Have you then stretched your commission
so far as to find a warranty for giving battle to his majesty's
cruisers?"

"Is there no king but George the Second? Perhaps she

5

bore the white flag, perhaps a Dane. But he was truly a gallant fellow; and there lies his berth, as empty as the day he was carried from it to be cast into the sea. He was a man fit to succeed to the command, should an evil star shine on my fate. I think I could die easier, were I to know this noble vessel was to be transmitted to one who would make such use of her as should be."

"Doubtless your owners would provide a successor, in the event of such a calamity."

"My owners are very reasonable," returned the other, casting another searching glance at his guest, which compelled Wilder to lower his own eyes to the cabin floor; "they seldom trouble me with importunities or orders."

"They are indulgent! I see that flags at least were not forgotten in your inventory: do they also give you permission to wear any of those ensigns, as you may please?"

As this question was put, the expressive and understanding looks of the two seamen met. The captain drew a flag from the half-open locker, where it had caught the attention of his visiter, and, letting the roll unfold itself on the deck, he answered,—

"This is the lily of France, you see. No bad emblem of your stainless Frenchman. An escutcheon of pretence without spot, but, nevertheless, a little soiled by use. Here you have the calculating Dutchman; plain, substantial, and cheap. It is a flag I little like. If the ship be of value, her owners are not often willing to dispose of her without a price. This is your swaggering Hamburger. He is rich in the possession of one town, and makes his boast of it in these towers. Of the rest of his mighty possessions he wisely says nothing in his allegory. These are the crescents of Turkey; a moonstruck nation, that believe themselves the inheritors of heaven. Let them enjoy their birthright in peace; it is seldom they are found looking for its blessings on the high seas;—and these, the little satellites that play about the mighty moon, your barbarians of Africa. I hold but little communion with these wide-trowsered gentry, for they seldom deal in aught gainful. And yet," he added, glancing his eye at the silken divan, before which Wilder was seated, "I have met the rascals; nor have we parted entirely without communication. Ah! here comes the man I like; your gorgeous Spaniard! This field of yellow reminds one of the riches of his mines; and this crown! one might fancy it of beaten gold, and stretch forth a hand to grasp the treasure. What a blazonry is this for a galleon! Here is the humbler Portuguese; and yet is he not without a wealthy look. I have often fancied there were true Brazilian diamonds in this kingly bauble. Yonder crucifix, which you see hanging in pious proximity to my state-room door, is a specimen of the sort I mean." Wilder turned his head to throw a look on the valuable emblem, that was really suspended from the bulk-head, within a few inches of the spot the other named. After satisfying his curiosity, he was in the act of giving his attention again to the flags, when he detected another of those penetrating, but stolen glances, with which his companion so often read the countenance of his associates. It is probable that the captain was endeavouring to discover the effect his profuse display of wealth had produced on the mind of his visiter. Let that be as it would, Wilder smiled; for, at that moment, the idea first occurred that the ornaments of the cabin had been thus studiously arranged with an expectation of his arrival, and with the wish that their richness might strike him favourably. The other caught the expression of his eye; and perhaps he mistook its meaning, when he suffered his construction of what it said to animate him to pursue his whimsical analysis of the flags, with an air still more cheerful and vivacious than before.

"These double-headed monsters are land birds, and seldom

risk a flight over deep waters," he continued; "they are not for
me. Your hardy, valiant Dane; your sturdy Swede; a nest of
smaller fry," he continued, passing his hand rapidly over a dozen
little rolls as they lay, each in its own repository, "who spread
their bunting like larger states; and your luxurious Neapolitan.
Ah! here come the keys of heaven! This is a flag to die under;
I lay yard-arm and yard-arm, once, under that very bit of bunting, with a heavy corsair from Algiers——"

"What! Did you choose to fight under the banners of the
Church?"

"In mere devotion. I pictured to myself the surprise that
would overcome the barbarian when he should find that we did
not go to prayers. We gave him but a round or two, before he
swore that Allah had decreed he might surrender. There was a
moment, while I luffed-up on his weather-quarter, I believe, that
the Mussulman thought the whole of the sacred conclave was
afloat, and that the downfall of Mahomet and his offspring was
nigh. I provoked the conflict, I will confess, in showing him
these peaceful keys, which he is dull enough to think open half
the strong boxes of Christendom."

"When he had confessed his error, you let him go?"

"Hum!—with my blessing. There was some interchange
of commodities between us, and we parted. I left him smoking
his pipe, in a heavy sea, with his fore-top-mast over the side, his
mizzenmast under his counter, and some six or seven holes in
his bottom, that let in the water just as fast as the pumps
discharged it. You see he was in a fair way to acquire his portion of the inheritance. But Heaven had ordained it all, and he
was satisfied!"

"And what flags are these which you have passed? They
seem rich and many."

"These are England; like herself, aristocratic, party-coloured,
and a good deal touched by humour. Here is bunting to note

all ranks and conditions, as if men were not made of the same flesh, and the people of one kingdom might not all sail honestly under the same emblems. Here is my Lord High Admiral; your St. George; your field of red, and of blue, as chance may give you a leader, or the humour of the moment prevail; the stripes of mother India, and the royal standard itself!"

"The royal standard!"

"Why not? a commander is termed 'a monarch in his ship.' Ay, this is the standard of the king; and, what is more, it has been worn in presence of an admiral!"

"This needs explanation!" exclaimed his listener, who seemed to feel much that sort of horror that a churchman would discover at the detection of sacrilege. "To wear the royal standard in presence of a flag! We all know how difficult, and even dangerous, it becomes, to sport a simple pennant, with the eye of a king's cruiser on us——"

"I love to flaunt the rascals!" interrupted the other, with a smothered, but bitter laugh. "There is pleasure in the thing! In order to punish, they must possess the power; an experiment often made, but never successful. You understand balancing accounts with the law, by showing a broad sheet of canvass. I need say no more."

"And which of all these flags do you most use?" demanded Wilder, after a moment of intense thought.

"As to mere sailing, I am as whimsical as a girl in her teens in the choice of her ribands. I will often show you a dozen in a day. Many is the worthy trader who has gone into port with his veritable account of this Dutchman, or that Dane, with whom he has spoken in the offing. As to fighting, though I have been known to indulge a humour, too, in that particular, still there is one which I most affect."

"And that is——"

The captain kept his hand for a moment on the roll he had

touched, and seemed to read the very soul of his visiter, so intent and keen was his look the while. Then, suffering the bunting to fall, a deep, blood-red field, without relief or ornament of any sort, unfolded itself, as he answered, with emphasis,—

"This."

"That is the colour of a rover!"

"Ay, it is *red!* I like it better than your gloomy fields of black, with death's heads, and other childish scare-crows. It threatens nothing; but merely says, 'Such is the price at which I am to be bought.' Mr. Wilder," he added, losing the mixture of irony and pleasantry with which he had supported the previous dialogue, in an air of authority, "we understand each other. It is time that each should sail under his proper colours. I need not tell you who I am?"

"I believe it is unnecessary," said Wilder. "If I can comprehend these palpable signs, I stand in presence of — of——"

"The Red Rover," continued the other, observing that he hesitated to pronounce the appalling name. "It is true; and I hope this interview is the commencement of a durable and firm friendship. I know not the secret cause, but from the moment of our meeting, a strong and indefinable interest has drawn me towards you. Perhaps I felt the void which my situation has drawn about me; — be that as it may, I receive you with a longing heart and open arms."

Though it must be very evident, from what preceded this open avowal, that Wilder was not ignorant of the character of the ship on board of which he had just ventured, yet did he not receive the acknowledgment without embarrassment. The reputation of this renowned freebooter, his daring, his acts of liberality and licentiousness so frequently blended, and his desperate disregard of life on all occasions, were probably crowding together in the recollection of our more youthful adventurer, and caused him to feel that species of responsible hesitation, to which we are all more or less subject on the occurrence of important events, be they ever so much expected.

"You have not mistaken my purpose, or my suspicions," he at length answered, "for I own I have come in search of this very ship. I accept the service; from this moment, you will rate me in whatever station you may think me best able to discharge my duty with credit."

"You are next to myself. In the morning the same shall be proclaimed on the quarter-deck; and, in the event of my death, unless I am deceived in my man, you will prove my successor. This may strike you as sudden confidence. It is so, in part, I must acknowledge; but our shipping lists cannot be opened, like those of the king, by beat of drum in the streets of the metropolis; and then am I no judge of the human heart, if my frank reliance on your faith does not in itself strengthen your good feelings in my favour."

"It does!" exclaimed Wilder, with sudden and strong emphasis.

The Rover smiled calmly, as he continued,—

"Young gentlemen of your years are apt to carry no small portion of their hearts in their hands. But notwithstanding this seeming sympathy, in order that you may have sufficient respect for the discretion of your leader, it is necessary that I should say we have met before. I was apprised of your intention to seek me out, and to offer to join me."

"It is impossible," cried Wilder. "No human being——"

"Can ever be certain his secrets are safe," interrupted the other, "when he carries a face as ingenuous as your own. It is but four-and-twenty hours since you were in the good town of Boston."

"I admit that much; but——"

"You will soon admit the rest. You were too curious in your enquiries of the dolt who declares he was robbed by us of his provisions and sails. The false-tongued villain! It may be well for him to keep from my path, or he may get a lesson that shall prick his honesty. Does he think such pitiful game as he would induce me to spread a single inch of canvass, or even lower a boat into the sea?"

"Is not his statement, then, true?" demanded Wilder, in a surprise he took no pains to conceal.

"True! Am I what report has made me? Look keenly at the monster, that nothing may escape you," returned the Rover, with a hollow laugh, in which scorn struggled to keep down the feelings of wounded pride. "Where are the horns, and the cloven foot? Snuff the air: is it not tainted with sulphur? But enough of this. I knew of your enquiries, and liked your mien. In short, you were my study; and though my approaches were made with some caution, they were sufficiently nigh to effect the object. You pleased me, Wilder; and I hope the satisfaction may be mutual."

The newly engaged buccaneer bowed to the compliment of his superior, and appeared at some little loss for a reply. As if to get rid of the subject at once, he hurriedly observed,—

"As we now understand each other, I will intrude no longer, but leave you for the night, and return to my duty in the morning."

"Leave me!" returned the Rover, stopping short in his walk, and fastening his eye keenly on the other. "It is not usual for my officers to leave me at this hour. A sailor should love his ship, and never sleep out of her unless on compulsion."

"We may as well understand each other," said Wilder quickly. "If it is to be a slave, and like one of the bolts, a fixture in the vessel, that you need me, our bargain is at an end."

"Hum! I admire your spirit, sir, much more than your dis-cretion. You will find me an attached friend, and one who little likes a separation, however short. Is there not enough to content you here? I will not speak of such low considerations as those which administer to the ordinary appetites. But you have been taught the value of reason — here are books; you have taste — here is elegance; you are poor — here is wealth."

" They amount to nothing, without liberty," coldly returned the other.

" And what is this liberty you ask? I hope, young man, you would not so soon betray the confidence you have just received. Our acquaintance is but short, and I may have been too hasty in my faith."

" I must return to the land," Wilder added, firmly, " if it be only to know that I am intrusted, and not a prisoner."

" There is a generous sentiment, or deep villany in all this," resumed the Rover, after a minute of thought. " I will believe the former. Declare to me that, while in the town of Newport, you will inform no soul of the true character of this ship."

" I will swear it," eagerly interrupted Wilder

" On this cross," rejoined the Rover, with a sarcastic laugh; " on this diamond-mounted cross! No, sir," he added, with a proud curl of the lip, as he cast the jewel contemptuously aside; " oaths are made for men who need laws to keep them to their promises; I need no more than the clear and unequivocal affirmation of a gentleman."

" Then, plainly and unequivocally do I declare, that, while in Newport, I will discover the character of this ship to no one, without your wish, or order, so to do. Nay, more——"

" No more. It is wise to be sparing of our pledges, and to say no more than the occasion requires. The time may come when you can do good to yourself, without harming me, by being unfettered by a promise. In an hour you shall land; that time will be needed to make you acquainted with the terms of your enlistment, and to grace my rolls with your name. — Roderick," he added, again touching the gong, " you are wanted, boy."

5 *

The same active lad that had made his appearance at the first summons, ran up the steps from the cabin beneath, and announced his presence again by his voice.

" Roderick," continued the Rover, " this is my future lieutenant, and, of course, your officer, and my friend. Will you take refreshment, sir? There is little that man needs, which Roderick cannot supply!"

" I thank you; I have need of none."

" Then have the goodness to follow the boy. He will show you into the dining apartment beneath, and give you the written regulations. In an hour, you will have digested the code, and by that time I shall be with you. Throw the light more upon the ladder, boy; you can descend *without* a ladder though, it would seem, or I should not, at this moment, have the pleasure of your company."

The intelligent smile of the Rover was unanswered by any corresponding evidence from the subject of his joke, that he found satisfaction in the remembrance of the awkward situation in which he had been left in the tower. The former caught the displeased expression of the other's countenance, as he gravely prepared to follow the boy, who already stood in the hatchway with a light. Advancing a step, with the grace and tones of a man of breeding, he said quickly,—

" Mr. Wilder, I owe you an apology for my seeming rudeness at parting on the hill. Though I believed you mine, I was not sure of my acquisition. You will readily see how necessary it might be, to one in my situation, to throw off a companion at such a moment."

Wilder turned with a countenance from which every shade of displeasure had vanished, and motioned to him to say no more.

" It was awkward enough, certainly, to find one's self in such a prison; but I feel the justice of what you say. I might have done the very thing myself, if the same presence of mind were at hand to help me."

"The good man, who grinds in the Newport ruin, must be in a sad way, since all the rats are leaving his mill," cried the Rover, beckoning his temporary adieus, as his companion followed the boy.

Wilder freely returned the open, cordial laugh; and then, as he descended, the cabin was left to him, who, a few minutes before, had been found in its quiet possession.

# CHAPTER VII.

The world affords no law to make thee rich;
Then be not poor, but break it, and take this.
*Apoth.* My poverty, but not my will, consents.
*Romeo and Juliet.*

THE Rover arrested his step, as the other disappeared, and stood
for more than a minute in an attitude of high and self-gratulating
triumph. He was exulting in his success. But though his intelligent face betrayed the satisfaction of the inward man, it was
illumined by no expression of vulgar joy. It was the countenance of one who was suddenly relieved from intense care, rather
than that of a man who was greedy of profiting by the services
of others. Indeed, it would not have been difficult for a close
observer to detect a shade of regret in the lightings of his seduc-
tive smile, or in the momentary flashes of his changeful eye.
The feeling, however, quickly passed away, and his whole figure
and countenance resumed the ordinary careless mien in which he
most indulged in his hours of ease.

After allowing sufficient time for the boy to conduct Wilder to
the cabin below, and to put him in possession of the regulations
for the police of the ship, the captain again touched the gong,
and once more summoned the former to his presence. The lad
had, however, to approach the elbow of his master, and to speak
thrice, before the other was conscious that he had answered
his call.

"Roderick," said the Rover, after a long pause, " are you
there?"

"I am here," added a low, and a mournful voice.

"Ah! you gave him the regulations?"

"I did."

"And he reads?"

"He reads."

"It is well. I would speak to the general. Roderick, you must have need of rest; good night; let the general be summoned to a council and—Good night, my Roderick."

The boy made an assenting reply; but, instead of springing with his former alacrity to execute the order, he lingered a moment near his master's chair. Failing, however, in his wish to catch his eye, he reluctantly descended the stairs which led into the lower cabins, and was seen no more that night.

It is needless to describe the manner in which the general made his second appearance. It differed in no particular from his former *entrée*, except that, on this occasion, the whole of his person was developed. He appeared a tall, upright form, that was far from being destitute of natural proportions, but which had been so exquisitely drilled into simultaneous movement, that the several members had so far lost the power of volition as to render it impossible for any one of them to stir, without producing something like a correspondent demonstration in all of its fellows. This rigid and well-regulated personage, after making a military bow to his superior, helped himself to a chair, in which, after some little time lost in preparation, he seated himself in silence. The Rover seemed conscious of his presence, for he acknowledged his salute by a gentle inclination of his own head; though he did not appear to think it necessary to suspend his ruminations the more on that account. At length, however, he turned short upon his companion, and said abruptly,—

"General, the campaign is not finished."

"What remains? The field is won, and the enemy is a prisoner."

Ay, your part of the adventure is well achieved, but much

of mine remains to be done.   You saw the youth in the lower cabin ?"

"I did."

"And how do you like his appearance?"

"Maritime."

"That is as much as to say you like him not."

"I like discipline."

"I am much mistaken if you do not find him to your taste on the quarter-deck.   Let that be as it may, I have still a favour to ask of you."

"A favour!—it is getting late."

"Did I say 'a favour?' there is duty to be done."

"I wait your orders."

"It is necessary that we use great precaution; for, as you know——"

"I wait your orders," laconically repeated the other.

The Rover compressed his mouth, and a smile struggled about the nether lip; but it changed into a look half bland, half authoritative, as he continued,—

"You will find two seamen in a skiff alongside the ship; the one is white, and the other is black.   These men you will have conducted into the vessel — into one of the forward state-rooms — and you will have them both thoroughly intoxicated."

"It shall be done," returned he who was called the general, rising, and marching with long strides towards the door of the cabin.

"Pause a moment," added the Rover: "what agent will you use?"

"Nightingale has the strongest head but one in the ship."

"He is too far gone already.   I sent him ashore to look about for any straggling seamen who might like our service; and I found him in a tavern, with all the fastenings off his tongue declaiming like a lawyer who had taken a fee from both parties.

Besides, he had a quarrel with one of these very men, and it is probable they would get to blows in their cups."

"I will do it myself. My nightcap is waiting for me; and it is only to lace it a little tighter than common."

The Rover seemed content with this assurance; for he expressed his satisfaction with a familiar nod of the head. The soldier was now about to depart, when he was again interrupted,—

"One thing more, general: there is your captive."

"Shall I make him drunk too?"

"By no means. Let him be conducted hither."

The general made an ejaculation of assent, and left the cabin. "It were weak," thought the Rover, as he resumed his walk up and down the apartment, "to trust too much to an ingenuous face and youthful enthusiasm. I am deceived if the boy has not had reason to think himself disgusted with the world, and ready to embark in any romantic enterprise; but still, to be deceived might be fatal; therefore will I be prudent, even to excess of caution. He is tied in an extraordinary manner to these two seamen. I would I knew his history! But that will come in proper time. The men must remain as hostages for his own return, and for his faith. If he prove false, why, they are seamen; and many men are expended in this wild service of ours! It is well arranged; and no suspicion of any plot on our part will wound the sensitive pride of the boy, if he be, as I would gladly think, a true man."

Such was, in a great manner, the train of thought in which the Rover indulged, for many minutes after his military companion had left him. His lips moved; smiles, and dark shades of thought, in turn, chased each other from his speaking countenance, which betrayed all the sudden and violent changes that denoted the workings of a busy spirit within. While thus engrossed in mind, his step became more rapid, and at times, he gesticulated a little extravagantly, when he found himself, in a sudden turn, unexpectedly by a form that seemed to rise on his sight like a vision.

While most engaged in his own humours, two powerful seamen had, unheeded, entered the cabin; and, after silently depositing a human figure in a seat, they withdrew without speaking. It was before this personage that the Rover now found himself. The gaze was mutual, long, and uninterrupted by a syllable from either party. Surprise and indecision held the Rover mute, while wonder and alarm appeared to have literally frozen the faculties of the other. At length the former, suffering a quaint and peculiar smile to gleam for a moment across his countenance, said abruptly,—

"I welcome Sir Hector Homespun!"

The eyes of the confounded tailor — for it was no other than that garrulous acquaintance of the reader who had fallen into the toils of the Rover — the eyes of the good-man rolled from right to left, embracing in their wanderings the medley of elegance and warlike preparation that they every where met, never failing to return, from each greedy look, to devour the figure that stood before him.

"I say, welcome Sir Hector Homespun!" repeated the Rover.

"The Lord will be lenient to the sins of the miserable father of seven small children!" ejaculated the tailor. "It is but little, valiant pirate, than can be gotten from a hard-working, upright tradesman, who sits from the rising to the setting sun, bent over his labour."

"These are debasing terms for chivalry, Sir Hector," interrupted the Rover, laying his hand on the little riding-whip, which had been thrown carelessly on the cabin table, and tapping the shoulder of the tailor with the same, as if he were a sorcerer, and would disenchant the other with a touch. "Cheer up, honest and loyal subject: fortune has at length ceased to frown: it is but a few hours since you complained that no custom came to your shop from this vessel, and now are you in a fair way to do the business of the whole ship."

"Ah! honourable and magnanimous Rover," rejoined Homespun, whose fluency returned with his senses, "I am an impoverished and undone man. My life has been one of weary and probationary hardships. Five bloody and cruel wars——"

"Enough! I have said that fortune was just beginning to smile. Clothes are as necessary to gentlemen of our profession as to the parish priest. You shall not baste a seam without your reward. Behold!" he added, touching the spring of a secret drawer, which flew open, and discovered a confused pile of gold, in which the coins of nearly every Christian people were blended, "we are not without the means of paying those who serve us faithfully."

The sudden exhibition of a hoard of wealth, which not only greatly exceeded any thing of the kind he had ever before witnessed, but which actually surpassed his limited imaginative powers, was not without its effect on the sensitive feelings of the good-man. After feasting on the sight for the few moments that his companion left the treasure exposed to view, he turned to the envied possessor of so much gold, and demanded — the tones of increased confidence gradually stealing into his voice, as the inward man felt additional motives of encouragement,—

"And what am I expected to perform, mighty seaman, for my portion of this wealth?"

"That which you daily perform on the land—to cut, to fashion, and to sew. Perhaps, too, your talent at a masquerade dress may occasionnally be taxed."

"Ah! they are lawless and irreligious devices of the enemy, to lead men into sin and worldly abominations. But, worthy mariner, there is my disconsolate consort, Desire; though stricken in years, and given to wordy strife, yet is she the lawful partner of my bosom, and the mother of a numerous offspring."

" She shall not want. This is an asylum for distressed husbands. Your men, who have not force enough to command at
home, come to my ship as to a city of refuge. You will make
the seventh who has found peace by fleeing to this sanctuary.
Their families are supported by ways best known to ourselves, and
all parties are content. This is not the least of my benevolent
acts."

" It is praiseworthy and just, honourable captain; and I hope
that Desire and her offspring may not be forgotten. The labourer
is surely worthy of his hire; and if, peradventure, I should toil
in your behalf, through stress of compulsion, I hope the good
woman, and her young, may fatten on your liberality."

" You have my word; they shall not be neglected."

" Perhaps, just gentlemen, if an allotment should be made in
advance from that stock of gold, the mind of my consort would
be relieved, her enquiries after my fate not so searching, and her
spirit less troubled. I have reason to understand the temper of
Desire; and am well identified, that, while the prospect of want
is before her eyes, there will be a clamour in Newport. Now
that the Lord has graciously given me the hopes of a respite,
there can be no sin in wishing to enjoy it in peace."

Although the Rover was far from believing, with his captive,
that the tongue of Desire could disturb the harmony of his ship,
he was in the humour to be indulgent. Touching the spring
again, he took a handful of the gold, and extending it towards
Homespun, demanded,—

" Will you take the bounty and the oath? The money will
then be your own."

" The Lord defend us from the evil one, and deliver us all from
temptation!" ejaculated the tailor. " Heroic Rover, I have a
dread of the law. Should any evil overcome you, in the shape
of a king's cruiser, or a tempest cast you on the land, there might
be danger in being contaminated too closely with your crew. Any

little services which I may render, on compulsion, will be overlooked, I humbly hope; and I trust to your magnanimity, honest
and honourable commander, that the same will not be forgotten
in the division of your upright earnings."

"This is but the spirit of cabbaging, a little distorted," muttered the Rover, as he turned lightly on his heel, and tapped the
gong, with an impatience that sent the startling sounds through
every cranny of the ship. Four or five heads were thrust in at
the different doors of the cabin, and the voice of one was heard,
desiring to know the wishes of their leader.

"Take him to his hammock," was the sudden order.

The good-man Homespun, who, from fright or policy, appeared
to be utterly unable to move, was quickly lifted from his seat,
and conveyed to the door which communicated with the quarter-
deck.

"Pause," he exclaimed, to his unceremonious bearers, as they
were about to transport him to the place designated by their captain; "I have one word yet to say. Honest and loyal rebel,
though I do not accept your service, neither do I refuse it in an
unseemly and irreverent manner. It is a sore temptation, and I
feel it at my fingers' ends. But a covenant may be made between us, by which neither party shall be a loser, and in which
the law shall find no grounds of displeasure. I would wish,
mighty commodore, to carry an honest name to my grave, and I
would also wish to live out the number of my days; for, after
having passed with so much credit and unharmed, through five
bloody and cruel wars——"

"Away with him!"

Homespun vanished, as if magic had been employed in trans-
porting him, and the Rover was again left to himself. His
meditations were not interrupted for a long time, by human footstep or voice. That breathing stillness, which unbending and
stern discipline can alone impart, pervaded the ship. A lands-

man seated in the cabin, might have fancied himself, although surrounded by a crew of lawless and violent men, in the solitude of a deserted church, so suppressed and deadened were even those sounds that were absolutely necessary. They were heard at times, it is true, the high and harsh notes of some reveller, who appeared to break forth in the strains of a sea song, which, as they issued from the depths of the vessel, and were not very musical in themselves, broke on the silence like the first discordant strains of a new practitioner on a bugle. But even these interruptions gradually grew less frequent, and finally became inaudible. At length the Rover heard a hand fumbling about the handle of the cabin door, and then his military friend once more made his appearance.

There was that in the step, the countenance, and the whole air of the general, which proclaimed that his recent service, if successful, had not been achieved without great personal hazard. The Rover, who had started from his seat the moment he saw who entered, instantly demanded his report.

"The white is so drunk, that he cannot lie down without holding on to the mast; but the negro is either a cheat, or his head is made of flint."

"I hope you have not too easily abandoned the design."

"I would as soon batter a mountain! My retreat was not made a minute too soon."

The Rover fastened his eyes on the general, in order to assure himself of the precise condition of his subaltern, and changed his purpose.

"It is well. We will now retire for the night."

The other carefully dressed his tall person, and brought his face in the direction of the little hatchway so often named. Then, by a sort of desperate effort, he essayed to march to the spot, with his customary military step. As one or two erratic movements, and crossings of the legs, were not commented on by his captain, the worthy martinet descended the stairs, as he believed, with sufficient dignity, the moral man not being in the precise state which is the best adapted to discover any little blunders that might be made by his physical coadjutor. The Rover looked at his watch; and, after allowing sufficient time for the deliberate retreat of the general, he stepped lightly on the stairs, and descended also.

The lower apartments of the vessel, though less striking in their equipments than the upper cabin, were arranged with great attention to neatness and comfort. A few offices for the servants occupied the extreme after-part of the ship, communicating by doors with the dining apartment of the secondary officers; or, as it was called in technical language, the "ward-room." On each side of this, again, were the state-rooms, an imposing name by which the dormitories of those who are entitled to the honours of the quarter-deck are called. Forward of the ward-room, came the apartments of the minor officers; and, immediately in front of them, the corps of the individual who was called the general was lodged, forming, by their discipline, a barrier between the more lawless seamen and their superiors.

There was little departure, in this disposition of the accommodations, from the ordinary arrangements of vessels of war of the same description and force as the Rover; but Wilder had not failed to remark, that the bulkheads which separated the cabins from the berth-deck, or the part occupied by the crew, were far stouter than common, and that a small howitzer was at hand, to be used, as a physician might say, internally, should occasion require. The doors were of extraordinary strength, and the means of barricadoing them resembled more a preparation for battle, than the usual securities against petty encroachments on private property. Muskets, blunderbusses, pistols, sabres, half-pikes, &c., were fixed to the beams and carlings, or were made to serve as ornaments against the different bulkheads, in a profusion that plainly told they were there as much for use as for show. In short, to the eye of a seaman, the whole betrayed a state of things, in which the superiors felt that their whole security against the violence and insubordination of their inferiors depended on their influence and their ability to resist, united; and that the former had not deemed it prudent to neglect any of the precautions which might aid their comparatively less powerful physical force.

In the principal of the lower apartments, or the ward-room, the Rover found his newly enlisted lieutenant, apparently busy in studying the regulations of the service in which he had just embarked. Approaching the corner in which the latter had seated himself, the former said, in a frank, encouraging, and even confidential manner,—

"I hope you find our laws sufficiently firm, Mr. Wilder?"

"Want of firmness is not their fault; if the same quality can always be observed in administering them, it is well," returned the other, rising to salute his superior. "I have never found such rigid rules, even in——"

"Even in what, sir?" demanded the Rover, perceiving that his companion hesitated.

"I was about to say, even in his majesty's service," returned Wilder, slightly colouring. "I know not whether it may be a fault, or a recommendation, to have served in a king's ship."

"It is the latter; at least I, for one, should think it so, since I learned my trade in the same service."

"In what ship?" eagerly interrupted Wilder.

"In many," was the cold reply. "But, speaking of rigid rules, you will soon perceive that, in a service where there are no courts on shore to protect us, nor any sister cruisers to look after our welfare, no small portion of power is necessarily vested in the commander. You find my authority a good deal extended."

"A little unlimited," said Wilder, with a smile that might have passed for ironical.

"I hope you will have no occasion to say that it is arbitrarily executed," returned the Rover, without observing, or perhaps without letting it appear that he observed, the expression of his companion's countenance. "But your hour is come; you are at liberty to land."

The young man thanked him, with a courteous inclination of the head, and expressed his readiness to go. As they ascended the ladder into the upper cabin, the captain expressed his regret that the hour, and the necessity of preserving the incognito of his ship, would not permit him to send an officer of his rank ashore in the manner he could wish.

"But then there is the skiff in which you came off, still alongside, and your own two stout fellows will soon twitch you to yon point. Apropos of those two men, are they included in our arrangements?"

"They have never quitted me since my childhood, and would not wish to do it now."

"It is a singular tie that unites two men so oddly constituted, to one so different by habits and education from themselves," returned the Rover, glancing his eye keenly at the other, and withdrawing it the instant that he perceived his interest in the answer was observed.

"It is," Wilder calmly replied; "but as we are all seamen, the difference is not so great as one would at first imagine. I will now join them, and take an opportunity to let them know that they are to serve in future under your orders."

The Rover suffered him to leave the cabin, following to the quarter-deck, with a careless step, as if he had come abroad to breathe the open air of the night.

The weather had not changed, but it still continued dark, though mild. The same stillness as before reigned on the decks of the ship; and nowhere, with a solitary exception, was a human form to be seen, amid the collection of dark objects that rose on the sight, all of which Wilder well understood to be necessary fixtures in the vessel. The exception was the same individual who had first received our adventurer, and who still paced the quarter-deck, wrapped, as before, in a watch-coat. To this personage the youth now addressed himself, announcing his intention temporarily to quit the vessel. His communication was received with a respect that satisfied him that his new rank was already known, although, as it would seem, it was to be made to succumb to the superior authority of the Rover.

"You know sir, that no one, of whatever station, can leave the ship at this hour, without an order from the captain," was the steady reply.

"So I presume; but I have the order, and transmit it to you. I shall land in my own boat."

The other, seeing a figure within hearing, which he well knew to be that of his commander, waited an instant, to ascertain if what he heard was true. Finding that no objection was made, he merely indicated the place where the other would find his boat.

"The men have left it!" exclaimed Wilder, stepping back in surprise, as he was about to descend the vessel's side.

"Have the rascals run?"

"Sir, they have not run; neither are they rascals. They are in this ship, and must be found."

The other waited to witness the effect of these authoritative words, too, on the individual who still lingered in the shadow of a mast. As no answer was, however, given from that quarter, he saw the necessity of obedience. Intimating his intention to seek the men, he passed into the forward parts of the vessel, leaving Wilder, as he thought, in sole possession of the quarter-deck. The latter was, however, soon undeceived. The Rover advancing carelessly to his side, made an allusion to the condition of his vessel, in order to divert the thoughts of his new lieutenant, who by his hurried manner of pacing the deck, he saw, was beginning to indulge in uneasy meditations.

"A charming sea-boat, Mr. Wilder," he continued, "and one that never throws a drop of spray abaft her mainmast. She is just the craft a seaman loves; easy on her rigging, and lively in a sea. I call her the 'Dolphin,' from the manner in which she cuts the water; and, perhaps, because she has as many colours as that fish, you will say. —Jack must have a name for his ship, you know, and I dislike your cut-throat appellations, your 'Spit-fires,' and 'Bloody-murders.'"

"You were fortunate in finding such a vessel. Was she built to your orders?"

"Few ships, under six hundred tons, sail from these colonies that are not built to serve my purposes," returned the Rover, with a smile; as if he would cheer his companion by displaying the mine of wealth that was opening to him, through the new connection he had made.

"This vessel was originally built for his most faithful majesty; and, I believe, was either intended as a present or a scourge to to the Algerines; but—but she has changed owners, as you see, and her fortune is a little altered; though how, or why, is a trifle with which we will not, just now, divert ourselves. I think she is all the better handled for the transfer. I have had her in port; she has undergone some improvements, and is now alto-gether suited to a running trade."

"You then venture, sometimes, inside the forts?"

"When you have leisure, my private journal may afford some interest," the other evasively replied. "I hope, Mr. Wilder, you find the vessel in such a state that a seaman need not blush for her?"

"Her beauty and neatness first caught my eye, and induced me to make closer enquiries into her character."

"You were quick in seeing that she was kept at a single

anchor !" returned the other laughing. " But I never risk any
thing without a reason; not even the loss of my ground tackle.
It would be no great achievement, for so warm a battery as this
I carry, to silence yonder apology for a fort; but in doing it, we
might receive an unfortunate hit, and, therefore, I keep ready
for an instant departure."

" It must be a little awkward to fight in a war where one cannot lower his flag in any emergency," said Wilder, more like
one who mused, than one who intended to express the opinion
aloud.

" The bottom is always beneath us," was the laconic answer.
" But to you I may say, that I am, on principle, tender on my
spars. They are examined daily, like the heels of a racer; for
it often happens that our valour must be well tempered by discretion."

" And how and where do you refit, when damaged in a gale,
or in a fight?"

" Hum ! We contrive to refit, sir, and to take the sea again
in tolerable condition."

He stopped; and Wilder, perceiving that he was not yet
deemed entitled to entire confidence, continued silent. In this
pause the officer returned, followed by the black alone. A few
words served to explain the condition of Fid. It was very apparent that the young man was not only disappointed, but that he
was deeply mortified. The frank and ingenuous air, however,
with which he turned to the Rover, to apologise for the derelic-
tion of his follower, satisfied the latter that he was far from sus-
pecting any improper agency in bringing about his awkward condition.

" You know the character of seamen too well, sir," he said,
" to impute this oversight to my poor fellow as a heinous fault.
A better sailor never lay on a yard, or stretched a ratlin, than

Dick Fid; but I must allow that he carries the quality of good fellowship to excess."

"You are fortunate in having one man left you to pull the boat ashore," carelessly returned the other.

"I am more than equal to that little exertion myself; nor do I like to separate the men. With your permission, the black shall be berthed, too, in the ship to-night."

"As you please. Empty hammocks are not scarce among us, since the last brush."

Wilder then directed the negro to return to his mess-mate, and to watch over him so long as he should be unable to look after himself. The black, who was far from being as clear-headed as common, willingly complied. The young man then took leave of his companions, and descended into the skiff. As he pulled, with vigorous arms, away from the dark ship, his eyes were cast upward with a seaman's pleasure on the order and neatness of her gear, and thence they fell on the frowning mass of the hull. A light-built, compact form was seen standing on the heel of the bowsprit, apparently watching his movements; and, notwithstanding the gloom of the clouded starlight, he was enabled to detect, in the individual who took so much apparent interest in his proceedings, the person of the Rover.

# CHAPTER VIII.

——What is yon gentleman?
Nurse. The son and heir of old Tiberio.
Juliet. What's he that follows there, that would not dance?
Nurse. Marry, I know not.

*Romeo and Juliet.*

THE sun was just heaving up out of the field of waters in which the blue islands of Massachusetts lie, when the inhabitants of Newport were seen opening their doors and windows, and preparing for the different employments of the day, with the freshness and alacrity of people who had wisely adhered to the natural allotments of time in seeking their rests, or in pursuing their pleasures. The morning salutations passed cheerfully from one to another as each undid the slight fastenings of his shop; and many a kind enquiry passed from one to the other concerning a daughter's fever, or the rheumatism of some aged grandam. As the landlord of the "Foul Anchor" was so wary in protecting the character of his house from any unjust imputations of unseemly revelling, so was he among the foremost in opening his doors, to catch any transient customer who might feel the necessity of washing away the damps of the past night with an invigorating stomachic. This cordial was then very generally taken, in the British provinces, under the various names of "bitters," "juleps," "morning drams," "fogmatics," &c. as the situation of different districts appeared to require particular preventives. The custom is getting a little into disuse, it is true;

but still it retains much of that sacred character which is the consequence of antiquity. It is not a little extraordinary that this venerable and laudable practice of washing away the unwholesome impurities engendered in the human system, at a time when, as it is entirely without any moral protector, it is left exposed to the attacks of all the evils to which flesh is heir, should subject the American to the witticisms of his European brother. We are not among the least grateful to those foreign philanthropists who take so deep an interest in our welfare as seldom to let any republican foible pass without applying to it, as it merits, the caustic application of their purifying monarchial pens. We are, perhaps, the more sensible of this generosity, because we have had occasion to witness, that so great is their zeal in behalf of our infant States, (robust, and a little unmanageable, perhaps, but still infant,) they are wont, in the warmth of their ardour to reform Cis-atlantic sins, to overlook some of their own backslidings. Numberless are the moral missionaries that the mother-country, for instance, has sent among us, on these pious and benevolent errands. We can only regret that their efforts have been crowned with so little success. It was our fortune to be familiarly acquainted with one of these worthies, who never lost an opportunity of declaiming, above all, against the infamy of the particular practice to which we have just alluded. The ground he took was so broad, that he held it to be not only immoral, but, what was hideous, it was ungenteel, to swallow any thing stronger than small beer, before the hour allotted to dinner. After that important period, it was not only permitted to assuage the previous mortifications of the flesh, but, so liberal did he show himself in the indulgence, after the clock had settled the point of orthodoxy, that he was regularly carried to bed at midnight, from which he as regularly issued, in the course of the following morning, to discourse again on the deformities of premature drunkenness. And here we would take occasion to say, that, as to our own insignificant person, we eschew the abomination altogether; and only regret that those of the two nations, who find pleasure in the practice, could not come to some amicable understanding as to the precise period of the twenty-four hours, when it is permitted to such Christian gentlemen as speak English to steep their senses in liquor, without bringing scandal on good breeding. That the negotiators who formed the last treaty of amity should have overlooked this important moral topic, is another evidence that both parties were so tired of an unprofitable war as to patch up a peace in a hurry. It is not too late to name a commission for this purpose; and, in order that the question may be fairly treated on its merits, we presume to suggest to the Executive the propriety of nominating, as our commissioner, some confirmed advocate of the system of "juleps." It is believed our worthy and indulgent mother can have no difficulty in selecting a suitable coadjutor from the ranks of her numerous and well-trained diplomatic corps.

With this manifestation of our personal liberality, united to so much interest in the proper, and we hope final, disposition of this important question, we may be permitted to resume the narrative, without being set down as advocates for morning stimulants, or evening intoxication; which is a very just division of the whole subject, as we believe, from an observation that is far from being limited.

The landlord of the "Foul Anchor," as has just been said, was early a-foot, to gain an honest penny from any of the supporters of the former system, who might chance to select his bar for their morning sacrifices to Bacchus, in preference to that of his neighbour, he who endeavoured to entice the lieges by exhibiting a red-faced man in a scarlet coat, that was called the "Head of George the Second." The activity of the alert publican did not go without its reward. The tide of custom set strongly, for the first half-hour, towards the haven of his hospitable bar; nor did he appear entirely to abandon the hopes of a further influx, even after the usual period of such arrivals began to pass away. Finding, however, that his customers were beginning to depart on their several pursuits, he left his station, and appeared at the outer door, with a hand in each pocket, as if he found a secret pleasure in the jingling of their new tenants. A stranger, who had not entered with the others, and who, of course, had not partaken of the customary libations, was standing at a little distance, with a hand thrust into the bosom of his vest, apparently more occupied with his own reflections than with the success of the publican. This figure caught the understanding eye of the latter, who conceived that no man, who had recourse to the proper morning stimulants, could wear so meditative a face at that early period in the cares of the day, and that, consequently, something was yet to be gained by opening a communication between them.

"A clean air, this, friend, to brush away the damps of the night," he said, snuffing the really delicious and invigorating breathings of a fine October morning. "It is such purifiers as this, that give our island its character, and make it, perhaps, the very healthiest, as it is universally admitted to be the beautifulest spot in creation. — A stranger here, 't is likely?"

"But quite lately arrived, sir," was the reply.

"A seafaring man, by your dress? and one in search of a ship, as I am ready to qualify to?" continued the publican, chuckling at his own penetration. "We have many such that pass hereaway; but people mustn't think, because Newport is so flourishing, that berths can always be had for asking. Have you tried your luck in the capital of the Bay-province?"

"I left Boston no later than the day before yesterday."

"What! couldn't the proud townsfolk* find you a ship? Ay,

---

* Boston was called the *town* of Boston, not being incorporated as a city, until a period comparatively recent. The government was that of a "town" until it had more than fifty thousand inhabitants.

they are a mighty people at talking, and it is n't often that they put their candle under the bushel; and yet there are what I call good judges, who think Narragansett Bay is in a fair way, shortly, to count as many sail as Massachusetts   Yonder is a wholesome brig, that is going, within the week, to turn her horses into rum and sugar; and here is a ship that hauled into the stream no longer ago than yesterday sun-down. That is a noble vessel, and her cabins are fit for a prince! She 'll be off with the change of the wind; and I dare say a good hand would n't go a-begging aboard her just now. Then, there is a slaver, off the fort, if you like a cargo of wool-heads for your money."

"Is it thought the ship in the inner harbour will sail with the first wind?" demanded the stranger.

"It is, downright. My wife is a full cousin to the wife of the collector's clerk; and I have it quite straight that the papers are ready, and that nothing but the wind detains them.   I keep some short scores, you know, friend, with the blue-jackets, and it behoves an honest man to look to his interests in these hard times. Yes, there she lies; a well-known ship, the 'Royal Caroline.' She makes a regular v'yage once a year between the provinces and Bristol, touching here out and home to give us certain supplies, and to wood and water; and then she goes home, or to the Carolinas, as the case may be."

"Pray, sir, has she much of an armament?" continued the stranger, who began to lose his thoughtful air, in the more evident interest he was beginning to take in the discourse.

"Yes, yes; she is not without a few bull-dogs, to bark in defence of her own rights, and to say a word in support of his majesty's honour, too, God bless him! — Judy! you Jude!" he shouted, at the top of his voice, to a negro girl who was gathering kindling-wood among the chips of a ship-yard, "scamper over to neighbour Homespun's, and rattle away at his bed-room windows; the man has over-slept himself: it is not common to hear seven o'clock strike, and the thirsty tailor not appear for his bitters."

A short cessation took place in the dialogue, while the wench was executing her master's orders. The summons produced no other effect than to draw a shrill reply from Desire, whose voice penetrated through the thin board coverings of the little dwelling, as readily as sound would be conveyed through a sieve. In another moment a window was opened, and the worthy housewife thrust her disturbed visage into the fresh air of the morning.

"What next! what next!" demanded the offended, and, as she was fain to believe, neglected wife, under the impression that it was her truant husband making a tardy return to his domestic allegiance, who had thus presumed to disturb her slumbers. "Is it not enough that you have eloped from my bed and board, for a whole night, but you must break in on the natural rest of a whole family, seven blessed children, without counting their mother? O, Hector! Hector! an example are you getting to be to the young and giddy, and a warning will you yet prove to the unthoughtful!"

"Bring hither the black book," said the publican to his wife, who had been drawn to a window by the lamentations of Desire; "I think the woman said something about starting on a journey between two days; if such has been the philosophy of the good man, it behoves honest people to look into their accounts. Ay, as I live, 'Keziah, you have let the limping beggar get seventeen and sixpence into arrears, and that for such trifles as morning-drams and nightcaps!"

"You are wrathy, friend, without reason; the man has made a garment for the boy at school, and found the——"

"Hush, good woman," interrupted her husband, returning the book, and making a sign for her to retire; "I dare say it will all come round in proper time, and the less noise we make about the backslidings of a neighbour, the less will be said of

6 *

our own transgressions.    A worthy and hard-working mechanic, sir," he continued, addressing the stranger : " but a man who could never get the sun to shine in at his windows, though, Heaven knows, the glass is none too thick for such a blessing."

" And do you imagine, on evidence as slight as this we have seen, that such a man has actually absconded ?"

" Why, it is a calamity that has befallen his betters !" returned the publican, interlocking his fingers across the rotundity of his person, with an air of grave consideration.    " We innkeepers, who live as it were in plain sight of every man's secrets — for it is after a visit to us that one is most apt to open his heart — should know something of the affairs of a neighbourhood. If the good man Homespun could smooth down the temper of his companion as easily as he lays a seam in its place, the thing might not occur, but —— Do you drink this morning, sir ?"

" A drop of your best."

" As I was saying," continued the other, furnishing his customer according to his desire, " if a tailor's goose would take the wrinkles out of the ruffled temper of a woman, as it does out of the cloth, and then, if after it had done this task, a man might eat it, as he would yonder bird hanging behind my bar —— Perhaps you will have occasion to make your dinner with us, too, sir ?"

" I cannot say I shall not," returned the stranger, paying for the dram he had barely tasted; " it greatly depends on the result of my enquiries concerning the different vessels in the port."

" Then would I, though perfectly disinterested, as you know, sir, recommend you to make this house your home, while you sojourn in the town.    It is the resort of most of the seafaring men ; and I may say this much of myself, without conceit — no man can tell you more of what you want to know, than the landlord of the 'Foul Anchor.'"

" You advise an application to the commander of this vessel in the stream, for a berth: will she sail so soon as you have named?"

" With the first wind. I know the whole history of the ship, from the day they laid the blocks for her keel, to the minute when she let her anchor go where you now see her. The great southern heiress, General Grayson's fine daughter, is to be a passenger; she, and her over-looker, government-lady, I believe they call her — a Mrs. Wyllys — are waiting for the signal, up here, at the residence of Madam de Lacey; she that is the relict of the rear admiral of that name, who is full sister to the general, and, therefore, an aunt to the young lady, according to my reckoning. Many people think the two fortunes will go together; in which case, he will be not only a lucky man, but a rich one, who gets Miss Getty Grayson for a wife."

The stranger, who had maintained rather an indifferent manner during the close of the foregoing dialogue, appeared now disposed to enter into it, with a degree of interest suited to the sex and condition of the present subject of their discourse. After waiting to catch the last syllable that the publican chose to expend his breath on, he demanded, a little abruptly,—

" And you say the house near us, on the rising ground, is the residence of Mrs. de Lacey?"

" If I did, I know nothing of the matter. By 'up here,' I mean half a mile off. It is a place fit for a lady of her quality, and none of your elbowy dwellings, like these crowded about us. One may easily tell the house, by its pretty blinds and its shades. I 'll engage there are no such shades in all Europe, as the very trees that stand before the door of Madam de Lacey."

" It is very probable," muttered the stranger, who, not appearing quite as sensitive in his provincial admiration as the publican, had already relapsed into his former musing air. Instead of pushing the discourse, he suddenly turned the subject, by making some common-place remark; and then, repeating the probability of his being obliged to return, he walked deliberately away, taking the direction of the residence of Mrs. de Lacey. The observing publican would, probably, have found sufficient matter for observation in this abrupt termination of the interview, had not Desire, at that precise moment, broken out of her habitation, and diverted his attention, by the peculiarly lively manner in which she delineated the character of her delinquent husband.

The reader has probably, ere this, suspected that the individual who had conferred with the publican, as a stranger, was not unknown to himself. It was, in truth, no other than Wilder. But, in the completion of his own secret purposes, the young mariner left the wordy war in his rear; and, turning up the gentle ascent, against the side of which the town is built, he proceeded towards the suburbs.

It was not difficult to distinguish the house he sought, among a dozen other similar retreats, by its "shades," as the innkeeper, in conformity with a provincial use of the word, had termed a few really noble elms that grew in the little court before its door. In order, however, to assure himself that he was right, he confirmed his surmises by actual enquiry, and continued thoughtfully on his path.

The morning had, by this time, fairly opened, with every appearance of another of those fine, bland, autumnal days for which the climate is, or ought to be, so distinguished. The little air there was came from the south, fanning the face of our adventurer, as he occasionally paused in his ascent, to gaze at the different vessels in the harbour, like a mild breeze in June. In short, it was just such a time as one, who is fond of strolling in the fields, is apt to seize on with rapture, and which a seaman sets down as a day lost in his reckoning.

Wilder was first drawn from his musings by the sound of a dialogue that came from persons who were evidently approaching.

There was one voice, in particular, that caused his blood to thrill, he knew not why, and which appeared, unaccountably even to himself, to set in motion every latent faculty of his system. Profiting by the formation of the ground, he sprang unseen up a little bank, and approaching an angle in a low wall, he found himself in the immediate proximity of the speakers.

The wall enclosed the garden and pleasure-grounds of a mansion, that he now perceived was the residence of Mrs. de Lacey. A rustic summer-house, which in the proper season had been nearly buried in leaves and flowers, stood at no great distance from the road. By its elevation and position it commanded a view of the town, the harbour, the isles of Massachusetts to the east, those of the Providence Plantations to the west, and to the south an illimitable expanse of ocean. As it had now lost its leafy covering, there was no difficulty in looking directly into its centre, through the rude pillars which supported its little dome. Here Wilder discovered the very party of whose conversation he had been a listener the previous day, while caged with the Rover, in the left of the ruin. Though the admiral's widow and Mrs. Wyllys were most in advance, evidently addressing some one who, like himself, was in the public road, the young sailor soon detected the more enticing person of the blooming Gertrude in the background. His observations were, however, interrupted by a reply from the individual who as yet was unseen. Directed by the voice, Wilder was soon enabled to perceive the person of a man in green old age, who, seated on a stone by the wayside, appeared to be resting his weary limbs, while he answered certain interrogations that were made from the summer-house. His head was white, and the hand which grasped a long walking-staff, sometimes trembled; but there was that in the costume, the manner, and the voice of the speaker, which furnished sufficient evidence of his having once been a veteran of the sea.

"Lord! your ladyship, ma'am," he said, in tones that were getting tremulous, even while they retained the deep intonations of his profession, "we old sea-dogs never stop to look into an almanack to see which way the wind will come after the next thaw, before we put to sea. It is enough for us, that the sailing orders are aboard, and that the captain has taken leave of his lady."

"Ah! the very words of the poor lamented admiral!" exclaimed Mrs. de Lacey, who had great satisfaction in pursuing the discourse with a superannuated mariner. "And then you are of opinion, honest friend, that when a ship is ready she should sail, whether the wind is——"

"Here is another follower of the sea, opportunely come to lend us his advice," interrupted Gertrude, with a hurried air, as if to divert the attention of her aunt from something very like a dogmatical termination of an argument that had just occurred between her and Mrs. Wyllys; "perhaps he may serve as an umpire."

"True," said the latter. "Pray, what do *you* think of the weather to-day, sir? would it be profitable to sail in such a time, or not?"

The young mariner reluctantly withdrew his eyes from the blushing Gertrude, who, in her eagerness to point him out, had advanced to the front, and was now shrinking back, timidly, to the centre of the building again, like one who already repented of her temerity. He then fastened his look on her who put the question; and so long and riveted was his gaze, that she saw fit to repeat it, believing that what she had first said was not properly understood.

"There is little faith to be put in the weather, madam," was the dilatory reply. "A man has followed the sea to but little purpose who is tardy in making that discovery."

There was something so sweet and gentle, at the same time

that it was manly, in the voice of Wilder, that the ladies, by a common impulse, were won to listen. The neatness of his attire, which, while it was strictly professional, was worn with an air of smartness, and even of gentility, that rendered it difficult to sup-pose he was not entitled to lay claim to a higher station in society than that in which he actually appeared, aided him also, in pro-ducing a favourable impression. Bending her head, with a man-ner that was intended to be polite, a little more perhaps in self-respect than out of consideration to the other, Mrs. de Lacey resumed the discourse.

"These ladies," she said, "are about to embark in yonder ship for the province of Carolina, and we were consulting concerning the quarter in which the wind will probably blow next. But in such a vessel, it cannot matter much, I should think, sir, whether the wind were fair or foul."

"I think not," was the reply. "She looks to me like a ship that will not do much, let the wind be as it may."

"She has the reputation of being a very fast sailer. Reputa-tion! we know she is such, having come from home to the Colo-nies in the incredibly short passage of seven weeks! But sea-men have their favourites and prejudices, I believe, like us poor mortals ashore. You will therefore excuse me, if I ask this honest veteran for an opinion on this particular point also. What do you imagine, friend, to be the sailing qualities of yonder ship — she with the peculiarly high top-gallant booms, and such con-spicuous round tops?"

A smile struggled on the lip of Wilder, but he continued silent. On the other hand, the old mariner arose, appearing to examine the ship like one who perfectly comprehended the some-what untechnical language of the admiral's widow.

"The ship in the inner harbour, your ladyship," he answered, when his examination was finished, "which is, I suppose, the vessel that madam means, is just such a ship as does a sailor's eye good to look at. A gallant and a safe boat she is, as I will swear; and as to sailing, though she may not be altogether a witch, yet is she a fast craft, or I'm no judge of blue water, or of those that live on it."

"Here is at once an extraordinary difference of opinion!" exclaimed Mrs. de Lacey. "I am glad, however, you pronounce her safe; for, although seamen love a fast-sailing vessel, these ladies will not like her the less for the security. I presume, sir, you will not dispute her being *safe?*"

"The very quality I should most deny," was the laconic answer of Wilder.

"It is very remarkable! This is a veteran seaman, sir, and he appears to think differently."

"He may have seen more, in his time, than myself, madam; but I doubt whether he can, just now, see as well. This is a great distance to discover the merits or demerits of a ship: I have been nigher."

"Then you really think there is danger to be apprehended, sir?" demanded the soft voice of Gertrude, whose fears had gotten the better of her diffidence.

"I do. Had I mother, or sister," touching his hat, and bowing to his fair interrogator, as he uttered the latter word with emphasis, "I would hesitate to let her embark in that ship. On my honour, ladies, I do assure you, that I think this very vessel in more danger than any ship which has left, or probably will leave, a port in the provinces this autumn."

"This is extraordinary!" observed Mrs. Wyllys. "It is not the character we have received of the vessel, which has been greatly exaggerated, or she is entitled to be considered as uncommonly convenient and safe. May I ask, sir, on what circumstances you have founded this opinion?"

"They are sufficiently plain. She is too lean in the harping and too full in the counter, to steer. Then, she is as wall-sided as a church, and stows too much above the water-line. Besides this, she carries no head sail, but all the press upon her will be aft, which will jam her into the wind, and, more than likely, throw her aback. The day will come when that ship will go down stern foremost."

His auditors listened to this opinion, which Wilder delivered in an oracular and very decided manner, with that sort of secret faith and humble dependence, which the uninstructed are very apt to lend to those who are initiated in the mysteries of any imposing profession. Neither of them had certainly a very clear perception of his meaning; but there were danger and death in his very words. Mrs. de Lacey felt it incumbent on her own particular advantages, however, to manifest how well she comprehended the subject.

"These are certainly very serious evils!" she gravely rejoined. "It is quite unaccountable that my agent should have neglected to mention them. Is there any other quality, sir, that strikes your eye at this distance, and which you deem alarming?"

"Too many. You observe that her top-gallant masts are fidded abaft; none of her lofty sails set flying; and then, madam, she has depended on bobstays and gammonings for the security of that very important part of a vessel, the bowsprit."

"Too true! too true!" said Mrs. de Lacey, with a start of professional horror. "These things had altogether escaped me; but I see them all plain enough, now they are mentioned. Such neglect is highly culpable; more especially to rely on bobstays and gammonings for the security of a bowsprit! Really, Mrs. Wyllys, I can never consent that my niece should embark in such a vessel."

The calm eye of Wyllys had been fastened on the countenance of Wilder while he was speaking, and she now turned it with undisturbed serenity on the admiral's widow.

" Perhaps the danger has been a little magnified," she observed. " Let us enquire of this other seaman what he thinks on these points.   And do you see all these serious dangers to be apprehended, friend, in trusting ourselves, at this season of the year, in a passage to the Carolinas, aboard of yonder ship?"

" Lord, madam !" said the grey-headed mariner, with a chuckling laugh, " these are new-fashioned faults and difficulties, if they be faults and difficulties at all !   In my time, such matters were never heard of; and I confess I am so stupid as not to understand half the young gentleman has been saying."

" It is some time, I fancy, old man, since you were last at sea," Wilder coolly observed.

" Some five or six years since the last time, and fifty since the first."

" Then you do not see the same causes for apprehension ?" Mrs. Wyllys once more demanded.

" Old and worn out as I am, lady, if her captain will give me a berth aboard her, I will thank him for the same as a favour."

" Misery seeks any relief," whispered Mrs. de Lacey, bestowing on her companions a significant glance, that paid no great compliment to the old man's motives.   " I incline to the opinion of the younger seaman ; he supports it with substantial, professional reasons."

Mrs. Wyllys suspended her questions, just as long as complaisance to the last speaker seemed to require ; and then she resumed them as follows, addressing her next enquiry to Wilder.

" And how do you explain this difference in judgment, between two men who ought both to be so well qualified to decide correctly ?"

" I believe there is a well-known proverb which will answer that question," returned the young man, smiling : " but some allowance must be made for the improvements in ships ; and, perhaps, some little deference to the stations we have respectively filled on board them."

"Both very true. Still, one would think the changes of half a dozen years cannot be so very considerable, in a profession that is so exceedingly ancient."

"Your pardon, madam: they require constant practice to be known. Now, I dare say that yonder worthy old tar is ignorant of the manner in which a ship, when pressed by her canvass, is made 'to cut the waves with her taffrail.'"

"Impossible!" cried the admiral's widow; "the youngest and the meanest mariner must have been struck with the beauty of such a spectacle."

"Yes, yes," returned the old tar, who wore the air of an offended man, and who, probably, had he been ignorant of any part of his art, was not just then in the temper to confess it; "many is the proud ship that I have seen doing the very same; and, as the lady says, a grand and comely sight it is!"

Wilder was confounded. He bit his lip, like one who was over-reached either by excessive ignorance or exceeding cunning; but the self-complacency of Mrs. de Lacey spared him the necessity of an immediate reply.

"It would have been an extraordinary circumstance, truly," she said, "that a man should have grown white-headed on the seas, and never have been struck with so noble a spectacle. But then, my honest tar, you appear to be wrong in overlooking the striking faults in yonder ship, which this, a—a—this gentleman has just, and so properly, named."

"I do not call them faults, your ladyship. Such is the way my late brave and excellent commander always had his own ship rigged; and I am bold to say that a better seaman, or a more honest man, never served in his majesty's fleet."

"And you have served the king! How was your beloved commander named?"

"How should he be! By us, who knew him well, he was called Fair-weather; for it was always smooth water, and prosperous times, under his orders; though on shore, he was known as the gallant and victorious Rear-Admiral de Lacey."

"And did my late revered and skilful husband cause his ships to be rigged in this manner?" said the widow, with a tremour in her voice that bespoke how much, and how truly, she was overcome by surprise and gratified pride.

The aged tar lifted his bending frame from the stone, gazed wistfully at the relict of him he had just named, and bowing low, he answered,—

"If I have the honour of seeing my admiral's lady, it will prove a joyful sight to my old eyes! Sixteen years did I serve in his own ship, and five more in the same squadron. I dare say your ladyship may have heard him speak of the captain of the main-top, Bob Bunt?"

"I dare say — I dare say. He loved to talk of those who served him faithfully."

"Ay, God bless him, and make his memory glorious! He was a kind officer, and one that never forgot a friend, whether his duty kept him on a yard or in the cabin. He was the sailor's friend, that very same admiral!"

"This is a grateful man!" said Mrs. de Lacey, wiping her eyes, "and I dare say a most competent judge of a vessel. And are you quite sure, worthy friend, that my late revered husband had all his ships arranged like the one of which we have been talking?"

"Very sure, madam; for with my own hands did I assist to rig them."

"Even to the bobstays?"

"And the gammonings, my lady. Were the admiral alive and here, he would call yon 'a safe and well-fitted ship,' as I am ready to swear "

Mrs. de Lacy turned, with an air of great dignity and entire decision, to Wilder, as she continued,—

"I have, then, made a small mistake in memory, which is not surprising, when one recollects that he who taught me so much of the profession is no longer here to continue his lessons. We are much obliged to you, sir, for your opinion, but we must think that you have over-rated the danger."

"On my honour, madam," interrupted Wilder, laying his hand on his heart, and speaking with singular emphasis, "I am sincere in what I say. I do affirm that I believe there will be great danger in embarking in yonder ship; and I call Heaven to witness, that in so saying, I am actuated by no malice to her commander, her owners, or any connected with her."

"We dare say, sir, you are very sincere. We only think you are a little in error," returned the admiral's widow, with a commiserating, and what she intended for a condescending, smile. "We are your debtors for your good intentions, at least. Come, worthy veteran, we must not part here. You will gain admission by knocking at my door; and we shall talk further of these matters."

Then bowing coolly to Wilder, she led the way up the garden, followed by all her companions. The step of Mrs. de Lacey was proud, like the tread of one conscious of all her advantages; while that of Wyllys was slow, as if she were buried in thought. Gertrude kept close to the side of the latter, her face hid beneath the shade of a gipsy hat. Wilder fancied that he could discover the stolen and anxious glance that she threw back towards one who had excited a decided emotion in her sensitive bosom, though it was a feeling no more attractive than alarm. He lingered until they were lost amid the shrubbery. Then, turning to pour out his disappointment on his brother tar, he found that the old man had made such good use of his time, as to be already within the gate, most probably felicitating himself on the prospect of reading the reward of his recent adulation.

# CHAPTER IX.

He ran this way, and leaped this orchard wall.
*Shakspeare*

WILDER retired from the field like a defeated man. Accident, or, as he was willing to term it, the sycophancy of the old mariner, had counteracted his own little artifice; and he was now left without the remotest chance of being again favoured with such another opportunity of effecting his purpose. We shall not, at this period of the narrative, enter into a detail of the feelings and policy which induced our adventurer to plot against the apparent interests of those with whom he had so recently associated himself; it is enough for our present object, that the facts themselves should be distinctly set before the reader.

The return of the disappointed young sailor towards the town was moody and slow. More than once he stopped short in the descent, and fastened his eyes, for minutes together, on the different vessels in the harbour. But in these frequent halts, no evidence of the particular interest he took in any one of the ships escaped him. Perhaps his gaze at the southern trader was longer and more earnest, than at any other; though his eye, at times, wandered curiously, and even anxiously, over every craft that lay within the shelter of the haven.

The customary hour for exertion had now arrived, and the sounds of labour were beginning to be heard, issuing from every quarter of the place. The songs of the mariners were rising on

the calm of the morning, with their peculiar, long-drawn intonations. The ship in the inner harbour was among the first to
furnish this proof of the industry of her people, and of her approaching departure. It was only as these movements caught
his eye, that Wilder seemed to be thoroughly awakened from his
abstraction, and to pursue his observations with an undivided
mind. He saw the seamen ascend the rigging, in that lazy manner which is so strongly contrasted by their activity in moments
of need; and here and there a human form was showing itself
on the black and ponderous yards. In a few moments, the fore-
top sail fell from its compact compass on the yard into graceful
and careless festoons. This the attentive Wilder well knew, was,
among all trading vessels, the signal of sailing. In a few more
minutes, the lower angles of this important sail were drawn to
the extremities of the corresponding spar beneath; and then the
heavy yard was seen slowly ascending the mast, dragging after
it the opening folds of the sail, until the latter was tightened at
all its edges, displaying itself in one broad, snow-white sheet of
canvass. Against this wide surface the light currents of air fell,
and as often receded; the sail bellying and collapsing in a manner to show that, as yet, they were powerless. At this point the
preparations appeared suspended, as if the mariners, having thus
invited the breeze, were awaiting to see if their invocation was
likely to be attended with success.

It was a natural transition for him, who so closely observed
these indications of departure in the ship so often named, to turn
his eyes on the vessel which lay without the fort, in order to witness the effect so manifest a signal had produced in her also.
But the closest and the keenest scrutiny could detect no sign of
any bond of interest between the two. While the former was
making the movements just described, the latter lay at her anchors, without the smallest proof that man existed within the
mass of her black and inanimate hull. So quiet and motionless

did she seem, that one who had never been instructed in the
matter, might readily have believed her a fixture in the sea, some
symmetrical and enormous excrescence, thrown up by the waves,
with its mazes of lines and pointed fingers, or one of those fan-
tastic monsters that are believed to exist in the bottom of the
ocean, darkened by the fogs and tempests of ages. To the understanding eye of Wilder, however, she exhibited a very different spectacle. He easily saw, through all this apparently drowsy
quietude, those signs of readiness which none but a seaman could
discover. The cable, instead of stretching in a long declining
line towards the water, was "short," or nearly "up and down,"
as it is equally termed in technical language, just "scope" enough
being allowed out-board to resist the power of the lively tide that
acted on the deep keel of the vessel. All her boats were in the
water, so disposed and prepared, as to convince him they were
in a state to be employed in towing in the shortest possible time.
Not a sail, or a yard, was out of its place, undergoing those repairs and examinations which the mariner is wont to make, when
lying within the security of a suitable haven; nor was there a
single rope wanting, amid the hundreds which interlaced the blue
sky that formed the back-ground of the picture, that might be
necessary in bringing every art of facilitating motion into use.
In short, the vessel, while seeming least prepared, was most in a
condition to move, or, if necessary, to resort to her means of
offence and defence. The boarding-nettings, it is true, were
triced to the rigging, as on the previous day; but a sufficient
apology was to be found for this act of extreme caution, in the
war, which exposed her to attacks from the light French cruisers,
that so often ranged from the islands of the West Indies, along
the whole coast of the continent, and in the position the ship
had taken, without the ordinary defences of the harbour. In
this state, the vessel, to one who knew her real character,
appeared like some beast of prey, or venomous reptile, that lay

in an assumed lethargy, to delude the unconscious victim within the limits of its leap, or nigh enough to receive the deadly blow of its fangs.

Wilder shook his head, in a manner which said plainly enough how well he understood this treacherous tranquillity, and continued his walk towards the town, with the same deliberate step as before. He had whiled away many minutes unconsciously, and would probably have lost the reckoning of as many more, had not his attention been suddenly diverted by a slight touch on the shoulder. Starting at this unexpected diversion, he turned, and saw, that, in his dilatory progress, he had been overtaken by the seaman whom he had last met in that very society in which he would have given so much to have been included himself.

"Your young limbs should carry you ahead, master," said the latter, when he had succeeded in attracting the attention of Wilder, "like a 'Mudian going with a clean full; and yet I have fore-reached upon you with my old legs, in such a manner as to bring us again within hail."

"Perhaps you enjoy the extraordinary advantage of 'cutting the waves with your taffrail,'" returned Wilder with a sneer. "There can be no accounting for the headway one makes, when sailing in that remarkable manner."

"I see, brother, you are offended that I followed your motions, though, in so doing, I did no more than obey a signal of your own setting. Did you expect an old sea-dog like me, who has stood his watch so long in a flag-ship, to confess ignorance in any matter that of right belongs to blue water? How the devil was I to know that there is not some sort of craft, among the thousands that are getting into fashion, which sails best stern foremost? They say a ship is modelled from a fish; and, if such be the case, it is only to make one after the fashion of a crab, or an oyster, to have the very thing you named."

7

"It is well, old man. You have had your reward, I suppose, in a handsome present from the admiral's widow, and you may now lie-by for a season, without caring much as to the manner in which they build their ships in future. Pray, do you intend to shape your course much further down this hill?"

"Until I get to the bottom."

"I am glad of it, for it is my especial intention to go up it again. As we say at sea, when our conversation is ended, 'A good time to you!'"

The old seaman laughed, when he saw the young man turn abruptly on his heel, and begin to retrace the very ground along which he had just before descended.

"Ah! you have never sailed with a rear-admiral," he said, continuing his own course in the former direction, and picking his way with a care suited to his age and infirmities. "No, there is no getting the finish, even at sea, without a cruise or two under a flag, and that at the mizen, too!"

"Intolerable old hypocrite," muttered Wilder between his teeth. "The rascal has seen better days, and is now perverting his knowledge to juggle a foolish woman. I am well quit of the knave, who, I dare say, has adopted lying for his trade, now labour is unproductive. I will go back. The coast is quite clear, and who can say what may happen next?"

Most of the foregoing paragraph was actually uttered in the suppressed manner already described, while the rest was merely meditated, which, considering the fact that our adventurer had no auditor, was quite as well as if he had spoken it through a trumpet. The expectation thus vaguely expressed, however, was not likely to be soon realised. Wilder sauntered up the hill, endeavouring to assume the unconcerned air of an idler, if by chance his return should excite attention; but though he lingered long in open view of the windows of Mrs. de Lacey's villa, he was not able to catch another glimpse of its tenants. There were very evident symptoms of the approaching journey, in the trunks and packages that left the building for the town, and in the hurried and busy manner of the few servants that he occasionally saw; but it would seem that the principal personages of the establishment had withdrawn into the secret recesses of the building, probably for the very natural purpose of confidential communion and affectionate leave-taking. He was turning, vexed and disappointed, from his anxious and fruitless watch, when he once more heard female voices on the inner side of the low wall against which he had been leaning. The sounds approached; nor was it long before his quick ears again recognised the musical voice of Gertrude.

"It is tormenting ourselves, without sufficient reason, my dear madam," she said, as the speakers drew sufficiently nigh to be distinctly overheard, "to allow any thing that may have fallen from such a — such an individual, to make the slightest impression."

"I feel the justice of what you say, my love," returned the mournful voice of her governess, "and yet am I so weak as to be unable entirely to shake off a sort of superstitious feeling on this subject. Gertrude, would you not wish to see that youth again?"

"Me, ma'am!" exclaimed her *élève*, in a sort of alarm. "Why should you, or I, wish to see an utter stranger again? and one so low — not low perhaps; — but one who is surely not altogether a very suitable companion for——"

"Well-born ladies, you would say. Why do you imagine the young man to be so much our inferior?"

Wilder thought there was a melody in the intonations of the youthful voice of the maiden, which in some measure excused the personality, as she answered,—

"I am certainly not so fastidious in my notions of birth and station as aunt de Lacey," she said, laughing; "but I should forget some of your own instructions, dear Mrs. Wyllys, did I not feel that education and manners make a sensible difference in the opinions and characters of all us poor mortals."

" Very true, my child. But I confess I saw or heard nothing that induces me to believe the young man, of whom we are speaking, either uneducated or vulgar. On the contrary, his language and pronunciation were those of a gentleman, and his air was quite suited to his utterance. He had the frank and simple manner of his profession; but you are not now to learn that youths of the first families in the provinces, or even in the kingdom, are often placed in the service of the marine."

" But they are officers, dear madam : this — this individual wore the dress of a common mariner."

" Not altogether. It was finer in its quality, and more tasteful in its fashion, than is customary. I have known admirals do the same in their moments of relaxation. Sailors of condition often love to carry about them the testimonials of their profession, without any of the trappings of their rank."

" You then think he was an officer — perhaps in the king's service ?"

"He might well have been so, though the fact, that there is no cruiser in the port, would seem to contradict it. But it was not so trifling a circumstance that awakened the unaccountable interest that I feel. Gertrude, my love, it was my fortune to have been much with seamen in early life. I seldom see one of that age, and of that spirited and manly mien, without feeling emotion. But I tire you; let us talk of other things."

"Not in the least, dear madam," Gertrude hurriedly interrupted. " Since you think the stranger a gentleman, there can be no harm — that is, it is not quite so improper, I believe — to speak of him. Can there then be the danger he would make us think, in trusting ourselves in a ship of which we have so good a report?"

"There was a strange, I had almost said wild, admixture of irony and concern in his manner, that is inexplicable! He certainly uttered nonsense part of the time; but then he did not appear to do it without a serious object. Gertrude, you are not as familiar with nautical expressions as myself; and perhaps you are ignorant that your good aunt, in her admiration of a profession that she has certainly a right to love, sometimes makes——"

"I know it — I know it; at least I often think so," the other interrupted, in a manner which plainly manifested that she found no pleasure in dwelling on the disagreeable subject. "It was exceedingly presuming, madam, in a stranger, however, to amuse himself, if he did it, with so amiable and so trivial a weakness, if indeed weakness it be."

"It was," Mrs. Wyllys steadily continued; "and yet he did not appear to me like one of those empty minds that find pleasure in exposing the follies of others. You may remember, Gertrude, that yesterday, while at the ruin, Mrs. de Lacey made some remarks expressive of her admiration of a ship under sail?"

"Yes, yes, I remember them," said the niece, a little impatiently.

"One of her terms was particularly incorrect, as I happen to know from my own familiarity with the language of sailors."

"I thought as much by the expression of your eye," returned Gertrude; "but——"

"Listen, my love. It certainly was not remarkable that a lady should make a trifling error in the use of so peculiar a language; but it is singular that a seaman himself should commit the same fault in precisely the same words. This the youth of whom we are speaking did; and, what is no less surprising, the old man assented to the same, just as if they had been correctly uttered."

"Perhaps," said Gertrude, in a low tone, "they may have heard, that attachment to this description of conversation is a foible of Mrs. de Lacey. I am sure, after this, dear madam, you cannot any longer consider the stranger a gentleman!''

"I should think no more about it, love, were it not for a feeling I can neither account for nor define. I would I could again see him!''

A slight exclamation from her companion interrupted her words; and, the next instant, the subject of her thoughts leaped the wall, apparently in quest of the rattan that had fallen at the feet of Gertrude, occasioning her alarm. After apologising for his intrusion, and recovering his lost property, Wilder was slowly preparing to retire, as if nothing had happened. There was a softness and delicacy in his manner, which was probably intended to convince the younger of the ladies that he was not entirely without some claims to the title she had recently denied him, and which was certainly not without its effect. The countenance of Mrs. Wyllys was pale; her lip quivered, though the steadiness of her voice proved it was not with alarm, and she hastily said—

"Remain a moment, sir, if your presence is not required else-where. There is something so remarkable in this meeting, that I could wish to improve it."

Wilder bowed, and again faced the ladies whom he had just been about to quit, like one who felt he had no right to intrude a moment longer than had been necessary to recover that which had been lost by his pretended awkwardness. When Mrs. Wyllys found that her wish was so unexpectedly realised, she hesitated as to the manner in which she should next proceed.

"I have been thus bold, sir," she said, in some embarrassment, "on account of the opinion you so lately expressed concerning the vessel which now lies ready to put to sea, the instant she is favoured with a wind."

"The Royal Caroline?" Wilder carelessly replied.

"That is her name, I believe."

"I hope, madam, that nothing which I have said," he hastily

continued, " will have an effect to prejudice you against the ship
I will pledge myself that she is made of excellent materials, and
then I have not the least doubt but she is very ably commanded."

" And yet have you not hesitated to say, that you consider a
passage in this very vessel more dangerous than one in any other
ship that will probably leave a port of the provinces in many
months to come."

" I did," answered Wilder, with a manner not to be mistaken.

" Will you explain your reasons for this opinion ?"

" If I remember rightly, I gave them to the lady whom I had
the honour to see an hour ago."

" That individual, sir, is no longer here, neither is she to trust
her person in the vessel. This young lady and myself, with our
attendants, will be the only passengers."

" I understood it so," returned Wilder, keeping his gaze
riveted on the speaking countenance of Gertrude.

" And, now that there is no apprehension of any mistake, may
I ask you to repeat the reasons why you think there will be
danger in embarking in the ' Royal Caroline ?' "

Wilder started, and even had the grace to colour, when he met
the attentive look with which Mrs. Wyllys awaited his answer.

" You would not have me repeat, madam," he stammered,
" what I have already said on the subject ?"

" I would not, sir ; once will suffice for such an explanation ;
still I am persuaded you have other reasons for your words."

" It is exceedingly difficult for a seaman to speak of ships in
any other than technical language, which must be the next thing
to being unintelligible to one of your sex. You have never been
at sea, madam ?"

" Very often."

" Then I may hope, possibly, to make myself understood.
You must be conscious, madam, that no small part of the safety
of a ship depends on the very material point of keeping her right

side uppermost: sailors call it 'making her stand up.' Now, I need not say, I am quite sure, to a lady of your intelligence, that if the Caroline fall on her beam there will be imminent hazard to all on board?"

"Nothing can be clearer; the same risk would be incurred in any other vessel."

"Without doubt, if any other vessel should trip. But I have pursued my profession for many years, without meeting with such a misfortune, but once. Then, the fastenings of the bow-sprit——"

"Are good as ever came from the hand of a rigger," said a voice behind them.

The whole party turned and beheld, at a little distance, the old seaman already introduced, mounted on some object on the other side of the wall, against which he was very coolly leaning, and whence he overlooked the whole of the interior of the grounds.

"I have been at the water-side to look at the boat, at the wish of Madam de Lacey, the widow of my late noble commander and admiral; and, let other men think as they may, I am ready to swear that the 'Royal Caroline' has as well-secured a bowsprit as any ship that carries the British flag! Ay, nor is that all I will say in her favour; she is throughout neatly and lightly sparred, and has no more of a wall-side than the walls of yonder church tumble-home. I am an old man, and my reckoning has got to the last leaf of the log-book; therefore it is little interest that I have, or can have, in this brig or that schooner; but this much will I say, which is, that it is just as wicked, and as little likely to be forgiven, to speak scandal of a wholesome and stout ship, as it is to talk amiss of a Christian."

The old man spoke with energy, and with a show of honest indignation, which did not fail to make an impression on the ladies, at the same time that it brought certain ungrateful admonitions to the conscience of the understanding Wilder.

"You perceive, sir," said Mrs. Wyllys, after waiting in vain for the reply of the young seaman, "that it is very possible for two men, of equal advantages, to disagree on a professional point. Which am I to believe?"

"Whichever your own excellent sense should tell you is most likely to be correct. I repeat, and in a sincerity to whose truth I call Heaven to witness, that no mother or sister of mine should, with my consent, embark in the Caroline."

"This is incomprehensible," said Mrs. Wyllys, turning to Gertrude, and speaking only for her ear. "My reason tells me we have been trifled with by this young man; and yet his protestations are so earnest, and apparently so sincere, that I cannot shake off the impression they have made. To which of the two, my love, do you feel most inclined to yield credence?"

"You know how very ignorant I am, dear madam, of all these things," said Gertrude, dropping her eyes to the faded sprig she was plucking: "but to me that old wretch has a very presuming and vicious look."

"You then think the younger most entitled to belief?"

"Why not, since you think he is a gentleman?"

"I know not that his superior situation in life entitles him to greater credit. Men often obtain such advantages to abuse them. —I am afraid, sir," continued Mrs. Wyllys, turning to the expecting Wilder, "that, unless you see fit to be more frank, we shall be compelled to refuse you our faith, and must persevere in the intention to profit by the opportunity of the 'Royal Caroline,' to get to the Carolinas."

"From the bottom of my heart, madam, I regret the determination."

"It may still be in your power to change it, by being explicit."

Wilder appeared to muse; once or twice his lips moved, as if he were about to speak. Mrs. Wyllys and Gertrude awaited his

7 *

intentions with evident interest; but, after a long and seemingly
hesitating pause, he disappointed both, by saying,—

"I am sorry that I have not the ability to make myself better
understood. It can only be the fault of my dulness; for I again
affirm that the danger is as apparent to my eyes as the sun at
noonday."

"Then we must continue blind, sir,' returned Mrs. Wyllys,
with a cold salute. "I thank you for your good intentions; but
you cannot blame us for not consenting to follow advice which is
buried in so much obscurity. Although in our own grounds, we
shall be pardoned the rudeness of leaving you. The hour ap-
pointed for our departure has arrived."

Wilder returned the grave bow of Mrs. Wyllys, with one quite
as formal as her own, though he bent with greater grace, and
with more cordiality, to the deep hurried courtesy of Gertrude
Grayson. He remained in the precise spot in which they left
him, until he saw them enter the villa; and he even fancied he
could catch the anxious expression of another timid glance which
the latter threw in his direction, as her light form appeared to
float from before his sight. Placing one hand on the wall, the
young sailor then leaped into the highway. As his feet struck
the ground, the slight shock seemed to awake him from his
abstraction, and he became conscious that he stood within six feet
of the old mariner, who had now twice stepped so rudely between
him and the object he had so much at heart. The latter did not
allow him time to give utterance to his disappointment, for he
was the first himself to speak.

"Come, brother," he said, in friendly, confidential tones, and
shaking his head, like one who wished to show to his companion
that he was aware of the deception he had attempted to practise;
"come, brother, you have stood far enough on this tack, and it
is time to try another. I've been young myself in my time,
and I know what a hard matter it is to give the devil a wide

berth, when there is fun to be found in sailing in his company. But old age brings us to our reckonings; and when life is getting on short allowance with a poor fellow, he begins to think of being sparing with his tricks, just as water is saved in a ship when the calms set in, after it has been spilt about decks like rain, for weeks and months on end. Thought comes with grey hairs, and no one is the worse for providing a little of it among his other small stores."

"I had hoped, when I gave you the bottom of the hill, and took the top myself," returned Wilder, without even deigning to look at his disagreeable companion, " that we had parted company for ever. As you seem, however, to prefer the high ground, I leave you to enjoy it at your leisure; I shall now descend into the town."

The old man shuffled after him, with a gait that rendered it difficult for Wilder, who was by this time in a fast walk, to out-strip him without resorting to the undignified expedient of actual flight. Vexed alike with himself and his tormentor, he was tempted to offer some violence to the latter; and then, recalled to his recollection by the dangerous impulse, he moderated his pace, and continued his route, with a determination to be superior to any emotions that such a pitiful object could excite.

"You were going under such a press of sail, young master," said the stubborn old mariner, who still kept a pace or two in his rear, "that I had to set every thing to hold way with you; but you now seem to be getting reasonable, and we may as well lighten the passage by a little profitable talk. You had nearly made the oldish lady believe the good ship 'Royal Caroline' was the flying Dutchman."

"And why did you see fit to undeceive her?" bluntly de-manded Wilder.

" Would you have a man, who has followed blue water fifty years, scandalize wood and iron after so wild a manner? The character of a ship is as dear to an old sea-dog as the character of his wife or his sweetheart."

" Hark ye, friend : you live, I suppose, like other people, by eating and drinking?"

" A little of the first, and a good deal of the last," returned the other, with a chuckle.

" And you get both, like most seamen, by hard work, great risk, and the severest exposure?"

" Hum! 'Making our money like horses, and spending it like asses!' — that is said to be the way with us all."

" Now, then, you have an opportunity of making some with less labour; you may spend it to suit your own fancy. Will you engage in my service for a few hours, with this for your bounty, and as much more for wages, provided you deal honestly?"

The old man stretched out a hand, and took the guinea which Wilder had showed over his shoulder without appearing to deem it at all necessary to face his recruit.

" It's no sham?" said the latter, stopping to ring the metal on a stone.

" 'T is gold, as pure as ever came from the mint."

The other very coolly pocketed the coin; and then, with a certain hardened and decided way, as if he were ready for any thing, he demanded,—

" What hen-roost am I to rob for this?"

" You are to do no such pitiful act; you have only to perform a little of that which, I fancy, you are no stranger to. Can you keep a false log?"

" Ay; and swear to it, on occasion. I understand you. You are tired of twisting the truth like a new-laid rope, and you wish to turn the job over to me."

" Something so. You must unsay all you have said concerning yonder ship; and, as you have had cunning enough to get on the weather-side of Mrs. de Lacey, you must improve your advantage, by making matters a little worse than I have represented them to be  Tell me, that I may judge of your qualifications, did you, in truth, ever sail with the worthy rear-admiral?"

"As I am an honest and religious Christian, I never heard of the worthy old man before yesterday. Oh! you may trust me in these matters! I am not likely to spoil a history for want of facts."

"I think you will do. Now listen to my plan——"

"Stop, worthy messmate," interrupted the other: "'stones can hear,' they say on shore; we sailors know that the pumps have ears on board a ship: have you ever seen such a place as the 'Foul Anchor' tavern in this town?"

"I have been there."

"I hope you like it well enough to go again. Here we will part. You shall haul on the wind, being the lightest sailer, and make a stretch or two among these houses, until you are well to windward of yonder church. You will then have plain sailing down upon hearty Joe Joram's, where is to be found as snug an anchorage, for an honest trader, as in any inn in the colonies. I will keep away down this hill, and, considering the difference in our rate of sailing, we shall not be long after one another in port."

"And what is to be gained by so much manœuvring? Can you listen to nothing which is not steeped in rum?"

"You offend me by the word. You shall see what it is to send a sober messenger on your errands, when the time comes. But, suppose we are seen speaking to each other on the highway —why, as you are in such low repute just now, I shall lose my character with the ladies altogether."

"There may be reason in that. Hasten, then, to meet me; for, as they spoke of embarking soon, there is not a minute to lose."

"No fear of their breaking ground so suddenly," returned the old man, holding the palm of his hand above his head to catch the wind. "There is not yet air enough to cool the burning cheeks of that young beauty; and, depend on it, the signal will not be given to them until the sea-breeze is fairly come in."

Wilder waved his hand, and stepped lightly along the road the other had indicated to him, ruminating on the figure which the fresh and youthful charms of Gertrude had extorted from one even as old and as coarse as his new ally. His companion followed his person, for a moment, with an amused look and an ironical cast of the eye; and then he also quickened his pace, in order to reach the place of rendezvous in sufficient season.

# CHAPTER X.

Forewarn him, that he use no scurrilous words.
*Winter's Tale.*

As Wilder approached the "Foul Anchor," he beheld every symptom of a strong excitement existing within the bosom of the hitherto peaceful town. More than half the women, and perhaps one-fourth of all the men, within a reasonable proximity of that well-known inn, were assembled before its door, listening to one of the former sex, who declaimed in tones so shrill and penetrating, as not to leave the proprietors of the curious and attentive countenances in the outer circle of the crowd the smallest rational ground of complaint on the score of impartiality. Our adventurer hesitated, with the sudden consciousness of one but newly embarked in such enterprises as that in which he had so recently enlisted, when he first saw these signs of commotion; nor did he determine to proceed, until he caught a glimpse of his aged confederate, elbowing his way through the mass of bodies, with a perseverance and an energy that promised to bring him right speedily into the very presence of her who uttered such piercing plaints. Encouraged by this example, the young man advanced, but was content to take his position in a situation that left him entire command of his limbs, and, consequently, in a condition to make a timely retreat, should the latter measure prove expedient.

"I call on you, Earthly Potter, and you, Preserved Green,

and you, Faithful Wanton," cried Desire, as he came within hearing, pausing to catch a morsel of breath, before she proceeded in her affecting appeal to the neighbourhood; "and you too, Upright Crook, and you too, Relent Flint, and you, Wealthy Poor,* to be witnesses and testimonials in my behalf. You, and all and each of you can qualify, if you will, that I have ever been a slaving and loving consort of the man who has deserted me in my age, leaving so many of his own children on my hands, to feed and to rear, besides——"

"What certainty is there," interrupted the landlord of the "Foul Anchor" most inopportunely, "that the good man has absconded? It was a merry day, the one that is just gone, and it is quite in reason to believe your husband was, like some others I can name — a thing I shall not be so unwise as to do — a little of what I call how-come-ye-so, and that his nap holds on longer than common. I'll engage we shall all see the honest tailor creeping out of some of the barns shortly, as fresh and as ready for his bitters as if he had not wet his throat with cold water since the last time of general rejoicing."

A low but pretty general laugh followed this effort of tavern wit, though it failed in exciting even a smile on the disturbed visage of Desire, which, by its doleful outline, appeared to have taken leave of all its risible properties for ever.

"Not he, not he," exclaimed the disconsolate consort of the good-man; "he has not the heart to get himself courageous in loyal drinking, on such an occasion as a merry-making on account of his majesty's glory : he was a man altogether for work; and it is chiefly for his hard labour that I have reason to complain. After being so long used to rely on his toil, it is a sore cross to a dependent woman, to be thrown suddenly and altogether on

---

* This whimsical collection of names may strike the reader as over charged, and yet they are all taken from the local history of Rhode Island.

herself for support. But I'll be revenged on him, if there's law to be found in Rhode Island, or in the Providence Plantations! Let him dare to keep his pitiful image out of my sight the lawful time, and then, when he returns, he shall find himself, as many a vagabond has been before him, without wife, as he will be without a house to lay his graceless head in." * Then, catching a glimpse of the enquiring face of the old seaman, who by this time had worked his way to her very side, she abruptly added, " Here is a stranger in the place, and one who has lately arrived! Did you meet a straggling runaway, friend, in your journey hither?"

"I had too much trouble in navigating my old hulk on dry land, to log the name and rate of every craft I fell in with," returned the other, with infinite composure; "and yet, now you speak of such a thing, I do remember to have come within hail of a poor fellow, just about the beginning of the morning-watch, somewhere hereaway, up in the bushes between this town and the bit of a ferry that carries one on to the main."

" What sort of a man was he?" demanded five or six anxious voices, in a breath; among which the tones of Desire, however, maintained their supremacy, rising above those of all the others like the strains of a first-rate artist flourishing a quaver above the more modest trills of the rest of the troupe.

" What sort of a man! Why, a fellow with his arms rigged athwart-ship, and his legs stepped like those of all other Christians, to be sure : but, now you speak of it, I remember that he

---

* It would seem, from this declaration, that certain legal antiquarians, who have contended that the community is indebted to Desire for the unceremonious manner of clipping the nuptial knot, which is so well known to exist, even to this hour, in the commmunity of which she was a member, are entirely in the wrong. It evidently did not take its rise in her example, since she clearly alludes to it as a means before resorted to by the injured innocents of her own sex.

had a bit of a sheep-shank in one of his legs, and rolled a good deal as he went ahead."

"It was he!" added the same chorus of voices. Five or six of the speakers instantly stole out of the throng, with the intention of hurrying after the delinquent, in order to secure the payment of certain small balances of account, in which the unhappy and much traduced good-man stood indebted to the several parties. Had we leisure to record the manner in which these praiseworthy efforts to save an honest penny were conducted, the reader might find much subject of amusement in the secret diligence with which each worthy tradesman endeavoured to outwit his neighbour on the occasion, as well as in the cunning subterfuges which were adopted to veil their real designs, when all met at the ferry, deceived and disappointed in their object. As Desire, however, had neither legal demand on, nor hope of favour from, her truant husband, she was content to pursue, on the spot, such further enquiries in behalf of the fugitive as she saw fit to make. It is possible the pleasures of freedom, in the shape of the contemplated divorce, were already floating before her active mind, with the soothing perspective of second nuptials, backed by the influence of such another picture as might be drawn from the recollections of her first love; the whole having a manifest tendency to pacify her awakened spirit, and to give a certain portion of directness and energy to the subsequent interrogatories.

"Had he a thieving look?" she demanded, without attending to the manner in which she was so suddenly deserted by all those who had just expressed the strongest sympathy in her loss. "Was he a man that had the air of a sneaking runaway?"

"As for his head-piece, I will not engage to give a very true account," returned the old mariner; "though he had the look of one who had been kept, a good deal of his time, in the lee-scuppers. If I should give an opinion, the poor devil has had too much——"

"Idle time, you would say: yes, yes; it has been his misfortune to be out of work a good deal latterly, and wickedness has got into his head, for want of something better to think of. Too much——"

"Wife," interrupted the old man emphatically. Another general, and a far less equivocal laugh at the expense of Desire, succeeded this blunt declaration. Nothing intimidated by such a manifest assent to the opinion of the hardy seaman, the undaunted virago resumed,—

"Ah! you little know the suffering and forbearance I have endured with the man in so many long years. Had the fellow you met the look of one who had left an injured woman behind him?"

"I can't say there was any thing about him which said, in so many words, that the woman he had left at her moorings was more or less injured," returned the tar, with commendable discrimination; "but there was enough about him to show, that, however and wherever he may have stowed his wife, if wife she was, he had not seen fit to leave all her outfit at home. The man had plenty of female toggery around his neck; I suppose he found it more agreeable than her arms."

"What!" exclaimed Desire, looking aghast; "has he dared to rob me? What had he of mine? not the gold beads?"

"I'll not swear they were gold."

"The villain!" continued the enraged termagant, catching her breath like a person that had just been submerged in water longer than is agreeable to human nature, and forcing her way through the crowd with such vigour as soon to be in a situation to fly to her secret hoards, in order to ascertain the extent of her misfortune; "the sacrilegious villain! to rob the wife of his bosom, the mother of his own children, and——"

"Well, well," again interrupted the landlord of the "Foul Anchor," with his unseasonable voice, "I never before heard the

good-man suspected of roguery, though the neighbourhood was
ever backward in calling him chicken-hearted."

The old seaman looked the publican full in the face, with much
meaning in his eye, as he answered,—

"If the honest tailor never robbed any but that virago, there
would be no great thieving sin to be laid to his account; for
every bead he had about him wouldn't serve to pay his ferryage.
I could carry all the gold on his neck in my eye, and see none
the worse for it.   But it is a shame to stop the entrance into a
licensed tavern with such a mob, as if it were an embargoed
port; and so I have sent the woman after her valuables, and all
the idlers, as you see, in her wake."

Joe Joram gazed on the speaker like a man enthralled by some
mysterious charm; neither answering, nor altering the direction
of his eye, for near a minute.   Then, suddenly breaking out in
a deep and powerful laugh, as if he were not backward in enjoying the artifice, which certainly had produced the effect of removing
the crowd from his own door to that of the absent tailor, he
flourished his arm in the way of greeting, and exclaimed,—

"Welcome, Tarry Bob; welcome, old boy, welcome!   From
what cloud have you fallen? and before what wind have you
been running, that Newport is again your harbour?"

"Too many questions to be answered in an open roadstead,
friend Joram; and altogether too dry a subject for a husky conversation.   When I am berthed in one of your inner cabins,
with a mug of flip and a kid of good Rhode Island beef within
grappling distance, why, as many questions as you choose, and
as many answers, you know, as suits my appetite."

"And who's to pay the piper, honest Bob? whose ship's
purser will pay your check now?" continued the publican, showing the old sailor in, however, with a readiness that seemed to
contradict the doubt expressed by his words, of any reward for
his extraordinary civility.

" Who ?" interrupted the other, displaying the money so lately received from Wilder, in such a manner that it might be seen by the few by-standers who remained, as if he would himself furnish a sufficient apology for the distinguished manner in which he was received ; " who but this gentleman ? I can boast of being backed by the countenance of his sacred majesty himself, God bless him ! "

" God bless him ! " echoed several of the loyal lieges ; and that, too, in a place which has since heard such different cries, and where the same words would now excite nearly as much surprise, though less alarm, than an earthquake.

" God bless him ! " repeated Joram, opening the door of an inner room, and pointing the way to his customer, " and all that are favoured with his countenance ! Walk in, old Bob ; you shall soon grapple with half an ox."

Wilder, who had approached the outer door of the tavern as the mob receded, witnessed the retreat of the two worthies into the recesses of the house, and immediately entered the bar-room himself. While deliberating on the manner in which he should arrive at a communication with his new confederate, without attracting too much attention to so odd an association, the landlord returned in person to relieve him. After casting a hasty glance around the apartment, his look settled on our adventurer, whom he approached in a manner half doubting, half decided.

What success, sir, in looking for a ship ?" he demanded, now recognising, for the first time, the stranger with whom he had before held converse that morning. " More hands than places to employ them ? "

" I am not sure it will so prove. In my walk on the hill I met an old seaman, who——"

" Hum ! " interrupted the publican, with an intelligible, though stolen, sign to follow. " You will find it more convenient, sir, to take your breakfast in another room." Wilder followed his conductor, who left the public apartment by a different door from that by which he had led his other guest into the interior of the house, wondering at the air of mystery that the innkeeper saw fit to assume on the occasion. After leading him by a circuitous passage, the latter showed Wilder, in profound silence, up a private stairway into the very attic of the building. Here he rapped lightly at a door, and was bid to enter by a voice that caused our adventurer to start by its deepness and severity. On finding himself, however, in a low and confined room, he saw no other occupant than the seaman who had just been greeted by the publican as an old acquaintance, and by a name to which he might, by his attire, well lay claim to be entitled — that of Tarry Bob. While Wilder was staring about him, a good deal surprised at the situation in which he was placed, the landlord retired, and he found himself alone with his confederate. The latter was already engaged in discussing the fragment of the ox just mentioned, and in quaffing of some liquid that seemed equally adapted to his taste, although sufficient time had not certainly been allowed to prepare the beverage he had seen fit to order. Without allowing his visiter leisure for much further reflection, the old mariner made a motion to him to take the only vacant chair in the room, while he continued his employment on the sirloin with as much assiduity as if no interruption had taken place.

"Honest Joe Joram always makes a friend of his butcher," he said, after ending a draught that threatened to drain the mug to the bottom. "There is such a flavour about his beef, that one might mistake it for the fin of a halibut. You have been in foreign parts, shipmate, or I may call you 'messmate,' since we are both anchored nigh the same kid — but you have doubtless been in foreign countries?"

"Often; I should else be but a miserable seaman."

" Then, tell me frankly, have you ever been in the kingdom that can furnish such rations — fish, flesh, fowl, and fruits — as this very noble land of America, in which we are now both moored ? and in which I suppose we both of us were born ?"

" It would be carrying the love of home a little too far, to believe in such universal superiority," returned Wilder, willing to divert the conversation from his real object, until he had time to arrange his ideas, and assure himself he had no other auditor but his visible companion. " It is generally admitted that England excels us in all these articles."

" By whom ? by your know-nothings and bold talkers. But I, a man who has seen the four quarters of the earth, and no small part of the water besides, give the lie to such empty boasters. We are colonies, friend, we are colonies; and it is as bold in a colony to tell the mother that it has the advantage in this or that particular, as it would be in a foremast Jack to tell his officer he was wrong, though he knew it to be true. I am but a poor man, Mr. —— By what name may I call your honour ?"

" Me ! my name ? — Harris."

" I am but a poor man, Mr. Harris; but I have had charge of a watch in my time, old and rusty as I seem, nor have I spent so many long nights on deck without keeping thoughts at work, though I may not have overhaul'd as much philosophy, in so doing, as a paid parish priest, or a fee'd lawyer. Let me tell you, it is a disheartening thing to be nothing but a dweller in a colony. It keeps down the pride and spirit of a man, and lends a hand in making him what his masters would be glad to have him. I shall say nothing of fruits, and meats, and other eatables, that come from the land of which both you and I have heard and know too much, unless it be to point to yonder sun, and then to ask the question, whether you think King George has the power to make it shine on the bit of an island where he lives, as it shines here on his broad provinces of America ?"

" Certainly not; and yet you know that every one must allow that the productions of England are so very much supe‧rior——"

" Ay, ay; a colony always sails under the lee of its mother. Talk does it all, friend Harris. Talk, talk, talk; a man can talk himself into a fever, or set a ship's company by the ears. He can talk a cherry into a peach, or a flounder into a whale. Now here is the whole of this long coast of America, and all her rivers, and lakes, and brooks, swarming with such treasures as any man might fatten on; and yet his majesty's servants, who come among us, talk of their turbots and their sole, and their carp, as if the Lord had only made such fish, and the devil had let the others slip through his fingers, without asking leave."

Wilder turned and fastened a look of surprise on the old man, who continued to eat, however, as if he had uttered nothing but what might be considered as a matter-of-course opinion.

" You are more attached to your birth-place than loyal, friend," said the young mariner, a little austerely.

" I am not fish-loyal, at least. What the Lord made, one may speak of, I hope, without offence. As to the government, that is a rope twisted by the hands of man, and——"

" And what?" demanded Wilder, perceiving that the other hesitated.

" Hum! Why I fancy man will undo his own work, when he can find nothing better to busy himself in. No harm in saying that either, I hope?"

" So much, that I must call your attention to the business that has brought us together. You have not so soon forgotten the earnest-money you received?"

The old sailor shoved the dish from before him; and, folding his arms, he looked his companion full in the eye, as he calmly answered,—

" When I am fairly enlisted in a service, I am a man to be

counted on. I hope you sail under the same colours, friend Harris?"

"It would be dishonest to do otherwise. There is one thing you will excuse—before I proceed to detail my plans and wishes, I must take occasion to examine this closet in order to be sure that we are actually alone."

"You will find little there except the toggery of some of honest Joe's female gender. As the door is not fastened with any extraordinary care, you have only to look for yourself, since seeing is believing."

Wilder did not seem disposed to wait for this permission; he opened the door while the other was speaking, and finding that the closet actually contained little else than the articles named by his companion, he turned away, like a man who was disappointed.

"Were you alone when I entered?" he demanded, after a thoughtful pause.

"Honest Joram, and yourself."

"No one else?"

"None that I saw," returned the other, his manner betraying slight uneasiness; "if you think otherwise, let us overhaul the room. Should my hand fall on a listener, the salute will not be light."

"Hold—answer me a single question; who bade me enter?"

Tarry Bob, who had risen with a good deal of alacrity, now reflected in his turn, for an instant, and closed his musing by indulging in a low laugh.

"Ah! I see that you have got your ideas a little jammed. A man cannot talk the same, with a small portion of ox in his mouth, as if his tongue had as much sea-room as a ship four-and-twenty hours out."

"Then, it was you."

"I'll swear to that much," returned Bob, resuming his seat

8

like one who had settled the whole affair to his entire satisfaction ; "and now, friend Harris, if you are ready to lay bare your mind, I'm just as ready to look at it."

Wilder did not appear to be quite as well content with the explanation as his companion; but he drew a chair and prepared to open his subject.

"I am not to tell you, friend, after what you have heard and seen, that I have no very strong desire that the lady with whom we have both spoken this morning, and her companion, should sail in the 'Royal Caroline.' I suppose it is enough for our purposes that you should know the fact; the reason why I prefer they should remain where they are, can be of no moment as to the duty you are to undertake."

"You need not tell an old seaman how to gather in the slack of a running idea," cried Bob, chuckling and winking at his companion, in a way that displeased the latter by its familiarity; "I have not lived fifty years on blue water, to mistake it for the skies."

"You then fancy, sir, that my motive is no secret to you?"

"It needs no spy-glass to see, that, while the old people say, 'Go,' the young people would like to stay where they are."

"You do both of the young people much injustice, then; until yesterday, I never laid eyes on the person you mean."

"Ah! I see how it is; the owners of the 'Caroline' have not been so civil as they ought, and you are paying them a small debt of thanks !"

"That is possibly a means of retaliation that might suit your taste," said Wilder, gravely; "but which is not much in accordance with mine. The whole of the parties are utter strangers to me."

"Hum! I suppose you belong to the vessel in the outer harbour; and, though you don't hate your enemies, you love your friends. We must contrive the means to coax the ladies to take passage in the slaver."

"God forbid!"

"God forbid! Now I think, friend Harris, you set up the backstays of your conscience a little too taut. Though I cannot, and do not, agree with you in all you have said concerning the 'Royal Caroline,' I see no reason to doubt that we shall have but one mind about the other vessel. I call her a wholesome-looking and well-proportioned craft, and one that a king might sail in with comfort."

"I deny it not; still I like her not."

"Well, I am glad of that; and, since the matter is fairly between us, master Harris, I have a word or two to say concerning that very ship. I am an old sea-dog, and one not easily blinded in the trade. Do you not find something, that is not in character for an honest trader, in the manner in which they have laid that vessel at her anchors, without the fort, and the sleepy look she bears, at the same time that any one may see she is not built to catch oysters, or to carry cattle to the islands?"

"As you have said, I think her a wholesome and a tight-built ship. Of what evil practices, however, do you suspect her? — perhaps she robs the revenue?"

"Hum! I am not sure it would be pleasant to smuggle in such a vesssel, though your contraband is a merry trade, after all. She has a pretty battery, as well as one can see from this distance."

"I dare say her owners are not tired of her yet, and would gladly keep her from falling into the hands of the French."

"Well, well, I may be wrong; but, unless sight is going with my years, all is not as it would be on board that slaver provided her papers were true, and she had the lawful name to her letters of marque. What think you, honest Joe, in this matter?"

Wilder turned impatiently and found that the landlord had

entered the room, with a step so light as to have escaped his attention, which had been drawn to his companion with a force that the reader will readily comprehend. The air of surprise with which Joram regarded the speaker was certainly not affected; for the question was repeated, and in still more definite terms, before he saw fit to reply.

"I ask you, honest Joe, if you think the slaver in the outer harbour of this port a true man?"

"You come across one, Bob, in your bold way, with such startling questions," returned the publican, casting his eyes obliquely around him, as if to make sure of the character of his audience, "such stirring opinions, that really I am often non-plushed to know how to get the ideas together to make a saving answer."

"It is droll enough, truly, to see the landlord of the 'Foul Anchor' dumb-founded," returned the old man, with perfect composure in mien and eye. "I ask you, in plain English, if you do not suspect something wrong about that slaver?"

"Wrong! Good heavens, Mister Robert, recollect what you are saying. I would not, for the custom of his majesty's lord high admiral, have any discouraging words uttered in my house against the reputation of any virtuous and fair-dealing slavers! The Lord protect me from blacking the character of any honest subject of the king!"

"Do you see nothing wrong, worthy and tender Joram, about the ship in the outer harbour?" repeated Mister Robert, without moving eye, limb, or muscle.

"Well, since you press me so hard for an opinion, and seeing that you are a customer who pays freely for what he orders, I will say, that, if there is any thing unreasonable, or even illegal, in the deportment of the gentlemen——"

"You sail so nigh the wind, friend Joram," coolly interrupted the old man, "as to keep every thing shaking, your teeth included. Just bethink you of a plain answer: have you seen any thing wrong about the slaver?"

"Nothing, on my conscience, then," said the publican, puffing not unlike a cetaceous fish that had come to the surface to breathe; "as I am an unworthy sinner, sitting under the preaching of good and faithful Dr. Dogma, nothing — nothing."

"No! Then are you a duller man than I had rated you at! Do you *suspect* nothing?"

"Heaven protect me from suspicions! The devil besets all our minds with doubts; but weak and evil inclined is he who submits to them. The officers and crew of that ship are free drinkers, and as generous as princes; moreover, as they never forget to clear the score before they leave the house, I call them — honest!"

"And I call them — pirates!"

"Pirates!" echoed Joram, fastening his eye, with marked distrust, on the countenance of the attentive Wilder. "'Pirate' is a harsh word, Mister Robert, and should not be thrown in any gentleman's face, without testimony enough to clear one in an action of defamation, should such a thing get fairly before twelve sworn and conscientious men. But I suppose you know what you say, and before whom you say it."

"I do; and now, as it seems that your opinion in this matter amounts to just nothing at all, you will please——"

"To do any thing you order," cried Joram, delighted to change the subject.

"To go and ask the customers below if they are dry," continued the other, beckoning for the publican to retire by the way he entered, with the air of one who felt certain of being obeyed. As soon as the door was closed on the retiring landlord, he turned to his remaining companion, and continued, "You seem as much struck aback as unbelieving Joe himself, at what you have just heard?"

"It is a harsh suspicion, and should be well supported, old man, before you venture to repeat it. What pirate has lately been heard of on this coast?"

"There is the well-known Red Rover," returned the other, dropping his voice, and casting a furtive look around him, as if even he thought extraordinary caution was necessary in uttering the formidable name.

"But he is said to keep chiefly in the Caribbean Sea."

"He is a man to be any where, and every where. The king would pay him well who put the rogue into the hands of the law."

"A thing easier planned than executed," Wilder thoughtfully answered.

"That is as it may be. I am an old fellow, and fitter to point out the way than to go ahead; but you are like a newly fitted ship, with all your rigging tight, and your spars without a warp in them. What say you to make your fortune by selling the knaves to the king? It is only giving the devil his own a few months sooner or later."

Wilder started, and turned away from his companion like one who was little pleased by the manner in which he expressed himself. Perceiving the necessity of a reply, however, he demanded,—

"And what reason have you for believing your suspicions true? or what means have you for effecting your object, if true, in the absence of the royal cruisers?"

"I cannot swear that I am right; but, if sailing on the wrong tack, we can only go about when we find out the mistake. As to means, I confess they are easier named than mustered."

"Go, go: this is idle talk; a mere whim of your old brain," said Wilder coldly; "and the less said the soonest mended. All this time we are forgetting our proper business. I am half inclined to think, Mister Robert, you are holding out false lights, in order to get rid of the duty for which you are already half paid."

There was a look of satisfaction in the countenance of the old tar, while Wilder was speaking, that might have struck his companion, had not the young man risen, to pace the narrow room, with a thoughtful and hurried step.

" Well, well," the former rejoined, endeavouring to disguise his contentment, in his customary selfish but shrewd expression, " I am an old dreamer, and often have I thought myself swimming in the sea, when I have been safe moored on dry land! I believe there must soon be a reckoning with the devil, in order that each may take his share of my poor carcass, and I be left the captain of my own ship. Now for your honour's orders."

Wilder returned to his seat, and disposed himself to give the necessary instructions to his confederate, in order that he might counteract all he had already said in favour of the outward-bound vessel.

# CHAPTER XI.

——- The man is, notwithstanding, sufficient;—three thousand ducats; —- I think I may take his bond.— *Merchant of Venice.*

As the day advanced, the appearance of a fresh sea-breeze setting in gradually grew stronger; and, with the increase of the
wind, were to be seen all the symptoms of an intention to leave
the harbour on the part of the Bristol trader. The sailing of a
large ship was an event of much more importance in an American port sixty years ago than at the present hour, when a score
is frequently seen to arrive and depart from one haven in a single
day. Althongh claiming to be inhabitants of one of the principal towns of the colony, the good people of Newport did not
witness the movements on board the "Caroline" with that species of indolent regard which is the fruit of satiety in sights as
well as in graver things, and with which, in the course of time,
the evolutions of even a fleet come to be contemplated. On the
contrary, the wharfs were crowded with boys, and indeed with
idlers of every growth. Even many of the more considerate
and industrious of the citizens were seen loosening the close grasp
they usually kept on the precious minutes, and allowing them to
escape uncounted, though not entirely unheeded, as they yielded
to the ascendency of curiosity over interest, and strayed from
their shops, and their work-yards, to gaze upon the noble spectacle of a moving ship.

The tardy manner in which the crew of the "Caroline" made

their preparations, however, exhausted the patience of more than one time-saving citizen. Quite as many of the better sort of the spectators had left the wharfs as still remained, and yet the vessel had spread to the breeze but the solitary sheet of canvass which has been already named. Instead of answering the wishes of hundreds of weary eyes, the noble ship was seen sheering about her anchor, inclining from the passing wind, as her bows were alternately turned to the right and to the left, like a restless courser, restrained by the grasp of the groom, chafing his bit, and with difficulty keeping those limbs upon the earth with which he is shortly to bound around the ring. After more than an hour of unaccountable delay, a rumour was spread among the crowd that an accident had occurred, by which some important individual belonging to the complement of the vessel was severely injured. But this rumour passed away also, and was nearly forgotten, when a sheet of flame issued from a bow-port of the " Caroline," driving before it a cloud of curling and mounting smoke, and was succeeded by the roar of artillery. A bustle, like that which usually precedes the immediate announcement of a long-expected event, took place among the weary expectants on the land, and every one now seemed to feel quite certain, that whatever might have occurred, it was settled that the ship should proceed.

Of all this delay, the several movements on board, the subsequent signal for sailing, and of the impatience in the crowd, Wilder had been a close observer. Posted with his back against the upright fluke of a condemned anchor, on a wharf a little apart from that occupied by most of the spectators, he had remained an hour in the same position, scarcely bending his look to his right hand or to his left. When the gun was fired he started, not with the nervous impulse which had made a hundred others do precisely the same thing, but to turn a glance along the streets that came within the range of his eye. From this hasty

8 *

and uneasy examination, he soon returned into his former reclining posture, though the wandering of his glances, and the whole
expression of his countenance, would have told an observer that
some event to which the young mariner looked forward with
excessive interest was on the eve of its consummation.    As
minute after minute, however, rolled by, his composure was gradually restored, and a smile of satisfaction lighted his features,
while his lips moved like those of a man who expressed his pleasure in a soliloquy.  In the midst of these agreeable meditations,
the sound of  many voices met his ears ; and, turning, he saw a
large  party within a few yards of where he stood.   He was not
slow to detect among them the forms of Mrs. Wyllys and Gertrude, attired  in such a manner as to leave no doubt that they
were on the eve of embarking.

A cloud, driving before the sun, does not produce a greater
change in the aspect of the earth, than was wrought in the expression of Wilder's countenance by this unexpected sight.   He
was just implicitly relying on the success of an artifice, which,
though sufficiently shallow, he flattered himself was deep enough
to act on the timidity and credulity of woman ; and now he was
suddenly awoke from his self-gratulation, to prove the utter disappointment of his hopes.   Muttering a suppressed but deep exe-
cration against the perfidy of his confederate, he shrunk as much
as possible behind the fluke of the anchor, fastening his eyes sullenly on the ship.

The party which accompanied the travellers to the water-side
was, like all other parties made to take leave of valued friends,
taciturn and restless.    Those who spoke, did so with a rapid and
impatient utterance, as if they wished to hurry the very separation they regretted ; and the features of those who said nothing
looked full of meaning.   Wilder heard several affectionate and
warm-hearted wishes given, and promises extorted, from youthful
voices, all of which were answered in the mournful tones of Ger-

trude, and yet he obstinately refused to bend even a stolen look in the direction of the speakers.

At length, a footstep within a few feet of him induced a hasty glance aside. His eye met that of Mrs. Wyllys. The lady started, as well as our young mariner, at the sudden recognition; but, recovering her self-possession, she observed, with admirable coolness,—

"You perceive, sir, that we are not to be deterred from an enterprise once undertaken, by any ordinary dangers."

"I hope you may not have reason, madam, to repent your courage."

A short, but painfully thoughtful pause succeeded, on the part of Mrs. Wyllys. Casting a look behind her, in order to ascertain that she was not overheard, she drew a step nigher to the youth, and said, in a voice even lower than before,—

"It is not yet too late. Give me but the shadow of a reason for what you have said, and I will wait for another ship. My feelings are foolishly inclined to believe you, young man, though my judgment tells me there is but too much probability that you trifle with our womanish fears."

"Trifle! On such a matter I would trifle with none of your sex; and least of all with you!"

"This is extraordinary! For a stranger it is inexplicable! Have you a fact, or a reason, which I can plead to the friends of my young charge?"

"You know them already."

"Then, sir, I am compelled, against my will, to believe your motive is one that you have some powerful considerations for wishing to conceal," coldly returned the disappointed and even mortified governess. "For your own sake, I hope it is not un-worthy. I thank you for all that is well intended: if you have spoken aught which is otherwise, I forgive it."

They parted, with the restraint of people who feel that distrust exists between them. Wilder again shrank behind his cover, maintaining a proud position, and a countenance that was grave to austerity. His situation, however, compelled him to become an auditor of most of what was now said.

The principal speaker, as was meet on such an occasion, was Mrs. de Lacey, whose voice was often raised in sage admonitions and professional opinions, blended in a manner that all would admire, though none of her sex but they who had enjoyed the singular good fortune of sharing in the intimate confidence of a flag-officer, might ever hope to imitate.

"And now, my dearest niece," concluded the relict of the rear-admiral, after exhausting her breath and her stores of wisdom, in numberless exhortations to be careful of her health, to write often, to repeat the actual words of her private message to her brother the general, to keep below in gales of wind, to be particular in the account of any extraordinary sights she might have the good fortune to behold in the passage, and, in short, in all other matters likely to grow out of such a leave-taking; "and now, my dearest niece, I commit you to the mighty deep, and One far mightier — to Him who made it. Banish from your thoughts all recollections of any thing you may have heard concerning the imperfections of the 'Royal Caroline;' for the opinion of the aged seaman who sailed with the lamented admiral assures me they are all founded in mistake." ["The treacherous villain!" muttered Wilder.] "Who spoke?" said Mrs. de Lacey; but, receiving no reply, she continued: — "His opinion is also exactly in accordance with my own, on more mature reflection. To be sure, it is culpable neglect to depend on bobstays and gammonings for the security of the bowsprit; but even this is an oversight which, as my old friend has just told me, may be remedied by 'preventers and lashings.' I have written a note to the master — Gertrude, my dear, be careful ever to call the master of the ship *Mister* Nichols; for none but those who bear his majesty's commission are entitled to be termed *captains ;* it is an honourable station, and should always be treated with reverence, it being in fact, next in rank to a flag-officer—I have written a note to the master on the subject, and he will see the neglect repaired : and so, my love, God bless you ; take the best possible care of yourself; write me by every opportunity ; remember my kindest love to your father, and be very minute in your description of the whales."

The eyes of the worthy and kind-hearted widow were filled with tears, and there was a touch of nature in the tremour of her voice, that produced a sympathetic feeling in all who heard her. The final parting took place under the impressions of these kind emotions, and, before another minute, the oars of the boat which bore the travellers to the ship were stirring the water.

Wilder listened to the well-known sounds with a feverish interest, that he might have found it difficult to explain to himself. A light touch on the elbow first drew his attention from the disagreeable subject. Surprised at the circumstance, he faced the intruder, who appeared to be a lad of apparently some fifteen years. A second look was necessary to tell the abstracted young mariner that he again saw the attendant of the Rover ; he who has already been introduced in our pages under the name of Roderick.

" Your pleasure ? " he demanded, when his amazement at being thus interrupted had a little subsided.

" I am directed to put these orders into your own hands," was the answer.

" Orders ! " repeated the young man with a curling lip. " The authority should be respected which issues its mandates through such a messenger."

" The authority is one that it has ever proved dangerous to disobey," gravely returned the boy.

" Indeed ! Then will I look into the contents without delay, lest I fall into some fatal negligence. Are you bid to wait an answer ?"

On raising his eyes from the note, after breaking its seal, the young man found that the messenger had already vanished. Perceiving how useless it would be to pursue so light a form, amid the mazes of lumber that loaded the wharf, and most of the adjacent shore, he opened the letter and read as follows :—

" An accident has disabled the master of the outward-bound ship called the ' Royal Caroline !' Her consignee is reluctant to intrust her to the officer next in rank ! but sail she must. I find she has credit for speed. If you have any credentials of *character* and *competency*, profit by the occasion, and earn the station you are finally destined to fill. You have been named to some who are interested, and you have been sought diligently. If this reach you in season, be on the alert, and be decided. Show no surprise at any co-operation you may unexpectedly meet. My agents are more numerous than you probably believe. The reason is obvious; gold is yellow, though I am

" RED."

The signature, the matter, and the style of this letter, left Wilder in no doubt as to its author. Casting a glance around him, he sprang into a skiff; and, before the boat of the travellers had reached the ship, that of Wilder had skimmed the water over half the distance between her and the land. As he plied his sculls with vigorous and skilful arms, he soon stood upon her decks. Forcing his way among the crowd of attendants from the shore, that are apt to cumber a departing ship, he reached the part of the vessel where a circle of busy faces told him he should find those most concerned in her fate. Until now, he had hardly breathed clearly, much less reflected on the character of his sudden enterprise. It was too late, however, to retreat, had he been so disposed, or to abandon his purpose without incurring the hazard of exciting dangerous suspicions. A single instant served to recall his thoughts, ere he demanded,—

" Do I see the owner of the ' Caroline?' "

" The ship is consigned to our house," returned a sedate, deliberate, and shrewd-looking individual, in the attire of a wealthy thrifty trader.

" I have heard that you have need of an experienced officer?"

" Experienced officers are comfortable things to an owner in a vessel of value," returned the merchant. " I hope the ' Caroline' is not without her portion."

" But I had heard, one to supply her commander's place, for a time, was greatly needed?"

" If her commander were incapable of doing his duty, such a thing might certainly come to pass. Are you seeking a berth?"

" I have come to apply for the vacancy."

" It would have been wiser, had you first ascertained there existed a vacancy to fill. But you have not come to ask authority in such a ship as this, without sufficient testimony of your ability and fitness?"

" I hope these documents may prove satisfactory," said Wilder, placing in his hands a couple of unsealed letters.

During the time the other was reading the certificates, for such they proved to be, his shrewd eye was looking over his spectacles at the subject of their contents, and returning to the paper, in alternate glances, in such a way as to render it very evident that he was endeavouring to assure himself of the fidelity of the words he read, by actual observation.

" Hum! This is certainly very excellent testimony in your favour, young gentleman; and — coming, as it does, from two so respectable and affluent houses as Spriggs, Boggs, and Tweed, and Hammer and Hacket — entitled to great credit. A richer and broader-bottomed firm than the former is not to be found in his majesty's colonies; and I have great respect for the latter, though envious people do say that they overtrade a little."

"Since, then, you esteem them so highly, I shall not be considered hasty in presuming on their friendship?"

"Not at all, not at all, Mr. —— a — a —" glancing his eye again into one of the letters; "ay, Mr. Wilder; there is never any presumption in a fair offer, in a matter of business. Without offers to sell and offers to buy, our property would never change hands, sir, ha! ha! ha! never change to a profit, you know, young gentleman."

"I am aware of the truth of what you say, and therefore I beg leave to repeat my offer."

"All perfectly fair and perfectly reasonable; but you cannot expect us, Mr. Wilder, to make a vacancy expressly for you to fill, though it must be admitted that your papers are excellent — as good as the note of Spriggs, Boggs, and Tweed themselves — not to make a vacancy expressly——"

"I had supposed the master of the ship so seriously injured——"

"Injured, but not seriously," interrupted the wary consignee, glancing his eye around at sundry shippers, and one or two spectators, who were within ear-shot; "injured certainly, but not so much as to quit the vessel. No, no, gentlemen; the good ship, 'Royal Caroline,' proceeds on her voyage, as usual, under the care of that old and well-tried mariner, Nicholas Nichols."

"Then, sir, I am sorry to have intruded on your time at so busy a moment," said Wilder, bowing with a disappointed air, and falling back a step, as if about to withdraw.

"Not so hasty — not so hasty; bargains are not to be concluded, young man, as you let a sail fall from the yard. It is possible that your services may be of use, though not, perhaps, in the responsible situation of master. At what rate do you value the title of 'captain?'"

"I care little for the name, provided the trust and the authority are mine."

"A very sensible youth!" muttered the discreet merchant;
"and one who knows how to distinguish between the shadow
and the substance! A gentleman of your good sense and
character must know, however, that the reward is always proportioned to the nominal dignity. If I were acting for myself,
in this business, the case would be materially changed, but,
as an agent, it is a duty to consult the interest of my principal."

"The reward is of no account," said Wilder, with an eagerness
that might have overreached itself, had not the individual with
whom he was bargaining fastened his thoughts on the means of
cheapening the other's services, with a steadiness from which
they rarely swerved, when bent on so commendable an object as
saving. "I seek for service."

"Then service you shall have; nor will you find us niggardly
in the operation. You cannot expect an advance for a run of no
more than a month; nor any perquisites in the way of stowage,
since the ship is now full to her hatches; nor, indeed, any great
price in the shape of wages, since we take you chiefly to accom-
modate so worthy a youth, and to honour the recommendations
of so respectable a house as Spriggs, Boggs, and Tweed; but
you will find us liberal, excessively liberal. Stay — how know
we that you are the person named in the invoi— I should say,
recommendation?"

"Does not the fact of possessing the letters establish my character?"

"It might in peaceable times, when the realm was not scourged
by war. A description of the person should have accompanied
the documents, like a letter of advice with the bill. As we take
you at some risk in this matter, you are not to be surprised that
the price will be affected by the circumstance. We are liberal;

I believe no house in the colonies pays more liberally; but then we have a character for prudence too."

"I have already said, sir, that the price shall not interrupt our bargain."

"Good : there is pleasure in transacting business on such liberal and honourable views; and yet I wish a notarial seal, or a description of the person, had accompanied the letters. This is the signature of Robert Tweed; I know it well, and would be glad to see it at the bottom of a promissory note for ten thousand pounds : that is, with a responsible endorser; but the uncertainty is much against your pecuniary interest, young man, since we become, as it were, underwriters that you are the individual named."

"In order that your mind may be at ease on this subject, Mr. Bale," said a voice from among the little circle that was listening, with characteristic interest, to the progress of the bargain, "I can testify, or, should it be necessary, qualify to the person of the gentleman."

Wilder turned in some haste, and in no little astonishment, to discover the acquaintance whom chance had thrown in so extraordinary, and possibly in so disagreeable a manner, across his path; and that, too, in a portion of the country where he wished to believe himself an entire stranger. To his utter amazement, he found that the new speaker was no other than the landlord of the "Foul Anchor."—Honest Joe stood with a perfectly composed look, and with a face that might readily have been trusted to confront a far more imposing tribunal, awaiting the result of his testimony on the wavering mind of the consignee.

"Ah ! you have lodged the gentleman for a night, and you can testify that he is a punctual paymaster, and a civil inmate. But I want documents fit to be filed with the correspondence of the owners *at home*."

"I know not what sort of testimony you think fit for such

good company," returned the unmoved publican, holding up his hand with an air of admirable innocence; "but if the sworn declaration of a housekeeper is of the sort you need, you are a magistrate, and may begin to say over the words at once."

"Not I, not I, man. Though a magistrate, the oath is informal, and would not be binding in law. But what do you know of the person in question?"

"That he is as good a seaman, for his years, as any in the colonies. There may be some of more practice and greater experience — I dare say such are to be found — but as to activity, watchfulness, and prudence, it would be hard to find his equal — especially for prudence."

"You then are quite certain that this person is the individual named in these papers?"

Joram received the certificates with the same admirable coolness he had maintained from the commencement, and prepared to read them with the most scrupulous care. In order to effect this necessary operation, he had to put on his spectacles (for the landlord of the "Foul Anchor" was in the wane of life), and Wilder fancied that he stood, during the process, a notable example of how respectable depravity may become, in appearance, when supported by a reverend air.

"This is all very true, Mr. Bale," continued the publican, removing his glasses, and returning the papers. "They have forgotten to say any thing of the manner in which he saved the 'Lively Nancy,' off Hatteras, and how he ran the 'Peggy and Dolly' over the Savannah bar, without a pilot, blowing great guns from the northward and eastward at the time; but I, who followed the water, as you know, in my younger days, have often heard both circumstances mentioned among seafaring men, and I am a judge of the difficulty. I have an interest in this ship, neighbour Bale, (for though a rich man, and I a poor one, we are nevertheless neighbours) — I say I have an interest in this ship;

since she is a vessel that seldom quits Newport without leaving
something to jingle in my pocket, or I should not be here to-day
to see her lift her anchor."

As the publican concluded, he gave audible evidence that his
visit had not gone unrewarded, by raising a music that was no
less agreeable to the ears of the thrifty merchant than to his own.
The two worthies laughed in an understanding way, and like
men who had found a particular profit in their intercourse with
the "Royal Caroline." The latter then beckoned Wilder apart;
and, after a little further preliminary discourse, the terms of the
young mariner's engagement were finally settled. The true master of the ship was to remain on board, both as a security for the
insurance, and in order to preserve her reputation; but it was
frankly admitted that his hurt, which was no less than a broken
leg, and which the surgeons were then setting, would probably
keep him below for a month to come. During the time he was
kept from his duty, his functions were to be discharged by our
adventurer. These arrangements occupied another hour, and
then the consignee left the vessel, perfectly satisfied with the
prudent and frugal manner in which he had discharged his duty
towards his principal. Before stepping into the boat, however,
with a view to be equally careful of his own interests, he took an
opportunity to request the publican to make a proper and legal
affidavit of all that he knew of his own knowledge concerning
the officer just engaged. Honest Joram was liberal of his promises: but, as he saw no motive, now that all was so happily
effected, for incurring useless risks, he contrived to evade their
fulfilment; finding, no doubt, his apology for this breach of faith,
in the absolute poverty of his information, when the subject came
to be duly considered in his own mind.

It is unnecessary to relate the bustle, the reparation of half
forgotten, and consequently neglected business, the duns, good
wishes, injunctions to execute commissions in some distant port,

and all the confused, and seemingly interminable, duties that crowd themselves into the last ten minutes that precede the sailing of a merchant-vessel, more especially if she is fortunate, or rather unfortunate, enough to have passengers. A certain class of men quit a vessel, in such a situation, with the reluctance that they would part with any other well-established means of profit, creeping down her sides as lazily as the leech, filled to repletion, rolls from his bloody repast. The common seaman, with an attention divided by the orders of the pilot and the adieus of acquaintances, runs in every direction but the right one; and perhaps at the only time in his life, seems ignorant of the uses of the ropes he has so long been accustomed to handle. Notwithstanding all these vexatious delays and customary encumbrances, the "Royal Caroline" finally got rid of all her visiters but one; and Wilder was enabled to indulge in a pleasure that a seaman alone can appreciate — that of clear decks and an orderly ship's company.

## CHAPTER XII.

——Good: speak to the mariners: fall to 't yarely, or we run ourselves aground. — *Tempest.*

A GOOD deal of the day had been wasted during the time occupied by the scenes just related. The breeze had come in steady, but far from fresh. So soon, however, as Wilder found himself left without the molestation of idlers from the shore, and the busy interposition of the consignee, he cast his eyes about him, with the intention of immediately submitting the ship to its power. Sending for the pilot, he communicated his determination, and withdrew himself to a part of the deck whence he might take a proper survey of the materials of his new command, and where he might reflect on the unexpected and extraordinary situation in which he found himself.

The " Royal Caroline" was not entirely without pretensions to her lofty name. She was a vessel of that happy size in which comfort and convenience are equally consulted. The letter of the Rover affirmed she had a reputation for speed; and her young and intelligent commander saw, with great inward satisfaction, that she was not destitute of the means of enabling him to exhibit her properties. A healthy, active, and skilful crew, justly proportioned spars, little top-hamper, and an excellent trim, with a superabundance of light sails, offered all the advantages his experience could suggest. His eye lighted, as it glanced rapidly over these several particulars of his command,

and his lips moved like those of a man who uttered inward grat-
ulations, or who indulged in some vaunt, that propriety suggested
should go no farther than his own thoughts.

By this time the crew, under the orders of the pilot, were
assembled at the windlass, and had commenced heaving-in upon
the cable. The labour was of a nature to exhibit their individual
powers, as well as their collective force, to the greatest advantage.
Their motion was simultaneous, quick, and full of muscle. The
cry was clear and · cheerful. As if to feel his influence, our
adventurer lifted his own voice amid the song of the mariners,
in one of those sudden and inspiriting calls with which a sea-
officer is wont to encourage his people. His utterance was deep,
animated, and full of authority. The seamen started, like
mettled coursers when they first hear the signal, each man casting
a glance behind him, as if he would scan the qualities of his
new superior. Wilder smiled, like one satisfied with his success;
and, turning to pace the quarter-deck, he found himself once
more coufronted by the calm, considerate, but certainly astonished
eye of Mrs. Wyllys.

"After the opinions you were pleased to express of this vessel,"
said the lady, in a manner of the coldest irony, "I did not expect
to find you filling a place of so much responsibility here."

"You probably know, madam," returned the young mariner,
"that a sad accident has happened to her master?"

"I do; and I had heard that another officer had been found,
temporarily to supply his place. Still, I should presume, that,
on reflection, you will not think it remarkable I am amazed in
finding who this person is?"

"Perhaps you may have conceived, from our conversations, an
unfavourable opinion of my professional skill. I hope that on
this head you will place your mind at ease; for——"

"You are doubtless a master of the art! It would seem, at
least, that no trifling danger can deter you from seeking proper

opportunities to display this knowledge. Are we to have the pleasure of your company during the whole passage, or do you leave us at the mouth of the port?''

"I am engaged to conduct the ship to the end of her voyage."

"We may then hope that the danger you either saw or imagined is lessened in your judgment, otherwise you would not be so ready to encounter it in our company."

"You do me injustice, madam," returned Wilder, with warmth, glancing his eye unconsciously towards the grave but attentive Gertrude : "there is no danger that I would not cheerfully en-counter, to save you, or this young lady, from harm."

"Even this young lady must be sensible of so much chivalry !" Then, losing the constrained manner which she had hitherto maintained, in one more natural, and one far more in consonance with her usually mild and thoughtful mien, Mrs. Wyllys con-tinued, "You have a powerful advocate, young man, in the un-accountable interest which I feel in your truth; an interest that my reason would condemn. As the ship must need your ser-vices, I will no longer detain you. Opportunities cannot be wanting to enable us to judge both of your inclination and ability to serve us. Gertrude, my love, females are usually considered as encumbrances in a vessel; more particularly when there is any delicate duty to perform like this before us."

Gertrude started, blushed, and followed her governess to the opposite side of the quarter-deck, though a look from our adven-turer seemed to say, that he considered her presence any thing but an encumbrance. As the ladies took a position apart from every body, and one where they were least in the way of working the ship, at the same time that they could command an entire view of her manœuvres, the disappointed sailor was obliged to cut short a communication which he would gladly have con-tinued, until compelled to take the charge of the vessel from the hands of the pilot. By this time, however, the anchor was aweigh, and the seamen were actively engaged in the process of making sail. Wilder lent himself, with feverish excitement, to the duty; and, taking the words from the officer who was issuing the orders, he assumed the immediate superintendence in person.

As sheet after sheet of canvass fell from the yards, and became distended by the complicated mechanism, the interest that a seaman seldom fails to take in his vessel began to gain the ascendency over all other feelings. By the time every thing was set, from the royals down, and the ship was cast with her head towards the harbour's mouth, our adventurer had momentarily forgotten that he was a stranger among those he was in so extraordinary a manner selected to command, and how precious a stake was intrusted to his firmness and decision. Every thing being set to advantage, alow and aloft, and the ship brought close upon the wind, his eye scanned each yard and sail, from the truck to the hull, concluding by casting a glance along the outer side of the vessel, in order to see that not even the smallest rope was in the water to impede her progress. A small skiff, occupied by a boy, was towing under the lee, and as the mass of the vessel began to move, it was skipping along the surface of the water, light and buoyant as a feather. Perceiving it was a boat belonging to the shore, Wilder walked forward, and demanded who was its owner. A mate pointed to Joram, who at that moment ascended from the interior of the vessel, where he had been settling the balance due from a delinquent, or what was in his eyes the same thing, a departing debtor.

The sight of this man recalled Wilder to a recollection of all that had occurred that morning, and of the whole delicacy of the task he had undertaken to perform. But the publican, whose ideas appeared always concentrated when occupied on the subject of gain, seemed troubled by no particular emotions at the interview. He approached the young mariner, and saluting him by

9

the title of "Captain," wished him a good voyage, with the customary compliments which seamen express, when about to separate on such an occasion.

"A lucky trip you have made of it, Captain Wilder," he concluded, "and I hope your passage will be short. You'll not be
without a breeze this afternoon; and, by stretching well over towards Montauk, you'll be able to make such an offing, on the
other tack, as to run the coast down in the morning. If I am
any judge of the weather, the wind will have more easting in it
than you may happen to find to your fancy."

"And how long do you think my voyage is likely to last?"
demanded Wilder, dropping his voice so low as to reach no ear
but that of the publican.

Joram cast a furtive glance aside; perceiving that they were
alone, he suffered an expression of hardened cunning to take
possession of a countenance that ordinarily seemed set in dull,
physical contentment, and laying a finger on his nose, he muttered,—

"Didn't I tender the consignee a beautiful oath, Master Wilder?"

"You certainly exceeded my expectations with your prompti-
tude, and——"

"Information!" added the landlord of the Foul Anchor, perceiving the other a little at a loss for a word. "Yes, I have
always been remarkable for the activity of my mind in these
matters; but, when a man once knows a thing thoroughly, it is
a great folly to spend his breath in words."

"It is certainly a great advantage to be thoroughly instructed.
I suppose you improve your knowledge to a good account?"

"Ah! bless me, Master Wilder, what would become of us all,
in these difficult times, if we did not turn an honest penny in
every way that offers? I have brought up several fine children
in credit, and it sha'n't be my fault if I don't leave them some-

thing, too, besides my good name. Well, well, they say, 'A nimble sixpence is as good as a lazy shilling;' but give me the man
who don't stand shilly-shally when a friend has need of his good
word, or a lift from his hand. You always know where
to find such a man, as our politicians say, after they have gone
through thick and thin in the cause, be it right or be it
wrong."

" Very commendable principles! and such as will surely be
the means of exalting you in the world sooner or later! But
you forget to answer my question —Will the passage be long, or
short?"

" Heaven bless you, Master Wilder! Is it for a poor publican, like me, to tell the master of this noble ship which way the
wind will blow next? There is the worthy and notable Commander Nichols, lying in his state-room below, he could do anything with the vessel; and why am I to expect that a gentleman
so well recommended as yourself will do less? I expect to hear
that you have made a famous run, and have done credit to the
good word I have had occasion to say in your favour."

Wilder execrated, in his heart, the wary cunning of the rogue
with whom he was compelled, for the moment, to be in league;
for he saw plainly that a determination not to commit himself
a tittle further than he might conceive to be absolutely necessary,
was likely to render Joram too circumspect to answer his own
immediate wishes. After hesitating, a moment, to reflect, he
continued, hastily,—

" You see that the ship is gathering way too fast to admit of
trifling. You know of the letter I received this morning?"

" Bless me, Captain Wilder! Do you take me for a postmas-
ter? How should I know what letters arrive at Newport, and
what stop on the main?"

" As timid a villain as he is thorough!" muttered the young
mariner. " But this much you may surely say, am I to be fol-

lowed immediately ? or is it expected that I shall detain the ship in the offing, under any pretence that I can devise ?"

"Heaven keep you, young gentleman! These are strange questions, coming from one who is fresh off the sea to a man that has done no more than look at it from the land these five-and-twenty years. According to my memory, sir, you will keep the ship about south until you are clear of the islands; and then you must make your calculations according to the wind, in order not to get into the Gulf, where, you know, the stream will be setting you one way, while your orders say 'Go another.'"

"Luff! mind your luff, sir!" cried the pilot, in a reproving voice, to the man at the helm; "luff you can; on no account go to leeward of the slaver!"

Wilder and the publican started, as if they both found something alarming in the proximity of the vessel just named; and the former pointed to the skiff, as he said,—

"Unless you wish to go to sea with us, Mr. Joram, it is time your boat held its master."

"Ay, ay, I see you are fairly under way, and I must leave you, however much I like your company," returned the landlord of the Foul Anchor, bustling over the side, and getting into his skiff in the best manner he could.

"Well, boys, a good time to ye; a plenty of wind, and of the right sort, a safe passage out, and a quick return. Cast off."

His order was obeyed: the light skiff, no longer impelled by the ship, immediately deviated from its course; and, after making a little circuit, it became stationary, while the mass of the vessel passed on with the steadiness of an elephant from whose back a butterfly had just taken its flight. Wilder followed the boat with his eyes, for a moment; but his thoughts were recalled by the voice of the pilot, who again called, from the forward part of the ship,—

"Let the light sails lift a little, boy; let them lift, I say;

keep every inch you can, or you'll not weather the slaver. Luff, I say, sir; luff."

"The slaver!" muttered our adventurer, hastening to a part of the ship whence he could command a view of that important, and, to him, doubly interesting ship; "ay, the slaver! it may be difficult, indeed, to weather upon the slaver!"

He had unconsciously placed himself near Mrs. Wyllys and Gertrude, the latter of whom was leaning on the rail of the quarter-deck, regarding the strange vessel at anchor with a pleasure far from unnatural to her years.

"You may laugh at me, and call me fickle and perhaps credulous, dear Mrs. Wyllys," the unsuspecting girl said, just as Wilder took the position mentioned, "but I wish we were well out of this Royal Caroline, and that our passage was to be made in yonder beautiful ship."

"It is indeed a beautiful ship!" returned Wyllys; "but I know not that it would be safer, or more comfortable, than the one we are in."

"With what symmetry and order the ropes are arranged! and how like a bird it floats upon the water!"

"Had you particularised the duck, the comparison would have been nautical," said the governess, smiling mournfully; "you show capabilities, my love, to become one day a seaman's wife."

Gertrude blushed a little; and, turning back her head to answer in the playful vein of her governess, her eye met the look of Wilder fastened on herself. The colour on her cheek deepened to carnation, and she was mute; the large gipsy hat she wore serving to conceal both her face and the confusion which suffused it.

"You make no answer, child, as if you reflected seriously on the chances," continued Mrs. Wyllys, whose thoughtful and abstracted mien, however, proved she scarcely knew what she uttered

" The sea is too unstable an element for my taste," Gertrude coldly answered. " Pray tell me, Mrs. Wyllys, if the vessel we are approaching is a king's ship? She has a warlike, not to say a threatening, exterior."

" The pilot has twice called her a slaver."

" A slaver! How deceitful is all her beauty and symmetry! I will never trust to appearances again, since so lovely an object can be devoted to so vile a purpose."

" Deceitful, indeed!" said Wilder aloud, under an impulse that he found as irresistible as it was involuntary. " I will take upon myself to say, that a more treacherous vessel does not float the ocean, than yonder finely proportioned and admirably equipped——"

" Slaver!" added Mrs. Wyllys, who had time to turn, and to look her astonishment, before the young man appeared disposed to finish his sentence.

" Slaver!" he said, with emphasis, bowing at the same time, as if to thank her for the word.

After this interruption there was a profound silence. Mrs. Wyllys studied the disturbed features of the young man for a moment, with a countenance that denoted a singular, though a complicated, interest; and then she gravely bent her eyes on the water, deeply occupied with intense and painful reflection. The light symmetrical form of Gertrude continued leaning on the rail, it is true, but Wilder was unable to catch another glimpse of her averted face. In the mean while, events that were of a character to withdraw his attention from even so pleasing a study, were hastening to their accomplishment.

The ship, by this time, had passed between the little island and the point where Homespun embarked, and she might now be said to have fairly left the inner harbour. The slaver lay directly in her track, and every man in the vessel was watching with interest, to see whether they would be able to pass her weather-beam. The measure was desirable, because a seaman has a pride in keeping on the honourable side of every thing he encounters, but chiefly because, from the position of the stranger, it would be the means of preventing the necessity of tacking before the Caroline reached a point more advantageous for such a manœuvre. The reader will, however, readily understand that the interest of her new commander took its rise in feelings very different from professional pride, or momentary convenience.

Wilder felt, in every nerve, the probability that a crisis was at hand. It will be remembered that he was profoundly ignorant of the immediate intentions of the Rover. As the fort was not in a state for service, it would not be difficult for the latter to seize upon his prey in open view of the townsmen, and bear it off, in contempt of their feeble means of defence. The position of the two ships was favourable to such an enterprise. Unprepared, and unsuspecting, the Caroline, at no time a match for her powerful adversary, must fall an easy victim; nor would there be much reason to apprehend that a single shot from the battery could reach them, before the captor and his prize would be at such a distance as to render the blow next to impotent, if not utterly innocuous. The wild and audacious character of such an enterprise was in accordance with the reputation of the desperate freebooter, on whose caprice, alone, the act now seemed solely to depend.

Under these impressions, and with the prospect of such a speedy termination to his new-born authority, it is not to be considered wonderful that our adventurer awaited the result with an interest greatly exceeding that of any of those by whom he was surrounded. He walked into the waist of the ship, and endeavoured to read the plan of his secret confederates, by some of those indications that are familiar to a seaman. Not the smallest sign of any intention to depart, or in any manner to change her position, was discoverable in the pretended slaver.

She lay in the same deep, beautiful, but treacherous quiet, as that in which she had reposed throughout the whole of the eventful morning.    But a solitary individual could be seen amid the mazes of her rigging, or along the wide reaches of her spars. It was a seaman seated on the extremity of a lower yard, where he appeared to busy himself with one of those repairs that are so constantly required in the gear of a ship.    As the man was placed on the weather-side of his own vessel, Wilder instantly conceived the idea that he was thus stationed to cast a grapnel into the rigging of the Caroline, should such a measure become necessary, in order to bring the two ships foul of each other. With the view to prevent so rude an encounter, he instantly determined to defeat the plan.    Calling to the pilot, he told him the attempt to pass to windward was of very doubtful success, and reminded him that the safer way would be to go to leeward.

"No fear, no fear, captain," returned the stubborn conductor of the ship, who, as his authority was so brief, was only the more jealous of its unrestrained exercise, and who, like the usurper of a throne, felt a jealousy of the more legitimate power which he had temporarily dispossessed; "no fear of me, captain. I have trolled over this ground oftener than you have crossed the ocean, and I know the name of every rock on the bottom, as well as the town-crier knows the streets of Newport.    Let her luff, boy; luff her into the very eye of the wind; luff, you can——"

"You have the ship shivering as it is, sir; should you get us foul of the slaver, who is to pay the cost?"

"I am a general underwriter," returned the opinionated pilot: "my wife shall mend every hole I make in your sails with a needle no bigger than a hair, and with such a palm as a fairy's thimble!"

"This is fine talking, sir, but you are already losing the ship's way; and, before you have ended your boasts, she will be as fast iu irons as a condemned thief. Keep the sails full, boy; keep them a rap full, sir."

"Ay, ay, keep her a good full," echoed the pilot, who, as the difficulty of passing to windward became more obvious, began to waver in his resolution. "Keep her full-and-by—I have always told you full-and-by.—I dont know, captain, seeing that the wind has hauled a little, but we shall have tu pass to leeward yet; you will acknowledge that, in such case, we shall be obliged to go about."

Now, in point of fact, the wind, though a little lighter than it had been, was, if any thing, a trifle more favourable; nor had Wilder ever, in any manner, denied that the ship would not have to tack some twenty minutes sooner, by going to leeward of the other vessel, than if she had succeeded in her delicate experiment of passing on the more honourable side; but, as the vulgarest minds are always the most reluctant to confess their blunders, the discomfited pilot was disposed to qualify the concession he found himself compelled to make, by some salvo of the sort, that he might not lessen his reputation for foresight among his auditors.

"Keep her away at once," cried Wilder, who was beginning to change the tones of remonstrance for those of command; "keep the ship away, sir, while you have room to do it, or, by the——"

His lips became motionless; for his eye happened to fall on the pale features of the frightened Gertrude.

"I believe it must be done, seeing that the wind is hauling. Hard up, boy, and run her under the stern of the ship at anchor. Hold! keep your luff again; eat into the wind to the bone, boy; lift again; let the light sails lift. The slaver has run a warp directly across our track. If there's law in the Plantations, I'll have her captain before the courts for this!"

"What does the fellow mean?" demanded Wilder, jumping hastily on a gun, to get a better view.

His mate pointed to the lee quarter of the other vessel, where sure enough, a large rope was seen whipping the water, in the very process of being extended. The truth instantly flashed on the mind of our young mariner. The Rover lay secretly moored with a spring, with a view to bring his guns more readily to bear upon the battery should his defence become necessary, and he now profited by the circumstance, in order to prevent the trader from passing to leeward. The whole arrangement excited a good deal of surprise, and not a few execrations among the officers of the Caroline, though none but her commander had the smallest twinkling of the real reason why the kedge had thus been laid, and why a warp was so awkwardly stretched across their path. Of the whole number, the pilot alone saw cause to rejoice in the circumstance. He had, in fact, got the ship in such a situation as to render it nearly as difficult to proceed in one way as in the other; and he was now furnished with a sufficient justification, should any accident occur, in the course of the exceedingly critical manœuvre, from whose execution there was now no retreat.

"This is an extraordinary liberty to take in the mouth of a harbour," muttered Wilder, when his eyes put him in possession of the fact just related. "You must shove her by to windward, pilot; there is no remedy."

"I wash my hands of the consequences, as I call all on board to witness," returned the other, with an air of an offended man, though secretly glad of the appearance of being driven to the very measure he was a minute before so obstinately bent on executing. "Law must be called in here, if sticks are snapped or rigging parted. Luff to a hair, boy; luff her short into the wind, and try a half-board."

The man at the helm obeyed the order. Releasing his hold of its spokes, the wheel made a quick evolution; and the ship, feeling a fresh impulse of the wind, turned her head heavily to-

wards the quarter whence it came, the canvass fluttering with a
noise like that produced by a flock of water-fowl taking wing.
But, met by the helm again, she soon fell off as before, powerless from having lost her way, and settling bodily down towards
the fancied slaver, impelled by the air, which seemed to have lost
much of its force at the critical instant it was most needed.

The situation of the Caroline was one which a seaman will
readily understand. She had forged so far ahead as to lie directly
on the weather-beam of the stranger, but too near to enable her
to fall-off in the least, without imminent danger that the vessels
would fall foul of each other. The wind was inconstant, sometimes blowing in puffs, while at moments there was a lull. As
the ship felt the former, her tall masts bent gracefully towards
the slaver, as if to make the parting salute; but, relieved from
the momentary pressure of the inconstant air, she as often rolled
heavily to windward without advancing a foot. The effect of each
change, however, was to bring her still nigher to her dangerous
neighbour, until it became evident, to the judgment of the youngest seaman in the vessel, that nothing but a sudden shift of wind
could enable her to pass ahead, the more especially as the tide
was on the change.

The inferior officers of the Caroline were not delicate in making
their comments on the dulness which had brought them into so
awkward and so mortifying a position, and the pilot endeavoured
to conceal his vexation, by the number and vociferousness of his
orders. From blustering, he soon passed into confusion, until
the men themselves stood idle, not knowing which of the uncertain and contradictory mandates ought to be obeyed. In the
mean time, Wilder had folded his arms with an appearance of
entire composure, and taken his station near his female passengers. Mrs. Wyllys studied his eye, with the wish of ascertaining
by its expression the nature and extent of their danger, if danger
there might be in the approaching collision of two ships in water

that was perfectly smooth, and where one was stationary, and the motion of the other scarcely perceptible. The stern, determined look she saw settling about the brow of the young man, excited an uneasiness that she would not otherwise have felt, under circumstances that, in themselves, bore no very vivid appearance of hazard.

" Have we aught to apprehend, sir ? " demanded the governess, endeavouring to conceal from her charge the nature of her own disquietude.

" I told you, madam, the Caroline would prove an unlucky ship."

Both females regarded the peculiarly bitter smile with which Wilder made this reply as an evil omen, and Gertrude clung to her companion as to one on whom she had long been accustomed to lean.

" Why do not the mariners of the slaver appear, to assist us — to keep us from coming too nigh ? " anxiously demanded the latter.

" Why do they not, indeed ! — we shall see them, I think, ere long."

" You speak and look, young man, as if you thought there would be danger in the interview ! "

" Keep near to me," returned Wilder, in a voice that was nearly smothered by the manner in which he compressed his lips. " In every event, keep as nigh my person as possible."

" Haul the spanker-boom to windward," shouted the pilot; " lower away the boats, and tow the ship's head round — clear away the stream anchor—aft gib sheet—board main tack, again."

The astonished men stood like statues, not knowing whither to turn, some calling to the rest to do this or that, and some as loudly countermanding the order; when an authoritative voice was heard calmly to say,—

" Silence in the ship."

The tones were of that sort which, while they denote the self-possession of the speaker, never fail to inspire the inferior with a portion of the confidence of him who commands. Every face was turned towards the quarter of the vessel whence the sound proceeded, each ear ready to catch the smallest additional mandate. Wilder was standing on the head of the capstan, where he could command a full view on every side of him. With a quick and understanding glance, he had made himself a perfect master of the situation of his ship. His eye was at the instant fixed anxiously on the slaver to pierce the treacherous calm which still reigned on all about her, in order to know how far his exertions might be permitted to be useful. But it appeared as if the stranger lay like some enchanted vessel on the water, not a human form appearing about her complicated machinery, except the seaman already named, who still continued his employment, with as much indifference as if the Caroline was a hundred miles from the place where he sat. The lips of Wilder moved, whether in bitterness or in satisfaction it would be difficult to say; and he motioned to the attentive crew to be quick.

"Throw all aback — lay every thing flat to the masts, forward and aft," he said.

"Ay!" echoed the pilot, "lay everything flat to the masts."

"Is there a shore-boat alongside the ship?" demanded our adventurer.

The answer, from a dozen voices, was in the affirmative.

"Show that pilot into her."

"This is an unlawful order," exclaimed the other; "I forbid any voice but mine to be obeyed."

"*Throw* him in," repeated Wilder.

Amid the bustle and exertion of bracing round the yards, the resistance of the pilot produced little sensation. He was raised on the extended arms of the two mates, and after exhibiting his limbs in sundry contortions in the air, he was dropped into the

boat, with as little ceremony as a billet of wood. The end of
the painter was cast after him; and the discomfited guide was
left, with singular indifference, to his own meditations.

In the mean time, the order of Wilder was executed. Those
vast sheets of canvass which, a moment before, had been either
fluttering in the air, or were bellying inward or outward as they
touched or filled, as it is technically called, were now pressing
against their respective masts, impelling the vessel to retrace her
mistaken path. The manœuvre required the utmost attention, and the nicest delicacy in its direction. But her young
commander proved himself, in every particular, competent to the
task. Here, a sail was lifted; there, another was brought with
a flatter surface to the air; now, the lighter canvass was spread;
and now it disappeared, like thin vapour dispelled by the sun.
The voice of Wilder throughout, though calm, was breathing
with authority. The ship itself seemed, like an animated being,
conscious that her destinies were reposed in different, and more
intelligent, hands than before. Obedient to the new impulse
they had received, the immense clouds of canvass, with the tall
forest of spars and rigging, rolled to and fro; and then, having
overcome its state of rest, the vessel heavily yielded to the pressure and began to recede.

Throughout the whole of the time necessary to extricate the
Caroline, the attention of Wilder was divided between his own
ship and his inexplicable neighbour. Not a sound was heard to
issue from the imposing stillness of the latter. Not a single
anxious countenance, not even one lurking eye, was to be detected,
at any of the numerous outlets by which the inmates of an armed
vessel can look abroad upon the deep. The seaman on the yard
continued his labour, like a man unconscious of any thing but his
own employment. There was, however, a slow, though nearly
imperceptible motion in the ship itself, which was apparently
made, like the lazy movement of a slumbering whale, more

by listless volition, than through any agency of human hands.

Not the smallest of these changes escaped the keen examination of Wilder. He saw, that as his own ship retired, the side of the slaver was gradually exposed to the Caroline. The muzzles of the threatening guns gaped constantly on his vessel, as the eye of the crouching tiger follows the movement of its prey; and at no time, while nearest, did there exist a single instant that the decks of the latter ship could not have been swept by a general discharge from the battery of the former. As each successive order issued from his own lips, our adventurer turned his eye with increasing interest to ascertain whether he would be permitted to execute it; and never did he feel certain that he was left to the sole management of the Caroline, until he found that she had backed from her dangerous proximity to the other, and that, obedient to a new disposition of her sails, she was falling off before the light air, in a place where he could hold her entirely at command.

Finding that the tide was getting unfavourable, and the wind too light to stem it, the sails were drawn to the yards, and an anchor was dropped.

# CHAPTER XIII.

What have we here? A man or a fish?

*The Tempest*

THE Caroline now lay within a cable's length of the supposed
slaver. In dismissing the pilot, Wilder had assumed a responsibility from which a seaman usually shrinks; since, in the case
of any untoward accident in leaving the port, it would involve a
loss of insurance, and his own probable punishment. How far
he had been influenced in taking so decided a step, by a knowledge of his being beyond or above the reach of the law, will be
made manifest in the course of the narrative; the only immediate effect of the measure was, to draw the whole of his attention,
which had before been so much divided between his passengers
and the ship, to the care of the latter. But so soon as his vessel
was secured for a time at least, and his mind was no longer
excited by the expectation of a scene of immediate violence, our
adventurer found leisure to return to his former occupation.
The success of his delicate manœuvre had imparted to his countenance a glow of something like triumph, and his step as he
advanced towards Mrs. Wyllys and Gertrude was that of a man
who enjoyed the consciousness of having acquitted himself dexterously in circumstances that required no small exhibition of
professional skill. At least such was the construction the former
lady put upon his kindling eye and exulting air; though the
latter might, possibly, be disposed to judge of his motives with

greater indulgence. Both, however, were ignorant of the true reasons of his self-felicitation, for a sentiment more generous than either of them could imagine had a full share in his present feelings.

Let the cause of his exultation be what it would, Wilder no sooner saw the Caroline swinging to her anchor, and that his services were of no further immediate use, than he sought an opportunity to renew a conversation which had hitherto been so vague and so often interrupted. Mrs. Wyllys had been viewing the neighbouring vessel with a steady look; nor did she now turn her gaze from the motionless and silent object, until the young mariner was near her person. She was then the first to speak.

"Yonder vessel must possess an extraordinary, not to say an insensible crew!" exclaimed the governess, in a tone bordering on astonishment. "If such things were, it would not be difficult to fancy her a spectre ship."

"She is truly an admirably proportioned and a beautifully equipped trader!"

"Did my apprehensions deceive me? or were we in actual danger of getting the two vessels entangled?"

"There was certainly some reason for apprehension; but we are now safe."

"For which we have to thank your skill. The manner in which you have just extricated us from the late danger has a direct tendency to contradict all that you have foretold of that which is to come."

"I well know that my conduct may bear an unfavourable construction, but——"

"You thought it no harm to laugh at the weakness of three credulous females," resumed Mrs. Wyllys, smiling. "You have had your amusement, and now, I hope, you will be more disposed to pity what is said to be a natural infirmity of woman's mind."

The governess glanced her eye at Gertrude, with an expression that seemed to say it would be cruel to trifle further with the apprehensions of one so innocent and so young. The look of Wilder followed her own; and he answered with a sincerity that was well calculated to carry conviction,—

"On the faith which a gentleman owes to all of your sex, madam, what I have already told you I continue to believe"

"The gammonings and the top-gallant-masts!"

"No, no," interrupted the young mariner, slightly laughing, and at the same time colouring a good deal; "perhaps not all of that. But neither mother, wife, nor sister of mine, should make this passage in the Royal Caroline."

"Your look, your voice, and your air of good faith, form a strange contradiction to your words, young man; for, while the former almost tempt me to believe you honest, the latter have not a shade of reason to support them. Perhaps I ought to be ashamed of such a weakness, and yet I will acknowledge that the mysterious quiet which seems to have settled for ever on yonder ship, has excited an inexplicable uneasiness, that may in some way be connected with her character. She is certainly a slaver?"

"She is certainly beautiful!" exclaimed Gertrude.

"Very beautiful!" Wilder rejoined.

"There is a man still seated on one of her yards, who appears to be entranced in his occupation," continued Mrs. Wyllys, leaning her chin thoughtfully on a hand, as she gazed at the object of which she was speaking. "Not once, during the time we were in so much danger of getting the ships entangled, did that seaman bestow so much as a stolen glance towards us. He resembles the solitary individual in the city of the transformed; for not another mortal is there to keep him company, so far as we may discover."

"Perhaps his comrades sleep," said Gertrude.

"Sleep! Mariners do not sleep in an hour and a day like this! Tell me, Mr. Wilder (you that are a seaman should know), is it usual for the crew to sleep when a strange vessel is so nigh — near even to touching, I might almost say?"

"It is not."

"I thought as much; for I am not an entire novice in matters of your daring, your hardy, your *noble* profession!" returned the governess, with emphasis. "Had we gone foul of the slaver, do you think her crew would have maintained their apathy?"

"I think not."

"There is something in all this assumed tranquillity, which might induce one to suspect the worst. Is it known that any of her crew have had communication with the town since her arrival?"

"It is"

"I have heard that false colours have been seen on the coast, and that ships have been plundered, and their people and passengers maltreated, during the past summer. It is even thought that the famous Rover has tired of his excesses on the Spanish Main, and that a vessel was not long since seen in the Caribbean Sea, which was thought to be the cruiser of that desperate pirate!"

Wilder made no reply. His eyes, which had been fastened steadily, though respectfully, on those of the speaker, fell to the deck, and he appeared to await her further pleasure. The governess mused a moment; and then, with a change in the expression of her countenance which proved that her suspicion of the truth was too light to continue without further and better confirmation, she added,—

"After all, the occupation of a slaver is bad enough, and unhappily by far too probable, to render it necessary to attribute any worse character to the stranger. I would I knew the motive of your singular assertions, Mr. Wilder?"

"I cannot better explain them, madam: unless my manner produces its effect, I fail altogether in my intentions, which at least are sincere"

"Is not the risk lessened by your presence?"

"Lessened, but not removed."

Until now, Gertrude had rather listened, as if unavoidably, than seeming to make one of the party. But here she turned quickly, and perhaps a little impatiently, to Wilder, and while her cheeks glowed, she demanded, with a smile that might have brought even a more obdurate man to his confession,—

"Is it forbidden to be more explicit?"

The young commander hesitated, perhaps as much to dwell upon the ingenuous features of the speaker, as to decide upon his answer. The colour mounted into his own embrowned cheek, and his eye lighted with a gleam of pleasure; then, suddenly reminded that he was delaying to reply, he said,—

"I am certain, that in relying on your discretion, I shall be safe."

"Doubt not," returned Mrs. Wyllys. "In no event shall you ever be betrayed."

"Betrayed! For myself, madam, I have little fear. If you suspect me of personal apprehension, you do me great injustice."

"We suspect you of nothing unworthy," said Gertrude, hastily; "but — we are very anxious for ourselves."

"Then will I relieve your uneasiness, though at the expence of——"

A call, from one of the mates to the other, arrested his words for the moment, and drew his attention to the other ship.

"The slaver's people have just found out that their ship is not made to put in a glass case, to be looked at by women and children," cried the speaker, in tones loud enough to send his words into the fore-top, where the messmate he addressed was attending to some especial duty.

"Ay, ay," was the answer; "seeing us in motion, has put him in mind of his next voyage. They keep watch aboard the fellow, like the sun in Greenland; six months on deck, and six months below!"

The witticism produced, as usual, a laugh among the seamen, who continued their remarks in a similar vein, but in tones more suited to the deference due their superiors.

The eyes ef Wilder, however, had fastened on the other ship. The man so long seated on the end of the main-yard had disappeared, and another sailor was deliberately walking along the opposite quarter of the same spar, steadying himself by the boom, and holding in one hand the end of a rope, which he was apparently about to reeve in the place where it properly belonged. The first glance told Wilder that the latter was Fid, who was so far recovered from his debauch as to tread the giddy height with as much, if not greater, steadiness than he would have rolled along the ground, had his duty called him to terra firma. The countenance of the young man, which, an instant before, had been flushed with excitement, and which was beaming with the pleasure of an opening confidence, changed directly to a look of gloom and reserve. Mrs. Wyllys, who had lost no shade of the varying expression of his face, resumed the discourse with some earnestness, where he had seen fit so abruptly to break it off.

"You would relieve us," she said, "at the expense of——"

"Life, madam; but not of honour."

"Gertrude, we can now retire to our cabin," observed Mrs. Wyllys, with an air of cold displeasure, in which disappointment was a good deal mingled with resentment at the trifling of which she believed herself the subject. The eye of Gertrude was no less averted and distant than that of her governess, while the tint that gave lustre to its beam was brighter, if not quite so resentful As they moved past the silent Wilder, each dropped a distant salute, and then our adventurer found himself the sole occupant of the quarter-deck. While his crew were busied in

coiling ropes, and clearing the decks, their young commander
leaned his head on the taffrail (that part of the vessel which the
good relict of the rear-admiral had so strangely confounded with
a very different object in the other end of the ship), remaining
for many minutes in an attitude of abstraction. From this reverie he was at length aroused, by a sound like that produced by
the lifting and falling of a light oar into the water.

Believing himself about to be annoyed by visiters from the
land, he raised his head, casting a dissatisfied glance over the vessel's side, to see who was approaching.

A light skiff, such as is commonly used by fishermen in the
bays and shallow waters of America, was lying within ten feet
of the ship, and in a position where it was necessary to take some
little pains in order to observe it.

It was occupied by a single man, whose back was towards the
vessel, and who was apparently abroad on the ordinary business
of the owner of such a boat.

" Are you in search of rudder-fish, my friend, that you hang
so closely under my counter?" demanded Wilder. " The bay is
said to be full of delicious bass and other scaly gentlemen, that
would far better repay your trouble."

" He is well paid who gets the bite he baits for," returned
the other, turning his head, and exhibiting the cunning eye and
chuckling countenance of old Bob Bunt, as Wilder's recent and
treacherous confederate had announced his name to be.

" How now! Dare you trust yourself with me, in five-fathom
water, after the villanous trick you have seen fit——"

" Hist! noble captain, hist!" interrupted Bob, holding up a
finger, to repress the other's animation, and intimating, by a sign,
that their conference must be held in lower tones; " there is no
need to call all hands to help us through a little chat. In what
way have I fallen to leeward in your favour, captain?"

" In what way, sirrah! Did you not receive money, to give

such a character of this ship to the ladies as (you said youself) would make them sooner pass the night in a churchyard than trust foot on board her?"

"Something of the sort passed between us, captain; but you forget one half of the conditions, and I overlooked the other; I need not tell so expert a navigator, that two halves make a whole No wonder, therefore, that the affair dropped through between us."

"How! Do you add falsehood to perfidy? What part of my engagement did I neglect?"

"What part!" returned the pretended fisherman, leisurely drawing in a line, which the quick eye of Wilder saw, though abundantly provided with lead at the end, was destitute of the equally material implement, the hook; "what part, captain! No less a particular than the second guinea."

"It was to have been the reward of a service done, and not an earnest, like its fellow, to induce you to undertake the duty."

"Ah! you have helped me to the very word I wanted. I fancied it was not in earnest like the one I got, and so I left the job half finished."

"Half finished, scoundrel! you never commenced what you swore so stoutly to perform."

"Now are you on as wrong a course, my master, as if you steered due east to get to the Pole. I religiously performed one half of my undertaking; and, you will acknowledge, I was only half paid."

"You would find it difficult to prove that you even did that little."

"Let us look into the log. I enlisted to walk up the hill as far as the dwelling of the good admiral's widow, and there to make certain alterations in my sentiments, which it is not necessary to speak of between us."

"Which you did not make; but, on the contrary, which you thwarted, by telling an exactly contradictory tale."

" True."

" True, knave!—Were justice done you, an acquaintance with 1 rope's end would be your reward."

" A squall of words!—If your ship steer as wild as your ideas, captain, you will make a crooked passage to the south. Do you not think it an easier matter for an old man like me to tell a few lies, than to climb yonder long and heavy hill?   In strict justice, more than half my duty was done when I got into the presence of the believing widow; and then I concluded to refuse the half of the reward that was unpaid, and to take bounty from t'other side."

" Villain !" exclaimed Wilder, a little blinded by resentment, " even your years shall no longer protect you.   Forward, there ! send a crew into the jolly boat, sir, and bring me this old fellow in the skiff on board the ship.   Pay no attention to his outcries; I have an account to settle with him, that cannot be balanced without a little noise."

The mate to whom this order was addressed, and who had answered the hail, jumped on the rail where he got sight of the craft he was commanded to chase.   In less than a minute he was in the boat, with four men, and pulling round the bows of the ship, in order to get on the side necessary to effect his object. The self-styled Bob Bunt gave one or two strokes with his sculls, and sent the skiff some twenty or thirty fathoms off, where he lay, chuckling like a man who saw only the success of his cunning, without any apparent apprehensions of the consequences.   But the moment the boat appeared in view, he laid himself to the work with vigorous arms, and soon convinced the spectators that his capture was not easily to be achieved.

For some little time it was doubtful what course the fugitive meant to take; for he kept whirling and turning in swift and sudden circles, completely confusing and baffling his pursuers by his skilful and light evolutions.   But, tiring of this amusement, or perhaps apprehensive of exhausting his own strength, which was powerfully and most dexterously exerted, it was not long before he darted on in a perfectly straight line, taking the direction of the Rover.

The chase now grew hot and earnest, exciting the clamour and applause of most of the nautical spectators. The result, for a time, seemed doubtful; but, if any thing, the jolly boat, though some distance astern, began to gain, as it gradually overcame the resistance of the water. In a very few minutes, however, the skiff shot under the stern of the other ship, and disappeared, bringing the hull of the vessel in a line with the Caroline and its course. The pursuers were not long in taking the same direction; and then the seamen of the latter ship began, laughingly, to climb the rigging, in order to command a view over the intervening object.

Nothing, however, was to be seen beyond but water, and the still more distant island with its little fort. In a few minutes, the crew of the jolly boat were observed pulling back in their path, returning slowly, like men who were disappointed. All crowded to the side of the ship in order to hear the termination of the adventure; the noisy assemblage even drawing the two passengers from the cabin to the deck. Instead, however, of meeting the questions of their shipmates with the usual wordy narrative of men of their condition, the crew of the boat were silent and perplexed. Their officer sprang to the deck without speaking, and he immediately sought his commander.

"The skiff was too light for you, Mr. Knighthead," Wilder calmly observed as the other approached, having never moved, himself, from the place where he had been standing during the whole proceeding.

"Too light, sir! Are you acquainted with the man who pulled it?"

"Not particularly well; I only know him for a knave."

10

"He should be one, since he is of the family of the devil!"

"I will take on myself to say he is as bad as you appear to think, though I have little reason to believe he has any honesty to cast into the sea. What has become of him?"

"A question easily asked, but hard to answer. In the first place, though an old and a grey-headed fellow, he twitched his skiff along as if it floated in air. We were not a minute, or two at the most, behind him; but, when we got on the other side of the slaver, boat and man had vanished!"

"He doubled her bows while you were crossing the stern."

"Did you see him, then?"

"I confess we did not."

"It could not be, sir; since we pulled far enough ahead to examine on both sides at once; besides, the people of the slaver knew nothing of him."

"You saw the slaver's people?"

"I should have said her man; for there is seemingly but one hand on board her."

"And how was he employed?"

"He was seated in the chains, and seemed to have been asleep. It is a lazy ship, sir; and one that takes more money from her owners, I fancy, than it ever returns!"

"It may be so. Well, let the rogue escape. There is the prospect of a breeze coming in from the sea, Mr. Earing; we will get our top-sails to the mast-heads again, and be in readiness for it. I could like yet to see the sun set in the water."

The mates and the crew went cheerfully to their task, though many a curious question was asked by the wondering seamen, of their ship-mates who had been in the boat, and many a solemn answer was given, while they were again spreading the canvass to invite the breeze. Wilder turned, in the mean time, to Mrs. Wyllys, who had been an auditor of his short conversation with the mate.

"You perceive, madam," he said, "that our voyage does not commence without its omens."

"When you tell me, inexplicable young man, with the air of singular sincerity you sometimes possess, that we are unwise in trusting to the ocean, I am half inclined to put faith in what you say; but when you attempt to enforce your advice with the machinery of witchcraft, you only induce me to proceed."

"Man the windlass!" cried Wilder, with a look that seemed to tell his companions, If you are so stout of heart, the opportunity to show your resolution shall not be wanting. "Man the windlass there! We will try the breeze again, and work the ship into the offing while there is light.

The clattering of handspikes preceded the mariners' song. Then the heavy labour, by which the ponderous iron was lifted from the bottom, was again resumed, and, in a few more minutes, the ship was once more released from her hold upon the land.

The wind soon came fresh off the ocean, charged with the saline dampness of the element. As the air fell upon the distended and balanced sails, the ship bowed to the welcome guest; and then, rising gracefully from its low inclination, the breeze was heard singing, through the maze of rigging, the music that is so grateful to a seaman's ear. The welcome sounds, and the freshness of the peculiar air, gave additional energy to the movements of the men. The anchor was stowed, the ship cast, the lighter sails set, the courses had fallen, and the bows of the Caroline were throwing the spray before her, ere ten minutes more had gone by.

Wilder had now undertaken the task of running his vessel between the islands of Connannicut and Rhode. Fortunately for the heavy responsibility he had assumed, the channel was not difficult, and the wind had veered so far to the east as to give him a favourable opportunity, after making a short stretch to windward, of laying through in a single reach. But this stretch would bring him under the necessity of passing very near the Rover, or of losing no small portion of his 'vantage ground. He did not hesitate. When the vessel was as nigh the weather shore as his busy lead told him was prudent, the ship was tacked, and her head laid directly towards the still motionless and seemingly unobservant slaver.

The approach of the Caroline was more propitious than before. The wind was steady, and her crew held her in hand, as a skilful rider governs the action of a fiery and mettled steed.

Still the passage was not made without exciting a breathless interest in every soul in the Bristol trader. Each individual had his own secret cause of curiosity. To the seamen, the strange ship began to be the subject of wonder; the governess and her ward scarce knew the reasons of their interest; while Wilder was but too well instructed in the nature of the hazard that all but himself were running. As before, the man at the wheel was about to indulge his nautical pride, by going to windward; but, although the experiment would now have been attended with no hazard, he was commanded to proceed differently.

"Pass the slaver's lee-beam, sir," said Wilder with a gesture of authority; and then the young captain went himself to lean on the weather rail, like every other idler on board, to examine the object they were so fast approaching. As the Caroline came boldly up, seeming to bear the breeze before her, the sighing of the wind, as it murmured through the rigging of the stranger, was the only sound that issued from her. Not a single human 'ace, not even a secret and curious eye, was any where to be seen. The passage was rapid; and, as the two vessels lay with heads and sterns nearly in a line, Wilder thought it was to be made without the slightest notice from the imaginary slaver. He was mistaken. A light active form, in the undress attire of a naval officer, sprang upon the taffrail, and waved a sea-cap in salute. The instant the fair hair was blowing about the countenance of this individual, Wilder recognized the features of the Rover.

"Think you the wind will hold here, sir?" shouted the latter, at the top of his voice.

"It has come in fresh enough to be steady," was the answer.

"A wise mariner would get his offing in time; to me, there is a smack of West Indies about it."

"You believe we shall have it more at south?"

"I do: but a taut bow-line for the night will carry you clear."

By this time the Caroline had swept by, and she was now luffing, across the slaver's bows, into her course again. The figure on the taffrail waved the sea-cap in adieu, and disappeared.

"Is it possible that such a man can traffic in human beings?" exclaimed Gertrude, when the sounds of both voices had ceased.

Receiving no reply, she turned to regard her companion. The governess was standing like a being entranced, her eyes looking on vacancy. They had not changed their direction since the motion of the vessel had carried her beyond the view of the countenance of the stranger. Gertrude took her hand, and repeated the question, when the recollection of Mrs. Wyllys returned. Passing her hand over her brow, with a bewildered air, she forced a smile, as she said,—

"The meeting of vessels, or the renewal of any maritime experience, never fails to revive my earliest recollections, love. But surely that was an extraordinary being, who has at length shown himself in the slaver!"

"For a slaver, most extraordinary!"

Mrs. Wyllys leaned her head on a hand for an instant, and then turned to look for Wilder. The young mariner was standing near, watching the expression of her countenance, with an interest scarcely less remarkable than her own air of thought.

"Tell me, young man, is yonder individual the commander of the slaver?"

"He is."

"You know him?"

"We have met."

"And he is called——"

"The master of yon ship. I know no other name."

"Gertrude, we will seek our cabin. When we are quitting the land, Mr. Wilder will have the goodness to let us know."

The latter bowed his assent, and the ladies left the deck. The Caroline had now the prospect of getting speedily to sea. In order to effect this object, Wilder had every thing that would draw set to the utmost advantage. One hundred times, at least, however, did he turn his head, to steal a look at the vessel he left behind. She lay as when they passed—a regular, beautiful, but motionless object in the bay. From each of these furtive examinations, our adventurer invariably cast an excited and impatient glance at the sails of his own ship; ordering this to be drawn tighter to the spar beneath, or that to be more distended along its mast.

The effect of so much solicitude, united with so much skill, was to urge the Bristol trader through her element at a rate she had rarely, if ever surpassed  It was not long before the land ceased to be seen on her two beams, and then it was only to be traced in the blue islands in their rear, or in a long, dim horizon, to the north and west, where the vast continent stretched for countless leagues. The passengers were now summoned to take their parting look at the land, and the officers were seen noting their departures. Just before the day shut in, and ere the islands were entirely sunk into the waves, Wilder ascended to an upper yard, bearing a glass. His gaze, towards the haven he had left, was long, anxious, and occupied. But his descent was distinguished by a more quiet eye, and a calmer mien. A smile, like that of success, played about his lips; and he gave his orders clearly, and in a more cheerful voice. They were obeyed as briskly. The elder mariners pointed to the seas, as they cut through them, and affirmed that the Caroline had never made such progress. The mates cast the log, and nodded their approbation, as one announced to the other the unusual speed of the ship. In short, content and hilarity reigned on board; for it was thought that the passage was commenced under favourable auspices, and there was the hope of a speedy and a prosperous termination of the run. In the midst of these encouraging omens, the sun dipped into the sea, illumining, as it fell, a wide reach of the chill and gloomy element. Then the shades of night gathered over the illimitable waste.

# CHAPTER XIV.

So foul and fair a day I have not seen.
*Macbeth.*

THE first watch of the night brought no change. Wilder had joined his passengers, cheerful, and with that air of enjoyment which every officer of the sea is apt to exhibit, when he has disengaged his vessel from the land, and has fairly launched her on the trackless and fathomless abyss of the ocean. He no longer alluded to the hazards of the passage, but strove, by the thousand nameless assiduities which his station enabled him to manifest, to expel all recollection of what had passed from their minds. Mrs. Wyllys lent herself to his evident efforts to remove their apprehensions, and one, ignorant of what had occurred between them, would have thought the little party, around the evening's repast, was a contented and unsuspecting group of voyagers, who had commenced their enterprise under the happiest auguries.

Still there was that in the thoughtful eye and clouded brow of the governess, as at times she turned her bewildered look on our adventurer, which denoted a mind far from being at ease. She listened to the gay and peculiar, because professional, sallies of the young mariner, with smiles that were indulgent while they were melancholy, as if his youthful spirits, enlivened by touches of a humour that was thoroughly and quaintly nautical, recalled familiar but sad images to her fancy. Gertrude had less alloy in her pleasure. Home and a beloved and indulgent father were before her; and she felt, while the ship yielded to each fresh impulse of the wind, as if another of those weary miles, which had so long separated them, was passed.

During these short but pleasant hours, the mariner, who had been so oddly called to the command of the Bristol trader, appeared in a new character. Though his conversation was characterized by the frank manliness of a seaman, it was nevertheless tempered by the delicacy of one whose breeding had not been neglected. The beautiful mouth of Gertrude often struggled to conceal the smiles which dimpled her cheeks at his sallies, like a soft air ruffling the surface of some limpid spring; and once or twice, when the humour of Wilder came unexpectedly, and in stronger colours than common, across her youthful fancy, she yielded to an irresistible merriment.

One hour of the free intercourse of a ship can do more towards softening the cold exterior in which the world encrusts the best of human feelings, than weeks of the unmeaning ceremonies of the land. He who has not felt this truth, would do well to distrust his own companionable qualities. It would seem that man, when he finds himself in the solitude of the ocean, most feels his dependency on others for happiness. He yields to sentiments with which he trifled in the wantonness of security, and is glad to seek relief in the sympathies of his kind. A community of hazard makes a community of interest, whether person or property composes the stake. Perhaps a literal reasoner might add that, as each is conscious the condition and fortunes of his neighbour are the indexes of his own, they acquire value from their affinity to self. If this conclusion be true, Providence has happily so constituted some of the species, that the sordid feeling is too latent to be discovered; and least of all was any one of the three, who passed the first hours of the night around the cabin table of the Royal Caroline, to be included in this selfish class. The nature of the intercourse, which had rendered the first hours of their acquaintance so singularly equivocal, appeared to be forgotten in the freedom of the moment; or, if it were remembered at all, merely served to give the young seaman additional

10 *

interest in the eyes of the females, as much by the mystery of
the circumstances, as by the concern he had manifested in their
behalf.

The bell had struck eight; and the hoarse call was heard
which summoned another set of watchers to the deck, before the
party was aware of the lateness of the hour.

"It is the middle watch," said Wilder, smiling, when he
observed that Gertrude started at the strange sounds, listening
like a timid doe that catches the note of the hunter's horn.
"We seamen are not always musical, as you may judge by the
strains of the present spokesman.    There are, however, ears
in the ship to whom his notes are even more discordant than
to your own."

"You mean the sleepers?" said Mrs. Wyllys.

"I mean the watch below.   There is nothing so sweet to the
foremast mariner as his sleep; for it is the most precarious of all
his enjoyments: on the other hand, perhaps, it is the most treacherous companion the commander knows."

"And why is the rest of the superior so much less grateful
than that of the common man?"

"Because he pillows his head on responsibility."

"You are young, Mr. Wilder, for a trust like this you bear."

"It is a service which makes all prematurely old."

"Then why not quit it?" said Gertrude, a little hastily.

"Quit it!" he replied, gazing at her intently, while he suspended his reply.   "It would be like quitting the air I breathe."

"Have you so long been devoted to your profession?" resumed
Mrs. Wyllys, bending her thoughtful eye from the ingenuous
countenance of her pupil, once more towards the features of the
young man.

"I have reason to think I was born on the sea."

"Think! — You surely know your birthplace?"

"We are all of us dependent on the testimony of others."

said Wilder, smiling, "for the account of that important event. My earliest recollections are blended with the sight of the ocean, and I can hardly say that I am a creature of the land at all."

"You have, at least, been fortunate in those who have had the charge of your education and of your younger days."

"I have!" he answered with emphasis. Then shading his face an instant with his hands, he arose, and added, with a melancholy smile, "And now to my last duty for the twenty-four hours. Have you a disposition to look at the night? So skilful and so stout a sailor should not seek her berth, without passing an opinion on the weather."

The governess took his arm, and they ascended the stairs of the cabin in silence, each finding sufficient employment in meditation. She was followed by the more active Gertrude, who joined them on the weather side of the quarter-deck.

The night was misty rather than dark. A full and bright moon had arisen: but it pursued its path through the heavens, behind a body of dusky clouds, that was much too dense for the borrowed rays to penetrate. Here and there a straggling gleam appeared to find its way through a covering of vapour less dense than the rest, falling upon the water like the dim illumination of a distant taper. As the wind was fresh and easterly,* the sea seemed to throw upward from its agitated surface more light than it received; long lines of glittering foam following each other, and lending a distinctness to the waters, that the heavens themselves wanted. The ship was bowed low on its side; and, as it entered each rolling swell, a wide crescent of foam was driven a-head, the element appearing to gambol along its path But, though the time was propitious, the wind not absolutely adverse,

* The writer will not pretend to give the philosophical reason for the phenomenon; but he thinks that every seaman must have observed that the sea has more of the peculiar light alluded to in an eastern than in western breeze, especially within the limits of the Atlantic.

and the heavens rather gloomy than threatening, an uncertain (and, to a landsman, it might seem an unnatural,) light gave a character of the wildest loneliness to the view.

Gertrude shuddered on reaching the deck, while she murmured an expression of strange delight    Even Mrs. Wyllys gazed upon the dark waves, that were heaving and setting in the horizon, around which was shed most of that radiance that seemed so supernatural, with a deep conviction that she was now entirely in the hands of the Being who had created the waters and the land. But Wilder looked upon the scene as one fastens his gaze on a placid sky.   To him the view possessed neither novelty, nor dread, nor charm.   Not so with his more youthful and enthusiastic companion.   After the first sensations of awe had a little subsided, she exclaimed, in the ardour of admiration,—

" One such night would repay a month of imprisonment in a ship!   You must find great enjoyment in these scenes, Mr. Wilder; you, who have them always at command."

" There is pleasure to be found in them without doubt. — I would that the wind had veered a point or two.   I do not like the sky, nor yonder misty horizon, nor this breeze hanging so dead at east !"

" The vessel makes great progress," calmly returned Mrs. Wyllys, observing that the young man spoke without consciousness, and fearing the effect of his words upon the mind of her pupil. " If we are going on our course, there is the appearance of a quick and prosperous passage."

" True !" exclaimed Wilder, who had become conscious of his indiscretion.   " Quite probable, and very true. — Mr. Earing, the air is getting too heavy for that duck.   Hand all your topgallant sails, and haul the ship up closer.   Should the wind hang here at east-with-southing, we may want all the offing we can get."

The mate replied in the obedient manner which seamen use to

their superiors; and, after scanning the signs of the weather for a moment himself, he proceeded to see the order executed. While the men were on the yards furling the light canvass, the females walked apart, leaving the young commander to the uninterrupted discharge of his duty. But Wilder, so far from deeming it necessary to lend his attention to so ordinary a service, the moment after he had spoken, seemed perfectly unconscious that the mandate had issued from his mouth. He stood on the precise spot where the view of the ocean and the heavens first caught his eye, and his gaze still continued fastened on the aspect of the two elements. His look was always in the direction of the wind, which, though far from a gale, frequently fell upon the sails in heavy and sullen puffs. After a long examination, the young mariner muttered his thoughts to himself, and commenced pacing the deck rapidly. Still he would make sudden and short pauses, riveting his gaze on the point of the compass whence the blasts came, as if he distrusted the weather, and would fain penetrate the gloom of night, in order to relieve some painful doubt. At length his step became arrested, in one of those quick turns that he made at each end of his narrow walk. Mrs. Wyllys and Gertrude stood near at hand, and were enabled to read with distinctness the anxious character of his countenance, as his eye became suddenly fastened on a distant point of the ocean, though in a quarter exactly opposite to that in which his former looks had been directed.

"Do you see reason to distrust the weather?" asked the governess, when she thought his examination had endured long enough to become ominous of evil.

"One does not look to leeward for the signs of the weather, in a breeze like this."

"What is there, that you fasten your eye so intently?"

Wilder raised his arm, and was about to speak, when the limb suddenly fell.

"It was delusion!" he muttered, turning and pacing the deck more rapidly than ever.

His companions watched the extraordinary, and apparently unconscious, movements of the young commander with amazement, and not without a little secret dismay. Their own looks wandered over the expanse of troubled water to leeward, but nowhere could they see more than the tossing element, capped with those ridges of garish foam which served only to make the chilly waste more dreary and imposing.

"We see nothing," said Gertrude, when Wilder again stopped to gaze, as before, on the seeming void.

"Look!" he answered, directing their eyes with his finger: "is there nothing there?"

"Nothing."

"You look into the sea. Here, just where the heavens and the waters meet; along that streak of misty light, into which the waves are tossing themselves like little hillocks. There; now 'tis smooth again, and my eyes did not deceive me. — By heavens, it is a ship!"

"Sail, ho!" shouted a voice from a-top. The cry sounded, in the ears of our adventurer, like the croaking of a sinister spirit.

"Whereaway?" he sternly demanded.

"Here on our lee-quarter, sir," returned the seaman, at the top of his voice. "I make her out a ship close-hauled; but, for an hour past, she has looked more like a mist than a vessel."

"He is right," muttered Wilder; "and yet 'tis a strange thing that a ship should be just there."

"And why stranger than that we are here?"

"Why!" said the young man, regarding Mrs. Wyllys, who had put this question, with a perfectly unconscious eye, "I say 'tis strange she should be there. I would she were any where else, or steering northward."

" You give no reason. Are we always to have warnings from you," she continued, " without reasons? Do you deem us so utterly unworthy of a reason? or do you think us altogether incapable of reflection on a subject connected with the sea? You have failed to make the essay, and are too quick to decide without it. Try us this once. We may possibly deceive your expectations."

Wilder laughed faintly, and bowed, as if he recollected him-self. Still he entered into no explanation; but he turned his gaze on the quarter of the ocean where the strange sail was said to be. The females followed his example, and always with the same want of success. Gertrude expressed her disappointment aloud, and her complaints found their way to the ears of the young man.

" You see the streak of dim light," he said, again pointing across the waste. " The clouds have lifted a little there, but the spray of the sea is floating between us and the opening. Her spars look like the delicate work of a spider, against the sky; and yet you see there are all the proportions, with the three masts, of a noble ship."

Aided by these minute directions, Gertrude at length caught a glimpse of the faint object, and soon succeeded in giving the true direction to the look of her governess also. Nothing was visible but the dim outline, not unaptly described by Wilder himself as resembling a spider's web.

" It must be a ship!" said Mrs. Wyllys; " but at a vast distance."

" Hum! Would it were farther. I could wish that vessel any where but there."

" And why not there? Have you reason to dread an enemy has been waiting for us in this particular spot."

" No: still I like not her position. Would to God she were going north!"

"It is some vessel from the port of New York, steering to his majesty's islands in the Caribbean Seas?"

"Not so," said Wilder, shaking his head; "no vessel from under the heights of Navesink, could gain that offing with a wind like this."

"It is then some ship going into the same place, or perhaps a vessel bound for one of the bays of the middle colonies?"

"Her road would be too plain to be mistaken. See; the stranger is close upon a wind."

"It may be a trader, or a cruiser coming *from* one of the places I have named."

"Neither. The wind has had too much northing, the last two days, for that."

"It is a vessel that we have overtaken, and which, like ourselves, has come out of the waters of Long Island Sound."

"That, indeed, is our last hope," muttered Wilder.

The governess, who had put the foregoing questions in order to extract from the commander of the Caroline the information he so pertinaciously withheld, had now exhausted all her own knowledge on the subject, and was compelled to await his further pleasure in the matter, or resort to the less equivocal means of direct interrogation. But the busy state of Wilder's thoughts left her no immediate opportunity to pursue the subject. He soon summoned the officer of the watch to his councils, and they consulted together apart, for many minutes. The hardy, but far from quick-witted, seaman who filled the second station in the ship, saw nothing so remarkable in the appearance of a strange sail in the precise spot where the dim and nearly aërial image of the unknown vessel was still visible; nor did he hesitate to pronounce her some honest trader, bent, like themselves, on her purpose of lawful commerce. His commander thought otherwise, as will appear by the short dialogue that passed between them.

" Is it not extraordinary that she should be just there?" de-manded Wilder, after each, in turn, had made a closer examina-tion of the faint object, by the aid of an excellent night-glass.

" She would certainly be better off, here," returned the literal seaman, who had an eye only for the nautical situation of the stranger; " we should be none the worse for being a dozen leagues more to the eastward, ourselves. If the wind holds here at east-by-south-half-south, we shall have need of all that offing. I got jammed once between Hatteras and the Gulf——"

" Do you not perceive that she is where no vessel could or ought to be, unless she has run exactly the same course with our-selves?" interrupted Wilder. " Nothing, from any harbour south of New York, could have such northing, as the wind has held; while nothing from the colony of York would stand on this tack, if bound east; or would be there, if going southward."

The plain-going ideas of the honest mate were open to a rea-soning which the reader may find a little obscure; for his mind contained a sort of chart of the ocean, to which he could at any time refer, with a proper discrimination between the various winds and all the different points of the compass. When pro-perly directed, he was not slow to see the probable justice of his young commander's inferences; and then wonder, in its turn, began to take possession of his more obtuse faculties.

" It is downright unnatural, truly, that the fellow should be just there!" he replied, shaking his head, but meaning no more than that it was entirely out of the order of nautical propriety : " I see the reason of what you say, Captain Wilder; and I don't know how to explain it. It is a ship, to a moral certainty!"

" Of that there is no doubt. But a ship most strangely placed !"

" I doubled the Good-Hope in the year ' 46,' " continued the other, " and we saw a vessel lying, as it might be, here on our weather-bow — which is just opposite to this fellow, since he is on our lee-quarter — but there I saw a ship standing for an hour across our fore-foot, and yet, though we set the azimuth, not a degree did he budge, starboard or larboard, during all that time, which, as it was heavy weather, was, to say the least, something out of the common order"

"It was remarkable!" returned Wilder, with an air so vacant, as to prove that he rather communed with himself than attended to his companion.

"There are mariners who say that the Flying Dutchman cruises off that Cape, and that he often gets on the weather side of a stranger, and bears down upon him like a ship about to lay him aboard. Many is the king's cruiser, as they say, that has turned her hands up from a sweet sleep, when the look-outs have seen a double-decker come down in the night, with ports up, and batteries lighted; but then this can't be any such craft as the Dutchman, since she is, at the most, no more than a large sloop of war, if a cruiser at all."

"No," said Wilder, "this can never be the Dutchman."

"Yon vessel shows no lights; and, for that matter, she has such a misty look, that one might well question its being a ship at all. Then, again, the Dutchman is always seen to windward, and the strange sail we have here lies broad upon our lee-quarter!"

"It is no Dutchman," said Wilder, drawing a long breath, like a man awaking from a trance. "Main-top-mast-cross-trees, there!"

The man stationed aloft answered the hail in the customary manner, the short conversation that succeeded being necessarily maintained in shouts, rather than in speeches.

"How long have you seen the stranger?" was the first demand of Wilder.

"I have just come aloft, sir; but the man I relieved tells me more than an hour."

" And has the man you relieved come down? or who is that I see sitting on the lee side of the mast-head?"

"'Tis Bob Brace, sir; who says he cannot sleep, and so he stays upon the yard to keep me company."

" Send the man down. I would speak to him."

While the wakeful seaman was descending the rigging, the two officers continued silent, finding sufficient occupation in musing on what had already passed.

" Why are you not in your hammock?" said Wilder, a little sternly, to the man who, in obedience to his order, had descended to the quarter-deck.

" I am not sleep-bound, your honour, and I had a mind to pass another hour aloft."

" And why are you, who have two night-watches to keep already, so willing to enlist in a third?"

" To own the truth, sir, my mind has been a little misgiving about this passage, since the moment we lifted our anchor."

Mrs. Wyllys and Gertrude, who were auditors, insensibly drew nigher to listen, with a species of interest which betrayed itself by the thrilling of nerves, and an accelerated movement of the pulse

" And you have your doubts, sir!" exclaimed the captain, in a tone of slight contempt. " Pray, may I ask what you have seen on board here, to make you distrust the ship?"

" No harm in asking, your honour," returned the seaman, crushing the hat he held between two hands that had a gripe like a couple of vices, " and so I hope there is none in answering. I pulled an oar in the boat after the old man this morning, and I cannot say I liked the manner in which he got from the chase. Then, there is something in the ship to leeward that comes athwart my fancy like a drag, and I confess, your honour, that I should make but little headway in a nap, though I should try the swing of a hammock."

"How long is it since you made out the ship to leeward?"

"I will not swear that a real living ship has been made out at all, sir. Something I did see, just before the bell struck seven, and there it is, just as clear and just as dim, to be seen now, by them that have good eyes."

"And how did she bear when you first saw her?"

"Two or three points more upon the beam than now."

"Then we are passing her!" exclaimed Wilder, with a pleasure too evident to be concealed.

"No, your honour, no. You forget, sir, the ship has come closer to the wind since the middle watch was set."

"True," returned his young commander, in disappointment; "true, very true; too true. And her bearing has not changed since you first made her out?"

"Not by compass, sir. It is a quick boat, that, or it would never hold such way with the Royal Caroline, and that too upon a stiffened bow-line, which every body knows is the real play of this ship."

"Go, get you to your hammock. In the morning we may have a better look at the fellow."

"And — you hear me, sir," added the attentive mate, "do not keep the men's eyes open below, with a tale as long as the short cable, but take your own natural rest, and leave all others, that have clear consciences, to do the same."

"Mr. Earing," said Wilder, as the seaman reluctantly proceeded to his place of rest, "we will bring the ship upon the other tack, and get more easting while the land is so far from us. This course will be setting us upon Hatteras. Besides——"

"Yes, sir," the mate replied, observing his superior to hesitate, "as you were saying, — besides, no one can foretell the length of a gale, nor the real quarter from which it may come."

"Precisely. No one can answer for the weather. The men are scarcely in their hammocks; turn them up at once, sir, before their eyes are heavy, and we will get the ship's head the other way "

The mate instantly sounded the well-known cry which summoned the watch below to the assistance of their shipmates on deck. Little delay occurred, and not a word was uttered, but the short, authoritative mandates which Wilder saw fit to deliver from his own lips. No longer pressed up against the wind, the ship, obedient to her helm, gracefully began to incline her head from the waves, and to bring the wind abeam. Then, instead of breasting and mounting the endless hillocks, like a being that toiled heavily along its path, she fell into the trough of the sea, from which she issued like a courser, who, having conquered an ascent, shoots along the track with redoubled velocity. For an instant the wind appeared to lull, though the wide ridge of foam, which rolled along on each side the vessel's bows, sufficiently proclaimed that she was skimming before it. In another moment, the tall spars began to incline again to the west, and the vessel came swooping up to the wind, until her plunges and shocks against the seas were renewed as violently as before. When every yard and sheet were properly trimmed to meet the new position of the vessel, Wilder turned to get a glimpse of the stranger. A minute was lost in ascertaining the precise spot where he ought to appear; for, in such a chaos of water, and with no guide but the judgment, the eye was apt to deceive itself, by referring to the nearer and more familiar objects by which the spectator was surrounded.

"The stranger has vanished!" said Earing, with a voice in which mental relief and distrust were oddly manifesting themselves.

"He should indeed be on this quarter; but I see him not!"

"Ay ay, sir; this is the way that the midnight cruiser off the Hope is said to come and go. There are men who have seen that vessel shut in by a fog, in as fine a starlight night as was ever met in a southern latitude. But then this cannot be the Dutch

man, since it is so many long leagues from the pitch of the Cape
to the coast of North America."

"Here he lies; and, by heaven, he has already gone about!"

The truth of what Wilder affirmed was sufficiently evident
to the eye of a seaman. The same diminutive and misty tracery,
as before, was to be seen on the light back-ground of the horizon,
looking not unlike the faintest shadows cast upon some brighter
surface by the deception of the phantasmagoria. But to the
mariners, who so well knew how to distinguish between the different lines of her masts, it was very evident that her course had
been suddenly and dexterously changed, and that she was now
steering no longer to the south and west, but, like themselves,
holding her way towards the north-cast, or broadly off towards
the middle of the Atlantic. The fact appeared to make a sensible impression on them all; though probably, had their reasons
been sifted, they would have been found to be entirely different.

"That fellow has truly tacked!" said Earing, after a long
meditative pause, and with a voice in which awe was beginning
to get the ascendency of doubt. "Long as I have followed the
sea, have I never before seen a vessel tack against such a head
beating sea. He must have been all shaking in the wind, when
we gave him the last look, or we should not have lost sight of
him."

"A lively and quick-working vessel might do it," said Wilder;
"especially if strong-handed."

"Ay, the hand of Beelzebub is always strong; and a light
job would he make of even a more difficult manœuvre!"

"Mr. Earing," interrupted Wilder, "we will pack upon the
Caroline, and try our sailing with this stranger. Get the main
tack aboard, and set the top-gallant sail."

The slow-minded mate would have remonstrated against the
order, had he dared; but there was that in the calm manner of
his young commander, which admonished him of the hazard.

He was not wrong, however, in considering the duty he was now to perform as one that was not entirely free from risk. The ship was already moving under quite as much canvass as he deemed it prudent to show at such an hour, and with so many threatening symptoms of heavier weather hanging about the horizon. The necessary orders were, however, repeated as promptly as they had been given. The seamen had already begun to consider the stranger, and to converse among themselves concerning his appearance and situation; and they obeyed with an alacrity that might perhaps have been traced to a secret but common wish to escape from his vicinity. The sails were successively and speedily set; and then each man folded his arms, and stood gazing steadily and intently at the shadowy object to leeward, in order to witness the effect of the change.

The Royal Caroline seemed, like her crew, sensible of the necessity of increasing her speed. As she felt the pressure of the broad sheets of canvass that had just been distended, the ship bowed lower, appearing to recline on the bed of water which rose under her lee nearly to the scuppers. On the other side, the dark planks and polished copper lay bare for many feet, though often washed by the waves that came sweeping along her length, green and angrily, still capped, as usual, with crests of lucid foam. The shocks, as the vessel tilted against the billows, were becoming every moment more severe; and, from each encounter, a bright cloud of spray arose, which either fell glittering on the deck, or drove, in brilliant mist, across the rolling water, far to leeward.

Wilder long watched the ship with a clouded brow, but with the steady intelligence of a seaman. Once or twice, when she trembled, and appeared to stop in her violent encounter with a wave as suddenly as if she had struck a rock, his lips severed, and he was about to give the order to reduce the sail; but a glance at the misty-looking image in the western horizon caused him to change his purpose. Like a desperate adventurer, who had cast his fortunes on some hazardous experiment, he appeared to await the issue with a resolution as haughty as it was unconquerable.

"The top-gallant is bending like a whip," muttered the careful Earing, at his elbow.

"Let it go; we have spare spars enough to put in its place."

"I have always found the Caroline leaky, after she has been strained by driving her against the sea."

"We have our pumps."

"True, sir; but in my poor judgment, it is idle to think of outsailing a craft that the devil commands, if he does not altogether handle."

"One will never know that, Mr. Earing, till he tries."

"We gave the Dutchman a chance of that sort; and, I must say, we not only had the most canvass spread, but much the best of the wind; and what good did it do? there he lay, under his three topsails, driver, and jib; and we, with studding-sails alow and aloft, couldn't alter his bearing a foot."

"The Dutchman is never seen in a northern latitude."

"Well, I cannot say he is," returned Earing, in a sort of compelled resignation; "but he who has put that flyer off the Cape may have found the cruise so profitable, as to wish to send another ship into these seas."

Wilder made no reply. He had either humoured the superstitious apprehension of his mate enough, or his mind was too intent on its principal object to dwell longer on a foreign subject.

Notwithstanding the seas that met her advance, in such quick succession as greatly to retard her progress, the Bristol trader had soon toiled her way through a league of the troubled element. At every plunge she took, the bows divided a mass of water that appeared to be fast getting more vast and more violent, and more than once the struggling hull was nearly buried forward, in some wave which it had equal difficulty in mounting or penetrating.

The mariners narrowly watched the smallest movements of their vessel. Not a man left her deck for hours. The superstitious awe, which had taken such deep hold of the untutored faculties of the chief mate, had not been slow in extending its influence to the meanest of her crew. Even the accident which had befallen her former commander, and the sudden and mysterious manner in which the young officer who now trod the quarter-deck, so singularly firm and calm under circumstances deemed so imposing, had their influence in heightening the wild impression. The impunity with which the Caroline bore such a press of canvass, under the circumstances in which she was placed, added to their kindling admiration; and, ere Wilder had determined in his own mind on the powers of his ship, in comparison with those of the vessel that so strangely hung in the horizon, he was himself becoming the subject of unnatural and revolting suspicions to his own crew.

## CHAPTER XV.

—— I' the name of truth
Are ye fantastical, or that indeed
Which outwardly ye show ?
*Macbeth.*

SUPERSTITION is a quality that seems indigenous to the ocean.
Few common mariners are exempt from its influence, in a greater
or less degree; though it is found to exist, among the seamen
of different people, in forms that are tempered by their respective
national habits and peculiar opinions.   The sailor of the Baltic
has his secret rites, and his manner of propitiating the gods of
the wind; the Mediterranean mariner tears his hair and kneels
before the shrine of some impotent saint, when his own hand
might better do the service he implores; while the more skilful
Englishman sees the spirits of the dead in the storm, and hears
the cries of a lost messmate in the gusts that sweep the waste he
navigates.   Even the better instructed and still more reasoning
American has not been able to shake off entirely the secret influence of a sentiment that seems to be the concomitant of his
condition.

There is a majesty in the might of the great deep, that has a
tendency to keep open the avenues of that dependent credulity
which more or less besets the mind of every man, however he
may have fortified his intellect by thought.   With the firmament
above him, and wandering on an interminable waste of water,
the less gifted seaman is tempted, at every step of his pilgrimage,

to seek the relief of some propitious omen. The few which are supported by scientific causes, give support to the many that have their origin only in his own excited and doubting fancy. The gambols of the dolphin, the earnest and busy passage of the porpoise, the ponderous sporting of the unwieldy whale, and the screams of the marine birds, have all, like the signs of the ancient soothsayers, their attendant consequences of good or evil. The confusion between things which are explicable, and things which are not, gradually brings the mind of the mariner to a state in which any exciting and unnatural sentiment is welcome, if it be for no other reason than that, like the vast element on which he passes his life, it bears the impression of what is thought a supernatural, because it is an incomprehensible, cause.

The crew of the Royal Caroline were all from that distant island that has been, and still continues to be, the hive of nations, which are probably fated to carry her name to a time when the site of her own fallen power shall be sought as a curiosity, like the remains of a city in a desert.

The whole events of the day had a tendency to arouse the latent superstition of these men. It has already been said, that the calamity which had befallen their former commander, and the manner in which a stranger had succeeded to his authority, had their influence in increasing their disposition to doubt. The sail to leeward appeared most inopportunely for the character of our adventurer, who had not yet enjoyed a fitting opportunity to secure the confidence of his inferiors, before such untoward circumstances occurred as threatened to deprive him of it for ever.

There has existed but one occasion for introducing to the reader the mate who filled the station in the ship next to that of Earing. He was called Knighthead; a name that was, in sound at least, indicative of a certain misty obscurity that beset his superior member. The qualities of his mind may be appreciated by the few reflections he saw fit to make on the escape of the old mariner whom Wilder had intended to punish. As this in-dividual was but one degree removed from the common men in situation, he was much more nearly associated with them in habits and opinions than Earing. His influence among them was accordingly much greater than that of his brother mate, while his authority was less, and his sentiments were very gene-rally received as the rule by which all things, that did not ac-tually depend on the mere right to command, were to be judged.

After the ship had been wore, and during the time that Wil-der, with a view to lose sight of his unwelcome neighbour, was endeavouring to urge her through the seas in the manner already described, this stubborn and mystified tar remained in the waist of the vessel, surrounded by a few of the older and more expe-rienced seamen, holding converse on the remarkable appearance of the phantom to leeward, and of the extraordinary manner in which their unknown officer saw fit to attest the enduring qual-ities of their own vessel. We shall commence our relation of the dialogue at a point where Knighthead saw fit to discontinue his distant innuendos, in order to deal more directly with the subject he had under discussion.

"I have heard it said, by older seafaring men than any in this ship," he continued, "that the devil has been known to send one of his mates aboard a lawful trader, to lead her astray among shoals and quicksands, in order that he might make a wreck, and get his share of the salvage among the souls of the people. What man can say who gets into the cabin, when an unknown name stands first in the shipping-list of a vessel?"

"The stranger is shut in by a cloud!" exclaimed one of the mariners, who, while he listened to the philosophy of his officer, still kept an eye riveted on the mysterious object to leeward.

"Ay, ay; it would occasion no surprise to me to see that

craft steering into the moon! Luck is like a fly-block and its
yard: when one goes up, the other comes down. They say the
red-coats ashore have had their turn of fortune, and it is time
we honest seamen look out for our squalls. I have doubled the
Horn, brothers, in a king's ship, and I have seen the bright
cloud that never sets, and I have held a living corposant in my
own hand. But these are things which any man may look on,
who will go upon a yard in a gale, or ship aboard a South-sea-
man; still, I pronounce it uncommon for a vessel to see her
shadow in the haze, as we have ours at this moment; there it
comes again! — hereaway, between the after-shroud and the
backstay — or for a trader to carry sail in a fashion that would
make every knee in a bomb-ketch work like a tooth-brush
fiddling across a passenger's mouth, after he has had a smart
bout with the sea-sickness."

"And yet the lad holds the ship in hand," said the oldest
of all the seamen, who kept his gaze fastened on the proceedings
of Wilder: "he is driving her through it in a mad manner, I
will allow; but yet, so far, he has not parted a yarn."

"Yarns!" repeated the mate, in a tone of contempt; "what
signify yarns, when the whole cable is to snap, and in such a
fashion as to leave no hope for the anchor, except in a buoy
rope? Hark ye, old Bill; the devil never finishes his jobs by
halves. What is to happen will happen bodily; and no easing-
off, as if you were lowering the captain's lady into a boat, and he
on deck to see fair play."

"Mr. Knighthead knows how to keep a ship's reckoning in
all weathers!" said another, whose manner sufficiently announced
the dependence he himself placed on the capacity of the second
mate.

"And no credit to me for the same. I have seen all services,
and handled every rig, from a lugger to a double-decker! Few
men can say more in their own favour than myself; for the little

I know has been got by much hardship, and small schooling
But what matters information, or even seamanship, against witchcraft, or the workings of one whom I don't choose to name, seeing
there is no use in offending any gentleman unnecessarily? I
say, brothers, that this ship is packed upon in a fashion that no
prudent seaman ought to, or would, allow "

A common murmur announced that most, if not all, of his
hearers were of the same mind.

"Let us examine calmly and reasonably, and in a manner
becoming enlightened Englishmen, into the whole state of the
case," the mate continued, casting an eye obliquely over his
shoulder, to make sure that the individual of whose displeasure
he stood in so salutary awe was not actually at his elbow. "We
are all of us, to a man, native-born islanders, without a drop of
foreign blood among us; not so much as a Scotchman or an
Irishman in the ship. Let us therefore look into the philosophy
of this affair, with the judgment which becomes our breeding.
In the first place, here is honest Nicholas Nichols slips from this
here water-cask, and breaks me a leg! Now, brothers, I've
known men to fall from tops and yards, and lighter damage
done. But what matters it, to a certain person, how far he
throws his man, since he has only to lift a finger to get us all
hanged? Then comes me aboard here a stranger, with a look
of the colonies about him, and none of your plain-dealing, out-
and-out, smooth English faces, such as a man can cover with the
flat of his hand——"

"The lad is well enough to the eye," interrupted the old
mariner.

"Ay, therein lies the whole deviltry of this matter! He is
good-looking, I grant ye; but it is not such good-looking as an
Englishman loves. There is a meaning about him that I don't
like; I never likes too much meaning in a man's countenance,
seeing that it is not always easy to understand what he would be

doing. Then, this stranger gets to be master of the ship, or, what is the same thing, next to master; while he who should be on deck giving his orders in a time like this, is lying in his berth unable to tack himself, much less to put the vessel about; and yet no man can say how the thing came to pass."

" He drove a bargain with the consignee for the station, and right glad did the cunning merchant seem to get so tight a youth to take charge of the Caroline."

"A merchant, after all, like the rest of us, is made of nothing better than clay; and, what is worse, it is seldom that, in putting him together, he is dampened with salt water. Many is the trader that has doused his spectacles, and shut his account-books, to step aside to overreach his neighbour, and then come back to find that he has overreached himself. Mr. Bale no doubt thought he was doing the clever thing for the owners, when he shipped this Mr. Wilder; but then, perhaps, he did not know that the vessel was sold to——. It becomes a plain-going seaman to have a respect for all he sails under; so I will not, unnecessarily, name the person who, I believe, has got, whether he came by it in a fair purchase or not, no small right in this vessel."

"I have never seen a ship got out of irons more handsomely than he handled the Caroline this very morning."

Knighthead indulged in a low, but what to his listeners appeared to be an exceedingly meaning, laugh.

" When a ship has a certain sort of captain, one is not to be surprised at any thing," he answered, the instant his merriment ceased. " For my own part, I shipped to go from Bristol to the Carolinas and Jamaica, touching at Newport out and home; and I will say, boldly, I have no wish to go anywhere else. As to backing the Caroline from her awkward berth alongside the slaver, why, it was well done; too well for so young a mariner. Had I done the thing myself, it could not have been better. But what think you, brothers, of the old man in the skiff?

There was a chase, and an escape, such as few old sea-dogs have the fortune to behold! I have heard of a smuggler that was chased a hundred times by his majesty's cutters, in the chops of the Channel, and which always had a fog handy to run into, but from which no man could truly say he ever saw her come out again! This skiff may have plied between the land and that Guernseyman, for any thing I know to the contrary; but it is not a boat I wish to pull a scull in."

"That *was* a remarkable flight!" exclaimed the elder seaman, whose faith in the character of our adventurer began to give way gradually, before such an accumulation of testimony.

"I call it so; though other men may possibly know better than I, who have only followed the water five-and-thirty years. Then, here is the sea getting up in an unaccountable manner! and look at these rags of clouds, which darken the heavens; and yet there is light enough, coming from the ocean, for a good scholar to read by!"

"I've often seen the weather as it is now."

"Ay, who has not? It is seldom that any man, let him come from what part he will, makes his first voyage as captain. Let who will be out to-night upon the water, I'll engage he has been there before. I have seen worse-looking skies, and even worse-looking water than this; but I never knew any good come of either. The night I was wrecked in the bay of——"

"In the waist there!" cried Wilder.

Had a warning voice arisen from the turbulent and rushing ocean itself, it would not have sounded more alarming in the startled ears of the conscious seamen, than this sudden hail. Their young commander found it necessary to repeat it, before even Knighthead, the proper and official spokesman, could muster resolution to answer.

"Get the fore-top-gallant-sail on the ship, sir," continued

Wilder, when the customary reply let him know that he had been heard.

The mate and his companions regarded each other, for a moment, in dull admiration ; and many a melancholy shake of the head was exchanged, before one of the party threw himself into the weather-rigging, proceeding aloft with a doubting mind, in order to loosen the sail in question.

There was certainly enough, in the desperate manner with which Wilder pressed the canvass on the vessel, to excite distrust, either of his intentions or judgment, in the opinions of men less influenced by superstition than those it was now his lot to command. It had long been apparent to Earing, and his more ignorant, and consequently more obstinate, brother officer, that their young superior had the same desire to escape from the spectral-looking ship, which so strangely followed their movements, as they had themselves. They only differed in the mode ; but this difference was so very material that the two mates consulted together apart, and then Earing, something stimulated by the hardy opinions of his coadjutor, approached his commander with the determination of delivering the results of their united judgments, with the directness which he thought the occasion now demanded But there was that in the steady eye and calm mien of Wilder that caused him to touch on the dangerous subject with a discretion and circumlocution that were a little remarkable for the individual. He stood watching the effect of the sail recently spread, for several minutes, before he even presumed to open his mouth. But a terrible encounter, between the vessel and a wave that lifted its angry crest apparently some dozen feet above the approaching bows, gave him courage to proceed, by admonishing him afresh of the danger of continuing silent.

" I do not see that we drop the stranger, though the ship is wallowing through the water so heavily," he commenced, determined to be as circumspect as possible in his advances.

11 *

Wilder bent another of his frequent glances on the misty object in the horizon, and then turned his frowning eye towards the point whence the wind proceeded, as if he would invite its heaviest blasts; he, however, made no answer.

"We have ever found the crew discontented at the pumps, sir," resumed the other, after a sufficient pause for the reply he in vain expected : "I need not tell an officer, who knows his duty so well, that seamen rarely love their pumps."

"Whatever I may find necessary to order, Mr. Earing, this ship's company will find it necessary to execute."

There was a settled air of command in the manner with which this tardy answer was given, that did not fail of its effect. Earing recoiled a step submissively, affecting to be lost in consulting the driving masses of clouds; then, summoning his resolution, he attempted to renew the attack in a different quarter.

"Is it your deliberate opinion, Captain Wilder," he said, using the title to which the claim of our adventurer might well be questioned, with a view to propitiate him,—"is it then your deliberate opinion, that the Royal Caroline can, by any human means, be made to drop yonder vessel?"

"I fear not," returned the young man, drawing a breath so long, that all his secret concern seemed struggling in his breast for utterance.

"And, sir, with proper submission to your better education and authority in this ship, I *know* not. I have often seen these matches tried in my time; and well do I know that nothing is gained by straining a vessel with the hope of getting to windward of one of these flyers!"

"Take the glass, Earing, and tell me under what canvass the stranger is going, and what you think his distance may be," said Wilder, without appearing to advert at all to what the other had just observed.

The honest and really well-meaning mate deposited his hat on the quarter-deck, and did as desired. When his look had been long, grave, and deeply absorbed, he closed the glass with the palm of his broad hand, and replied in the manner of one whose opinion was sufficiently matured,—

"If yonder sail had been built and fitted like other craft," he said, "I should not be backward in pronouncing her a full-rigged ship, under three single-reefed topsails, courses, spanker, and jib."

"Has she no more?"

"To that I would qualify, provided an opportunity were given me to make sure that she is, in all respects, like other vessels."

"And yet, Earing, with all this press of canvass, by the compass we have not left her a foot."

"Lord, sir," returned the mate, shaking his head like one who was well convinced of the folly of such efforts, "if you were to split every cloth in the main-course, you will never alter the bearings of that craft an inch, till the sun shall rise! Then, indeed, such as have eyes that are good enough, might perhaps see her sailing about among the clouds; though it has never been my fortune, be it bad or be it good, to fall in with one of these cruisers after the day has fairly dawned."

"And the distance?" said Wilder; "you have not yet spoken of her distance."

"That is much as people choose to measure. She may be here, nigh enough to toss a biscuit into our tops; or she may be there, where she seems to be, hull down in the horizon."

"But, if where she seems to be?"

"Why, she *seems* to be a vessel of about six hundred tons, and, judging from appearances only, a man might be tempted to say she was a couple of leagues, more or less, under our lee."

"I put her at the same! Six miles to windward is not a little advantage in a hard chase. By heavens, Earing, I'll drive the Caroline out of water, but I'll leave him!"

"That might be done, if the ship had wings like a curlew, or a sea-gull; but, as it is, I think we are more likely to drive her under."

"She bears her canvass well, so far. You know not what the boat can do when urged."

"I have seen her sailed in all weathers, Captain Wilder, but——"

His mouth was suddenly closed. A vast black wave reared itself between the ship and the eastern horizon, and came rolling onward, seeming to threaten to engulf all before it. Even Wilder watched the shock with breathless anxiety, conscious, for the moment, that he had exceeded the bounds of sound discretion in urging his ship so powerfully against such a mass of water. Luckily the sea broke a few fathoms from the bows of the Caroline, sending its surge in a flood of foam upon her decks. For half a minute the forward part of the vessel disappeared, as if, unable to mount the swell, it were striving to go through it, and then she heavily emerged, gemmed with a million of the scintillating insects of the ocean. The ship stopped, trembling in every joint of her massive and powerful frame, like some affrighted courser; and, when she resumed her course, it was with a moderation that appeared to warn those who governed her movements of their indiscretion.

Earing faced his commander in silence, perfectly conscious that nothing he could utter contained an argument like this. The seamen no longer hesitated to mutter their disapprobation aloud, and many a prophetic opinion was ventured concerning the consequences of such reckless risks. To all this Wilder turned an insensible ear. Firm in his secret purpose, he would have braved a greater hazard to accomplish his object. But a distinct though smothered shriek, from the stern of the vessel, reminded him of the fears of others. Turning quickly on his heel, he approached the still trembling Gertrude and her governess, who had both been, throughout the whole of those long and tedious hours, inobtrusive, but deeply interested, observers of his smallest movements.

"The vessel bore that shock so well, I have great reliance on her powers," he said, in a soothing voice, but with words that were intended to lull her into a blind security. "With a firm ship, a thorough seaman is never at a loss."

"Mr. Wilder," returned the governess, "I have seen much of this terrible element on which you live. It is vain to think of deceiving me. I know that you are urging the vessel beyond what is usual. Have you sufficient motive for this hardihood?"

"Madam, — I have!"

"And is it, like so many of your motives, to continue locked for ever in your own breast? or may we, who are equal participators in its consequences, claim to share equally in the reason?"

"Since you know so much of the profession," returned the young man, slightly laughing, but in a way that rendered what he had said more alarming by the sounds produced in the unnatural effort, "you need not be told, that, in order to get a ship to windward, it is necessary to show her canvass."

"You can, at least, answer one of my questions more directly. Is this wind sufficiently favourable to pass the dangerous shoals of the Hatteras?"

"I doubt it."

"Then why not return to the place whence we came?"

"Will you consent to that?" demanded the youth, with the swiftness of thought.

"I would go to my father," said Gertrude, with a rapidity so nearly resembling his own, that the ardent girl appeared to want breath to utter the little she said.

"And I am willing, Mr. Wilder, to abandon this ship entirely," calmly resumed the governess. "I require no explanation of all your mysterious warnings: restore us to our friends in Newport, and no further questions shall ever be asked."

"It might be done!" muttered our adventurer; "it might be done! A few busy hours would do it, with this wind. — Mr. Earing!"

The mate was instantly at his elbow. Wilder pointed to the dim object to leeward; and, handing him the glass, desired that he would take another view. Each again looked, in turn, long and closely.

"He shows no more sail!" said the commander impatiently, when his own prolonged gaze was ended.

"Not a cloth, sir. But what matters it to such a craft, how much canvass is spread, or how the wind blows?"

"Earing, I think there is too much southing in this breeze; and there is more brewing in yonder streak of dusky clouds on our beam. Let the ship fall off a couple of points or more, and take the strain off the spars by a pull upon the weather-braces."

The simple-minded mate heard the order with an astonishment he did not care to conceal. There needed no explanation to teach one of his experience that the effect would be to go over the same track they had just passed; and that it was, in substance, abandoning the objects of the voyage. He presumed to defer his compliance in order to remonstrate.

"I hope there is no offence for an elderly seaman, like myself, Captain Wilder, in venturing an opinion on the weather," he said. "When the pocket of the owner is interested, my judgment approves of going about, for I have no taste for land that the wind blows on, instead of off. But by easing the ship with a reef or two, she would always be jogging seaward; and all we gain would be clear gain, because it is so much off the Hatteras. Besides, who can say that to-morrow, or the next day, we sha'n't have a puff out of America, here at north-west?"

"A couple of points fall off and a pull upon your weather braces," said Wilder, in a way to show that he was in earnest.

It would have exceeded the peaceful and submissive disposition of the honest Earing to delay any longer. The orders were given to the inferiors; and, as a matter of course, they were obeyed—though ill-suppressed and portentous sounds of discontent, at the undetermined, and seemingly unreasonable, changes in their officer's mind, might have been heard issuing from the mouths of Knighthead and the other veterans of the crew.

To all these symptoms of disaffection Wilder remained utterly indifferent. If he heard them at all, he either disdained to yield them any notice, or, guided by a temporising policy, he chose to appear unconscious of their import. In the meantime the vessel, like a bird whose wing had wearied with struggling against the tempest, and which inclines from the gale to choose an easier course, glided swiftly away, quartering the crests of the waves, or sinking gracefully into their troughs, as she yielded to the force of a wind that was now made to be favourable. The sea rolled on, in a direction no longer adverse to her course; and, by receding from the breeze, the quantity of sail spread was no longer trying to her powers of endurance. Still, in the opinion of all her crew, she had quite enough canvass exposed to a night of so portentous aspect. But not so in the judgment of the stranger who was charged with the guidance of her destinies. In a voice that still admonished his inferiors of the danger of disobedience, he commanded several broad sheets of studding-sails to be set in quick succession. Urged by these new impulses, the ship went careering over the waves, leaving a train of foam in her track, that rivalled, in its volume and brightness, the tumbling summit of the largest swell.

When sail after sail had been set, until even Wilder was obliged to confess to himself that the Royal Caroline, staunch as she was, would bear no more, our adventurer began to pace the deck again, and to cast his eyes about him to watch the fruits of

his new experiment. The change in the course of the Bristol
trader had made a corresponding change in the apparent direction
of the stranger, who yet floated in the horizon like a diminutive
and misty shadow. Still the unerring compass told the watchful
mariner, that she continued to maintain the same relative position
as when first seen.* No effort, on the part of Wilder, could
alter her bearing an inch. Another hour soon passed away,
during which, as the log told him, his own ship had rolled through
three leagues of water, and still there lay the stranger in the
west, as if he were merely a lessened shadow of herself, cast by
the Caroline upon the distant and dusky clouds. An alteration
in his course exposed a broader surface of his canvass to the eyes
of those who watched him, but in nothing else was there a visible
change. If his sail had been materially increased, the distance
and the obscurity prevented even the understanding Earing from
detecting it. Perhaps the excited mind of the worthy mate was
too much disposed to believe in the miraculous powers possessed
by his unaccountable neighbour, to admit of the full exercise of
his experienced faculties on the occasion; but even Wilder, who
vexed his sight, in often-repeated examinations, was obliged to
confess to himself, that the stranger seemed to glide across the
waste of waters, more like a body floating in the air, than a ship
resorting to the known expedients of mariners.

Mrs. Wyllys and her charge, by this time, had retired to their
cabin; the former secretly felicitating herself on the prospect of
soon quitting a vessel that had commenced its voyage under such
sinister circumstances, as to have deranged the equilibrium of
even her governed and well-disciplined mind. Gertrude was left
in ignorance of the change. To her uninstructed eye, all appeared
the same on the wilderness of the ocean; Wilder having it in

---

* The reader will understand that the *apparent* direction of a ship at
sea, seen from the deck of another, changes with the change of course,
but that the *true* direction can only be varied by a change of relative
position.

his power to alter the direction of his vessel as often as he pleased, without his fairer and more youthful passenger being any the wiser.

Not so with the intelligent commander of the Caroline himself. To him there was neither obscurity nor doubt in the midst of his midnight path. His eye had long been familiar with every star that rose from out the dark and ragged outline of the sea, nor was there a blast that swept across the ocean, that his burning cheek could not tell from what quarter of the heavens it poured out its power. He knew, and understood, each inclination made by the bows of his ship: his mind kept even pace with her windings and turnings, in all her trackless wanderings; and he had little need to consult any of the accessories of his art, to tell him what course to steer, or in what manner to guide the movements of the nice machine he governed. Still he was unable to explain the extraordinary evolutions of the stranger. The smallest change he ordered seemed rather anticipated than followed; and his hopes of eluding a vigilance that proved so watchful, was baffled by a facility of manœuvring, and a superiority of sailing, that really began to assume, even to his intelligent eyes, the appearance of some unaccountable agency.

While our adventurer was engaged in the gloomy musings that such impressions were not ill adapted to excite, the heavens and the sea began to exhibit new aspects. The bright streak which had so long hung along the eastern horizon, as if the curtain of the firmament had been slightly opened to admit a passage for the winds, was now suddenly closed; and heavy masses of black clouds began to gather in that quarter, until vast volumes of the vapour were piled upon the water, blending the two elements in one. On the other hand, the gloomy canopy lifted in the west, and a long belt of lurid light was shed athwart the view. In this flood of bright and portentous mist the stranger still floated, though there were moments when his faint and fanciful outlines seemed to be melting into air.

## CHAPTER XVI.

———Yet again? What do you here? Shall we give o'er and drown? Have you a mind to sink? — *Tempest.*

Our watchful adventurer was not blind to these sinister omens. No sooner did the peculiar atmosphere by which the mysterious image that he so often examined was suddenly surrounded, catch his eye, than his voice was raised in the clear, powerful, and exciting notes of warning.

"Stand by," he called aloud, " to in-all-studding-sails! Down with them!" he added, scarcely giving his former words time to reach the ears of his subordinates. " Down with every rag of them, fore and aft the ship! Man the top-gallant clew-lines, Mr. Earing. Clew up, and clew down! In with every thing, cheerily, men! — In!"

This was a language to which the crew of the Caroline were no strangers, and it was doubly welcome, since the meanest seaman amongst them had long thought that his unknown commander had been heedlessly trifling with the safety of the vessel, by the hardy manner in which he disregarded the wild symptoms of the weather. But they undervalued the keen-eyed vigilance of Wilder. He had certainly driven the Bristol trader through the water at a rate she had never been known to go before; but, thus far, the facts themselves gave evidence in his favour, since no injury was the consequence of what they deemed temerity. At the quick sudden order just given, however, the whole ship was in an uproar. A dozen seamen called to each other, from different parts of the vessel, each striving to lift his voice above the roaring ocean; and there was every appearance of a general and inextricable confusion; but the same authority which had so unexpectedly aroused them into activity, produced order from their ill-directed though vigorous efforts.

Wilder had spoken, to awaken the drowsy and to excite the torpid. The instant he found each man on the alert, he resumed his orders with a calmness that gave a direction to the powers of all, and yet with an energy that he well knew was called for by the occasion. The enormous sheets of duck, which had looked like so many light clouds in the murky and threatening heavens, were soon seen fluttering wildly, as they descended from their high places, and, in a few minutes, the ship was reduced to the action of her more secure and heavier canvass. To effect this object, every man in the ship exerted his powers to the utmost, under the guidance of the steady but rapid mandates of their commander. Then followed a short and apprehensive pause. All eyes were turned towards the quarter where the ominous signs had been discovered; and each individual endeavoured to read their import, with an intelligence correspondent to the degree of skill he might have acquired, during his particular period of service on that treacherous element which was now his home.

The dim tracery of the stranger's form had been swallowed by the flood of misty light, which, by this time, rolled along the sea like drifting vapour, semi-pellucid, preternatural, and seemingly tangible. The ocean itself appeared admonished that a quick and violent change was nigh. The waves ceased to break in their former foaming and brilliant crests, and black masses of the water lifted their surly summits against the eastern horizon, no longer shedding their own peculiar and lucid atmosphere around them. The breeze which had been so fresh, and which had even blown with a force that nearly amounted to a gale, was lulling and becoming uncertain, as it might be awed by the more violent power that was gathering along the borders of the sea, in the direction of the neighbouring continent. Each moment, the eastern puffs of air lost their strength, becoming more and more feeble, until, in an incredibly short period, the heavy sails were heard flapping against the masts. A frightful and ominous calm succeeded. At this instant, a gleam flashed from the fearful obscurity of the ocean, and a roar, like that of a sudden burst of thunder, bellowed along the waters. The seamen turned their startled looks on each other, standing aghast, as if a warning of what was to follow had come out of the heavens themselves. But their calm and more sagacious commander put a different construction on the signal. His lip curled, in high professional pride, and he muttered with scorn,—

"Does he imagine that we sleep? Ay, he has got it himself, and would open our eyes to what is coming! What does he conjecture we have been about, since the middle watch was set?"

Wilder made a swift turn or two on the quarter-deck, turning his quick glances from one quarter of the heavens to another; from the black and lulling water on which his vessel was rolling, to the sails; and from his silent and profoundly expectant crew, to the dim lines of spars that were waving above his head, like so many pencils tracing their curvilinear and wanton images over the murky volumes of the superincumbent clouds.

"Lay the after-yards square!" he said, in a voice which was heard by every man on deck, though his words were apparently spoken but little above his breath. The creaking of the blocks, as the spars came slowly and heavily round to the indicated posi-tion, contributed to the imposing character of the moment, sounding like notes of fearful preparation.

"Haul up the courses!" resumed Wilder with the same elo-quent calmness of manner. Then, taking another glance at the threatening horizon, he added slowly but with emphasis, "Furl them—furl them both. Away aloft, and hand your courses!"

he continued in a shout; "roll them up, cheerily; in with them, boys, cheerily; in !"

The conscious seamen took their impulses from the tones of their commander. In a moment, twenty dark forms were leaping up the rigging, with the alacrity of so many quadrupeds. In another minute, the vast and powerful sheets of canvass were effectually rendered harmless, by securing them in tight rolls to their respective spars. The men descended as swiftly as they had mounted to the yards; and then succeeded another breathing pause. At this appalling moment, a candle would have sent its flame perpendicularly towards the heavens. The ship, missing the steadying power of the wind, rolled heavily in the troughs of the seas, which began to lessen at each instant, as if the startled element was recalling into the security of its own vast bosom that portion of its particles which had so lately been permitted to gambol madly over its surface. The water washed sullenly along the side of the ship, or, as she labouring rose from one of her frequent falls into the hollows of the waves, it shot back into the ocean from her decks in glittering cascades. Every hue of the heavens, every sound of the element, and each dusky and anxious countenance, helped to proclaim the intense interest of the moment. In this brief interval of expectation and inactivity, the mates again approached their commander.

"It is an awful night, Captain Wilder!" said Earing, presuming on his rank to be the first to speak.

"I have known far less notice given of a shift of wind," was the answer.

"We have had time to gather in our kites, 't is true, sir; but there are signs and warnings that come with this change which the oldest seaman must dread!"

"Yes,' continued Knighthead, in a voice that sounded hoarse and powerful, even amid the fearful accessories of that scene; " yes, it is no trifling commission that can call people that I shall not name out upon the water in such a night as this. It was in just such weather that I saw the Vesuvius ketch go to a place so deep, that her own mortar would not have been able to have sent a bomb into the open air, had hands and fire been there fit to let it off!"

"Ay; and it was in such a time that the Greenlandman was cast upon the Orkneys, in as flat a calm as ever lay on the sea."

"Gentlemen," said Wilder, with a peculiar and perhaps an ironical emphasis on the word, "what would ye have? There is not a breath of air stirring, and the ship is naked to her topsails!"

It would have been difficult for either of the two malcontents to give a very satisfactory answer to this question. Both were secretly goaded by mysterious and superstitious apprehensions, that were powerfully aided by the more real and intelligible aspect of the night; but neither had so far forgotten his manhood, and his professional pride, as to lay bare the full extent of his own weakness, at a moment when he was liable to be called upon for the exhibition of qualities of a more positive and determined character. The feeling that was uppermost betrayed itself in the reply of Earing, though in an indirect and covert manner.

"Yes, the vessel is snug enough now," he said, "though eyesight has shown us it is no easy matter to drive a freighted ship through the water as fast as one of those flying craft aboard which no man can say who stands at the helm, by what compass she steers, or what is her draught!"

"Ay," resumed Knighthead, "I call the Caroline fast for an honest trader. There are few square-rigged boats who do not wear the pennants of the king, that can eat her out of the wind on a bowline, or bring her into their wake with studding-sails set. But this is a time and an hour to make a seaman think. Look at yon hazy light, here in with the land, that is coming so fast down upon us, and then tell me whether it comes from the coast of America, or whether it comes from out of the stranger who has been so long running under our lee, but who has got, or is fast getting, the wind of us at last, while none here can say how, or why. I have just this much, and no more, to say : give me for consort a craft whose captain I know, or give me none !"

"Such is your taste, Mr. Knighthead," said Wilder, coldly; "mine may, by some accident, be different."

"Yes, yes," observed the more cautious and prudent Earing, "in time of war, and with letters of marque aboard, a man may honestly hope the sail he sees should have a stranger for her master; or otherwise he would never fall in with an enemy. But, though an Englishman born myself, I should rather give the ship in that mist a clear sea, seeing that I neither know her nation nor her cruise. Ah, Captain Wilder, this is an awful sight for the morning watch ! Often and often have I seen the sun rise in the east, and no harm done; but little good can come of a day when the light first breaks in the west. Cheerfully would I give the owners the last month's pay, hard as it has been earned, did I but know under what flag the stranger sails."

"Frenchman, Don, or Devil, yonder he comes !" cried Wilder. Then, turning towards the attentive crew, he shouted, in a voice that was appalling by its vehemence and warning, " Let run the after-halyards ! round with the fore-yard; round with it, men, with a will ! "

These were cries that the startled crew but too well understood. Every nerve and muscle were exerted to execute the orders, to be in readiness for the tempest. No man spoke; but each expended the utmost of his power and skill in direct and manly efforts. Nor was there, in verity, a moment to lose, or a particle of human strength expended here, without a sufficient object.

The lurid and fearful-looking mist, which, for the last quarter of an hour, had been gathering in the north-west, was driving down upon them with the speed of a race-horse. The air had already lost the damp and peculiar feeling of an easterly breeze; and little eddies were beginning to flutter among the masts — precursors of the coming squall. Then, a rushing, roaring sound was heard moaning along the ocean, whose surface was first dimpled, next ruffled, and finally covered with a sheet of clear, white, and spotless foam. At the next moment, the power of the wind fell upon the inert and labouring Bristol trader.

While the gust was approaching, Wilder had seized the slight opportunity afforded by the changeful puffs of air to get the ship as much as possible before the wind; but the sluggish movement of the vessel met neither the wishes of his own impatience nor the exigencies of the moment. Her bows slowly and heavily fell off from the north, leaving her precisely in a situation to receive the first shock on her broadside. Happy it was, for all who had life at risk in that defenceless vessel, that she was not fated to receive the whole weight of the tempest at a blow. The sails fluttered and trembled on their massive yards, bellying and collapsing alternately for a minute, and then the rushing wind swept over them in a hurricane.

The Caroline received the blast like a stout and buoyant ship as she was, yielding to its impulse until her side lay nearly incumbent on the element; and then, as if the fearful fabric were conscious of its jeopardy, it seemed to lift its reclining masts again, struggling to work its way through the water.

" Keep the helm-a-weather! Jam it a-weather, for your life!" shouted Wilder, amid the roar of the gust.

The veteran seaman at the wheel obeyed the order with steadiness, but in vain did he keep his eyes on the margin of his head sail, to watch the manner in which the ship would obey its power. Twice more, in as many moments, the giddy masts fell towards the horizon, waving as often gracefully upward, and then they yielded to the mighty pressure of the wind, until the whole machine lay prostrate on the water.

" Be cool !" said Wilder, seizing the bewildered Earing by the arm, as the latter rushed madly up the steep of the deck; "it is our duty to be calm : bring hither an axe."

Quick as the thought which gave the order, the admonished mate complied, jumping into the mizzen-channels of the ship, to execute with his own hands the mandate that he knew must follow.

"Shall I cut?" he demanded, with uplifted arms, and in a voice that atoned for his momentary confusion, by its steadiness and force.

" Hold !—Does the ship mind her helm at all ?"

" Not an inch, sir."

" Then cut," Wilder clearly and calmly added.

A single blow sufficed for the discharge of this important duty. Extended to the utmost powers of endurance, by the vast weight it upheld, the lanyard struck by Earing no sooner parted, than each of its fellows snapped in succession, leaving the mast dependent on its wood for the support of all the ponderous and complicated hamper it upheld. The cracking of the spar came next; and the whole fell, like a tree that had been snapped at its foundation.

" Does she fall off ?" called Wilder, to the observant seaman at the wheel.

" She yielded a little, sir; but this new squall is bringing her up again."

" Shall I cut ?" shouted Earing from the main-rigging, whither he had leaped, like a tiger who had bounded on his prey.

" Cut."

A louder and more imposing crash succeeded this order, though not before several heavy blows had been struck into the massive mast itself. As before, the sea received the tumbling maze of spars, rigging, and sails; the vessel surging, at the same instant, from its recumbent position, and rolling far and heavily to windward.

12

"She rights! she rights!" exclaimed twenty voices which had been mute, in a suspense that involved life and death.

"Keep her dead away!" added the calm but authoritative voice of the young commander. "Stand by to furl the fore-top-sail—let it hang a moment to drag the ship clear of the wreck—cut, cut—cheerily, men—hatchets and knives—cut *with* all, and cut *off* all!"

As the men now worked with the vigour of hope, the ropes that still confined the fallen spars to the vessel were quickly severed; and the Caroline, by this time dead before the gale, appeared barely to touch the foam that covered the sea. The wind came over the waste in gusts that rumbled like distant thunder, and with a power that seemed to threaten to lift the ship from its proper element. As a prudent and sagacious seaman had let fly the halyards of the solitary sail that remained, at the moment the squall approached, the loosened but lowered topsail was now distended in a manner that threatened to drag after it the only mast which still stood. Wilder saw the necessity of getting rid of the sail, and he also saw the utter impossibility of securing it. Calling Earing to his side, he pointed out the danger, and gave the necessary order.

"The spar cannot stand such shocks much longer," he concluded; "should it go over the bows, some fatal blow might be given to the ship at the rate she is moving. A man or two must be sent aloft to cut the sail from the yards."

"The stick is bending like a willow whip," returned the mate, "and the lower mast itself is sprung. There would be great danger in trusting a hand in that top, while these wild squalls are breathing around us."

"You may be right," returned Wilder, with a sudden conviction of the truth of what the other had said. "Stay you then here; if any thing befall me, try to get the vessel into port as far north as the Capes of Virginia, at least;—on no account attempt Hatteras, in the present condition of——"

"What would you do, Captain Wilder?" interrupted the mate, laying his hand on the shoulder of his commander, who had already thrown his sea-cap on the deck, and was preparing to divest himself of some of his outer garments.

"I go aloft to ease the mast of that topsail, without which we lose the spar, and possibly the ship."

"I see that plain enough, sir; but, shall it be said that another did the duty of Edward Earing? It is your business to carry the vessel into the Capes of Virginia, and mine to cut the topsail adrift. If harm comes to me, why, put it in the log, with a word or two about the manner in which I played my part. That is the most proper epitaph for a sailor."

Wilder made no resistance. He resumed his watchful and reflecting attitude, with the simplicity of one who had been too long trained to the discharge of certain obligations himself, to manifest surprise that another should acknowledge their imperative character. In the mean time, Earing proceeded steadily to perform what he had just promised. Passing into the waist of the ship, he provided himself with a suitable hatchet, and then, without speaking a syllable to any of the mute but attentive seamen, he sprang into the fore-rigging, every strand and rope-yarn of which was tightened by the strain nearly to snapping. The understanding eyes of his observers comprehended his intention; and with precisely the same pride of station as had urged him to the dangerous undertaking, four or five of the oldest mariners jumped upon the rattlings, to mount into an air that apparently teemed with a hundred hurricanes.

"Lie down out of that fore-rigging," shouted Wilder, through a deck trumpet; "lie down; all, but the mate, lie down!" His words were borne past the inattentive ears of the excited and mortified followers of Earing, but for once they failed of their effect. Each man was too earnestly bent on his purpose to listen to the sounds of recall. In less than a minute, the whole were scattered along the yards, prepared to obey the signal of their officer. The mate cast a look about him; perceiving that the time was comparatively favourable, he struck a blow upon the large rope that confined one of the lower angles of the distended and bursting sail to the yard. The effect was much the same as would be produced by knocking away the key-stone of an ill-cemented arch. The canvass broke from its fastenings with a loud explosion, and, for an instant, it was seen sailing in the air ahead of the ship, as if it were sustained on wings. The vessel rose on a sluggish wave—the lingering remains of the former breeze—and settled heavily over the rolling surge, borne down alike by its own weight and the renewed violence of the gusts. At this critical instant, while the seamen aloft were still gazing in the direction in which the little cloud of canvass had disappeared, a lanyard of the lower rigging parted, with a crack that reached the ears of Wilder.

"Lie down!" he shouted wildly through his trumpet; "down by the backstays; down for your lives; every man of you, down!"

A solitary individual profited by the warning, gliding to the deck with the velocity of the wind. But rope parted after rope, and the fatal snapping of the wood followed. For a moment, the towering maze tottered, seeming to wave towards every quarter of the heavens; and then, yielding to the movements of the hull, the whole fell, with a heavy crash, into the sea. Cord, lanyard, and stay snapped like thread, as each received in succession the strain of the ship, leaving the naked and despoiled hull of the Caroline to drive before the tempest, as if nothing had occurred to impede its progress.

A mute and eloquent pause succeeded the disaster. It seemed as if the elements themselves were appeased by their work, and something like a momentary lull in the awful rushing of the winds might have been fancied. Wilder sprang to the side of the vessel, and distinctly beheld the victims, who still clung to their frail support. He even saw Earing waving his hand in adieu with a seaman's heart, like a man who not only felt how desperate was his situation, but who knew how to meet it with resignation. Then the wreck of spars, with all who clung to it, was swallowed up in the body of the frightful, preternatural-looking mist which extended on every side of them, from the ocean to the clouds.

"Stand by, to clear away a boat!" shouted Wilder, without pausing to think of the impossibility of one's swimming, or of effecting the least good, in so violent a tornado.

But the amazed and confounded seamen who remained needed no instruction in this matter. Not a man moved, nor was the smallest symptom of obedience given. The mariners looked wildly around them, each endeavouring to trace in the dusky countenance of some shipmate his opinion of the extent of the evil; but not a mouth opened among them all.

"It is too late — it is too late!" murmured Wilder; "human skill and human efforts could not save them!"

"Sail, ho!" Knighthead shouted in a voice that was teeming with superstitious awe.

"Let him come on," returned his young commander, bitterly; "the mischief is ready done to his hands!"

"Should this be a true ship, it is our duty to the owners and the passengers to speak her, if a man can make his voice heard in this tempest," the second mate continued, pointing, through the haze, at the dim object that was certainly at hand.

"Speak her! — passengers!" muttered Wilder, involuntarily repeating his words. "No; any thing is better than speaking her. Do you see the vessel that is driving down upon us so fast?" he sternly demanded of the watchful seaman who still clung to the wheel of the Caroline.

"Ay, ay, sir."

"Give her a berth — sheer away hard to port — perhaps he may pass us in the gloom, now we are no higher than our decks. Give the ship a broad sheer, I say, sir."

The usual laconic answer was given ; and, for a few moments, the Bristol trader was seen diverging a little from the line in which the other approached ; but a second glance assured Wilder that the attempt was useless. The strange ship (every man on board felt certain it was the same that had so long been seen hanging in the north-western horizon) came on through the mist, with a swiftness that nearly equalled the velocity of the tempestuous winds themselves. Not a thread of canvass was seen on board her. Each line of spars, even to the tapering and delicate top-gallant masts, was in its place, preserving the beauty and symmetry of the whole fabric ; but nowhere was there the smallest fragment of a sail opened to the gale. Under her bows rolled a volume of foam that was even discernible amid the universal agitation of the ocean ; and, as she came within sound, the sullen roar of the water might have been likened to the noise of a cascade. At first, the spectators on the decks of the Caroline believed they were not seen, and some of the men called madly for lights, in order that the disasters of the night might not terminate in an encounter.

"Too many see us there already !" said Wilder.

"No, no," muttered Knighthead ; "no fear but we are seen ; and by such eyes, too, as never yet loooked out of mortal head !"

The seamen paused. In another instant, the long-seen and mysterious ship was within a hundred feet of them. The very power of that wind, which was wont usually to raise the billows, now pressed the element, with the weight of mountains, into its bed. The sea was every where a sheet of froth, but the water did not rise above the level of the surface. The instant a wave lifted itself from the security of the vast depths, the fluid was borne away before the tornado in glittering spray. Along this frothy but comparatively motionless surface, then, the stranger came booming with the steadiness and grandeur with which a cloud is seen sailing in the hurricane. No sign of life was discovered about her. If men looked out from their secret places, upon the straitened and discomfited wreck of the Bristol trader, it was covertly, and as darkly as the tempest before which they drove. Wilder held his breath, for the moment the stranger was nighest, in the very excess of suspense; but, as he saw no signal of recognition, no human form, nor any intention to arrest, if possible, the furious career of the other, a smile gleamed across his countenance, and his lips moved rapidly, as if he found pleasure in being abandoned to his distress. The stranger drove by, like a dark vision; and, ere another minute, her form was beginning to grow less distinct, in the body of spray to leeward.

"She is going out of sight in the mist!" exclaimed Wilder, when he drew his breath, after the fearful suspense of the few last moments.

"Ay, in mist or clouds," responded Knighthead, who now kept obstinately at his elbow, watching, with the most jealous distrust, the smallest movement of his unknown commander.

"In the heavens, or in the sea, I care not, provided he be gone."

"Most seamen would rejoice to see a strange sail, from the hull of a vessel shaved to the deck like this."

"Men often court their destruction, from ignorance of their own interests. Let him drive on, say I, and pray I! He goes four feet to our one; and I ask no better favour than that this hurricane may blow until the sun shall rise."

Knighthead started, and cast an oblique glance, which resembled denunciation, at his companion. To his superstitious mind, there was profanity in thus invoking the tempest, at a moment when the winds seemed already to be pouring out their utmost wrath.

" This is a heavy squall, I will allow," he said, "and such a one as many mariners pass whole lives without seeing; but he knows little of the sea who thinks there is not more wind where this comes from."

" Let it blow!" cried the other, striking his hands together a little wildly; " I pray for wind!"

All the doubts of Knighthead, as to the character of the young stranger who had so unaccountably got possession of the office of Nicholas Nichols, if any remained, were now removed. He walked forward among the silent and thoughtful crew, with the air of a man whose opinion was settled. Wilder, however, paid no attention to the movements of his subordinate, but contined pacing the deck for hours; now casting his eyes at the heavens, and now sending frequent and anxious glances around the limited horizon, while the Royal Caroline still continued drifting before the wind, a shorn and naked wreck.

## CHAPTER VI.

Sit still, and hear the last of our sea sorrow.
*Shakspeare.*

THE weight of the tempest had been felt at that hapless moment when Earing and his unfortunate companions were precipitated from their giddy elevation into the sea. Though the wind continued to blow long after this fatal event, it was with a constantly diminishing power. As the gale decreased, the sea began to rise, and the vessel to labour in proportion. Then followed two hours of anxious watchfulness on the part of Wilder, during which the whole of his professional knowledge was needed, in order to keep the despoiled hull from becoming a prey to the greedy waters. His consummate skill, however, proved equal to the task that was required at his hands; and, just as the symptoms of day were becoming visible along the east, both wind and waves were rapidly subsiding together. During the whole of this doubtful period, our adventurer did not receive the smallest assistance from any of the crew, with the exception of two experienced seamen whom he had previously stationed at the wheel. But to this neglect he was indifferent; since little more was required than his own judgment, seconded, as it faithfully was, by the exertions of the mariners more immediately under his eye.

The day dawned on a scene entirely different from that which had marked the tempestuous deformity of the night. The whole fury of the winds appeared to have been expended in their precocious effort. From the moderate gale, to which they had fallen by the end of the middle watch, they further altered to a vacil-

12 *

lating breeze; and, ere the sun rose, the changeful element subsided into a flat calm. The sea went down as suddenly as the power which had raised it vanished; and, by the time the broad golden light of the sun was shed fairly and fully upon the unstable ocean, it lay unruffled and polished, though still gently heaving in swells so long and heavy as to resemble the placid respiration of a sleeping infant.

The hour was still early, and the serene appearance of the sky gave every promise of a day which might be passed in devising the expedients necessary to bring the ship under the command of her people.

"Sound the pumps!" said Wilder, observing that the crew were appearing from the different places in which they had bestowed their cares and their persons together, during the later hours of the night.

"Do you hear me, sir?" he added, sternly, observing that no one moved to obey his order. "Let the pumps be sounded, and the ship cleared of every inch of water."

Knighthead, to whom Wilder addressed himself, regarded his commander with an oblique and sullen eye, exchanging intelligent glances with his comrade before he saw fit to make the smallest motion towards compliance. But there was still that in the authoritative mien of his superior, which induced him to comply. The dilatory manner in which the seamen performed the duty was quickened, however, as the rod ascended, and the well-known signs of a formidable leak met their eyes. The experiment was repeated with greater activity, and with more precision.

"If witchcraft can clear the hold of a ship that is already half full of water," said Knighthead, casting another menacing glance towards the attentive Wilder, "the sooner it is done the better; for the whole cunning of something more than a bungler will be needed, to make the pumps of the Royal Caroline suck!"

"Does the ship leak?" demanded his superior, with a quick-ness which proclaimed how important the intelligence was deemed

"Yesterday, I would have boldly put my name to the articles of any craft that floats the ocean; and, had the captain asked me if I understood her nature and character, as certain as that my name is Francis Knighthead, I should have told him, yes. But I find that the oldest seaman may still learn something of the water; though it should be got in crossing a ferry in a flat."

"What mean you, sir?" demanded Wilder, who, for the first time, began to note the mutinous looks assumed by his mate, no less than the threatening manner in which he was seconded by the crew. "Have the pumps rigged without delay, and clear the ship of water."

Knighthead slowly complied with the former part of this order; and, in a few moments, every thing was arranged to commence the necessary, and, as it would seem, the urgent duty of pumping. But no man lifted his hand to the laborious employment. Wilder, who had taken the alarm, was not slow in detecting this reluctance, and he repeated the order more sternly, calling to two of the seamen, by name, to set the example of obedience. The men hesitated, giving an opportunity to the mate to confirm them by his voice, in their mutinous intentions.

"What need of hands to work a pump in a vessel like this?" he said, coarsely laughing, secret terror struggling strangely at the same time with open malice. "After what we have seen this night, none here will be amazed should the vessel begin to spout out the brine like a whale."

"What am I to understand by this hesitation and by this language?" said Wilder, approaching Knighthead with a firm step, and an eye that threw back the defiance of his inferior, in more than equal measure. "Is it you, who should be foremost in exertion at a moment like this, who dare to set an example of disobedience?"

The mate recoiled a pace, aud his lips moved; still he uttered no audible reply. Wilder ordered him, in a calm authoritative tone, to lay his own hands to the brake. Knighthead then found his voice, making a flat refusal. At the next moment, he was felled to the feet of his indignant commander, by a blow he had neither the address nor the power to resist. This act of decision was succeeded by a single moment of breathless indecision among the crew; and then the common cry, and the general rush upon our defenceless and solitary adventurer, were signals for open hostility. A shriek from the quarter-deck arrested the struggle, just as a dozen hands were laid violently upon the person of Wilder, and, for the moment, there was a truce. The cry came from Gertrude, and happily it possessed sufficient influence to check the savage intentions of a set of beings rude and unnurtured enough to be guilty of any act of violence when their passions were thoroughly aroused. Wilder was reluctantly released; and the surly mariners turned towards her whose interference had stopped, if it had not changed, their intentions.

During the more momentous hours of the night that was past, the very existence of the passengers had been forgotten by those whose duty kept them on deck. If they had been recalled at all to the recollection of any, it was at those fleeting moments when the mind of the young seaman, who directed the movements of the ship, found leisure to catch stolen glimpses of softer scenes than the wild warring of the elements that was raging before his eyes. Knighthead had named them, as he would have made allusion to a part of the cargo, but their fate had little influence on his hardened nature. Mrs. Wyllys and her charge had therefore remained below during the whole period, perfectly unapprised of the disasters of the intervening time. Buried in the recesses of their berths, they had heard the roaring of the winds, and the incessant washing of the waters; but these usual accompaniments of a storm served to conceal the crashing of

masts, and the hoarse cries of the mariners. During the moments of terrible suspense, while the Bristol trader lay on her
side, the better-informed governess had, indeed, some fearful
glimmerings of the truth; but, conscious of her uselessness, and
unwilling to alarm her less instructed companion, she had sufficient self-command to be mute. The subsequent silence, and
comparative calm, induced her to believe that she had been mistaken in her apprehensions; and, long ere morning dawned, both
she and Gertrude had sunk into refreshing slumbers. They had
risen and mounted to the deck together, and were still in the first
burst of their wonder at the desolation which met their eyes, when
the long-meditated attack on Wilder was made.

"What means this awful change?" demanded Mrs. Wyllys,
with a lip that quivered, and a cheek which, notwithstanding the
extraordinary power she possessed over her feelings, was blanched
to the colour of death.

The eye of Wilder was glowing, and his brow was dark as
those heavens from which they had just so happily escaped, as he
answered, still menacing his assailants with an arm,—

"It means mutiny, madam — rascally, cowardly mutiny!"

"Could mutiny strip a vessel of her masts, and leave her a
helpless log upon the sea?"

"Hark ye, madam!" roughly interrupted the mate; "to you
I will speak freely; for it is well known who you are, and that
you came on board the Caroline a paying passenger. This night
I have seen the heavens and the ocean behave as I have never
seen them behave before. Ships have been running afore the
wind, light and buoyant as corks, with all their spars stepped and
steady, when other ships have been shaved of every mast as the
razor sweeps the chin. Cruisers have been fallen in with, sailing
without living hands to work them; and, altogether, no man here
has ever before passed a middle watch like the one gone by."

"And what has this to do with the violence I have just wit

nessed? Is the vessel fated to endure every evil? — Can *you* explain this, Mr. Wilder?"

"You cannot say, at least, you had no warning of danger," returned Wilder bitterly.

"Ay, the devil is obliged to be honest on compulsion," resumed the mate. "Each of his imps sails with his orders; and, thank Heaven! however willing he may be to overlook them, he has neither courage nor power to do so. Otherwise, a peaceful voyage would be such a rarity in these unsettled times, that few men would be found hardy enough to venture on the water for a livelihood. — A warning! we will own you gave us open and frequent warning. It was a notice that the consignee should not have overlooked, when Nicholas Nichols met with the hurt, as the anchor was leaving the bottom. I never knew an accident happen at such a time, and no evil come of it. Then we had a warning with the old man in the boat; besides the never-failing ill-luck of sending the pilot violently out of the ship. As if all this was n't enough, instead of taking a hint and lying peaceably at our anchors, we got the ship under way, and left a safe and friendly harbour of a Friday, of all the days in a week! * So far from being surprised at what has happened, I only wonder at still finding myself a living man; the reason of which is simply this, that I have given my faith where faith is due, and not to unknown mariners and strange commanders. Had Edward Earing done the same, he might still have had a plank between him and the bottom; but, though half inclined to believe in the truth,

---

* The superstition, that Friday is an evil day, was not peculiar to Knighthead: it prevails, more or less, among seamen, to this hour. An intelligent merchant of Connecticut had a desire to do his part in eradicating an impression that is sometimes inconvenient. He caused the keel of a vessel to be laid on a Friday; she was launched on a Friday; named "The Friday;" and sailed on her first voyage on a Friday. Unfortunately for the success of this well-intentioned experiment, neither vessel nor crew were ever again heard of!

he had, after all too much leaning to superstition and credulity."

This laboured profession of faith in the mate, though sufficiently intelligible to Wilder, was still an enigma to his female
listeners. But Knighthead had not formed his resolution by
halves; neither had he gone thus far, with any intention to stop
short of the whole design. In summary words he explained to
Mrs. Wyllys the desolate condition of the ship, and the utter
improbability that she could continue to float many hours; since
actual observation had told him that her lower hold was already
half full of water.

"And what is to be done?" demanded the governness, casting a glance of bitter distress towards the pallid and attentive
Gertrude. "Is there no strange sail in sight to take us from the
wreck? or must we perish in our helplessness?"

"God protect us from any more strange sails!" exclaimed the
surly Knighthead. "We have the pinnace hanging at the stern,
and here must be land yet some forty leagues to the north-west
water and food are plenty, and twelve stout hands can soon pull
a boat to the continent of America; that is, provided America is
left where it was seen no later than at sunset yesterday."

"You propose to abandon the vessel?"

"I do. The interest of the owners is dear to all good seamen,
but life is sweeter than gold."

"The will of Heaven be done! But surely you meditate no
violence against this gentleman, who, I am quite certain, has
governed the vessel in very critical circumstances, with a discretion beyond his years!"

Knighthead muttered his intentions, whatever they might be,
to himself; and he walked apart, apparently to confer with the
men, who seemed but too well disposed to second any of his views,
however mistaken or lawless. During the few moments of suspense that succeeded, Wilder was silent and composed, a smile

resembling that of contempt struggling about his lip, and maintaining the air rather of one who had power to decide on the fortunes of others, than of a man who knew that his own fate was at that very moment in discussion. When the dull minds of the seamen had arrived at their conclusion, the mate advanced to proclaim the result. Indeed, words were unnecessary, in order to make known a very material part of their decision; for some of the men proceeded instantly to lower the stern-boat into the water, while others set about supplying it with the necessary means of subsistence.

"There is room for all the Christians in the ship to stow themselves in this pinnace," resumed Knighthead; "as for those that place their dependence on any particular persons, why, let them call for aid where they have been used to receive it."

"From all which I am to infer that it is your intention," said Wilder, calmly, "to abandon the wreck and your duty?"

The half-awed but still resentful mate returned a look in which fear and triumph struggled for the mastery, as he answered,—

"You, who know how to sail a ship without a crew, can never want a boat! Besides, you shall never say to your friends, whoever they may be, that we leave you without the means of reaching the land, if you are indeed a land-bird at all. There is the launch!"

"There is the launch! but well do you know, that, without masts, our united strengths could not lift it from the deck; else would it not be left."

"They that took the masts out of the Caroline can put them in again," rejoined a grinning seaman: "it will not be an hour after we leave you, before a shear-hulk will come alongside to step the spars again, and then you may go cruise in company."

Wilder was superior to a reply. He began to pace the deck, thoughtful it is true, but composed and entirely self-possessed. In the mean time, as a common desire to quit the wreck as soon as possible actuated the men, their preparations advanced with great activity. The wondering and alarmed females had hardly time to think clearly on the extraordinary situation in which they found themselves, before they saw the form of the helpless master borne past them to the boat; in another minute they were summoned to take their places at his side.

Thus called upon to act, they began to feel the imperious necessity of decision. Remonstrances they feared would be useless; for the fierce and malignant looks which were cast, from time to time, at Wilder as the labour proceeded, proclaimed the danger of awakening such obstinate and ignorant minds into renewed acts of violence. The governess bethought her of an appeal to the wounded man; but the look of wild care which he had cast about him, on being lifted to the deck, and the expression of bodily and mental pain that gleamed across his rugged features, as he buried them in the blankets by which he was enveloped, too plainly announced that little assistance was to be expected from him.

"What remains for us to do?" she at length demanded of the seemingly insensible object of her concern.

"I would I knew!" he answered quickly, casting a keen but hurried glance around the whole horizon. "It is not at all improbable that they will reach the shore. Four-and-twenty hours of calm will assure it."

"If otherwise?"

"A blow at north-west, or from any quarter off the land, will prove their ruin."

"And the ship?"

"If deserted, she must sink."

"Then will I speak in your favour to these hearts of flint! I know not why I feel such interest in your welfare, inexplicable young man, but I would suffer much, rather than leave you to incur this peril."

"Stop, dearest madam," said Wilder, respectfully arresting her movement with his hand. "I cannot leave the vessel."

"We know not yet. The most stubborn natures may be subdued; even ignorance can be made to open its ears at the voice of entreaty. I may prevail."

"There is one temper to be quelled — one reason to convince — one prejudice to conquer, over which you have no power."

"Whose is that?"

"My own."

"What mean you, sir? Surely you are not weak enough to suffer resentment against such beings to goad you to an act of madness?"

"Do I seem mad?" demanded Wilder. "The feeling by which I am governed may be false, but, such as it is, it is grafted on my habits, my opinions; I will say, my principles. Honour forbids me to quit a ship that I command, while a plank of her is afloat."

"Of what use can a single arm prove at such a crisis?"

"None," he answered, with a melancholy smile. "I must die, in order that others, who may be serviceable hereafter, should do their duty."

Both Mrs. Wyllys and Gertrude regarded his kindling eye, but otherwise placid countenance, with looks whose concern amounted to horror. The former read, in the very composure of his mien, the unalterable character of his resolution; and the latter, shuddering as the prospect of the cruel fate which awaited him crowded on her mind, felt a glow about her own youthful heart that almost tempted her to believe his self-devotion commendable. But the governess saw new reasons for apprehension in the determination of Wilder. If she had hitherto felt reluctance to trust herself and her ward with a band like that which now possessed the sole authority, it was more than doubly increased by the rude and noisy summons she received to hasten and take her place among them.

"Would to Heaven I knew in what manner to decide!" she exclaimed. "Speak to us, young man; counsel us, as you would counsel a mother and a sister."

"Were I so fortunate as to possess relatives so near and dear, nothing should separate us at a time like this."

"Is there hope for those who remain on the wreck?"

"But little."

"And in the boat?"

It was near a minute before Wilder made an answer. He again turned his eye to the bright and broad horizon, studying the heavens, in the direction of the distant continent, with infinite care. No omen that could indicate the probable character of the weather escaped his vigilance, while his countenance reflected the various emotions by which he was governed.

"As I am a man," he said with fervour, "and one who is bound not only to counsel but to protect your sex, I distrust the time. I think the chance of being seen by some passing sail equal to the probability that those who adventure in the pinnace will ever reach the land."

"Then let us remain," said Gertrude, the blood, for the first time since her re-appearance on deck, rushing in a torrent into her colourless cheeks. "I like not the wretches who would be our companions in that boat."

"Away, away!" impatiently shouted Knighthead. "Each minute of light is a week of life to us all, and every moment of calm, a year. Away, away, or we leave you!"

Mrs. Wyllys answered not, but she stood the image of doubt and indecision. The plash of oars was heard in the water, and, at the next moment, the pinnace was seen gliding over the element, impelled by the strong arms of six powerful rowers.

"Stay!" shrieked the governess, no longer undetermined, "receive my child, though you abandon me!"

A wave of the hand, and an indistinct rumbling in the coarse tones of the mate, were the answers to her appeal. A long, deep, and breathing silence followed among the deserted. The grim countenances of the seamen in the pinnace soon became confused and indistinct, and then the boat itself began to lessen on the eye, until it seemed no more than a dark and distant speck, rising and falling with the flow and reflux of the blue waters. During all this time, not even a whispered word was spoken. Each of the party gazed, until eyes grew dim, at the receding object; and it was only when his sight refused to convey the tiny image to his brain, that Wilder himself shook off the impression of the trance into which he had fallen. His look then turned on his companions, and he pressed his hand upon his forehead, as if the brain were bewildered by the responsibility he had assumed in advising them to remain. But the sickening apprehension passed away, leaving in its place a firmer mind, and a resolution, too often tried in scenes of doubtful issue, to be long or easily shaken from its calmness and self-possession.

"They are gone!" he said, breathing heavily, like one whose respiration had been long and unnaturally suspended.

"They are gone!" echoed the governess, turning an eye that was contracting with the intensity of her care, on the marble-like and motionless form of her pupil. "There is no longer hope."

The look that Wilder threw on the same silent but lovely statue was scarcely less expressive than the gaze of her, who had nurtured her infancy. His brow grew thoughtful, and his lips became compressed, while he gathered all the resources of his fertile imagination and varied experience.

"Is there hope?" demanded the governess, who was watching the change of his working countenance, with an attention that never swerved.

The gloom passed away from his features, and the smile that lighted them was like the radiance of the sun, as it breaks through the blackest vapours of the gust.

"There is !" he said with firmness; "our case is not yet desperate."

"Then, may He who rules the ocean and the land receive the praise !" cried the grateful governess, giving vent to her long suppressed agony in a flood of tears.

Gertrude cast herself upon the neck of Mrs. Wyllys, and for a minute their unrestrained emotions were mingled.

"And now, dearest madam," said Gertrude, leaving the arms of her governess, "let us trust to the skill of Mr. Wilder; he has foreseen and foretold this danger; equally well may he predict our safety."

"Foreseen and foretold !" returned the other, in a manner to show that her faith in the professional prescience of the stranger was not altogether so unbounded as that of her more youthful and ardent companion. "No mortal could have foreseen this awful calamity; and, least of all, foreseeing it, would he have sought to incur its danger ! Mr. Wilder, I will not annoy you with requests for explanations that might now be useless, but you will not refuse to communicate your grounds of hope."

Wilder hastened to relieve a curiosity that he knew must be as painful as it was natural. The mutineers had left the largest, and much the safest, of the two boats belonging to the wreck, from a desire to improve the calm, well knowing that hours of severe labour would be necessary to launch it into the ocean from the place it occupied between the stumps of the two principal masts. This operation, which might have been executed in a few minutes with the ordinary purchases of the ship, would have required all their strength united, and that, too, to be exercised with a discretion and care that would have consumed too many of those moments which they rightly deemed to be so precious

at that wild and unstable season of the year. Into this little ark
Wilder proposed to convey such articles of comfort and necessity
as he might hastily collect from the abandoned vessel; and then,
entering it with his companions, to await the critical instant when
the wreck should sink from beneath them.

"Call you this hope?" exclaimed Mrs. Wyllys, when his short
explanation was ended, her cheek blanching with disappointment.
"I have heard that the gulf, which foundering vessels leave,
swallows all lesser objects that are floating nigh!"

"It sometimes happens. For worlds I would not deceive you;
and I now say that I think our chance for escape equal to that
of being ingulfed with the vessel."

"This is terrible!" murmured the governess; "but the will
of Heaven be done! Cannot ingenuity supply the place of
strength, and the boat be cast from the decks before the fatal moment shall arrive?"

Wilder shook his head in the negative.

"We are not so weak as you may think us," said Gertrude.
"Give a direction to our efforts, and let us see what may yet be
done.  "Here is Cassandra," she added — turning to the black
girl already introduced to the reader, who stood behind her young
and ardent mistress with the mantle and shawls of the latter
thrown over her arm, as if about to attend her on an excursion
for the morning — "here is Cassandra, who alone has nearly the
strength of a man."

"Had she the strength of twenty, I should despair of launching the boat without the aid of machinery. But we lose time in
words: I will go below in order to judge of the probable duration
of our doubt; and then to our preparations. Even you, fair and
fragile as you seem, lovely being, may aid in the latter."

He then pointed out such lighter objects as would be necessary
to their comfort, should they be so fortunate as to get clear of
the wreck, and advised their being put into the boat without

delay. While the three females were thus usefully employed, he descended into the hold of the ship, in order to note the increase of the water, and to make his calculations on the time that would elapse before the sinking fabric must entirely disappear. The fact proved their case to be more alarming than even Wilder had been led to expect. Stripped of her masts, the vessel had laboured so heavily as to open many of her seams; and, as the upper works began to settle beneath the level of the ocean, the influx of the element was increasing with frightful rapidity. As the young mariner looked understandingly about him, he cursed, in the bitterness of his heart, the ignorance and superstition that had caused the desertion of the crew. There existed, in reality, no evil that exertion and skill could not have remedied; but, deprived of aid, he saw the folly of even attempting to procrastinate a catastrophe that was now unavoidable. Returning with a heavy heart to the deck, he immediately set about those dispositions which were necessary to afford them the only chance of escape.

While his companions deadened the sense of apprehension by their lighter employment, Wilder stepped the two masts of the boat, and disposed of the sails and the other implements that might be useful in the event of success. Thus occupied, a couple of hours flew by, as if minutes were compressed into moments. At the expiration of that period, his labour ceased. He then cut the gripes that had kept the launch in its place when the ship was in motion, leaving it standing upright on its wooden beds, but in no other manner connected with the hull, which, by this time, had settled so low as to create the apprehension, that, at any moment, it might sink from beneath them. After this measure of precaution was taken, the females were summoned to the boat, lest the crisis might be nearer than he supposed; for he well knew that a foundering ship was like a tottering wall, liable at any moment to yield to the impulse of the downward pressure.

He then commenced the scarcely less necessary operation of selection among the chaos of articles with which the ill-directed zeal of his companions had so cumbered the boat, that there was hardly room to dispose of their more precious persons. Notwithstanding the often repeated and vociferous remonstrances of the negress, boxes, trunks, and packages flew from the launch, Wilder having no consideration for more than their ultimate safety. The boat was soon cleared of what, under their circumstances, was literally lumber; leaving, however, far more than enough to meet all their wants, and not a few of their comforts, in the event that they should escape the greedy element.

Then, and not till then, did the exertions of Wilder relax. He had arranged his sails, ready to be hoisted in an instant: he had carefully examined that no straggling rope connected the boat to the wreck, to draw them under with the foundering mass; and he had assured himself that food, water, compass, and the imperfect instruments that were then in use to ascertain the position of a ship, were carefully disposed of in their several places, and ready to his hand. When all was in a state of preparation, he disposed of himself in the stern of the boat, and endeavoured, by the composure of his manner, to inspire his less resolute companions with a portion of his own firmness.

The bright sunshine was sleeping in a thousand places on every side of the silent and deserted wreck. The sea had subsided to such a state of rest, that it was only at long intervals that the huge and helpless mass on which the ark of the expectants lay was lifted from its dull quietude, to roll heavily, for a moment, in the washing waters, and then to settle lower and lower into the absorbing element. Still the disappearance of the hull was slow,—it was even tedious to those who looked forward with so much impatience to its total immersion, as to the crisis of their own fortunes.

During these hours of weary and awful suspense, the discourse between the watchers, though conducted in tones of confidence, and often of tenderness, was broken by long intervals of musing silence.  Each forbore to dwell upon the danger of their situation, in consideration of the feelings of the rest; but neither could conceal the imminent risk they ran, from that jealous love of life which was common to them all.  In this manner, minutes, hours, and the day itself, rolled by, and the darkness was seen stealing along the deep, gradually narrowing the boundary of their view towards the east, until the whole of the empty scene was limited to a little dusky circle around the spot on which they lay.  To this change succeeded another fearful hour, during which it appeared that death was about to visit them, environed by its most revolting horrors.  The heavy plunge of the wallowing whale, as he cast his huge form upon the surface of the sea, was heard, accompanied by the mimic blowings of a hundred imitators that followed in the train of the monarch of the ocean. It appeared to the alarmed and feverish imagination of Gertrude, that the brine was giving up all its monsters; and notwithstanding the calm assurances of Wilder that these accustomed sounds were rather the harbingers of peace than signs of any new danger, they filled her mind with images of the secret recesses over which they seemed suspended by a thread, and painted them replete with the disgusting inhabitants of the caverns of the deep. The intelligent seaman himself was startled, when he saw on the surface of the water the dark fins of the voracious shark stealing around the wreck, apprised by his instinct that the contents of the devoted vessel were shortly to become the prey of his tribe.  Then came the moon, with its mild and deceptive light, to throw the delusion of its glow on the varying but frightful scene.

" See," said Wilder, as the luminary lifted its pale and melancholy orb out of the bed of the ocean; "we shall at least have light for our hazardous launch!"

"Is it at hand?" demanded Mrs. Wyllys, summoning all the resolution she could in so trying a situation.

13

"It is. The ship has already brought her scuppers to the water. Sometimes a vessel will float until saturated with the brine. If ours sink at all, it will be soon."

"If at all! Is there the smallest hope that she can float?"

"None!" said Wilder, pausing to listen to the hollow sounds which issued from the depths of the vessel, as the water broke through her divisions, in passing from side to side, and which sounded like the groaning of some heavy monster in the last agony of nature. "None: she is already losing her level!"

His companions saw the change; but not for the empire of the world could either of them have uttered a syllable. Another low, threatening, rumbling sound was heard, and the pent air beneath blew up the forward part of the deck, with an explosion like that of a gun.

"Now grasp the ropes I have given you!" cried Wilder, breathless with his eagerness to speak.

His words were smothered by the rushing and gurgling of waters. The vessel made a plunge like a dying whale; and, raising its stern high into the air, it glided into the depths of the sea, like the leviathan seeking his secret places. The motionless boat was lifted with the ship, until it stood in an attitude fearfully approaching to the perpendicular. As the wreck descended, the bows of the launch met the element, burying themselves nearly to filling; but, buoyant and light, they rose again, and, struck powerfully on the stern by the settling mass, the little ark shot ahead, as if driven by the hand of man. Still, as the water rushed into the vortex, every thing within its influence yielded to the suction; and, at the next instant, the launch was seen darting down the declivity, as if eager to follow the vast machine of which it had so long formed a dependent, through the same gaping whirlpool, to the bottom: but it rose, rocking, to the surface, and, for a moment, was tossed and whirled like a bubble in the eddies of a pool; after which the ocean moaned and slept again.

## CHAPTER XVIII.

——Every day some sailor's wife,
The masters of some merchant, and the merchant,
Have just our theme of woe.
*Tempest.*

"WE are safe!" said Wilder, who had stood with his person firmly braced against a mast, steadily watching the manner of their escape. "Thus far, at least, are we safe; for which may Heaven alone be praised, since no art of mine could avail us a feather."

The females had buried their faces in the folds of the vestments and clothes on which they were sitting; nor did even the governess raise her countenance, until twice assured by her companion that the imminency of the risk was past. Another minute went by, during which Mrs. Wyllys and Gertrude were rendering their thanksgivings, in a manner and in words less equivocal than the expression which had just broken from the lips of the young seaman. When this grateful duty was performed, they stood erect, as if emboldened by the offering to look their situation more steadily in the face.

On every side lay the seemingly illimitable waste of waters To them, their small and frail tenement was the world. So long as the ship, sinking and dangerous as she was, remained beneath them, there had appeared to be a barrier between their existence and the ocean. A single minute had deprived them of even this failing support, and they now found themselves cast upon the sea in a vessel that might be likened to one of the bubbles of the element. Gertrude felt, at that instant, that she would have given half her hopes in life for the mere sight of the vast and nearly untenanted continent which stretched for so many thousands of miles along the west, and kept the world of waters to their limits.

But the rush of emotions that belonged to their forlorn condition soon subsided, and their thoughts returned to the study of the means necessary to further safety. Wilder had anticipated these feelings; and, even before Mrs. Wyllys and Gertrude recovered their recollections, he was occupied, aided by the terrified but loquacious Cassandra, in arranging the contents of the boat in such a manner as would enable her to move through the element with the least possible resistance.

" With a well-trimmed ship, and a fair breeze," cried our adventurer cheerfully, so soon as his little task was ended, " we may yet hope to reach the land in one day and another night. I have seen the hour when, in this good launch, I would not have hesitated to run the length of the American coast, provided——"

" You have forgotten your provided," said Gertrude, observing that he hesitated, probably from a reluctance to express any exception to the opinion which might increase the fears of his companions.

" Provided it were two months earlier in the year," he added, with less confidence.

" The season is, then, against us : it only requires the greater resolution in ourselves !"

Wilder turned his head to regard the fair speaker, whose placid countenance, as the moon silvered her features, expressed any thing but the force necessary to endure the hardships he knew she was liable to encounter, before they might hope to gain the continent. After musing, he lifted his open hand towards the south-west, and held its palm some little time to the air of the night

"Any thing is better than idleness, for people in our condition," he said. "There are some symptoms of the breeze coming in this quarter; I will be ready to meet it."

He then spread his two lug-sails; and, trimming aft the sheets, placed himself at the helm, like one who expected his services might be shortly needed. The result did not disappoint him. Ere long, the light canvass of the boat began to flutter; and then, as he brought the bows in the proper direction, the little vessel commenced moving slowly along its blind and watery path.

The wind, charged with the dampness of night, soon came fresher upon the sails. Wilder urged the latter reason as a motive for the females to seek their rest beneath a little canopy of tarpaulings, which his foresight had provided, and on mattresses he had brought from the ship. Perceiving that their protector wished to be alone, Mrs. Wyllys and her pupil did as desired; and, in a few minutes, if not asleep, no one could have told that any other than our adventurer had possession of the solitary launch.

The middle hour of the night went by, without any material change in the prospects of these lonely travellers. The wind had freshened to a smart breeze; and, by the calculations of Wilder, he had already moved across several leagues of ocean, directly in a line for the eastern end of that long and narrow isle that separates the waters which wash the shores of Connecticut from those of the open sea. The minutes flew swiftly by; for the time was propitious, and the thoughts of the young seaman were busy with the recollections of a short but adventurous life. He leaned forward to catch the gentle respiration of those who slept. Then his form fell back into its seat, and his lip moved as he gave inward utterance to the wayward fancies of his imagination. But at no time, not even in the midst of his greatest abandonment to reverie and thought, did he forget the constant, and nearly instinctive, duties of his station. A rapid glance at the heavens, an oblique look at the compass, and an occasional, but more protracted, examination of the pale face of the melancholy moon, were the usual directions taken by his practised eyes. The latter was still in the zenith; and Wilder saw with uneasiness that she was shining through an atmosphere without a haze. He would have better liked those portentous and watery circles by which she is so often environed, and which are thought to foretell the tempest, than the hard and dry medium through which her beams fell so clear upon the face of the waters. The humidity with which the breeze had commenced was also gone; and, in its place, the sensitive organs of the seaman detected the often grateful, though at that moment unwelcome, taint of the land. All these were signs that the airs from the continent were about to prevail, and (as he dreaded, from certain wild-looking, long, narrow clouds, that were gathering over the western horizon,) to prevail with the force that was usual at that turbulent season.

If any doubts had existed in the mind of Wilder as to the accuracy of his prognostics, they would have been effectually solved about the commencement of the morning watch. At that hour the inconstant breeze began again to die; and, even before its last breathing was felt upon the flapping canvass, it was met by counter currents from the west. Our mariner saw at once that the struggle was now truly to commence, and he made his dispositions accordingly. The square sheets of duck, which had so long been exposed to the mild airs of the south, were reduced to one-third their original size, by double reefs; and several of the more cumbrous of the remaining articles, such as were of doubtful use to persons in their situation, were cast, without pausing to hesitate, into the sea. Nor was this care without a sufficient object. The air soon came sighing heavily over the deep from the north-west, bringing with it the chilling asperity of the inhospitable regions of the Canadas.

"Ah! well do I know you," muttered Wilder, as the first puff of this unwelcome wind struck his sails, and forced the little boat to bend to its power in passing; " well do I know you, with your fresh-water flavour and your smell of the land! Would to God you had blown your fill upon the lakes, without coming down to drive many a weary seaman back upon his wake, and to eke out a voyage, already too long, by your bitter colds and steady obstinacy!"

" Do you speak?" said Gertrude, half appearing from beneath her canopy, and then shrinking back, shivering, into its cover again, as she felt the influence in the change of air.

" Sleep, lady, sleep," he answered, for he liked not, at such a moment, to be disturbed by even her gentle voice.

" Is there new danger?" she asked, stepping lightly from the mattress, unwilling to disturb the repose of her governess. " You need not fear to tell me the worst: I am a soldier's child!"

He pointed to the signs so well comprehended by himself, but continued silent.

" I feel that the wind is colder than it was, but I see no other change."

" And do you know whither the boat is going?"

" To the land, I think. You assured us of that, and I do not believe you would willingly deceive."

" You do me justice; as a proof of it, I will now tell you that you are mistaken. I know that to your eyes all points of the compass, on this void, must seem the same; but I cannot so easily deceive myself."

" And we are not sailing for our homes?"

" So far from it, that, should this course continue, we must cross the whole Atlantic before we can again see land."

Gertrude made no reply, but retired, in sorrow, to the side of her governess. In the mean time, Wilder, left to himself, began to consult his compass and the direction of the wind. Perceiving that he might approach nearer to the continent of

America by changing the position of the boat, he wore round, and brought its head as nigh up to the south-west as the wind would permit.

But there was little hope in this trifling change. At each minute the power of the breeze was increasing, until it freshened to a degree that compelled him to furl his after-sail. The slumbering ocean was not long in awakening; and, by the time the launch was snug under a close-reefed fore-sail, the boat was rising on the growing waves, or sinking into the momentary calm of their furrows. The dashing of the waters, and the rushing of the wind, which now began to sweep heavily across the waste, drew the females to the side of their protector. To their hurried and anxious questions he made considerate but brief replies, answering like a man who felt that the time was better suited to action than to words.

In this manner the lingering minutes of the night went by, loaded with a care that each moment rendered heavier, and which each successive freshening of the breeze had a tendency to render more and more anxious. The day came, only to give more distinctness to the cheerless prospect. The waves were looking green and angrily, while, here and there, large crests of foam were beginning to break on their summits—the certain evidence that a conflict betwixt the elements was at hand. Then came the sun over the ragged margin of the eastern horizon, climbing slowly into the blue arch above, which lay clear, chilling, distinct, and without a cloud.

Wilder noted all these changes with a closeness that proved how critical he deemed their case. He seemed rather to consult the signs of the heavens than to regard the tossings and rushings of the water, which dashed against the side of his little vessel in a manner that often appeared to threaten their total destruction. To the latter, however, he was too much accustomed to anticipate the true moment of alarm, though to the less instructed senses of his companions it already seemed so dangerous. It was to him as is the thunder when compared to the lightning, in the mind of the philosopher; or, rather, he knew that if harm might come from the one on which he floated, its ability to injure must first be called into action by the power of the sister element.

"What do you think of our case now?" asked Mrs. Wyllys, keeping her look fastened on his countenance, as if she would rather trust to its expression, than even to his words, for the answer.

"So long as the wind continue thus, we may yet hope to keep within the route of ships to and from the great northern ports; but, if it freshen to a gale, and the sea begin to break with violence, I doubt the ability of this boat to lie-to."

"Then our resource must be in endeavouring to run before the gale?"

"Then we must scud."

"What would be our direction, in such an event?" demanded Gertrude, to whose mind, in the agitation of the ocean, and the naked view on every hand, all idea of places and distances was lost in the most inextricable confusion.

"In such an event," returned our adventurer, regarding her with a look in which commiseration and indefinite concern were so singularly mingled, that her own mild gaze was changed into a timid and furtive glance, — "in such an event we should be leaving that land it is so important to reach."

"What 'em 'ere?" cried Cassandra, whose large dark eyes were rolling on every side of her, with a curiosity that no care or sense of danger could extinguish; "'em berry big fish on a water?"

"It is a boat!" cried Wilder, springing upon a thwart, to catch a glimpse of a dark object that was driving on the glittering crest of a wave, within a hundred feet of the spot where the

13 *

launch itself was struggling through the brine. "What, ho! — boat, ahoy! — holloa there! — boat, ahoy!"

The breathing of the wind swept by them, but no human sound answered his shout. They had already fallen between two seas, into a deep vale of water, where the narrow view extended no farther than the rolling barriers on each side.

"Merciful Providence!" exclaimed the governess, "can there be others as unhappy as ourselves?"

"It was a boat, or my sight is not as true as usual," returned Wilder, still keeping his stand, to watch the moment when he might catch another view. His wish was quickly realized. He had trusted the helm to the hands of Cassandra, who suffered the launch to vary a little from its course. The words were still on his lips, when the same black object came sweeping down the wave to windward, and a pinnace, bottom upwards, washed past them in the trough. Then followed a shriek from the negress, who abandoned the tiller, and, sinking on her knees, hid her face in her hands. Wilder instinctively caught the helm, bending his look at the same time in the direction of the object from which the eye of Cassandra had revolted. A human form was seen, erect, and half exposed, advancing in the midst of the broken crest which was still covering the dark declivity to windward with foam. For a moment it stood with the brine dripping from the drenched locks, like some being that had issued from the deep to turn its frightful features on the spectators; and then the lifeless body of a drowned man drove past the launch.

Not only Wilder, but Gertrude and Mrs. Wyllys had seen this startling spectacle so nigh them as to recognise the grim counte- nance of Knighthead, rendered stern and forbidding by death. Neither spoke or gave any other evidence of their intelligence. Wilder hoped that his companions had at least escaped the shock of recognising the victim; and the females themselves saw, in the hap'ess fortune of the mutineer, too much of their own probable though more protracted fate, to be able to give vent to the horror they felt in words. For some time, the elements were heard sighing a sort of hoarse requiem over their victims.

"The pinnace has filled!" Wilder at length ventured to say, when he saw by the pallid features of his companions that it was useless to affect reserve any longer. "Their boat was frail, and loaded to the water's edge."

"Think you all are lost?" observed Mrs. Wyllys, in a voice that scarcely amounted to a whisper. "All! not even a soul escaped?"

"There is no hope for any! Gladly would I part with an arm for the assistance of the poorest of those misguided seamen, who have hurried on their evil fortune by their own disobedience and ignorance."

"And of all the happy and thoughtless human beings who so lately left the harbour of Newport, we alone remain!"

"There is not another: this boat, and its contents, are the sole memorials of the Royal Caroline!"

"It was not within the ken of human knowledge to foresee this evil?" continued the governess, fastening her eye on the countenance of Wilder, as if she would ask a question which conscience told her, at the same time, betrayed a portion of that very superstition which had hastened the fate of the rude being they had so lately passed.

"It was not."

"And the danger to which you so often and so inexplicably alluded had no reference to this we have incurred?"

"It had not."

"It has gone with the change in our situation?"

"I hope it has."

"See!" interrupted Gertrude, laying a hand, in her haste, on the arm of Wilder. "Heaven be praised! yonder is something at last to relieve the view."

"It is a ship!" exclaimed her governess; but, an envious wave lifting its green side between them and the object, they sank into a trough, as if the vision had been placed momentarily before their eyes, merely to taunt them with its image. Wilder had caught, however, a glimpse of the well-known outlines of a ship against the heavens, as they descended. When the boat rose again, his look was properly directed, and he was enabled to be certain of the reality of the vessel. Wave succeeded wave, and moments followed moments, during which the stranger as often appeared and disappeared as the launch unavoidably rose and fell with the seas. These short and hasty glimpses sufficed, however, to convey all that was necessary to one who had been nurtured on that element where circumstances now exacted of him such constant and unequivocal evidence of his skill.

At the distance of a mile there was a ship rolling and pitching gracefully, and without any apparent shock, on those waves through which the launch was struggling with so much difficulty. A solitary sail was set to steady the vessel, and that so reduced by reefs, as to look like a little snowy cloud waving in the air. At times her tapering masts appeared pointing to the zenith, or rolling as if inclining against the wind; and then, again, with slow and graceful sweeps, they seemed to fall towards the ruffled surface of the ocean, as if to seek refuge from their endless motion in the bosom of the agitated element itself. There were moments when the long, low, and black hull was seen distinctly resting on the summit of a sea, and glittering in the sun-beams, with the water washing from her sides; and then, as boat and vessel sank together, all was lost to the eye, even to the attenuated lines of her tallest and most delicate spars.

Both Mrs. Wyllys and Gertrude bowed their faces to their knees, when assured of the truth of their hopes, and poured out their gratitude in silent and secret thanksgivings. The joy of Cassandra was more clamorous, and less restrained. The simple negress laughed, shed tears, and exulted, on the prospect that was now offered for the escape of her young mistress and herself from a death that the recent sight had set before her imagination in the most frightful form. But no answering look of congratulation was to be traced in the anxious eye of their companion.

"Now," said Mrs. Wyllys, seizing his hand in both her own, "we may surely hope to be delivered; and then will follow, brave and excellent young man, an opportunity of proving how highly we rate your services."

Wilder permitted this burst of feeling, but he neither spoke, nor exhibited himself the smallest sympathy in her joy.

"Surely you are not grieved, Mr. Wilder," added the wondering Gertrude, "that the prospect of escape from these awful waves is at length so mercifully held forth to us?"

"I would gladly die to shelter you from harm," returned the young sailor; "but——"

"This is not a time for any thing but gratitude," interrupted the governess: "I cannot hearken to any cold exceptions now; what means that 'but?'"

"It may not be as easy as you think to reach the ship—the gale may prevent—in short, many is the vessel that is seen at sea which cannot be spoken."

"Happily, such is not our cruel fortune. I understand your wish to dampen hopes that may possibly be thwarted; but I have too long and too often trusted this dangerous element, not to know that he who has the advantage of being to windward can speak, or not, as he shall please."

"You are right in saying we are to windward; and, were I in a ship, nothing would be easier than to run within hail of the stranger. That ship is certainly lying-to, and yet the gale is not fresh enough to bring so stout a vessel to so short canvass."

"They see us, then, and await our arrival?"

"No, no: thank God, we are not yet seen! This little rag

of ours is blended with the spray. They take it for a gull, or a comb of the sea, for the moment it is in view."

"And do you thank Heaven for this?" exclaimed Gertrude, regarding the anxious Wilder with a wonder that her more cautious governess had the power to restrain.

"Did I thank Heaven for not being seen? I may have mistaken the object of my thanks. It is an armed ship!"

"Perhaps a cruiser of the king's! We are the more likely to meet with a welcome reception. Delay not to hoist some signal, lest they increase their sail and leave us."

"You forget that the enemy is often found upon our coast. This might prove a Frenchman!"

"I have no fears of a generous enemy. Even a pirate would give shelter, and welcome, to females in our distress."

A profound silence succeeded. Wilder still stood upon the thwart, straining his eyes to read each sign that a seaman understands; nor did he appear to find much pleasure in the task.

"We will draw ahead," he said; "and, as the ship is lying on a different tack, we may yet gain a position that will leave us masters of our movements."

To this his companions knew not well how to make any objection. Mrs. Wyllys was so much struck with the remarkable air of coldness with which he met this prospect of refuge against the forlorn condition in which he had just before confessed they were placed, that she was much more disposed to ponder on the cause than to trouble him with questions she had the discernment to see would be useless. Gertrude wondered, while she was disposed to think he might be right, though she knew not why. Cassandra alone was rebellious. She made stout objections against even a moment's delay, assuring the inattentive young seaman, that, should any evil come to her young mistress by his obstinacy, General Gravson would be angered; and she left him to reflect on the results of a displeasure, that to her simple mind teemed with more danger than would attend the resentment of a monarch Provoked by his contumacious disregard of her remonstrances, the negress, forgetting her respect, and blinded by her fears for her whom she not only loved, but had been taught to reverence, seized the boat-hook, and, unperceived by Wilder, fastened to it one of the linen cloths that had been brought from the wreck, exposing the fluttering drapery above the diminished sail, ere her device caught the attention of her companions. Then, indeed, she lowered the signal, before the dark look of Wilder. Short as was the triumph of the negress, it was crowned with success.

The restrained silence, which is so apt to succeed a sudden burst of displeasure, was still reigning in the boat, when a cloud of smoke broke out of the side of the ship, the deadened roar of artillery, struggling heavily up against the wind, immediately after.

"It is now too late to hesitate," said Mrs. Wyllys; "we are seen, let the stranger be friend or enemy."

Wilder did not answer, but continued to watch the movements of the stranger. In another moment, the spars were seen receding from the breeze, and, in a couple of minutes more, the head of the ship was changed to the direction in which they lay Four or five broader sheets of canvass appeared in different parts of the complicated machinery, while the vessel inclined to the breeze. As she mounted on the seas, her bows seemed issuing from the element altogether and high jets of glittering spray were cast into the air, falling in gems upon the sails and rigging.

"It is now too late, indeed," murmured our adventurer, bearing up the helm of his own little craft, and letting its sheet slip through his hands, until the sail was bagging with the breeze nearly to bursting. The boat which had so long been labouring through the water, with a wish to cling as nigh as possible to the continent, flew over the seas, leaving a long trail of foam behind;

and, before either of the females had regained their entire self-possession, she was floating in the comparative calm that the hull of a large vessel never fails to create. A light form stood in the rigging of the ship, issuing the necessary orders for her manœuvres; and, in the midst of the confusion and alarm that such a scene was likely to cause in the bosom of woman, Gertrude and Mrs. Wyllys, with their two companions, were transferred in safety to the decks of the stranger. The moment they and their effects were secured, the launch was cut adrift, like useless lumber. Twenty mariners were then seen climbing among the ropes; and sail after sail was opened still wider, until, bearing the vast folds of all her canvass spread, the vessel was urged along her trackless course, like a swift cloud drifting through the thin medium of the upper air.

# CHAPTER XIX.

Now let it work : Mischief, thou art afoot,
Take then what course thou wilt !

SHAKSPEARE.

WHEN the velocity with which the vessel flew before the wind is properly considered, the reader will not be surprised to learn that, at the end of a week from the time when the foregoing incidents close, we are enabled to open the scene of the present chapter in a very different quarter of the same sea. It is unnecessary to follow the Rover in the windings of his devious and uncertain course, during which his keel furrowed more than a thousand miles of ocean, eluding more than one cruiser of the king, and avoiding sundry less dangerous rencounters, as much from inclination as any other visible cause. It is sufficient for our purpose to lift the curtain which must conceal her movements during this week, when the gallant vessel is in a milder climate, and, the season of the year considered, in a more propitious sea.

Exactly seven days after Gertrude and her governess became the inmates of a ship, whose character it is no longer necessary to conceal from the reader, though it remained a secret from the females, the sun rose upon her flapping sails, symmetrical spars, and dark hull, within sight of a few low, small, and rocky islands. The colour of the element would have told a seaman, had no mound of blue land been seen in the west, that the bottom of the sea was heaving up nearer to its surface, and that it was necessary to guard against the known and dreaded dangers of a coast. Wind there was none; for the vacillating and uncertain air which from time to time distended the lighter canvass of the vessel was the breathing of a morning that was breaking upon the main, so soft, mild, and bland as to impart to the sleeping ocean the appearance of a placid lake.

Every thing having life in the ship was up and stirring. Fifty stout and healthy-looking seamen were hanging in different parts of her rigging, some laughing and holding low converse with messmates who lay indolently on the neighbouring spars, and others leisurely performing the light duty that was the ostensible employment of the moment. More than as many others loitered carelessly about the decks below, somewhat similarly engaged; the whole having the appearance of men who were set to perform their trivial tasks, more to escape the imputation of idleness than from any actual necessity of their being executed. The quarter-deck, the hallowed spot of every vessel that pretends to discipline, was occupied by a set of seamen who could not lay much greater claim to activity. In short, the vessel partook of the character of the ocean and of the weather, both of which seemed to be reserving their powers to some occasion more suitable for their display.

Three or four young (and, considering the nature of their service, far from unpleasant looking,) men appeared in a sort of undress nautical uniform, in which the fashion of no people in particular was very studiously consulted. Notwithstanding the calm that reigned on all around them, each of them wore a short straight dirk at his girdle; and, as one of them bent over the side of the vessel, the handle of a little pistol was discovered through an opening in the folds of his professional frock. There were, however, no other immediate signs of distrust, by which an observer might infer that this armed precaution was more than the usual custom of the ship. A couple of grim and callous looking sentinels, attired and accoutred like soldiers of the land, contrary to marine usage, were posted on the line which separated the place sacred to uses of the officers from the forward part of the deck, bespeaking additional caution. Still, these arrangements were regarded by the seamen with incurious eyes—a proof that use had rendered them familiar.

The individual who has been introduced to the reader under the high-sounding title of General stood, upright and rigid as one of the masts of the ship, studying with a critical eye the equipments of his two mercenaries, and apparently as regardless of what was passing around him, as if he literally considered himself a fixture. One form, however, was to be distinguished from all around it, by the air of authority that breathed even in its repose. It was the Rover. He stood alone, none presuming to approach the spot where he had chosen to plant his person. There was a constant expression of investigation in his wandering eye, as it roved from object to object in the equipment of the vessel; and, at moments, as his eye examined the blue vacuum above him, the cloud that denotes a seaman's responsibility gathered about his brow. This lowering look became so marked, at times, that the fair hair which broke out in ringlets from beneath a black velvet sea-cap, from whose top depended a tassel of gold, could no longer impart to his countenance the gentleness which formed its natural expression in moments of quiet. Disdaining concealment, and as if he wished to announce the nature of the power he wielded, he wore his pistols openly in a leathern belt through which he had thrust, with the same disregard of concealment, a light and curved yatagan, which, by the chasings of its handle, had probably come from the manufactory of an eastern artisan.

On the deck of the poop, overlooking the rest, and retired from the crowd beneath, stood Mrs. Wyllys and her charge, neither of whom announced, in the slightest degree, by eye or air, that anxiety which might be supposed natural to females who found themselves in a condition so critical as that in which they were. On the contrary, while the former pointed out to the latter the hillock of pale blue which rose from the water, like a dark and strongly defined cloud in the distance, hope was strongly blended with the ordinary expression of her features. She also called to Wilder, in a cheerful voice; and the youth, who had long been standing, with a sort of jealous watchfulness, at the foot of the ladder which led from the quarter-deck, was at her side in an instant.

"I am telling Gertrude," said the governess, "that yonder is her home; that when the breeze shall be felt, we may speedily hope to reach it; but the wilfully timid girl insists that she cannot believe her senses, after the frightful risks we have run, until, at least, she shall see the dwelling of her childhood, and the face of her father. You have often been on this coast before, Mr. Wilder?"

"Often, madam."

"Then, you can tell us the name of the distant land we see?"

"Land!" repeated our adventurer, affecting a look of surprise; "is there land in view?"

"Is there land in view! Have not hours gone by since it was proclaimed from the masts?

"It may be so. We seamen are dull after a night of watching, and we often hear but little of what passes."

A suspicious glance was shot from the eye of the governess, as if she apprehended she knew not what.

"Has the sight of the cheerful, blessed soil of America, so soon lost its charm in your eye, that you approach it with so heedless an air? The infatuation of men of your profession, in favour of so dangerous and so treacherous an element, is an enigma I never could explain."

"Do seamen, then, really love their calling with so devoted an affection?" innocently demanded Gertrude.

"It is a folly of which we are at least accused," rejoined Wil der, turning his eye on the speaker, and smiling in a manner that had lost every shade of reserve.

" And justly ? "

" I fear, justly."

" Too justly ! " said Mrs. Wyllys, with emphasis ; "better than their quiet and peaceful homes ! "

Gertrude pursued the idea no further ; but her eye fell to the deck, as if she reflected on a perversity of taste which could render man so insensible to domestic pleasures, and incline him to court the dangers of which she had been a witness.

" I, at least, am free from the latter charge," exclaimed Wilder. " A ship has always been my home."

" Much of my life, too, has been wasted in one," continued the governess, who was pursuing, in her own mind, some images of a time long past. " Happy and miserable, alike, have been the hours that I have passed upon the sea ! Nor is this the first king's ship in which it has been my fortune to be thrown. And yet the customs seem changed since the days I mean ; or else my memory is beginning to lose some of the impressions of an age when memory is apt to be most tenacious. Is it usual, for instance, Mr. Wilder, to admit an utter stranger, like yourself, to exercise authority in a vessel of war ? "

" Certainly not."

" And yet you have been acting, as far as my recollections are true, as second here, since the moment we entered this vessel, wrecked and helpless fugitives from the waves."

Our adventurer again averted his eye, and evidently searched for words, ere he replied,—

"A commission is always respected. Mine procured for me the consideration you have witnessed."

" You are then an officer of the crown ? "

" Would any other authority be respected in a vessel of the crown ? Death had left a vacancy in the second station of this—

cruiser. Fortunately for the wants of the service, perhaps for myself, I was at hand to fill it."

"But, tell me farther," continued the governess, who appeared disposed to profit by the occasion to solve more doubts than one, "is it usual for the officers of a vessel of war to appear armed among their crew, in the manner I see here?"

"It is the pleasure of our commander."

"That commander is evidently a skilful seaman; but his caprices and tastes are as extraordinary as his mien. I have surely seen him before; and, it would seem, but lately."

Mrs. Wyllys was silent for several minutes. During the whole time, her eye was never averted from the form of the calm and motionless being who still maintained his attitude of repose, aloof from all that throng whom he had the address to render so entirely dependent on his authority. The governess studied the smallest peculiarity of his person, as if she would never tire of her gaze. Drawing a heavy and relieving breath, she remembered, however, that she was not alone, and that others were silently awaiting the process of her thoughts. Without manifesting embarrassment at an absence of mind that was far too common to surprise her pupil, she resumed the discourse where she had herself dropped it, turning again towards Wilder.

"Is Captain Heidegger an old acquaintance?" she demanded.

"We have met before."

"It should be a name of German origin by the sound. I am certain it is new to me. And yet there was a time when few officers of his rank were unknown to me, at least by name. Is his family of long standing in England?"

"That is a question he may better answer himself," said Wilder, glad to perceive that the subject of their discourse was approaching. "For the moment, madam, my duty calls me elsewhere."

Wilder withdrew with reluctance; and, had suspicion been

active in the breasts of either of his companions, they would not have failed to note the glance of distrust with which he watched the manner of his commander in making his salutations. There was nothing, however, in the air of the Rover that should have given ground to so much jealous vigilance. On the contrary, he was cold and abstracted, appearing to mingle in their discourse, more from a sense of the obligations of hospitality, than from any satisfaction that he might derive from the intercourse. Still, his deportment was kind, and his voice bland as the airs that were wafted from the healthful islands in view.

"There is a sight," he said, pointing towards the low blue ridges of the land, "that forms the landsman's delight, and the seaman's terror."

"Are seamen so averse to the view of regions where so many millions of their fellow-creatures find pleasure in dwelling?" demanded Gertrude (to whom he more particularly addressed his words), with a frankness that would, in itself, have sufficiently proved no glimmerings of his real character had ever dawned on her spotless and unsuspicious mind.

"Miss Grayson included," he returned, with a slight bow, and a smile, in which, perhaps, irony was concealed by playfulness. "After the risk you have run, even I, confirmed and obstinate sea-monster as I am, have no reason to complain of your distaste for our element. And yet, you see, it is not entirely without its charms. No lake, that lies within the limits of yonder continent, can be more calm and sweet than this bit of ocean. Were we a few degrees more southward, I would show you landscapes of rock and mountain — of bays, and of hill-sides sprinkled with verdure — of tumbling whales, and lazy fishermen, and distant cottages, and lagging sails — that would make a figure even in pages that the bright eye of a lady might love to read."

"And yet for most of your picture would you be indebted to the land. In return for this sketch, I would take you north, and show you black and threatening clouds — a green and angry sea — shipwrecks and shoals — cottages, hill-sides, and mountains, in the imagination only of the drowning man — and sails bleached by waters that contain the voracious shark, or the disgusting polypus."

Gertrude had answered in his own vein; but it was too evident from a tremour that stole into her voice, that memory was also busy with its frightful images. The Rover was not slow to detect the change. Desirous of banishing every recollection that might give her pain, he artfully, but delicately, gave a new direction to the discourse.

"There are people who think the sea has no amusements," he said. "To a pining, home-sick, sea-sick, miserable lubber, this may be true enough; but the man who has sufficient spirit to keep down the qualms of the animal, may tell a different tale. We have our balls regularly, for instance; and there are artists on board this ship, who, though they cannot, perhaps, make as accurate a right-angle with their legs as the first dancer of a ballet, can go through their figures in a gale of wind; which is more than can be said of the highest jumper of them all on shore."

"A ball, without females, would, at least, be thought an unsocial amusement, with us uninstructed people of terra firma."

"Hum! It might be all the better for a lady or two. Then have we our theatre. Farce, comedy, and the buskin, take their turns to help along the time. Yon fellow, that you see lying on the fore-topsail-yard, like an indolent serpent basking on the branch of a tree, will 'roar you as gently as any sucking-dove!' And here is a votary of Momus, who would raise a smile on the lips of a sea-sick friar. I believe I can say no more in his commendation."

"All this is well in the description;" returned Mrs. Wyllys; "but something is due to the merit of the — poet or painter shall I term you?"

" Neither, but a grave and veritable chronologer. However, since you doubt, and since you are so new to the ocean——"

" Pardon me !" the lady gravely interrupted. " On the contrary, I have seen much of it."

The Rover, who had rather suffered his unsettled glances to wander over the youthful countenance of Gertrude than towards her companion, now bent his eyes on the last speaker, where he kept them fastened so long as to create some little embarrassment in the subject of his gaze.

" You seem surprised that the time of a female should have been thus employed," she observed, with a view to arouse his attention to the impropriety of his observation.

" We were speaking of the sea, if I remember," he continued, like a man that was suddenly awakened from a reverie. " Ay, I know it was of the sea; for I had grown boastful in my panegyrics; I had told you that this ship was faster than——"

" Nothing !" exclaimed Gertrude, laughing at his blunder. " You were playing master of ceremonies at a nautical ball."

" Will you figure in a minuet ? Will you honour my boards with the graces of your person ? "

" I, sir ? and with whom ? With the gentleman who knows so well the manner of keeping his feet in a gale ? "

" You were about to relieve any doubts we might have concerning the amusements of seamen," said the governess, reproving the too playful spirit of her pupil, by a glance of her grave eye.

" Ay, it was the humour of the moment, nor will I balk it."

He turned to Wilder, who had posted himself within ear-shot of what was passing, and continued, —

" These ladies doubt our gaiety, Mr. Wilder. Let the boatswain give the magical wind of his call, and pass the word, ' To mischief,' among the people."

Our adventurer bowed his acquiescence, and issued the order

14

In a few moments, the individual who made acquaintance with the reader in the bar-room of the Foul Anchor appeared in the centre of the vessel, near the main hatchway, decorated as before with his silver chain and whistle, and accompanied by two mates, who were humbler scholars of the same gruff school. A long, shrill whistle followed from the instrument of Nightingale, who, when the sound had died away on the ear, roared, in his least sonorous tones,—

"All hands to mischief, ahoy!"

We have before had occasion to liken these sounds to the muttering of a bull, nor shall we see fit to disturb the comparison, since no other similitude so apt presents itself. The example of the boatswain was followed by each of his mates in turn, when the summons was deemed sufficient. However unintelligible and grum the call might sound in the ears of Gertrude, it produced no unpleasant effects on the organs of a majority of those who heard it. When the first note of the call mounted on the air, each idle and extended young seaman, as he lay stretched upon a spar, or hung dangling from a rattling, lifted his head, to catch the words that were to follow, as an obedient spaniel pricks his ears to catch his master's voice. But no sooner was the emphatic word pronounced, which preceded the long-drawn and customary exclamation with which Nightingale closed his summons, than the low murmur of voices, which had so long been maintained among the men, broke out in a common shout. Every symptom of lethargy disappeared in an instant. The young and nimble topmen bounded into the rigging of their respective masts, ascending the shaking ladders of ropes like so many squirrels hastening to their holes at the signal of alarm. The graver and heavier seamen of the forecastle, the quarter-gunners and quarter-masters, the less instructed and half-startled waisters, and the raw and actually alarmed after-guard, all hurried, by a sort of instinct, to their several points; the more practised to plot mischief against their shipmates, and the less intelligent, conscious of their ignorance, to concert the means of defence.

In an instant, the tops and yards were ringing with laughter and jokes, as each exulting mariner aloft proclaimed his device to his fellows, or urged his own inventions at the expense of some less ingenious mode of annoyance. On the other hand, the dis-trustful and often repeated glances that were thrown upward, from the men who had clustered on the quarter-deck and around the foot of the mainmast, sufficiently proclaimed the diffidence with which the novices on deck were about to enter into the expected contest of practical wit. The steady and more earnest seamen forward, however, maintained their places with a stern resolution which proved their reliance on their physical force, and on their long familiarity with the humours, as well as with the dangers of the ocean.

Another little cluster of men assembled, in the midst of the general clamour and confusion, with a haste and steadiness that announced both a consciousness of the entire necessity of unity on the present occasion, and the habit of acting in concert. These were the drilled and military dependants of the general, between whom and the less artificial seamen there existed not only an an-tipathy that might almost be called instinctive, but which, for ob-vious reasons, had been so strongly encouraged in the vessel of which we write, as often to manifest itself in turbulent and nearly mutinous broils. About twenty in number, they collected quickly; and, although obliged to dispense with their fire-arms in such an amusement, there was a sternness in the visage of each of the whiskered worthies, that showed how readily he could appeal to the bayonet that was suspended from his shoulder, should there be need. Their commander withdrew, with the rest of the officers, to the poop, in order that their presence should prove no encumbrance to the freedom of the sports.

A couple of minutes might have been lost in producing the different changes we have just related. But, so soon as the top-men were sure that no unfortunate laggard of their party was within reach of the resentment of the different groups beneath, they complied literally with the summons of the boatswain, by commencing their mischief.

Sundry buckets, most of which had been provided for the extinction of fire, were quickly pendent from as many whips * on the outer extremity of the different yards, and descending towards the sea. In spite of the awkward opposition of the men below, these leathern vessels were speedily filled and run up to the yards again. Many a gaping waister and rigid marine now made a more familiar acquaintance with the element on which he had enlisted than suited either his convenience or his humour. So long as the jokes were confined to these semi-initiated tyroes, the topmen enjoyed the fun with impunity; but, the instant the dignity of a quarter-gunner's person was invaded, the whole gang of petty officers and forecastle-men rose in a body to resent the insult. They made their retort with a readiness and dexterity that manifested how much at home the elder mariners were in all that belonged to their art. A small fire-engine was transferred to the head, and brought to bear on the nearest top, like a well-planted battery clearing the way for the expected charge. The laughing and chattering topmen were soon dispersed; some ascending beyond the power of the engine, and others retreating into the neighbouring top, along ropes and across giddy heights that would have seemed impracticable to any animal less agile than a squirrel or a monkey.

The marines were now summoned forward by the successful and malicious mariners, to improve their advantage. Thoroughly drenched already, and eager to resent their wrongs, a half-dozen

---

* A rope rove through a single block is termed a "whip" in nautical language.

of the soldiers, led on by a corporal, the coating of whose pow-
dered poll had been converted into a sort of paste by too great an
intimacy with a bucket of water, essayed to mount the rigging;
an exploit that to them was much more arduous than it would
have been to enter a breach. The waggish quarter-gunners and
quarter-masters, satisfied with their own success, stimulated them
to the enterprise; and Nightingale and his mates, while they
rolled their tongues into their cheeks, gave forth with their whis-
tles the cheering sound of "heave away!" The sight of these
adventurers, slowly and cautiously mounting the rigging, acted
on the scattered topmen very much in the manner that the appearance of so many flies, in the vicinity of a web, is known to
act on their concealed and rapacious enemy the spider. The sailors
aloft understood, by expressive glances from those below, that a
soldier was considered legal game. No sooner, therefore, had the
latter fairly entered into the toils, than twenty topmen rushed out
upon them, in order to make sure of their prizes. In an incredibly short space of time, the assailants were captured to a man.

Two or three of the aspiring adventurers were lashed where
they had been found, unable to make any resistance in a spot
where instinct itself irresistibly urged them to devote both hands
to the necessary duty of holding fast; while the rest were transferred, by means of whips, to different spars, very much in the manner that a light sail or a yard would have been swayed into its place.

In the midst of the clamorous rejoicings that attended this
success, one individual made himself conspicuous for the gravity
and business-like air with which he performed his particular part
of the comedy. Seated on the outer end of a lower yard, with
as much steadiness as if he had been placed on an ottoman, he
was gravely occupied in examining into the condition of a captive,
who had been run up at his feet, with an order from the waggish
captain of the top, "to turn-him-in for a jewel-block;" an appellation that is given to the blocks that are pendent from the ends of cer-

tain yards, and which appears to have been taken from the precious stones that are so often seen dangling from the ears of the fair.

"Ay, ay," muttered this deliberate and grave-looking tar, who was no other than Richard Fid, "the stropping you've sent up with the fellow is none of the best; and, if he squeaks so now, what will he do when you come to reeve a rope through him! By the Lord, masters, you should have furnished the lad a better outfit, if you meant to send him into good company aloft. Here are more holes in his jacket than there are cabin windows to a Chinese junk. Hilloa! — on deck there! — you Guinea, pick me up a tailor, and send him aloft to keep the wind out of this waister's tarpauling."

The athletic African, who, on account of his great strength, had been posted on the forecastle, cast an eye upward, and, with both arms thrust into his bosom, he rolled along the deck, with just as serious a mien as if he had been sent on a duty of the gravest kind. The uproar over-head had drawn a most helpless-looking mortal from a retired corner of the berth-deck to the ladder of the forward hatch, where, with a body half above the combings, a skein of strong coarse thread around his neck, a piece of bees'-wax in one hand, and a needle in the other, he stood staring about him with just that sort of bewildered air that a Chinese mandarin would manifest were he to be suddenly initiated into the mysteries of the ballet. On this object the eye of Scipio fell. Stretching out an arm, he cast him upon his shoulder, and, before the startled subject of his attack knew into whose hands he had fallen, a hook was passed beneath the waist-band of his trowsers, and he was half-way between the water and the spar, on his way to Fid.

"Have a care lest you let the man fall into the sea!" cried Wilder, sternly, from his stand on the distant poop.

"H'em a tailor, Masser Harry," returned the deliberate black; "if he clothes no 'trong, he nobody to blame but heself."

During this brief parlance, the good-man Homespun had safely arrived at the termination of his flight. Here he was suitably received by Fid, who raised him to his side; and, having placed him comfortably between the yard and the boom, he proceeded to secure him by a lashing that would give the tailor the proper disposition of his hands.

"Bouse a bit on this waister!" called out Richard, when he had properly secured the good-man; "so; belay all that."

He then put one foot on the neck of his prisoner, and, seizing his lower member as it swung uppermost, he coolly placed it in the lap of the awe-struck tailor.

"There, friend," he said, "handle your needle and palm now, as if you were at job-work. Your knowing handicraft always begins with the foundation, whereby he makes sure that his upper gear will stand."

"The Lord protect me, and all other sinful mortals, from an untimely end!" exclaimed Homespun, gazing at the vacant view from his giddy elevation, with a sensation a little resembling that with which the aëronaut, in his first experiment, regards the prospect beneath.

"Settle away this waister," again called Fid: "he interrupts rational conversation by his noise; and, as his gear is condemned by this here tailor, why, you may turn him over to the purser for a new outfit."

The real motive, however, of getting rid of his pendent companion was a twinkling of humanity that still glimmered through the rough humour of the tar, who well knew that his prisoner must hang where he did at a good deal of expense of bodily ease. As soon as his request was complied with, he turned to the good-man to renew the discourse with just as much composure as if they were both seated on the deck, or as if a dozen practical jokes of the same character were not in the process of enactment in as many different parts of the vessel.

"Why do you open your eyes, brother, in this port-hole fashion?" commenced the top-man. "This is all water that you see about you, except that hommoc of blue in the eastern board, which is a morsel of upland in the Bahamas, d'ye see."

"A sinful and presuming world is this we live in!" returned the good-man; "nor can any one tell at what moment his life is to be taken from him. Five bloody and cruel wars have I lived to see in safety, and yet am I reserved to meet this disgraceful and profane end at last."

"Well, since you have had your luck in the wars, you've the less reason to grumble at the bit of a surge you may have felt in your garments, as they run you up to this here yard-arm. I say, brother, I have known stouter fellows take the same ride, who never knew when or how they got down again."

Homespun, who did not more than half comprehend the allusion of Fid, now regarded him in a way that announced some little desire for an explanation, mingled with great admiration of the unconcern with which his companion maintained his position without the smallest aid from any thing but his self-balancing powers.

"I say, brother," resumed Fid, "that many a stout seaman has been whipt up to the end of a yard, who has started by the signal of a gun, and who has staid there just as long as the president of a court-martial was pleased to believe might be necessary to improve his honesty!"

"It would be a fearful and frightful trifling with Providence, in the least offending and conscientious mariner, to take such awful punishments in vain, by acting them in his sports: but doubly so do I pronounce it in the crew of a ship on which no man can say at what hour retribution and compunction are to alight. It seems to me unwise to tempt Providence by these provocating exhibitions."

Fid cast a glance of more than usual significance at the good-man, and even postponed his reply until he had freshened his ideas by an ample addition to the morsel of weed which he had kept all along thrust into one of his cheeks. Then, casting his eyes about him, in order to see that none of his noisy and riotous companions of the top were within ear-shot, he fastened a still more meaning look on the countenance of the tailor, and responded as follows :—

" Hark ye, brother, whatever may be the other good points of Richard Fid, his friends cannot say he is much of a scholar. This being the case, he has not seen fit to ask a look at the sailing orders on coming aboard this wholesome vessel. I suppose, howsomever, that they can be forthcoming at need, and that no honest man need be ashamed to be found cruising under the same."

" Ah ! Heaven protect such unoffending innocents as serve here against their will, when the allotted time of the cruiser shall be filled !" returned Homespun. " I take it, however, that you, as a seafaring and understanding man, have not entered into this enterprise without receiving the bounty, and knowing the whole nature of the service ?"

" The devil a bit have I entered at all, either in the Enterprise or in the Dolphin, as they call the craft. There is Master Harry, the lad on the poop there—he who hails a yard like a bull-whale roaring—I follow his signals d'ye see ; and it is seldom I bother him with questions as to what tack he means to lay his boat on next."

" What ! would you sell your soul in this manner to Beelzebub, and that, too, without a price ?"

" I say, friend, it may be as well to overhaul your ideas before you let them slip, in this no-man's fashion, from your tongue. I would wish to treat a gentleman, who has come aloft to pay me a visit, with such civility as may do credit to my top, though the crew be at mischief, d'ye see. But an officer like him I follow has a name of his own, without stopping to borrow one of the

14 *

person you've just seen fit to name. I scorn such a pitiful thing as a threat; but a man of your years needn't be told, that it is just as easy to go down from this here spar as it was to come up to it."

The tailor cast a glance beneath him into the brine, and hastened to do away the unfavourable impression which his last unfortunate interrogation had so evidently left on the mind of his brawny associate.

" Heaven forbid that I should call any one but by their given and family names, as the law commands," he said. " I meant merely to enquire, if you would follow the gentleman you serve to so unseemly and pernicious a place as a gibbet?"

Fid ruminated some little time, before he could muster his ideas to reply to so comprehensive a question. During this un-usual process, he agitated the weed, with which his mouth was nearly gorged, with great industry; and then, terminating both processes, by casting a jet of the juice nearly to the sprit-sail-yard, he said, in a very decided tone,—

" If I would n't may I be d———d ! After sailing in company for four-and-twenty years, I should be no better than a sneak, to part company because such a trifle as a gallows hove in sight."

" The pay of such a service should be both generous and punc-tual, and the cheer of the most encouraging character," the good-man observed, in a way which manifested that he would not be displeased were he to receive a circumstantial reply. Fid was in no disposition to balk his curiosity, but rather deemed himself bound, since he had entered on the subject, to leave no part of it unexplained.

" As for the pay, d'ye see," he said, " it is seaman's wages. I should despise myself to take less than falls to the share of the best foremast-hand in a ship, since it would be all the same as owning that I got my deserts. But Master Harry has a way of his own in rating men's services; and if his ideas get jammed in an affair of this sort, it is no marlingspike that I handle which can loosen them. I once just named the propriety of getting me a quarter-master's berth; but devil the bit would he be doing the thing, seeing, as he says himself, that I have a fashion of getting a little hazy at times, which would only be putting me in danger of disgrace; since everybody knows that the higher a monkey climbs in the rigging of a ship, the easier everybody on deck can see that he has a spar abaft which is n't human Then, as to cheer, it is seaman's fare; sometimes a cut to spare for a friend, and sometimes a hungry stomach."

"But then there are often divisions of the — a — a — the prize-money, in this successful cruiser?" observed the good-man, averting his face as he spoke, perhaps from a consciousness that it might betray an unseemly interest in the answer "I dare say, you receive amends for all your sufferings, when the purser gives forth the spoils?"

"Hark ye, brother," said Fid, again assuming a look of significance; "can you tell me where the Admiralty Court sits which condemns her prizes?"

The tailor returned the glance with interest; but an extraordinary uproar, in another part of the vessel, cut short the dialogue, just as there was a rational probability it might lead to some consolatory explanations between the parties.

As the action of the tale is shortly to be set in motion again, we shall refer the cause of the commotion to the opening of the succeeding chapter.

## CHAPTER IX.

—— Come, and get thee a sword, though made of a lath:
They have been up these two days.
                                                *King Henry VI.*

W<small>HILE</small> the little by-play that we have just related was enacting
on the fore-yard-arm of the rover, scenes that partook equally
of the nature of tragedy and farce were in the process of exhibition elsewhere. The contest between the possessors of the deck
and the active tenants of the top, was far from having reached its
termination. Blows had, in more than one instance, succeeded
to angry words; and, as the former was a part of the sports in
which the marines and waisters were on an equality with their
more ingenious tormentors, the war was beginning to be waged
with some appearances of a doubtful success. Nightingale, however, was always ready to recall the combatants to their sense of
propriety, with his well-known wind of the call, and his murmur-
ing voice. A long, shrill whistle, with the words " Good humour,
ahoy !" had hitherto served to keep down the rising tempers
of the different parties, when the joke bore too hard on the high-
spirited soldier, or the revengeful, though perhaps less mettle-
some, member of the after-guard. But an oversight on the part
of him who in common kept so vigilant an eye on the movements
of all beneath his orders, had nearly led to results of a more
serious nature.

No sooner had the crew commenced the rough sports we have
just related, than the vein which had induced the Rover momentarily to loosen the reins of discipline seemed suddenly to sub-

side. The gay and cheerful air that he had maintained in his dialogue with his female guests (or prisoners, whichever he might be disposed to consider them,) had disappeared in a thoughtful and clouded brow. His eye no longer lighted with those glimmerings of wayward and sarcastic humour in which he loved occasionally to indulge, but its expression became settled and austere. His mind had relapsed into one of those brooding reveries that so often obscured his mien, as a shadow darkens the golden tints of the ripe and waving corn.

While most of those who were not actors in the humorous achievements of the crew steadily regarded the same, some with wonder, others with distrust, and all with more or less of the humour of the hour, the Rover, to all appearance, was unconscious of all that was going on. It is true, that at times he raised his eyes to the active beings who clung like squirrels to the ropes, or suffered them to fall on the duller movements of the men below; but it was always with a vacancy which proved that the image they carried to the brain was dim and illusory. The looks he cast from time to time on Mrs. Wyllys and her fair and interested pupil betrayed the workings of the temper of the inward man. It was only in these brief but comprehensive glances that the feelings by which he was governed might have been, in any manner, traced to their origin. Still the nicest observer would have been puzzled, in endeavouring to pronounce on the entire character of the emotions uppermost in his mind. At instants, it might have been fancied that some unholy and licentious passion was getting the ascendency; and then, as his eye ran rapidly over the chaste and matronly, though still attractive, countenance of the governess, the look of doubt, as well as of respect, with which he gazed, was too obvious to be misinterpreted.

While the Rover was thus occupied, the sports proceeded, sometimes humorous and forcing smiles from the lips of the half-terrified Gertrude, but always tending to that violence and outbreaking of anger, which might, at any moment, set at nought the discipline of a vessel in which there were no other means of enforcing authority than such as its officers could, on the instant, command. Water had been so lavishly expended, that the decks were running with the fluid, more than one flight of spray having invaded the privileged precincts of the poop. Every ordinary device of similar scenes had been resorted to by the men aloft to annoy their less advantageously posted shipmates beneath; and such means of retaliation had been adopted as use or facility rendered obvious. Here, a hog and a waister were seen swinging against each other, pendent beneath a top; there, a marine, lashed in the rigging, was obliged to suffer the manipulation of a pet monkey, which, drilled to the duty and armed with a comb, was posted on his shoulder, with an air as grave and an eye as observant, as if he had been regularly educated in the art of the perruquier; and every where, some coarse and practical joke proclaimed the licentious liberty which had been momentarily accorded to a set of beings who were, in common, kept in that restraint which comfort, no less than safety, requires for the well-ordering of an armed ship.

In the midst of the noise and turbulence, a voice was heard, apparently issuing from the ocean, hailing the vessel by name, with the aid of a speaking-trumpet, that had been applied to the outer circumference of a hawse-hole.

" Who speaks the Dolphin?" demanded Wilder, when he perceived that the summons had fallen on the ears of his commander, without recalling him to the recollection of what was in action.

" Father Neptune is under your fore-foot."

" What wills the god?"

" He has heard that certain strangers have come into his dominions, and he wishes leave to come aboard the saucy Dolphin, to enquire into their errands, and to overhaul the log-book for their characters."

"He is welcome. Show the old man aboard through the head; he is too experienced a sailor to wish to come in by the cabin-windows."

Here the parlance ceased; for Wilder turned upon his heel, disgusted with his part of the mummery.

An athletic seaman soon appeared, seemingly issuing from the element whose deity he personated. Mops, dripping with brine, supplied the place of hoary locks; gulf-weed, of which acres were floating within a league of the ship, composed a sort of negligent mantle; and in his hand he bore a trident, made of three marling-spikes properly arranged, and borne on the staff of a half-pike. Thus accoutred, the god of the ocean, who was no less a personage than the captain of the forecastle, advanced with a suitable air of dignity along the deck, attended by a train of bearded water-nymphs and naïades, in costumes as grotesque as his own. Arrived on the quarter-deck, in front of the position occupied by the officers, the principal personage saluted the group, with a wave of his sceptre, and resumed the discourse as follows: Wilder, from the continued abstraction of his commander, finding himself under the necessity of maintaining one portion of the dialogue.

"A wholesome and prettily-rigged boat have you come out in this time, my son; and one well filled with a noble set of my children. How long is it since you left the land?"

"Some eight days."

"Hardly time enough to give the green-ones the use of their sea legs. I shall be able to find them, by the manner in which they hold on in a calm." [Here the General, who was standing with a scornful and averted eye, let go his hold of a mizzen-shroud, which he had grasped for no other visible reason than to render his person utterly immovable; Neptune smiled, and continued:]—" I sha'n't ask concerning the port you are last from, seeing that the Newport soundings are still hanging about the flukes of your anchors. I hope you haven't brought out many fresh hands with you, for I smell the stock-fish aboard a Baltic man, who is coming down with the trades, and who can't be more than a hundred leagues from this; I shall therefore have but little time to overhaul your people, in order to give them their papers."

" You see them all before you. So skilful a mariner as Neptune needs no advice when or how to tell a seaman."

" I shall then begin with this gentleman," continued the waggish head of the forecastle, turning towards the still motionless chief of the marines. " There is a strong look of the land about him; and I should like to know how many hours it is since he first floated over blue water?"

" I believe he has made many voyages; and I dare say has long since paid the proper tribute to your majesty."

" Well, well; the thing is like enough, tho'f I will say I have known scholars make better use of their time, if he has been as long on the water as you pretend. How is it with these ladies?"

" Both have been at sea before, and have a right to pass without a question," resumed Wilder, a little hastily.

" The youngest is comely enough to have been born in my dominions," said the gallant sovereign of the sea: " but no one can refuse to answer a hail that comes straight from the mouth of old Neptune; so, if it makes no great difference in your honour's reckoning, I will just beg the young woman to do her own talking." Then, without paying the least attention to the angry glance of Wilder, the sturdy representative of the god addressed himself directly to Gertrude " If, as report goes, my pretty damsel, you have seen blue water before this passage, you may be able to recollect the name of the vessel, and some other small particulars of the run?"

The face of Gertrude changed its colour from red to pale, as rapidly and as glowingly as the evening sky flushes and returns to its pearl-like loveliness; but she kept down her feelings sufficiently to answer with an air of entire self-possession,—

" Were I to enter into all these little particulars, it would detain you from more worthy subjects. Perhaps this certificate will convince you that I am no novice on the sea." As she spoke, a guinea fell from her white hand into the broad and extended palm of her interrogator.

" I can only account for my not remembering your ladyship, by the great extent and heavy nature of my business," returned the audacious freebooter, bowing with an air of rude politeness as he pocketed the offering. " Had I looked into my books before I came aboard this here ship, I should have seen through the mistake at once; for now I remember that I ordered one of my limners to take your pretty face, in order that I might show it to my wife at home. The fellow did it well enough, in the shell of an East-India oyster; I will have a copy set in coral, and sent to your husband, whenever you may see fit to choose one."

Then, repeating his bow, with a scrape of the foot he turned to the governess, in order to continue his examination.

" And you, madam," he said, " is this the first time you have ever come into my dominions, or not ?"

" Neither the first, nor the twentieth; I have often seen your majesty before."

" An old acquaintance ! In what latitude might it be that we first fell in with each other ?"

" I believe I first enjoyed that honour, quite thirty years since, under the Equator."

" Ay, ay, I'm often there, looking out for Indiamen and your homeward-bound Brazil traders. I boarded a particularly great number that very season, but can't say I remember your countenance."

"I fear that thirty years have made some changes in it," re-turned the governess, with a smile, which, though mournful, was far too dignified in its melancholy, to induce the suspicion that she regretted a loss so vain as that of her personal charms. "I was in a vessel of the king, and one that was a little remarkable for its size, since it was of three decks."

The god received the guinea, which was now secretly offered; but it would seem that success had quickened his covetousness, for, instead of returning thanks, he rather appeared to manifest a disposition to increase the amount of the bribe.

"All this may be just as your ladyship says," he rejoined; "but the interest of my kingdom, and a large family at home, make it necessary that I should look sharp to my rights. Was there a flag in the vessel?"

"There was."

"Then, it is likely they hoisted it, as usual, at the end of the jib-boom?"

"It was hoisted as is usual with a vice-admiral, at the fore."

"Well answered, for petticoats!" muttered the deity, a little baffled in his artifice. "It is d——d queer, saving your ladyship's presence, that I should have forgotten such a ship. Was there any thing of the extraordinary sort, that one would be likely to remember?"

The features of the governess had already lost their forced pleasantry in a shade of reflection, and her eye was fastened on vacancy, as she answered like one who thought, aloud,—

"I can, at this moment, see the arch and roguish manner with which that wayward boy, who then had but eight years, over-reached the cunning of the mimic Neptune, and retaliated for his devices by turning the laugh of all on board on his own head!"

"Was he but eight?" demanded a deep voice at her elbow.

"Eight in years, but mature in artifice," returned Mrs. Wyllys, seeming to awake from a trance, as she turned her eyes full upon the face of the Rover.

" Well, well," interrupted the captain of the forecastle, who cared not to continue an enquiry in which his dreaded commander saw fit to take a part, " I dare say it is all right. I will look into my journal; if I find it so, well—if not, why, it 's only giving the ship a head-wind, until I 've overhauled the Dane, and then it will be all in good time to receive the balance of the fee."

So saying, the god hurried past the officers, and turned his attention to the marine guard, who had grouped themselves in a body, secretly aware of the necessity each man might be under of receiving support from his fellows in so searching a scrutiny. Perfectly familiar with the career each individual among them had run in his present lawless profession, and secretly apprehensive that his authority might be suddenly forced from him, the chief of the forecastle selected a raw landsman from among them, ordering his attendants to drag the victim forward, where he believed they might act the cruel revels he contemplated with less danger of interruption. Already irritated by the laughs which had been created at their expense, and resolute to defend their comrade, the marines resisted. A long, clamorous, and angry dispute succeeded, during which each party maintained its right to pursue the course it had adopted. From words the disputants were not long in passing to the usual signs of hostilities. While the peace of the ship thus hung, as it were, suspended by a hair, the general saw fit to express the disgust of such an outrage upon discipline, which had, throughout the whole scene, possessed his mind.

" I protest against this riotous and unmilitary procedure," he said, addressing himself to his still abstracted and thoughtful superior. " I have taught my men, I trust, the proper spirit of soldiers; and there is no greater disgrace can happen to one of them than to lay hands on him, except it be in the regular and wholesome way of a cat. I give open warning to all, that if a finger is put upon one of my bullies, unless as I have said in the way of discipline, it will be answered with a blow."

As the general had not essayed to smother his voice, it was heard by his followers, and produced the effect which might have been expected. A vigorous thrust from the fist of the sergeant drew mortal blood from the visage of the god of the sea, at once establishing his terrestrial origin. Thus compelled to vindicate his manhood, in more senses than one, the stout seaman returned the salutation, with such additional embellishments as the exigencies of the moment seemed to require. Such an interchange of civilities, between two so prominent personages, was the signal of general hostilities among their respective followers. It was the uproar which attended this onset that caught the attention of Fid, who, the instant he saw the nature of the sports below, abandoned his companion on the yard, and slid down to the deck by the aid of a backstay, with as much facility as a monkey could have shown in the same manœuvre. His example was followed by all the topmen; and there was every appearance that the audacious marines would be borne down by the sheer force of numbers. But, stout in their resolution, and bitter in their hostility, these drilled warriors, instead of seeking refuge in flight, fell back upon each other for support. Bayonets were seen gleaming in the sun; while some of the seamen, in the exterior of the crowd, were already laying their hands on the half-pikes that formed a warlike ornament to the foot of the mast.

" Hold ! stand back, every man of you !" cried Wilder, dashing into the centre of the throng and forcing them aside, with a haste that was possibly quickened by the recollection of the increased danger that would surround the unprotected females, should the bands of subordination be once broken among so lawless and desperate a crew. " On your lives, fall back, and obey.

And you, sir, who claim to be so good a soldier, I call on you to bid your men refrain."

The general, however disgusted he might have been by the previous scene, had too many important interests involved in the interior peace of the vessel, not to exert himself at this appeal. He was seconded by all the inferior officers, who well knew that their lives, as well as their comfort, depended on staying the torrent that had so unexpectedly broken loose. But they only proved how hard it is to uphold an authority that is not established on the foundation of legitimate power. Neptune had cast aside his masquerade; and, backed by his stout forecastle-men, was preparing for a conflict that might speedily give him greater pretensions to immortal nature than those he had just rejected. Until now, the officers, partly by threats and partly by remonstrances, had so far controlled the outbreaking, that the time had been passed rather in preparations than in violence. But the marines had seized their arms; while two crowded masses of the mariners were forming on each side of the mainmast, abundantly provided with pikes, and such other weapons as could be made of the bars and handspikes of the vessel. One or two of the cooler heads among the latter had even proceeded so far as to clear away a gun, which they were pointing in-board, and in a direction that might have swept a moiety of the quarter-deck. In short, the broil had reached that pass when another blow struck from either side must have given up the vessel to plunder and massacre. The danger of such a crisis was heightened by the taunts that broke forth from profane lips, which were only opened to lavish the coarsest revilings on the persons and characters of their enemies.

During the five minutes that might have flown by in these sinister and threatening symptoms of insubordination, the individual who was chiefly interested in the maintenance of discipline had manifested the most extraordinary indifference to, or rather unconsciousness of, all that was passing near him. With his arms folded on his breast, and his eyes fastened on the placid sea, he stood motionless as the mast near which he had placed his person.   Long accustomed to the noise of scenes similar to the one he had himself provoked, he heard, in the confused sounds which rose unheeded on his ear, no more than the com‧ motion which ordinarily attended the license of such sports.

His subordinates in command, however, were far more active. Wilder had already beaten back the boldest of the seamen, and a space was cleared between the hostile parties, into which his assistants threw themselves, with the haste of men who knew how much was required at their hands.   This momentary success might have been pushed too far; for believing that the spirit of mutiny was subdued, our adventurer was proceeding to improve his advantage, by seizing the most audacious of the offenders, when his prisoner was immediately torn from his grasp by twenty of his confederates.

"Who's this, that sets himself up for a commodore aboard the Dolphin?" exclaimed a voice in the crowd, at a most unhappy moment for the authority of the new lieutenant.   "In what fashion did he come aboard us? or, in what service did he learn his trade?"

"Ay, ay," continued another sinister voice, "where is the Bristol trader he was to lead into our net, and for which we lost so many of the best days in the season, at a lazy anchor?"

A general and simultaneous murmur followed, which, had such testimony been wanting, would in itself have manifested that the unknown officer was scarcely more fortunate in his present than in his recent service.   Both parties united in condemning his interference, and from both sides were heard scornful opinions of his origin, mingled with unequivocal denunciations against his person.

Nothing daunted by these evidences of the danger he was in, our adventurer answered their taunts with the most scornful smiles, challenging a single individual of them all to dare to step forth, and maintain his words by suitable actions.

" Hear him ! " exclaimed his auditors. — " He speaks like a king's officer in chase of a smuggler ! " cried one. — " Ay, he's a bold 'un in a calm," said a second. — " He's a Jonah, that has slipped into the cabin-windows ! " cried a third ; " and while he stays in the Dolphin, luck will keep upon our weather-beam."— " Into the sea with him ! overboard with the upstart ! into the sea with him ! where he'll find that a bolder and a better man has gone before him ! " shouted a dozen at once ; some of whom immediately made very plain demonstrations of an intention to put their threat in execution. But two forms instantly sprang from the crowd, and threw themselves, like angry lions, between Wilder and his foes. The one who was foremost in the rescue faced short upon the advancing seamen, and, with a blow from an arm that was irresistible, levelled the representative of Neptune to his feet, as if he had been a waxen image of a man. The other was not slow to imitate his example ; and, as the throng receded before this secession from its own numbers, the latter, who was Fid, flourished a fist that was as big and almost as solid as a twelve-pound shot, while he vociferated, fairly frothing at the mouth with rage,—

" Away with ye, ye lubbers ! away with ye ! Would you run foul of a single man, and he an officer, and such an officer as ye never set eyes on before, except, mayhap, in the fashion that a cat looks upon a king ? I should like to see the man, among ye all, who can handle a heavy ship, in a narrow channel, as I have seen Master Harry here handle the saucy——"

" Stand back ! " cried Wilder, forcing himself between his defenders and his foes. " Stand back, I say, and leave me alone to meet the audacious villains."

" Overboard with him ! overboard with them all ! " cried the seamen, " he and his knaves together ! "

"Will you remain silent, and see murder done before your eyes?" exclaimed Mrs. Wyllys, rushing from her place of retreat, and laying a hand eagerly on the arm of the Rover.

He started like one who was awakened suddenly from a light sleep, looking her full and intently in the eye.

"See!" she added, pointing to the violent throng below, where every sign of a bloody struggle was exhibiting itself. "See, they kill your officer, and there is none to help him!"

The look of faded marble, which had so long been seated on his features, vanished. Taking in the whole nature of the scene at the glance, the blood came rushing into every vein and fibre of his face. Seizing a rope which hung from the yard above his head, he swung his person off the poop, and fell lightly into the very centre of the crowd. Both parties fell back, while a sudden silence succeeded to a clamour that a moment before would have drowned the roar of a cataract. Making a haughty and repelling motion with his arm, he spoke, and in a voice that, if any change could be noted, was even pitched on a key less high and threatening than common. But the lowest and the deepest of its intonations reached the most distant ear, so that no one who heard was left in doubt of its meaning.

"Mutiny!" he said, in a tone that strangely balanced between irony and scorn; "open, violent, and blood-seeking mutiny! Are ye tired of your lives, men? Is there one, among ye all, who is willing to make himself an example for the good of the rest? If there be, let him lift a hand, a finger, a hair. Let him speak, look me in the eye, or dare to show that life is in him, by sign, breath, or motion!"

He paused; and so general and absorbing was the spell produced by his presence and his mien, that, in all that crowd of fierce and excited spirits, there was not one so bold as to presume to brave his anger. Sailors and marines stood, alike passive, humbled, and obedient as faulty children, when arraigned before an authority from which they feel that escape is impossible. Perceiving that no voice answered, no limbs moved, nor even an eye among them all was bold enough to meet his own steady but glowing look, he continued, in the same deep and commanding tone,—

"It is well: reason has come of the latest; but, happily for ye all, it has returned. Fall back, fall back, I say; you taint the quarter-deck." — The men receded a pace or two on every side of him. — "Let those arms be stacked; it will be time to use them when I say there is need. And you, fellows, who have been so bold as to lift a pike without an order, have a care they do not burn your hands." — A dozen staves fell upon the deck together. — "Is there a drummer in this ship? let him appear!"

A terrified and cringing-looking being presented himself, having found his instrument by a sort of desperate instinct.

"Now speak, aloud, and let me know at once whether I command a crew of orderly and obedient men, or a set of miscreants that require some purifying before I can trust them."

The first few taps of the drum sufficed to tell the men that it was the "beat to quarters." Without hesitating, the crowd dissolved, and each of the delinquents stole silently to his station; the crew of the gun that had been turned inward managing to thrust it through its port again, with a dexterity that might have availed them greatly in time of combat. Throughout the whole affair, the Rover manifested neither anger nor impatience. Deep and settled scorn, with a high reliance on himself, had, indeed, been exhibited in his bearing, but not, for an instant, did it seem that he suffered passion to get the mastery of reason. And, now that he had recalled his crew to their duty, he appeared no more elated with his success than he had been daunted by the storm which, a minute before, had threatened the dissolution of his authority. Instead of pursuing his further purpose in haste, he

15

awaited the observance of the minutest form which etiquette, as well as use, had rendered customary on such occasions.

The officers approached to report their several divisions in readiness to engage, with exactly the same regularity as if an enemy had been in sight.  The topmen and sail-trimmers were enumerated, and found prepared; shot-slugs and stoppers were handled; the magazine was even opened; the arm-chests were emptied of their contents; and, in short, more than the ordinary preparation of an every-day exercise was observed.

"Let the yards be slung; the sheets and halyards stoppered," he said to the first lieutenant, who now displayed as intimate an acquaintance with the military as he had hitherto discovered with the nautical part of his profession.  "Give the boarders their pikes and boarding-axes, sir; we will show these fellows that we dare trust them with arms!"

The orders were obeyed to the letter; and then succeeded that deep and grave silence which renders a crew at quarters a sight so imposing even to those who have witnessed it from boyhood. In this manner, the skilful leader of this band of desperate marauders knew how to curb their violence with the fetters of discipline.  When he believed their minds brought within the proper limits, by the situation of restraint in which he had placed them, where they well knew that a word, or even an offensive look, would be met by instant punishment, he walked apart with Wilder, of whom he demanded an explanation of what had passed.

Whatever might have been the natural tendency of our adventurer to mercy, he had not been educated on the sea to look with lenity on the crime of mutiny.  Had his recent escape from the wreck of the Bristol trader been already banished from his mind, the impressions of a whole life still remained to teach the necessity of keeping tight those cords which experience has so often proved are absolutely necessary to quell such turbulent bands, when removed from the pale of society, the influence of woman, and when excited by the constant collision of tempers rudely provoked and equally disposed to violence. Though he "set down naught in malice," it is certain that he did "nothing extenuate," in the account he rendered. The whole of the facts were laid before the Rover, in the direct, unvarnished language of truth.

"One cannot keep these fellows to their duty by preaching," returned the irregular chief, when the other had done. "We have no 'Execution Dock' for our delinquents, no 'yellow-flag' for fleets to gaze at, no grave and wise-looking courts to thumb a book or two, and end by saying, 'Hang him.'—The rascals knew my eye was off them. Once before, they turned my vessel into a living evidence of that passage in the Testament which teaches humility to all, by telling us, 'that the last shall be first, and the first last.' I found a dozen round-abouts drinking and making free with the liquors of the cabin, and all the officers prisoners forward—a state of things, as you will allow, a little subversive of decency as well as decorum!"

"I am amazed you should have succeeded in restoring discipline!"

"I got among them single-handed, and with no other aid than a boat from the shore; but I ask no more than a place for my foot, and room for an arm, to keep a thousand such spirits in order. Now they know me, it is rare we misunderstand each other."

"You must have punished severely!"

"There was justice done.—Mr. Wilder, I fear you find our service a little irregular; but a month of experience will put you on a level with us, and remove all danger of such another scene." As the Rover spoke, he faced his recruit with a countenance that endeavoured to be cheerful, but whose gaiety could force itself no further than a frightful smile. "Come," he quickly added, "this time I set the mischief afoot myself; and as we are completely masters, we may afford to be lenient. Besides," glancing his eyes towards the place where Mrs. Wyllys and Gertrude still remained in deep suspense, awaiting his decision, "it may be well to consult the sex of our guests at such a moment."

Then, leaving his subordinate, the Rover advanced to the centre of the quarter-deck, whither he immediately summoned the principal offenders. The men listened to his rebukes, which were not altogether free from admonitory warnings of what might be the consequences of a similar transgression, like creatures who stood in presence of a being of a nature superior to their own. Though he spoke in his usual quiet tone, the lowest of his syllables went into the ears of the most distant of the crew; and, when his brief lesson was ended, the men stood before him, not only like delinquents who had been reproved though pardoned, but with the air of criminals who were as much condemned by their own consciousness as by the general voice. Among them all was only one seaman who, perhaps from past service, was emboldened to venture a syllable in his own justification.

"As for the matter with the marines," he said, "your honour knows there is little love between us, though I allow that a quarter-deck is no place to settle our begrudgings; but, as to the gentleman who has seen fit to step into the shoes of——"

"It is my pleasure that he should remain there," interrupted his commander. "Of his merit I alone am judge."

"Well, well, since it is your pleasure, sir, why, no man may dispute it. But no account has been rendered of the Bristol-man, and great expectations were had aboard here from that very ship. Your honour is a reasonable gentleman, and will not be surprised that the people who were on the look-out for an outward-bound West-Indiaman should be unwilling to take up with a battered and empty launch, in her stead."

"Ay, sir, if I will it, you shall take an oar, a tiller, a thole for your portion. No more of this! You saw the condition of his ship with your own eyes; and where is the seaman who has not, on some evil day, been compelled to admit that his art is nothing, when the elements are against him? Who saved this ship, in the very gust that has robbed us of our prize? Was it your skill? or was it that of a man who has often done it before, and who may one day leave you to your ignorance to manage your own interests? It is enough that I believe him faithful. There is no time to convince your dulness of the propriety of all that's done. Away, and send me the two men who so nobly stepped between their officer and mutiny."

Then came Fid, followed by the negro, rolling along the deck, and thumbing his hat with one hand, while the other sought an awkward retreat in a certain part of his vestments.

"You have done well, my lad; you and your messmate——"

"No messmate, your honour, seeing that he is a nigger," interrupted Fid. "The chap messes with the other blacks, but we take a pull at the can, now and then, in company."

"Your friend, then, if you prefer that term."

"Ay, ay, sir; we are friendly enough at odd times, though a breeze often springs up between us. Guinea has a d——d awkward fashion of luffing up in his talk; and your honour knows it isn't always comfortable to a white man to be driven to leeward by a black. I tell him it is inconvenient. He is a good enough fellow in the main, howsomever, sir; and as he is just an African bred and born, I hope you'll be good enough to overlook his little failings."

"Were I otherwise disposed," returned the Rover, "his steadiness and activity to-day would plead in his favour."

"Yes, yes, sir, he is somewhat steady, which is more than I can always say in my own behalf. Then, as for seamanship, there are few men who are his betters; I wish your honour would take the trouble to walk forward, and look at the heart he turned

into the mainstay, no later than the last calm; it takes the strain
as easy as a small sin sits upon a rich man's conscience."

"I am satisfied with your description: you call him Guinea?"

"Call him by any thing along that coast; for he is no way
particular, seeing he was never christened, and knows nothing at
all of the bearings and distances of religion. His lawful name
is S'ip, or Shipio Africa, taken, as I suppose, from the circumstance that he was first shipped from that quarter of the world.
But as respects names, the fellow is as meek as a lamb; you may
call him any thing, provided you don't call him too late to his
grog."

All this time, the African stood rolling his large dark eyes in
every direction except towards the speakers, perfectly content
that his long-tried shipmate should serve as his interpreter. The
spirit which had so recently been awakened in the Rover seemed
already to be subsiding; for the frown which had gathered on his
brow was dissipating in a look which bore rather the character of
curiosity than of any fiercer emotion.

"You have sailed long in company, my lads," he carelessly
continued, addressing his words to neither in particular.

"Full and by, in many a gale, and many a calm, your honour.
'T is four-and-twenty years the last equinox, Guinea, since Master
Harry fell athwart our hawse; and, then we had been together
three years in the Thunderer, besides the run we made round the
Horn, in the Bay privateer."

"Ah! you have been four-and-twenty years with Mr. Wilder. It is not so remarkable that you should set a value on his
life."

"I should as soon think of setting a price on the king's
crown!" interrupted the straight-going seaman. "I overheard
the lads, d' ye see, sir, just plotting to throw the three of us overboard, and so we thought it time to say something in our own
favour; and, words not always being at hand, the black saw fit

to fill up the time with something that might answer the turn quite as well. No, no, he is no great talker, that Guinea; nor, for that matter, can I say much in my own favour, in this particular; but seeing that we clapped a stopper on their movements, your honour will allow that we did as well as if we had spoken as smartly as a young midshipman fresh from college, who is always for hailing a top in Latin, you know, sir, for want of understanding the proper language."

The Rover smiled, and he glanced his eye aside, apparently in quest of our adventurer. Not seeing him at hand, he was tempted to push his enquiries a little further, though too much governed by self-respect to let the intense curiosity by which he was influenced escape him in any direct and manifest interrogation. But an instant's recollection recalled him to himself, and he discarded the idea as unworthy of his character.

"Your services shall not be forgotten. Here is gold," he said, offering a handful of the metal to the negro, as the one nearest his own person. "You will divide it, like honest shipmates; and you may ever rely on my protection."

Scipio drew back, and with a motion of his elbow, replied,—

"His honour will give 'em Masser Harry."

"Your Master Harry has enough of his own, lad; he has no need of money."

"S'ip no need 'em eider."

"You will please to overlook the fellow's manners, sir," said Fid, very coolly interposing his own hand, and deliberately pocketing the offering; "but I needn't tell as old a seaman as your honour, that Guinea is no country to scrape down the seams of a man's behaviour in. Homsomever, I can say this much for him, which is, that he thanks your honour just as heartily as if you had given him twice the sum. Make a bow to his honour, boy, and do some credit to the company you have kept. And now, since this little difficulty about the money is gotten over, by my presence of mind, with your honour's leave, I'll just step aloft, and cast loose the lashings of that bit of a tailor on the larboard fore-yard-arm. The chap was never made for a topman, as you may see, sir, by the fashion in which he crosses his lower stanchions. That fellow will make a carrick bend with his legs as easily as I could do the same with a yarn of white line!"

The Rover signed for him to retire; and, turning where he stood, he found himself confronted by Wilder. The eyes of the confederates met; and a slight colour bespoke the conscious-ness of the former. Regaining his self-possession on the instant, however, he smilingly alluded to the character of Fid; and then he directed his lieutenant to have the "retreat from quarters" beat.

The guns were secured, the stoppers loosened, the magazine closed, the ports lashed, and the crew withdrew to their several duties, like men whose violence had been completely subdued by the triumphant influence of a master spirit. The Rover then disappeared from the deck, which, for a time, was left to the care of an officer of the proper rank.

## CHAPTER XX.

Thief. 'T is in the malice of mankind, that he thus advises us; not to have us thrive in our mystery. — *Timon of Athens.*

Throughout the whole of that day, no change occurred in the weather. The sleeping ocean lay like a waving and glittering mirror, smooth and polished on its surface, though, as usual, the long rising and swelling of a heavy ground-swell announced the commotion that was in action at a distant place. From the time that he left the deck, until the sun laved its burnished orb in the sea, the Rover was seen no more. Satisfied with his victory, he no longer seemed to apprehend that it was possible any should be bold enough to plot the overthrow of his power. This apparent confidence in himself did not fail to impress his people favourably. As no neglect of duty was overlooked, nor any offence left to go unpunished, an eye that was not seen was believed to be ever on them, and an invisible hand was thought to be at all times uplifted, ready to strike or to reward. It was by a similar system of energy in moments of need, and of forbearance when authority was irksome, that this extraordinary man had so long succeeded, not only in keeping down domestic treason, but in eluding the address and industry of more open enemies.

When the watch was set for the night, however, and the ship lay in profound silence, the Rover was again seen walking swiftly to and fro across the poop, of which he was now the solitary occupant. The vessel had drifted in the Gulf stream so far to the northward, that the little mound of blue had long sunk below the

15 *

edge of the ocean; and she was again surrounded, far as human eye might see, by an interminable world of water. As not a breath of air was stirring, the sails had been handed, the naked spars rearing themselves, in the gloom of the evening, like those of a ship at anchor. In short, it was one of those hours of entire repose that the elements occasionally grant to such adventurers as trust their fortunes to the capricious and treacherous winds.

Even the men whose duty it was to be on the alert were emboldened by the general tranquillity to become careless on their watch, and to cast their persons between the guns, or on different portions of the vessel, seeking that rest which the forms of discipline and good order prohibited them from enjoying in their hammocks. Here and there, indeed, the head of a drowsy officer was seen nodding with the lazy heaving of the ship, as he leaned against the bulwarks, or rested his person on the carriage of some gun that was placed beyond the sacred limits of the quarter-deck. One form alone was erect and vigilant, maintaining a watchful eye over the whole. This was Wilder, whose turn it was again to keep the deck.

For two hours not the slightest communication occurred between the Rover and his lieutenant. Both rather avoided than sought the intercourse; for each had his own secret sources of meditation. After the long and unusual silence, the former stopped short in his walk, and looked steadily on the still motionless figure on the deck beneath him.

" Mr. Wilder," he at length said, "the air is fresher on this poop, and more free from the impurities of the vessel   Will you ascend ?"

The other complied; and they walked silently, and with even steps together, as seamen are wont to pace the deck in the hours of night.

" We had a troublesome morning, Wilder," the Rover resumed, unconsciously betraying the subject of his thoughts, and speaking always in a voice so guarded, that no ears but those of his new lieutenant could hear him : " were you ever so near that pretty precipice a mutiny, before ? "

" The man who is hit is nigher to danger than he who feels the wind of the ball."

" Ah ! you have then been bearded in your ship ! Give your-self no uneasiness on account of the personal animosity which a few of the fellows saw fit to manifest against yourself. I am acquainted with their most secret thoughts, as you shall shortly know."

" I confess that, in your place, I should sleep on a thorny pillow, with such evidences of the temper of my men before my mind. A few hours of disorder might deliver the vessel, on any day, into the hands of the government, and your own life to——"

" The executioner ! And why not yours ?" demanded the Rover so quickly as to give, in a slight degree, an air of distrust to his manner. " But the eye that has often seen battles seldom winks. Mine has too often and too steadily looked danger in the face, to be alarmed at the sight of a king's pennant. Besides, it is not usual for us to be on this ticklish coast; the islands and the Spanish Main are less dangerous cruising grounds."

" And yet have you ventured here at a time when success against the enemy has given the admiral leisure to employ a powerful force in your pursuit."

" I had a reason for it. It is not always easy to separate the commander from the man. If I have temporarily forgotten the obligations of the former in the wishes of the latter, so far, at least, no harm has come of it. I may have tired of chasing your indolent Don, and of driving guarda costas into port. This life of ours is full of excitement, which I love ; to me there is interest even in a mutiny !"

" I like not treason. In this particular, I confess myself like the boor who loses his resolution in the dark. While the enemy is in view, I hope you will find me true as other men; but sleeping over a mine is not an amusement to my taste."

"So much for want of practice! Hazard is hazard, come in what shape it may; and the human mind can as readily be taught to be indifferent to secret machinations as to open risk. Hush! Struck the bell six or seven?"

"Seven. You see the men slumber, as before. Instinct would wake them, were their hour at hand."

"'T is well. I feared the time had passed. Yes, Wilder, I love suspense; it keeps the faculties from dying, and throws a man upon the better principles of his nature. Perhaps I owe it to a wayward spirit, but, to me, there is sometimes enjoyment in an adverse wind."

"And in a calm?"

"Calms may have their charms for your quiet spirits; but in them there is nothing to be overcome. One cannot stir the elements, though one may counteract their workings."

"You have not entered on this trade of yours——"

"Yours!"

"I might, now, have said 'of ours,' since I, too, have become a rover."

"You are still in your noviciate," resumed the other, whose quick mind had already passed the point at which the conversation had arrived; "and high enjoyment had I in being the one who shrived you in your wishes. You manifested a skill in playing round your subject without touching it, which gives me hope of an apt scholar."

"But no penitent, I trust."

"That as it may be; we are all liable to have our moments of weakness, when we look on life as book-men paint it, and think of being probationers where we are put to enjoy. I angled for you as the fisherman plays with the trout. Nor did I overlook the danger of deception. You were faithful on the whole; though I protest against your ever again acting so much against my interests as to intrigue to keep the game from coming to my net."

"When, and how, have I done this? You have yourself admitted——"

"That the Royal Caroline was prettily handled, and wrecked by the will of Heaven; I speak of nobler quarries, now, than such as any hawk may fly at. Are you a woman-hater, that you would fain frighten the noble-minded woman, and the sweet girl, who are beneath our feet at this moment, from enjoying the high privilege of your company?"

"Was it treacherous to wish to save a woman from a fate like that, for instance, which hung over them both this very day? For, while your authority exists in this ship, I do not think there can be danger, even to her who is so lovely."

"By heavens, Wilder, you do me no more than justice. Before harm should come to that fair innocent, with this hand would I put the match into the magazine, and send her, all spotless as she is, to the place from which she seems to have fallen."

Our adventurer listened greedily to these words, though he little liked the strong language of admiration with which the Rover was pleased to clothe his generous sentiment.

"How did you know of my wish to serve them?" he demanded, after a pause, which neither seemed in any hurry to break.

"Could I mistake your language? I thought it plain enough when I heard it."

"Heard! My confession was then made when I least believed it."

The Rover did not answer; but his companion now understood, from his smile, that he had been the dupe of an audacious and completely successful masquerade, and that in the old seaman

Bob Bunt, he had in truth been communing with his commander in person. The deportment of Joram and the unaccountable disappearance of the skiff were now completely explained. Startled at discovering how intricate were the toils into which he had rushed, and possibly vexed at being so thoroughly over-reached, he made several turns across the deck without speaking.

"I confess myself deceived," he at length said, "and hence-forth I shall submit to you as a master from whom one may learn, but who can never be surpassed. The landlord of the Foul Anchor, at least, acted in his proper person, whoever might have been the aged seaman!"

"Honest Joe Joram! An useful man to a distressed mariner, you must allow. How did you like the Newport pilot?"

"Was he an agent too?"

"For the job merely. I trust such knaves no further than their own eyes can see. But, hist! Heard you nothing?"

"I thought a rope had fallen into the water."

"Ay, it is so. Now you shall find how thoroughly I overlook these turbulent gentlemen."

The Rover then cut short the dialogue, which was growing deeply interesting to his companion, and moved with a light step to the stern, over which he hung, for a few moments, by him-self, like a man who found a pleasure in gazing at the surface of the sea. But a slight noise, like that produced by agitated ropes, caught the ear of his companion, who placed himself at the side of his commander, where he did not wait long without gaining another proof of the manner in which he, as well as all the rest of the crew, were circumvented by the devices of their leader.

A man was guardedly, and, from his situation, with some dif-ficulty, moving round the quarter of the ship, by the aid of the ropes and mouldings, which afforded him sufficient means to effect his object. He soon reached a stern-ladder, where he stood sus-pended, endeavouring to discern which of the two forms that were overlooking his proceedings was that of the individual he sought.

" Are you there, Davis ? " said the Rover, in a voice but little above a whisper, first laying his hand lightly on Wilder, as if he would tell him to attend. " I fear you have been seen or heard."

" No fear of that, your honour. I got out at the port by the cabin bulkhead; the afterguard are all as sound asleep as if they had the watch below."

" It is well. What news do you bring from the people."

" Lord ! your honour may tell them to go to church, and the stoutest sea-dog of them all would n't dare to say he had forgotten his prayers."

" You think them in a better temper than they were ? "

" I know it, sir. Not but what the will to work mischief is to be found in two or three of the men; but they dare not trust each other. Your honour has such winning ways with you, that one never knows when he is on safe grounds in setting up to be master."

" This is ever the way with your disorganisers," muttered the Rover, just loud enough to be heard by Wilder. " A little more honesty might make them dangerous; as it is, their knavery defeats itself. And how did these fellows receive the lenity ? Did I well? or must there yet be punishment ? "

" It is better as it stands, sir. The people know you have a good memory, and they talk already of the danger of adding another reckoning to this they feel certain you have not forgotten. There is the captain of the forecastle, who is a little bitter as usual, and the more so, just now, on account of the knock-down blow he got from the black."

" He is a troublesome rascal; a settling day must come at last between us."

"It will be easy to expend him in boat-service, sir, and the ship's company will be all the better for his absence."

"Well, well; no more of him," interrupted the Rover a little impatiently, as if he liked not that his companion should look too deeply into the policy of his government, so early in his initiation. "I will see to him. If I mistake not, fellow, you overacted your own part to-day, and were a little too forward in leading on the trouble."

"I hope your honour will remember that the crew had been piped to mischief; besides, there could be no great harm in washing the powder off a few marines."

"Ay, but you pressed the point after your officer had seen fit to interfere. Be wary in future, lest you make the acting too true to nature, and get applauded in a manner quite as natural."

The fellow promised caution and amendment; and then he was dismissed with his reward in gold, and an injunction to be secret in his return. So soon as the interview was ended, the Rover and Wilder resumed their walk; the former having made sure that no eaves-dropper was at hand to pry into the secret of his connection with the spy. The silence was again long and thoughtful.

"Good ears" (recommenced the Rover) "are nearly as important, in a ship like this, as a stout heart. The rogues forward must not be permitted to eat of the fruit of knowledge, lest we, who are in the cabins, die."

"This is a perilous service in which we are embarked," observed his companion, involuntarily exposing his real thoughts.

The Rover made many turns across the deck, before he answered. When he spoke, it was in a voice so bland and gentle, that his words sounded more like the admonitory tones of a considerate friend, than like the language of a man who had long been associated with a set of beings so rude and unprincipled as those whom he commanded.

"You are still on the threshold of life, Mr. Wilder," he said, "and it is all before you to choose the path on which you will go. As yet, you have been present at no violation of what the world calls its laws; nor is it too late to say you never will be. I may have been selfish in my wish to gain you; but try me, and you will find that self, though often active, cannot, or does not, long hold its dominion over my mind. Say but the word, and you are free; it is easy to destroy the little evidence which exists of your having made one of my crew. The land is not far beyond that streak of fading light; before to-morrow's sun shall set, your foot may be on it."

"Then, why not both? If this irregular life be not fit for me, it is unfit for you. Could I hope——"

"What would you say?" calmly demanded the Rover, after waiting sufficiently long to be sure his companion hesitated to continue. "Speak freely; your words are for the ears of a friend."

"Then, as a friend will I unbosom myself. You say the land is here in the west. It would be easy for you and me, men nurtured on the sea, to lower this boat into the water; and, profiting by the darkness, long ere our absence could be known, we should be lost to the eye of any who might seek us."

"Whither would you steer?"

"To the shores of America, where shelter and peace might be found in a thousand secret places."

"Would you have a man, who has so long lived a prince among his followers, become a beggar in a land of strangers?"

"But you have gold. Are we not masters here? Who is there that might dare even to watch our movements, until we were pleased ourselves to throw off the authority with which we are clothed? Ere the middle watch was set, all might be done."

"Alone! Would you go alone?"

"No — not entirely — that is — it would scarcely become us,

as men, to desert the females to the brutal power of those we should leave behind."

"And would it become us, as men, to desert those who put faith in our fidelity? Mr. Wilder, your proposal would make me a villain! Lawless, in the opinion of the world, have I long been; but a traitor to my faith and plighted word, never! The hour may come when the beings whose world is in this ship shall part; but the separation must be open, voluntary, and manly. You never knew what drew me into the haunts of man, when we first met in the town of Boston?"

"Never," returned Wilder, in a tone of deep disappointment; for hope had caused his very heart to beat quicker.

"You shall hear. A sturdy follower had fallen into the hands of the minions of the law. It was necessary to save him. He was a man I little loved, but he was one who had been honest, after his own opinions. I could not desert the victim; nor could any but I effect his escape. Gold and artifice succeeded; the fellow is now here to sing the praises of his commander to the crew. Could I forfeit a good name, obtained at so much hazard?"

"You would forfeit the good opinions of knaves, to gain a reputation among those whose commendations are an honour."

"I know not. You little understand the nature of man, if you are now to learn that he has pride in maintaining a reputation for even vice, when he has once purchased notoriety by its exhibition. Besides, I am not fitted for the world, as it is found among your dependent colonists."

"You claim your birth, perhaps, from the mother-country?"

"I am no better than a poor provincial, sir; a humble satellite of the mighty sun. You have seen my flags, Mr. Wilder: but there was one wanting among them all; ay, and one which, had it existed, it would have been my pride, my glory, to have upheld with my heart's best blood!"

"I know not what you mean."

"I need not tell a seaman like you, how many noble rivers pour their waters into the sea along this coast of which we have been speaking — how many wide and commodious havens abound there — or how many sails whiten the ocean, that are manned by men who first drew breath on that spacious and peaceful soil?"

"Surely I know the advantages of my native country."

"I fear not," quickly returned the Rover. "Were they known as they should be, by you and others like you, the flag I mentioned would soon be found in every sea; nor would the natives of our country have to succumb to the hirelings of a foreign prince."

"I will not affect to misunderstand your meaning; for I have known others as visionary as yourself in fancying that such an event may arrive."

"May! — As certain as that star will set in the ocean, or that day is to succeed to night, it *must*. Had that flag been abroad, Mr. Wilder, no man would have ever heard the name of the Red Rover."

"The king has a service of his own, and it is open to all his subjects alike."

"I could be a subject of a king; but to be the subject of a subject, Wilder, exceeds the bounds of my poor patience. I was educated, I might almost have said, born, in one of his vessels; and how often have I been made to feel, in bitterness, that an ocean separated my birthplace from the footstool of his throne! Would you think it, sir; one of his commanders dared to couple the name of my country with an epithet I will not wound your ear by repeating?"

"I hope you taught the scoundrel manners."

The Rover faced his companion, and there was a ghastly smile on his face, as he answered,—

"He never repeated the offence. 'T was his blood or mine; dearly did he pay the forfeit of his brutality!"

"You fought like men, and fortune favoured the injured party?"

"We fought, sir. But I had dared to raise my hand against a native of the holy isle! It is enough, Mr. Wilder; the king rendered a faithful subject desperate, and he has had reason to repent it. Enough for the present; another time I may say more. Good night."

Wilder saw the figure of his companion descend the ladder to the quarter-deck; and then he was left to pursue the current of his thoughts alone, during the remainder of a watch which, to his impatience, seemed without an end.

# CHAPTER XXII.

She made good view of me; indeed, so much,
That sure, methought, her eyes had lost her tongue
For she did speak in starts distractedly.

*Twelfth Night.*

THOUGH most of the crew of the Dolphin slept, there were bright and anxious eyes still open in a different part of the vessel. The Rover had relinquished his cabin to Mrs. Wyllys and Gertrude, from the moment they entered the ship, and we shall shift the scene to that apartment (already sufficiently described to render the reader familiar with the objects it contained), resuming the action of the tale at an early part of the discourse just related in the preceding chapter.

It will not be necessary to dwell upon the feelings with which the females had witnessed the disturbances of that day; the conjectures and suspicions to which they gave rise may be apparent in what is about to follow. A mild soft light fell from the lamp of wrought and massive silver, that was suspended from the upper deck, obliquely upon the pensive countenance of the governess, while a few of its strongest rays lighted the more youthful features of her companion. The back-ground was occupied, like a dark shadow in a picture, by the dusky form of the slumbering Cassandra. At the moment when the curtain must be drawn from before this quiet scene, the pupil was seeking in the averted eyes of her instructress an answer to a question which the tongue of the latter appeared reluctant to accord.

"I repeat, my dearest madam," said Gertrude, "that the

fashion of these ornaments, no less than their materials, is extra-ordinary in a ship."

"And what would you infer from the fact?"

"I know not.   I would that we were safe in the house of my father."

"God grant it!  It may be imprudent to be longer silent.—Gertrude, frightful, horrible suspicions have been engendered in my mind by what we have this day witnessed."

The cheek of the young girl blanched, while she demanded an explanation with her eyes.

"I have long been familiar with the usages of a vessel of war," continued the governess, who had only paused in order to review the causes of her suspicions in her own mind, "but never have I seen such customs, as each hour unfolds in this vessel."

"Of what do you suspect her?"

The look of engrossing, maternal anxiety, that the lovely interrogator received in reply to this question, might have startled one whose mind had been more accustomed to muse on the depravity of human nature than the spotless being who received it; but to Gertrude it conveyed no more than a general and vague sensation of alarm.

"Why do you thus regard me, my governess—my mother?" she exclaimed, bending forward, and laying a hand imploringly on the arm of the other, as if to arouse her from a trance.

"Yes, I will speak.  It is safer that you should know the worst, than that your innocence should be liable to be abused. I distrust the character of this ship, and of all that belong to her."

"All!"

"Yes; of all."

"There may be wicked and evil-intentioned men in his majesty's fleet; but we are surely safe from them, since fear of punishment, if not fear of disgrace, will be our protection."

"I dread lest we find that the lawless spirits who harbour here submit to no laws except those of their own enacting, nor acknowledge any authority but that which exists among themselves."

"This would make them pirates!"

"And pirates, I fear, we shall find them.

"Pirates? What! all?"

"Even all. Where one is guilty of such a crime, it is clear that the associates cannot be free from suspicion."

"But, dear madam, we know that one among them, at least, is innocent; since he came with ourselves, and under circumstances that will not admit of deception."

"I know not. There are different degrees of turpitude, as there are different tempers to commit it! I fear that all who may lay claim to be honest, in this vessel, are here."

The eyes of Gertrude sank to the floor, and her lips quivered, partly in a tremour she could not control, and in part through an emotion that she found inexplicable to herself.

"Since we know whence our late companion came," she said, in an under tone, "I think you do him wrong, however right your suspicions may prove as to the rest."

"I may possibly be wrong as to him, I admit, but it is important that we know the worst. Command yourself, my love; our young attendant ascends: some knowledge of the truth may be gained from him."

Mrs. Wyllys gave her pupil an expressive sign to compose her features, while she herself resumed a calmness of mien that might have deceived one far more practised than the boy, who now came slowly into the cabin. Gertrude buried her face in a part of her attire, while the former addressed the youth, in a tone equally divided between kindness and concern.

"Roderick, child," she commenced, "your eyelids are getting heavy. The service of a ship must be new to you?"

"It is so old as to keep me from sleeping on my watch," coldly returned the boy.

"A careful mother would be better for one of your years, than the school of the boatswain. What is your age, Roderick?"

"I have seen years enough to be both wiser and better," he answered, not without a shade of thought on his brow. "Another month will make me twenty."

"Twenty! you trifle with my curiosity, urchin."

"Did I say twenty, madam? Fifteen would be much nearer to the truth."

"I believe you. And how many of those years have you passed upon the water?"

"But two, in truth; though I often think them ten; and yet there are times when they seem but a day!"

"You are romantic early, boy. And how do you like the trade of war?"

"War!"

"Of war. I speak plainly, do I not? Those who serve in a vessel that is constructed expressly for battle, follow the trade of war."

"Oh! yes; war is certainly our trade."

"And have you yet seen any of its horrors? Has this ship been in combat since your service began?"

"This ship!"

"Surely this ship: have you ever sailed in another?"

"Never."

"Then, it is of this ship that one must question you. Is prize-money plenty among your crew?"

"Abundant; they never want."

"Then the vessel and captain are both favourites. The sailor loves the ship and commander that give him an active life."

"Ay, madam; our lives are active here. And some there are among us, too, who love both ship and commander."

" And have you mother, or friend, to profit by your earnings?"

" Have I——"

Struck with the tone of stupor with which the boy responded to her queries, the governess turned her head, to cast a rapid glance at the language of his countenance. He stood in a sort of senseless amazement, looking her full in the face, but with an eye so vacant as to prove that he was not sensible of the image that filled it.

" Tell me, Roderick," she continued, careful not to awaken his jealousy by any sudden allusion to his manner, — " tell me of this life of yours. You find it merry?"

" I find it sad."

" 'T is strange. The young ship-boys are usually among the merriest of mortals. Perhaps your officer treats you with severity."

No answer was given.

" I am right: your captain is a tyrant."

" You are wrong: never has he said a harsh or unkind word to me."

" Ah! then he is gentle and kind. You are very happy, Roderick."

" I — happy, madam?"

" I speak plainly, and in English — happy."

" Oh! yes: we are all very happy here."

" It is well. A discontented ship is no paradise. And you are often in port, Roderick, to taste the sweets of the land?"

" I care but little for the land, madam, could I only have friends in the ship that love me."

" And have you not? Is not Mr. Wilder your friend?"

" I know but little of him; I never saw him before——"

" When, Roderick?"

" Before we met in Newport."

" In Newport!"

"Surely you know we both came from Newport, last?"

"Ah! I comprehend you. Then, your acquaintance with Mr. Wilder commenced at Newport? It was while the ship was lying off the fort?"

"It was. I carried him the order to take command of the Bristol trader. He had only joined us the night before."

"So lately! It was a young acquaintance, indeed. But I suppose your commander knew his merits?"

"It is so hoped among the people. But——"

"You were speaking, Roderick."

"None here dare question the captain for his reasons. Even *I* am obliged to be mute."

"Even *you!*" exclaimed Mrs. Wyllys, in a surprise that for the moment overcame her self-restraint. But the thought in which the boy was lost appeared to prevent his observing the sudden change in her manner. Indeed, so little did he know what was passing, that the governess touched the hand of Gertrude, and silently pointed out the insensible figure of the lad, without the slightest apprehension that the movement would be observed.

"What think you, Roderick," continued his interrogator, "would he refuse to answer *us* also?"

The boy started; and, as consciousness shot into his glance, it fell upon the countenance of Gertrude.

"Though her beauty be so rare," he answered, with vehemence, "let her not prize it too highly. Woman cannot tame his temper!"

"Is he then so hard of heart? Think you that a question from this fair one would be denied?"

"Hear me, lady," he said, with an earnestness that was no less remarkable than the plaintive softness of the tones in which he spoke; "I have seen more in the last two crowded years of my life than many youths would witness between childhood and the age of man. This is no place for innocence and beauty. Oh! quit the ship, if you leave it as you came, without a deck to lay your head under!"

"It may be too late to follow such advice," Mrs. Wyllys gravely replied, glancing her eye at the silent Gertrude as she spoke. "But tell me more of this extraordinary vessel, Roderick; you were not born to fill the station in which I find you?"

The boy shook his head, but remained with downcast eyes, apparently indisposed to answer.

"How is it that I find the Dolphin bearing different hues to-day from what she did yesterday? and why is it that neither then, nor now, does she resemble, in her paint, the slaver of Newport harbour?"

"And why is it," returned the boy, with a smile, in which melancholy struggled powerfully with bitterness, "that none can look into the secret heart of him who makes these changes at will? If all remained the same but the paint of the ship, one might still be happy in her!"

"Then, Roderick, you are not happy: shall I intercede with Captain Heidegger for your discharge?"

"I could never wish to serve another."

"How! Do you complain, and yet embrace your fetters?"

"I complain not."

The governess eyed him closely; and, after a moment's pause, she continued —

"Is it usual to see such riotous conduct among the crew as we have this day witnessed?"

"It is not. You have little to fear from the people; he who brought them under knows how to keep them down."

"They are enlisted by order of the king?"

"The king! — Yes, surely; a king who has no equal."

"But they dared to threaten the life of Mr. Wilder. Is a seaman, in a king's ship, usually so bold?"

The boy glanced a look at Mrs. Wyllys, as if he would say he understood her affected ignorance of the character of the vessel, but he chose to continue silent.

"Think you, Roderick," continued the governess, who no longer deemed it necessary to pursue her covert enquiries on that particular subject, — "think you, Roderick, that the Rov— that is, that Captain Heidegger will suffer us to land at the first port which offers?"

"Many have been passed since you reached the ship."

"Ay, many that are inconvenient; but when one shall be gained where his pursuits will allow his ship to enter?"

"Such places are not common."

"But, should it occur, do you think he will permit us to land? We have gold to pay him for his trouble."

"He cares not for gold. I never ask him for it, that he does not fill my hand."

"You must be happy, then. Plenty of gold will compensate for a cold look at times."

"Never!" returned the boy, with quickness and energy. "Had I the ship filled with the dross, I would give it all to bring a look of kindness into his eye."

Mrs. Wyllys started, no less at the fervid manner of the lad than at the language. Rising from her seat, she approached nigher to him, and in a situation where the light of the lamp fell fuller upon his person. She saw the large drop that broke out from beneath a long and silken lash to roll down a cheek which, though embrowned by the sun, was gradually blushing with the colour that stole into it, as her own gaze became more settled; and then her eyes fell slowly and keenly along the whole form of the lad, until they reached the feet that were so delicate, that they seemed barely able to uphold him. The usually mild countenance of the governess changed to a look of cold regard, and her whole form elevated itself in chaste matronly dignity, as she sternly asked,—

"Boy, have you a mother?"

"I know not," was the answer that came from lips that scarcely severed to permit the smothered sounds to escape.

"It is enough; another time I will speak further with you. Cassandra will in future do the service of this cabin; when I have need of you, the gong shall be touched."

The head of Roderick fell to his bosom. He shrunk from before the cold and searching eye which followed his form until it had disappeared through the hatch. The moment he had disappeared Mrs. Wyllys caught Gertrude to her bosom, straining the astonished but affectionate girl to her heart in a way to show how precious she was at that fearful moment.

A gentle tap at the door broke in upon the flood of reflections which were crowding on the mind of the governess. She gave the customary answer; and, before time was allowed for any interchange of ideas between her and her pupil, the Rover entered.

# CHAPTER XXIII.

*I melt, and am not of stronger earth than others. — Coriolanus.*

THE females received their visiter with a restraint, which will be easily understood when the subject of their recent conversation is recollected. The sinking of Gertrude's form was hurried, but her governess maintained the coldness of her air with greater self-composure. Still there was anxious concern in the watchful glance that she threw towards her guest, as if she would antici-pate the motive of his visit before he spoke.

The countenance of the Rover himself was thoughtful to gravity. He bowed as he came within the influence of the lamp, and his voice was heard muttering some low and hasty syllables, that conveyed no meaning to the ears of his listeners. Indeed, so great was the abstraction in which he was lost, that he had evidently prepared to throw his person on the vacant divan, without explanation or apology, like one who took possession of his own; though recollection returned just in time to prevent this breach of decorum. Smiling, and repeating his bow, with a still deeper inclination, he advanced with perfect self-possession to the table, where he expressed his fears that Mrs. Wyllys might deem his visit unseasonable, or perhaps not announced with sufficient cere-mony. During this short introduction his voice was bland as woman's, and his mien as courteous as if he actually felt him-self an intruder in the cabin of a vessel in which he was literally a monarch.

"But unseasonable as the hour is," he continued, "I should

have gone to my cot with a consciousness of not having discharged all the duties of an attentive and considerate host, had I forgotten to re-assure you of the tranquillity of the ship, after the scene you have witnessed. I have pleasure in saying, that the humour of my people is already expended, and that lambs, in their nightly folds, are not more placid than they are at this minute in their hammocks."

"The authority that so promptly quelled the disturbance is happily ever present to protect us," returned the cautious governess; "we repose entirely on your discretion and generosity."

"You have not misplaced your confidence. From the danger of mutiny, at least, you are exempt."

"And from all others, I trust."

"This is a wild and fickle element we dwell on," he answered, while he bowed his acknowledgment, taking the seat to which the other invited him by a motion of the hand; "but you know its character; and need not be told that we seamen are seldom certain of any of our movements. I loosened the cords of discipline myself to-day, and in some measure invited the broil that followed : but it is passed, like the hurricane and the squall; the ocean is not now smoother than the tempers of my knaves."

"I have often witnessed these rude sports in vessels of the king; but I do not remember to have known any more serious result than the settlement of some ancient quarrel, or some odd freak of nautical humour, which has commonly proved as harmless as it has been quaint."

"Ay; but the ship which often runs the hazard of the shoals gets wrecked at last," muttered the Rover. "I rarely give the quarter-deck up to the people, without keeping a vigilant watch on their humours; but—to-day——"

"You were speaking of to-day."

"Neptune, with his coarse devices, is no stranger to you, madam."

"I have seen the god in times past."

"'T was thus I understood it;—under the line?"

"And elsewhere."

"Elsewhere!" repeated the other in a tone of disappointment. "Ay, the sturdy despot is to be found in every sea; and hundreds of ships, and ships of size, too, are to be seen scorching in the calms of the Equator. It was idle to give the subject a second thought!"

"You have been pleased to observe something that has escaped my ear."

The Rover started; for he had again rather muttered than spoken the preceding sentence aloud. Casting a searching glance around him, as it might be to assure himself that no impertinent listener had found means to pry into the mysteries of a mind he seldom saw fit to lay open to the examination of his associates, he regained his self-possession, and resumed the discourse with a manner as undisturbed as if it had received no interruption.

"I had forgotten that your sex is as timorous as it is fair," he added, with a smile so insinuating and gentle, that the governess cast an involuntary and uneasy glance towards her charge, "or I might have been earlier with my assurances of safety."

"They are welcome even now."

"And your young and gentle friend," he continued, inclining towards Gertrude, though he still addressed his words to the governess; "her slumbers will be none the heavier for what has passed."

"The innocent seldom find an uneasy pillow."

"There is a holy and unsearchable mystery in that truth: the innocent pillow their heads in quiet! Would to God the guilty might find some refuge, too, against the sting of thought! But we live in a world, and in a time, when men cannot be sure even of themselves."

He then paused, and looked about him with a smile so haggard, that the anxious governess unconsciously drew nigher her pupil, like one who was ready to yield protection against the uncertain designs of a maniac. Her visiter, however, remained in a silence so long and deep, that she felt the necessity of removing the awkward embarrassment of their situation, by speaking herself.

"Do you find Mr. Wilder as much inclined to mercy as yourself?" she asked. "There would be merit in his forbearance, since he appeared to be the particular object of the anger of the mutineers."

"And yet you saw he was not without friends. You witnessed the devotion of the men who stood forth so bravely in his behalf?"

"I did; and find it remarkable that he should have been able, in so short a time, to conquer thus completely two so stubborn natures."

"Four-and-twenty years are not an acquaintance of a day."

"And does their friendship bear so old a date?"

"I have heard that time counted between them. It is very certain the youth is bound to those uncouth companions of his by some extraordinary tie! Perhaps this is not the first of their services."

Mrs. Wyllys looked grieved. Although prepared to believe that Wilder was a secret agent of the Rover, she had endeavoured to hope his connection with the freebooters was susceptible of some explanation more favourable to his character. However he might be implicated in the common guilt of those who pursued the reckless fortunes of that proscribed ship, it was evident he bore a heart too generous to wish to see her, and her young and guileless charge, the victims of the licentiousness of his associates. His

16 *

repeated and mysterious warnings no longer needed explanation. Indeed, all that had been dark and inexplicable, both in the previous and unaccountable glimmerings of her own mind, and in the extraordinary conduct of the inmates of the ship, was at each instant becoming capable of solution. She now remembered, in the person and countenance of the Rover, the form and features of the individual who had spoken the passing Bristol trader from the rigging of the slaver — a form which had unaccountably haunted her imagination, during her residence in his ship, like an image recalled from some dim and distant period. Then she saw at once the difficulty that Wilder might have in laying open a secret in which not only his life was involved, but which, to a mind that was not hardened in vice, involved a penalty not less severe—that of the loss of their esteem. In short, a good deal of that which the reader has found no difficulty in comprehending was also becoming clear to the faculties of the governess, though much still remained obscured in doubts that she could neither solve, nor yet entirely banish from her thoughts. On all these points she had leisure to reflect, for her guest, or host, whichever he might be called, seemed in nowise disposed to interrupt her reverie.

"It is wonderful," Mrs. Wyllys at length resumed, "that beings so uncouth should be influenced by the same attachments as those which unite the educated and the refined."

"It is wonderful, as you say," returned the other, like one awakening from a dream. "I would give a thousand of the brightest guineas that ever came from the mint of George II. to know the private history of that youth."

"Is he then a stranger to you?" demanded Gertrude, with the quickness of thought.

The Rover turned an eye on her, that was vacant for the moment, but into which consciousness and expression began to steal as he gazed, until the foot of the governess was trembling with the nervous excitement that pervaded her frame.

" Who shall pretend to know the heart of man ?" he answered, again inclining his head as it might be in acknowledgment of her perfect right to his homage. " All are strangers till we can read their thoughts."

" To pry into the mysteries of the human mind, is a privilege which few possess," coldly remarked the governess. " The world must be often tried and thoroughly known, before we can pretend to judge of the motives of those around us."

" And yet it is a pleasant world to those who have the heart to make it merry," cried the Rover, with one of those startling transitions which marked his manner. " To him who is stout enough to follow the bent of his humour, all is easy. Do you know, that the true secret of the philosopher is not in living for ever, but in living while he can ? He who dies at fifty, after his fill of pleasure, has had more of life than he who drags his feet through a century, bearing the burden of the world's caprices, and afraid to speak above his breath, lest, forsooth, his neighbour should find that his words were evil."

" And yet there are some who find their greatest pleasure in pursuing the practices of virtue."

" 'T is lovely in your sex to say it," he answered, with an air that the sensitive governess fancied was gleaming with the grow- ing licentiousness of a freebooter. She would now gladly have dismissed her visiter ; but a certain flashing of the eye, and a manner that was becoming gay by a species of unnatural effort, admonished her of the danger of offending one who acknowledged no law but his own will. Assuming a tone and a manner that were kind, while they upheld the dignity of her sex, and pointing to sundry instruments of music that formed part of the hetero- geneous furniture of the cabin, she adroitly turned the discourse by saying —

" One whose mind can be softened by harmony, and whose feelings are so evidently alive to the influence of sweet sounds, should not decry the pleasures of innocence.   This flute, and yon guitar, both call you master."

"And, finding these flimsy evidences about my person, you are willing to give me credit for the accomplishments you mention! Here is another mistake of miserable mortality!  Seeming is the every-day robe of honesty.  Why not give me credit for kneeling, morning and night, before that glittering bauble?" pointing to the diamond crucifix which hung, as usual, near the door of his own apartment.

"I hope, at least, that the Being whose memory is intended to be revived by that image, is not without your homage.   In the pride of his strength and prosperity, man may think lightly of the consolations that can flow from a power superior to humanity; but those who have oftenest proved their value, feel deepest the reverence which is their due."

The look of the governess was averted; but, profoundly filled with the feeling she expressed, her reflecting eye turned to him again, as she uttered the simple sentiment.   The gaze she met was earnest and thoughtful as her own.   Lifting a finger, he laid it on her arm, with a motion so light as to be scarcely perceptible, while he asked —

"Think you we are to blame, if our temperaments incline more to evil than power is given to resist?"

"It is only those who attempt to walk the path of life alone that stumble.   I shall not offend your manhood, if I ask, do you never commune with God?"

"It is long since that name has been heard in this vessel, lady, except to aid in that miserable scoffing and profanity which simpler language made too dull.  But what is He, that unknown Deity, more than what man in his ingenuity has seen fit to make him?"

"'The fool hath said in his heart, There is no God,'" she answered in a voice so firm, that it startled even the ears of one so long accustomed to the turbulence and grandeur of his wild profession. " 'Gird up now thy loins like a man; for I will demand of thee, and answer thou me. Where wast thou when I laid the foundations of the earth? Declare, if thou hast understanding.' "

The Rover gazed wildly on the flushed countenance of the speaker. Bending his face aside, he said aloud, rather giving utterance to his thoughts than pursuing the discourse —

" There is nothing more in this than what I have often heard, and yet it comes over my feelings with the freshness of native air! Lady, repeat thy words; change not a syllable, nor vary the slightest intonation of the voice, I pray thee."

Though much amazed, and even alarmed at the request, Mrs. Wyllys complied; delivering the holy language of the inspired writers with a fervour that found its support in the strength of her own faith. Her auditor listened like a being enthralled. For nearly a minute, neither eye nor attitude was changed, but he stood at the feet of her who had so simply and so powerfully asserted the majesty of God, motionless as the mast against which he leaned. It was long after her accents had ceased, that he drew a deep respiration, and again spoke.

" This is re-treading the whole path of life at a single stride," he said. " I know not why my pulses, which in common are like iron, beat so irregularly now. Lady, this little hand of thine might check a temper that has so often braved——"

He ceased; for his eye following his own hand, which had unconsciously touched that of Mrs. Wyllys, was fastened on the member he had named, which he appeared to study as if examining a relic. Drawing a sigh, like one who awakened from an agreeable illusion, he turned away, leaving the sentence unfinished.

" You would have music!" he recklessly exclaimed. " Then music there shall be, though its symphony be rung upon a gong!"

As he spoke, the wayward and vacillating being we have been attempting to describe struck the instrument so quick and powerfully as to drown all reply in the din.   Though deeply mortified that he had so quickly escaped from the influence she had partially acquired, and secretly displeased at the unceremonious manner in which he had seen fit to announce his independence again, the governess was aware of the necessity of concealing her disappointment.

"This is certainly not the harmony I invited," she said, when the overwhelming sounds had ceased to fill the ship; "nor do I think it of a quality to favour tho slumbers of those who are less dangerous in their hammocks than when awake."

"Fear nothing for them.  The seaman will sleep soundly with his ear near the port at which the cannon bellows, and he awakes at the call of the boatswain's whistle.  He is too deeply schooled in habit, to think he has heard more than a note of the flute; stronger and fuller than common, if you will, but still a sound that has no interest for him.   Another tap would have sounded the alarm of fire; these three touches say no more than music. It was the signal for the band.  The night is still, and favourable for their art, and we will listen to sweet sounds awhile."

His words were scarcely uttered before the low chords of wind instruments were heard without, where the men had probably stationed themselves by some previous order of their captain. The Rover smiled, as if he exulted in this prompt proof of the sort of despotic, or rather magical, power he wielded; and, throwing his form on the divan, he sat listening to the sounds which followed.

The strains which now rose upon the night, and which spread themselves soft and melodiously abroad upon the water, would have done credit to more regular artists.  The air was wild and melancholy, and, perhaps, it was the more in accordance with the present humour of the man for whose ear it was created.   Then, losing the former character, the whole power of the music was concentrated in softer and still gentler sounds, as if the genius who had given birth to the melody were pouring out the feelings of his soul in pathos. The temper of the Rover's mind answered to the changing expression of the music; and, when the strains were sweetest and most touching, he bowed his head like one who wept.

Though secretly under the influence of the harmony themselves, Mrs. Wyllys and her pupil could but gaze on the singularly constituted being into whose hands they had been cast by their evil fortune. The former was filled with admiration at the fearful contrariety of passions which could reveal themselves in the same individual, under so very different and so dangerous forms; while the latter, judging with the indulgence of her years, was willing to believe that a man whose emotions could be thus easily and kindly excited, was rather the victim of circumstances than the creator of his own habits.

"There is Italy in those strains," said the Rover, when the last chord died upon his ear; "sweet, indolent, luxurious, forgetful Italy! It has never been your chance, madam, to visit that land, so mighty in its recollections, and so impotent in its actual condition?"

The governess made no reply; but, bowing her head, in turn, her companions believed she was submitting also to the influence of the music. At length, impelled by another changeful impulse, the Rover advanced towards Gertrude; and, addressing her with a courtesy that would have done credit to a different scene, he said,—

"One who in common speaks music should not have neglected the gifts of nature. You sing?"

Had Gertrude possessed the power he affected to believe, her voice would have denied its services at his call. Bending to his compliment, she murmured her apologies in words that were barely audible. He listened intently; but, without pressing a point that it was easy to see was unwelcome, he turned away, and gave the gong a light quick tap.

" Roderick," he continued, when the light footsteps of the lad were heard upon the stairs that led into the cabin below, " do you sleep ? "

" The answer was slow and smothered; of course it was in the negative.

" Apollo was not absent at the birth of Roderick, madam. The lad can raise such sounds as have been known to melt the stubborn feeling of a seaman. Go, place yourself by the cabin door, good Roderick, and bid the music run a low accompaniment to your words."

The boy obeyed, stationing his slight form so much in shadow, that his countenance was not visible to those who sat within the stronger light of the lamp.

The instruments then commenced a gentle symphony, which was soon ended; and twice did they begin the air, but no voice was heard.

" Words, Roderick, words; we are but dull interpreters of the meaning of the flutes."

The boy then began in a full, rich, contralto voice, which betrayed a tremour, however, that threatened more than once to interrupt his song. The words, so far as they might be distinguished, ran as follows :—

> " The land was lying broad and fair
>     Behind the western sea ;
>   And holy solitude was there,
>     And sweetest liberty.

> " The ling'ring sun, at evening, hung
>     A glorious orb, divinely beaming
>   On silent lake and tree ;
>     And ruddy light was o'er all streaming,
>       Mark, man ! for thee ;
>       O'er valley, lake, and tree !

" And now a thousand maidens stray,
    Or range the echoing groves:
 While flutt'ring near, on pinions gay,
    Fan twice ten thousand loves.
  In that soft clime, at even time,
    Hope says——"

" Enough of this, good Roderick," impatiently interrupted his
master. " There is too much of the Corydon in that song for
the humour of a mariner. Sing us of the sea and its pleasures,
boy; and roll out the strains in a fashion that will suit a sailor's
fancy."

The lad was mute, perhaps in disinclination to the task, perhaps from inability to comply.

" What, Roderick! does the muse desert thee? or is thy memory getting dull? You see the child is wilful in his melody; he
must sing of loves and sunshine, or he fails. Now touch us a
stronger chord, my men, and put life into your cadences, while I
troll a sea air for the honour of the ship."

The band caught the humour of their master (for he well
deserved the name), sounding a powerful and graceful symphony,
to prepare the listeners for the song of the Rover. Those treacherous and beguiling tones which so often stole into his voice
when speaking, did not mislead expectation as to its powers. It
proved to be equally rich, full, deep, and melodious. Favoured
by these natural advantages, and aided by an exquisite ear, he
rolled out the following stanzas, in a manner that was singularly
divided between that of the reveller and the man of sentiment.
The words were probably original; for they smacked strongly of
his own profession, and were not entirely without a touch of
the peculiar taste of the individual.

" All hands, unmoor! unmoor!
 Hark to the hoarse, but welcome sound,
    Startling the seaman's sweetest slumbers,
 The groaning capstan's labouring round,

The cheerful fife's enlivening numbers;
And ling'ring idlers join the brawl,
And merry ship-boys swell the call,
    All hands unmoor! unmoor!

"The cry's 'A sail! a sail!'
Brace high each nerve to dare the fight,
    And boldly steer to seek the foeman;
One secret prayer to aid the right,
    And many a secret thought to woman!
Now spread the flutt'ring canvass wide,
And dash the foaming sea aside;
    The cry's 'A sail! a sail!'

"Three cheers for victory!
Hush'd be each plaint o'er fallen brave;
    Still ev'ry sigh to messmate given;
The seaman's tomb is in the wave;
    The hero's latest hope is heaven!
High lift the voice in revelry!
Gay raise the song, the shout, the glee;
    Three cheers for victory!"

When he had ended the song, and without waiting to listen
if any words of compliment were to succeed an effort that might
lay claim to great excellence both in tones and execution, he
arose; and, desiring his guests to command the services of his
band at pleasure, he wished them "soft repose and pleasant
dreams," and coolly descended into the lower apartments, apparently for the night.   Mrs. Wyllys and Gertrude, notwithstanding
they had been amused, or rather seduced, by the interest thrown
around a manner that was so wayward, while it was never gross,
felt a sensation, as he disappeared, like that produced by breathing
a freer air, after having been too long compelled to respire the
pent atmosphere of a dungeon.   The former regarded her pupil
with eyes in which open affection struggled with inward solicitude;
but neither spoke, since a slight movement near the door of the
cabin reminded them that they were not yet alone.

"Would you have further music, madam?" asked Roderick, stealing timidly out of the shadow as he spoke; "I will sing you to sleep, if you will; but I am choked when he bids me to be merry against my feelings."

The brow of the governess contracted, and she was evidently preparing herself to give a stern and repulsive answer; but the plaintive tones, and shrinking, submissive form of the other, pleaded so strongly to her heart, that the frown passed away, leaving in its place the reproving look which chastens the frown of maternal concern.

"Roderick," she said, "I thought we should have seen thee no more to-night!"

"You heard the gong. Although he can be so gay, and can raise such thrilling sounds in his pleasanter moments, you have never yet listened to him in anger."

"Is his anger so very fearful?"

"Perhaps to me it is more frightful than to others; but I find nothing so terrible as a word of his, when his mind is moody"

"Is he then harsh to thee?"

"Never."

"You contradict yourself, Roderick. He is, and he is not. Have you not said how terrible you find his moody language?"

"Yes; for I find it changed. Once he was never thoughtful or out of humour, but latterly he is not himself."

Mrs. Wyllys did not answer. The language of the boy was certainly much more intelligible to her than to her attentive, but unsuspecting, companion; for, while she motioned to the lad to retire, Gertrude manifested a desire to gratify the curious interest she felt in the life and manners of the freebooter. The signal, however, was authoritatively repeated, and the lad slowly, and with reluctance, withdrew.

The governess and her pupil then retired into their own state-room; and, after devoting many minutes to those nightly offerings and petitions which neither ever suffered any circumstances to cause them to neglect, they slept in the consciousness of innocence, and in the hope of an all-powerful protection. Though the bell of the ship regularly sounded the hours throughout the watches of the night, scarcely another sound arose, during the darkness, to disturb the calm which seemed to have settled equally on the ocean and all that floated on its bosom.

## CHAPTER XXIV.

—— But, for the miracle,
I mean our preservation, few in millions
Can speak like us.

*Tempest.*

DURING these moments of treacherous calm, the Dolphin might
have been likened to a slumbering beast of prey. But as nature
limits the period of repose to the creatures of the animal world,
so it would seem that the inactivity of the freebooters was not
doomed to any long continuance. With the morning sun a
breeze came across the water, breathing the flavour of the land,
and setting the sluggish ship again in motion. Throughout all
that day, with a wide reach of canvass spreading along her booms,
her course was held towards the south. Watch succeeded watch,
and night came after day, and still no change was made in her
direction. Then the blue islands were seen heaving up, one after
another, out of the sea. The prisoners of the Rover, for thus
the females were now constrained to consider themselves, silently
watched each hillock of green that the vessel glided past, each
naked and sandy key, or each mountain-side, until, by the calculations of the governess, they were already steering amid the
western Archipelago.

During all this time no question was asked which in the smallest
manner betrayed to the Rover the consciousness of his guests,
that he was not conducting them towards the promised port of
the continent. Gertrude wept for the sorrow of her father; but
her tears flowed in private, or were poured upon the bosom of her

governess.   Wilder she avoided, with an intuitive consciousness that he was no longer the character she had wished to believe; but to all in the ship she struggled to maintain an equal air and a serene eye.   In this deportment, safer than any impotent entreaties might have proved, she was strongly supported by her governess, whose knowledge of mankind had early taught her that virtue was never so imposing, as when it knew best how to maintain its equanimity.   On the other hand, both the commander of the ship and his lieutenant sought no other communication with the inmates of the cabin than courtesy appeared absolutely to require.

The former, as if repenting already of having laid so bare the capricious humours of his mind, withdrew gradually into himself, neither seeking nor permitting familiarity with any; while the latter appeared perfectly conscious of the constrained mien of the governess, and of the altered though still pitying eye of her pupil. Little explanation was necessary to acquaint Wilder with the reasons of this change.   Instead of seeking the means to vindicate his character, however, he rather imitated their reserve. Little else was wanting to assure his former friends of the nature of his pursuits; for even Mrs. Wyllys admitted to her charge, that he acted like one in whom depravity had not yet made such progress as to have destroyed that consciousness which is ever the surest test of innocence.

We shall not detain the narrative to dwell upon the natural regrets in which Gertrude indulged, as this sad conviction forced itself upon her understanding, nor to relate the gentle wishes in which she did not think it wrong to indulge, that one, who certainly was master of so many manly and generous qualities, might be made to see the error of his life, and to return to a course for which even her cold and nicely judging governess allowed nature had eminently endowed him.   The kind emotions that had been awakened in her bosom by the events of the last fortnight were not content to exhibit themselves in wishes alone; and that petitions more personal, and even more fervent than common, mingled in her prayers; but this is a veil which it is not our province to raise, the heart of one so pure and so ingenuous being the best repository for its own gentle feelings.

For several days the ship had been contending with the unvarying winds of those regions. Instead of struggling, however, like a cumbered trader, to gain some given port, the Rover suddenly altered her course, gliding through one of the many passages that intersect the islands, with the ease of a bird that is settling to its nest. A hundred different sails were seen, but all were avoided alike; the policy of the freebooters teaching them the necessity of moderation, in a sea so crowded with vessels of war. After the vessel had shot through one of the straits which divide the chain of the Antilles, it issued in safety on the more open sea which separates them from the Spanish Main. The moment the passage was effected, and a broad and clear horizon was seen stretching on every side of them, a manifest alteration occurred in the mien of every individual of the crew. The brow of the Rover himself lost the look of care, which had wrapped the whole man in a mantle of reserve, and his reserve disappeared, leaving him the reckless, wayward being we have described. Even the men, whose vigilance had needed no quickening in running the gauntlet of the cruisers which were known to swarm in the narrower seas, appeared to breathe a freer air, and sounds of merriment and thoughtless gaiety were once more heard in a place over which the gloom of distrust had been so long and so heavily cast.

On the other hand, the governess saw new ground for uneasiness in the course the vessel was taking. While the islands were in view, she had hoped that their captor only awaited a suitable occasion to place them in safety within the influence of the laws of some of the colonial governments. Her own observation told her there was so much of what was once good, if not noble, mingled with the lawlessness of the two principal individuals in the vessel, that she saw nothing that was visionary in such an expectation. Even the tales of the time, which recounted the desperate acts of the freebooter, with wild and fanciful exaggerations, did not forget to include numberless instances of even chivalrous generosity. In short, he bore the character of one who, while he declared himself the enemy of all, knew how to distinguish between the weak and the strong, and who often found as much gratification in repairing the wrongs of the former as in humbling the pride of the latter.

But all her agreeable anticipations from this quarter were forgotten when the last island of the group sank into the sea behind them, and the ship lay alone on an empty ocean. As if ready to throw aside his mask, the Rover ordered the sails to be reduced; and, neglecting the favourable breeze, the vessel was brought to the wind. No object calling for the immediate attention of her crew, the Dolphin came to a stand, in the midst of the waters, her officers and people abandoning themselves to their pleasures, or to idleness, as whim or inclination dictated.

"I had hoped that your convenience would have permitted us to land in some of his majesty's islands," said Mrs. Wyllys, speaking for the first time since her suspicions had been awakened on the subject of her quitting the ship, and addressing her words to the self-styled Captain Heidegger, just after the order to heave-to the vessel had been obeyed. "I fear you find it irksome to be so long dispossessed of your cabin."

"It cannot be better occupied," he rather evasively replied; though the observant and anxious governess fancied his eye was bolder, and his air under less restraint, than when she had before dwelt on the same topic. "If custom did not require that a ship should wear the colours of some people, mine should always sport those of the fair."

" And, as it is— —"

" As it is, I hoist the emblems that belong to the service I am in."

" In fifteen days, that you have been troubled with my presence, it has never been my good fortune to see those colours set."

" No !" exclaimed the Rover, glancing his eye quickly at her, as if to penetrate her thoughts. " Then shall the uncertainty cease on the sixteenth. — Who 's there, abaft ?"

" No one better nor worse than Richard Fid," returned the individual in question, lifting his head from a locker into which it had been thrust, while its owner searched for some mislaid implement, and who added a little quickly, when he ascertained by whom he was addressed, " Always at your honour's orders."

" Ah ! 'T is the friend of *our* friend," the Rover observed to Mrs. Wyllys, with an emphasis which the other understood. " He shall be my interpreter. — Come hither, lad ; I have a word to exchange with you."

" A thousand at your service, sir," returned Richard, comply- ing ; " for, though no great talker, I have always something uppermost in my mind which can be laid hold of at need."

" I hope you find that your hammock swings easily in my ship ?"

" I 'll not deny it, your honour ; an easier craft, especially upon a bowline, might be hard to find."

" And the cruise. I hope you also find the cruise such as a seaman loves ? "

" D'ye see, sir, I was sent from home with little schooling, and so I seldom make so free as to pretend to read the captain's orders."

" But still you have your inclinations," said Mrs. Wyllys firmly, determined to push the investigation even further than her companion had intended.

" I can't say that I 'm wanting in natural feeling, your lady- ship," returned Fid, endeavouring to manifest his admiration of

17

the sex, by the awkward bow he made to the governess as its representative, " tho'f crosses and mishaps have come athwart me as well as better men.   I thought as strong a splice was laid between me and Kate Whiffle as was ever turned into a sheet cable; but then came the law, with its regulations and shipping articles, luffing short athwart my happiness, and making a wreck at once of all the poor girl's hopes, and giving but a Flemish account of my comfort."

" It was proved that she had another husband!" dryly remarked the Rover.

" Four, your honour.   The girl had a love of company, and it grieved her to the heart to see an empty house; but then, as it was seldom more than one of us could be in port at a time, there was no such need to make the noise they did about the trifle. But envy did it all, sir; envy, and the greediness of the land-sharks.   Had every woman in the parish as many husbands as Kate, the devil a bit would they have taken up the precious time of judge and jury, in looking into the manner in which a wench like her kept a quiet household."

" And, since that unfortunate repulse, you have kept yourself altogether out of the bands of matrimony?"

" Ay, ay; *since*, your honour," returned Fid, giving his commander another of those droll looks, in which a peculiar cunning struggled with a more direct and straight-going honesty; " *since*, as you say rightly, sir; though they talked of a small matter of a bargain that I had made with another woman, myself; but, in overhauling the affair, they found that, as the shipping articles with poor Kate wouldn't hold together, why, they could make nothing at all of me; so I was white-washed like a queen's parlour, and sent adrift."

" And all this occurred after your acquaintance with Mr. Wilder?"

" Afore, your honour, afore.   I was but a younker in the time of it, seeing that it is four-and-twenty years, come May next, since I have been towing at the stern of Master Harry. But then, as I have had a sort of family of my own since that day, why, the less need, you know, to be berthing myself again in any other man's hammock."

"You were saying it is four-and-twenty years," interrupted Mrs. Wyllys, "since you made the acquaintance of Mr. Wilder?"

"Acquaintance! Lord, my lady, little did he know of acquaintances at that time; though, bless him! the lad has had occasion to remember it often enough since."

"The meeting of two men of so singular merit must have been somewhat remarkable?" observed the Rover.

"It was for that matter remarkable enough, your honour; though, as to the merit, notwithstanding Master Harry is often for overhauling that part of the account, I've set it down for just nothing at all."

"I confess, that, in a case where two men, both of whom are so well qualified to judge, are of different opinions, I feel at a loss to know which can have the right. Perhaps, by the aid of the facts, I might form a truer judgment."

"Your honour forgets the Guinea, who is altogether of my mind in the matter, seeing no great merit in the thing either. But, as you are saying, sir, reading the log is the only true way to know how fast a ship can go; and so, if this lady and your honour have a mind to come at the truth of the affair, why, you have only to say as much, and I will put it all before you in creditable language."

"There is reason in this proposition," returned the Rover, motioning to his companion to follow to a part of the poop where they were less exposed to the observations of inquisitive eyes. "Now, place the whole clearly before us; and then you may consider the merits of the question disposed of definitively."

Fid was far from discovering the smallest reluctance to enter on the required detail; and, by the time he had cleared his throat, freshened his supply of the weed, and otherwise disposed himself to proceed, Mrs. Wyllys had so far conquered her reluctance to pry clandestinely into the secrets of others, as to yield to a curiosity she found unconquerable, and to take the seat to which her companion invited her by a gesture of his hand.

"I was sent early to sea, your honour, by my father," commenced Fid, after these little preliminaries had been observed, "who was, like myself, a man that passed more of his time on the water than on dry ground; though, as he was nothing more than a fisherman, he generally kept the land aboard; which is, after all, little better than living on it altogether. Howsomever, when I went, I made a broad offing at once, fetching up on the other side of the Horn, the very first passage I made; which was no small journey for a new beginner; but then, as I was only eight years old——"

"Eight! you are speaking of yourself," interrupted the disappointed governess.

"Certain, madam; and, though genteeler people might be talked of, it would be hard to turn the conversation on any man who knows better how to rig or how to strip a ship. I was beginning at the right end of my story; but, as I fancied your ladyship might not choose to waste time in hearing concerning my father and mother, I cut the matter short by striking in at eight years old, overlooking all about my birth and name, and such other matters as are usually logged in your every-day narratives."

"Proceed," she rejoined, resorting to a compelled resignation.

"My mind is pretty much like a ship that is about to slip off its ways," resumed Fid. "If she makes a fair start, and there is neither jam nor dry-rub, smack she goes into the water, like a sail let run in a calm; but, if she once brings up, a good deal of labour is to be gone through to set her in motion again. Now, in order to wedge up my ideas, and to get the story slushed, so that I can slip through it with ease, it is needful to over-run the part which I have just let go; which is, how my father was a fisherman, and how I doubled the Horn. — Ah! here I have it again, clear of kinks, fake above fake, like a well-coiled cable; so that I can pay it out as easily as the boatswain's yeoman can lay his hand on a bit of ratling-stuff. Well, I doubled the Horn, as I was saying, and might have been the matter of four years cruising about among the islands and seas of those parts, which were none of the best known then, or, for that matter, now. After this, I served in his majesty's fleet a whole war, and got three wounds and as much honour as I could stow beneath hatches. Well, then I fell in with the Guinea — the black, my lady, that you see turning in a new clue-garnet-block for the starboard clue of the fore-course."

"Ay; then you fell in with the African," said the Rover.

"Then we made our acquaintance; and although his colour is no whiter than the back of a whale, I care not who knows it, after Master Harry, there is no man living who has an honester way with him, or in whose company I take greater satisfaction. To be sure, your honour, the fellow is sometimes contradictory, and has a great opinion of his strength, and thinks his equal is not to be found at a weather-earing, or in the bunt of a topsail; but then he is no better than a black, and one is not to be too particular in looking into the faults of such as are not actually his fellow-creatures."

"That would be uncharitable in the extreme."

"The very words the chaplain used to let fly aboard the Brunswick! It is a great thing to have schooling, your honour; since, if it does nothing else, it fits a man for a boatswain, and puts him in the track of steering the shortest course to Heaven. But, as I was saying, there was I and Guinea shipmates, and in a reason-

able way friends, for five years more; and then the time arrived
when we met with the mishap of the wreck in the West
Indies."

"What wreck?"

"I beg your honour's pardon; I never swing my head-yards
till I'm sure the ship won't luff back into the wind; and, before
I tell the particulars of the wreck, I will overrun my ideas,
to see that nothing is forgotten that should of right be first
mentioned."

The Rover, who saw, by the expression of her countenance,
how impatient his companion was becoming for a sequel that
approached so tardily, and how much she dreaded an interruption,
made a significant sign to her to permit the straight-going tar to
take his own course, as the best means of coming at the facts
they both longed so much to hear.  Left to himself, Fid soon
took the necessary review of the transactions, in his own quaint
manner; and, having happily found that nothing which he considered as germane to the narrative was omitted, he proceeded at
once to the more material, and what was to his auditors by far
the most interesting portion of his narrative.

"Well, as I was telling your honour," he continued, "Guinea
was then a maintopman, and I was stationed in the same place
aboard the Proserpine, a quick-going two-and-thirty, when we fell
in with a bit of a smuggler, between the islands and the Spanish
Main; and so the captain made a prize of her, and ordered her
into port; for which I have always supposed, as he was a sensible
man, he had his orders.  But this is neither here nor there,
seeing that the craft had got to the end of her rope, and foun-
dered in a heavy hurricane that came over us, mayhap a couple
of days' run to leeward of our haven.  Well, she was a small
boat; and, as she took it into her mind to roll over on her side
before she went to sleep, the master's mate in charge, and three
others, slid off her decks to the bottom of the sea, as I have

always had reason to believe, never having heard any thing of them since. It was here that Guinea first served me the good turn; for, though we had often before shared hunger and thirst together, this was the first time he ever jumped overboard to keep me from taking in salt water like a fish."

"He kept you from drowning with the rest?"

"I 'll not say just that much, your honour; for there is no knowing what lucky accident might have done the same good turn for me. Howsomever, seeing that I can swim no better nor worse than a double-headed shot, I have always been willing to give the black credit for as much, though little has ever been said between us on the subject; for no other reason, as I can see, than that settling-day has not yet come. Well, we contrived to get the boat afloat, and enough into it to keep soul and body together, and made the best of our way for the land, seeing that the cruise was, to all useful purposes, over in that smuggler. I needn't be particular in telling this lady of the nature of boat-duty, as she has lately had some experience in that way herself; but I can tell her this much : had it not been for that boat in which the black and myself spent the better part of ten days, she would have fared but badly in her own navigation."

"Explain your meaning."

"My meaning is plain enough, your honour, which is, that little else than the handy way of Master Harry in a boat could have kept the Bristol trader's launch above water, the day we fell in with it."

"But in what manner was your own shipwreck connected with the safety of Mr. Wilder?" demanded the governess, unable any longer to await the dilatory explanation of the prolix seaman.

"In a very plain and natural fashion, my lady, as you will say yourself, when you come to hear the pitiful part of my tale. Well, there were I and Guinea rowing about in the ocean, on short allowance of all things but work, for two nights and a day.

heading-in for the islands; for, though no great navigators, we could smell the land, and so we pulled away lustily; for you consider it was a race in which life was the wager, until we made, in the pride of the morning, as it might be here at east-and-by-south, a ship under bare poles; if a vessel can be called bare that had nothing better than the stumps of her three masts standing, and they without rope or rag to tell one her rig or nation. Howsomever, as there were three naked sticks left, I have always put her down for a full-rigged ship; and when we got nigh enough to take a look at her hull, I made bold to say she was of English build."

"You boarded her?" observed the Rover.

"A small task that, your honour, since a starved dog was the whole crew she could muster to keep us off. It was a solemn sight when we got on her decks, and one that bears hard on my manhood," continued Fid, with an air that grew more serious as he proceeded, "whenever I have occasion to overhaul the log-book of memory."

"You found her people suffering of want?"

"We found a noble ship as helpless as a halibut in a tub. There she lay, a craft of some four hundred tons, water-logged and motionless as a church. It always gives me great reflection, sir, when I see a noble vessel brought to such a strait; for one may liken her to a man who has been docked of his fins, and who is getting to be good for little else than to be set upon a cat-head to look out for squalls."

"The ship was then deserted?"

"Ay, the people had left her, sir, or had been washed away in the gust that had laid her over. I never could come at the truth of the particulars. The dog had been mischievous, I conclude, about the decks; and so he had been lashed to a timber-head, the which saved his life, since, happily for him, he found himself on the weather-side when the hull righted a little, after her spars gave way. Well, sir, there was the dog, and not much else as we could see, though we spent half a day in rummaging round, in order to pick up any small matter that might be useful; but then, as the entrances to the hold and cabin were full of water, why, we made no great affair of the salvage after all."

"And then you left the wreck?"

"Not yet, your honour. While knocking about among the bits of rigging and lumber above board, says Guinea, says he, 'Mister Dick, I hear some one making their plaints below.' Now, I had heard the same noises myself, sir; but had set them down as the spirits of the people moaning over their losses, and had said nothing of the same, for fear of stirring up the superstition of the black; for the best of them are no better than superstitious niggers, my lady; so I said nothing of what I had heard, until he saw fit to broach the subject himself. Then we both turned-to to listening with a will, and sure enough the groans began to take a human sound. It was a good while, howsomever, before I could make up whether it was any thing more than the complaining of the hulk itself; for you know, my lady, that a ship which is about to sink makes her lamentations just like any other living thing."

"I do, I do," returned the governess, shuddering; "I have heard them, and never will memory lose the recollection of the sounds!"

"Ay, I thought you might know something of the same, and solemn groans they are; but as the hulk kept rolling on the top of the sea, and no further signs of her going down, I began to think it best to cut into her abaft, in order to make sure that some miserable wretch had not been caught in his hammock, at the time she went over. Well, good will and an axe soon let us into the secret of the moans."

"You found a child?"

"And its mother, my lady. As good luck would have it, they
17*

were in a berth on the weather-side, and as yet the water had not reached them; but pent air and hunger had nearly proved as bad as the brine. The lady was in the agony when we got her out; and as to the boy, proud and strong as you now see him there on yonder gun, my lady, he was just so miserable, that it was no small matter to make him swallow the drop of wine and water that the Lord had left us, in order, as I have often thought since, to bring him up to be, as he at this moment is, the pride of the ocean!"

"But, the mother?"

"The mother had given the only morsel of biscuit she had to the child, and was dying in order that the urchin might live. I never could get rightly into the meaning of the thing, my lady, why a woman, who is no better than a Lascar in matters of strength, nor any better than a booby in respect of courage, should be able to let go her hold of life in this quiet fashion, when many a stout mariner would be fighting for each mouthful of air the Lord might see fit to give. But there she was, white as the sail on which the storm has long beaten, and limber as a pennant in a calm, with her poor skinny arm around the lad, holding in her hand the very mouthful that might have kept her own soul in the body a little longer."

"What did she, when you brought her to the light?"

"What did she!" repeated Fid, whose voice was getting thick and husky, "why, she did a d——d honest thing; she gave the boy the crumb, and motioned, as well as a dying woman could motion, that we should have an eye over him till the cruise of life was up."

"And was that all?"

"I have always thought she prayed; for something passed between her and one who was not to be seen, if a man might judge by the fashion in which her eyes were turned aloft, and her lips moved. I hope, among others, she put in a good word for Richard Fid; for certain she had as little need to be asking for herself as any body. But no man will ever know what she said, seeing that her mouth was shut from that time for ever after."

" She died?"

" Sorry am I to say it. But the poor lady was past swallow-ing when she came into our hands, and then it was but little we had to offer her. A quart of water, with, mayhap, a gill of wine, a biscuit, and a handful of rice, was no great allowance for two hearty men to pull a boat some seventy leagues within the tropics. Howsomever, when we found no more was to be got from the wreck, and that, since the air had escaped by the hole we had cut, she was settling fast, we thought it best to get out of her; and sure enough we were none too soon, seeing that she went under just as we had twitched the jolly-boat clear of the suction."

" And the boy—the deserted child!" exclaimed the governess, whose eyes had now filled to overflowing.

" There you are all aback, my lady. Instead of deserting him, we brought him away with us, as we did the only other living creature to be found about the wreck. But we had still a long journey before us, and, to make the matter worse, we were out of the track of the traders. So I put it down as a case for a council of all hands, which was no more than I and the black, since the lad was too weak to talk, and little could he have said otherwise in our situation. So I begun myself, saying, says I, ' Guinea, we must either eat this here dog, or this here boy. If we eat the boy, we shall be no better than the people in your own country,' who, you know, my lady, are cannibals, ' but if we eat the dog, poor as he is, we may make out to keep soul and body together, and to give the child the other matters.' So Guinea, he says, says he, ' I 've no occasion for food at all : give 'em to the boy,' says he, ' seeing that he is little and has need of strength.' Howsomever, Master Harry took no great fancy to the dog, which we soon finished between us, for the plain reason that he was so thin. After that, we had a hungry time of it ourselves; for, had we not kept up life in the lad, you know, there was so little of it that it would soon have slipt through our fingers."

"And you fed the child, though fasting yourselves?"

"No, we wer'n't altogether idle, my lady, seeing that we kept our teeth jogging on the skin of the dog, though I will not say that the food was over savoury; and then, as we had no occasion to lose time in eating, we kept the oars going so much the livelier. Well, we got in at one of the islands after a time, though neither I nor the nigger had much to boast of as to strength or weight when we made the first kitchen we fell in with."

"And the child?"

"Oh! he was doing well enough; for, as the doctors after-wards told us, the short allowance on which he was put did him no harm."

"You sought his friends?"

"Why, as for that matter, my lady, so far as I have been able to discover, he was with his best friends already. We had neither chart nor bearings by which we knew how to steer in search of his family. His name he called Master Harry, by which it is clear he was a gentleman born, as indeed any one may see by looking at him; but not another word could I learn of his relations or country, except that, as he spoke the English language and was found in an English ship, there is a natural reason to believe he is of English build himself."

"Did you not learn the name of the ship?" demanded the attentive Rover, in whose countenance the traces of a lively interest were very distinctly discernable.

"Why, as to that matter, your honour, schools were scarce in my part of the country; and in Africa, you know, there is no great matter of learning; so that, had her name been out of water, which it was not, we might have been bothered to read it Howsomever, there was a horse-bucket kicking about her decks, and which, as luck would have it, got jammed in with the pumps in such a fashion that it did not go overboard until we took it with us. Well, this bucket had a name painted on it; and, after we had leisure for the thing, I got Guinea, who has a natural turn at tattooing, to rub it into my arm in gunpowder, as the handiest way of logging these small particulars. Your honour shall see what the black has made of it."

So saying, Fid very coolly doffed his jacket, and laid bare to the elbow one of his brawny arms, on which the blue impression was still very plainly visible. Although the letters were rudely imitated, it was not difficult to read, in the skin, the words "Ark, of Lynnhaven."

"Here, then, you had a clue at once to find the relatives of the boy," observed the Rover, after he had deciphered the letters.

"It seems not, your honour; for we took the child with us aboard the Proserpine, and our worthy captain carried sail hard after the people; but no one could give any tidings of such a craft as the 'Ark, of Lynnhaven;' and, after a twelvemonth, or more, we were obliged to give up the chase."

"Could the child give no account of his friends?" demanded the governess.

"But little, my lady; for the reason that he knew but little about himself. So we gave the matter over altogether; I and Guinea, and the captain, and all of us, turning-to to educate the boy. He got his seamanship of the black and myself, and may-hap some little of his manners also; and his navigation and Latin of the captain, who proved his friend till such a time as he was able to take care of himself, and, for that matter, some years afterwards."

" And how long did Mr. Wilder continue in a king's ship?" asked the Rover, in a careless and apparently an indifferent manner.

" Long enough to learn all that is taught there, your honour," was the evasive reply.

" He came to be an officer, I suppose?"

" If he didn't, the king had the worst of the bargain. But what is this I see hereaway, atween the backstay and the vang? It looks like a sail! or is it only a gull flapping his wings before he rises?"

" Sail, ho!" called the look-out from the mast-head. " Sail, ho!" was echoed from top and deck; the glittering though distant object having struck a dozen vigilant eyes at the same instant. The Rover was compelled to lend his attention to a summons so often repeated; and Fid profited by the circumstance to quit the poop, with the hurry of one who was not sorry for the interruption. Then the governess arose too, and, thoughtful and melancholy, she sought the privacy of her cabin.

# CHAPTER XXV.

Their preparation is to-day by sea.
*Antony and Cleopatra.*

"SAIL, ho!" in the little frequented sea in which the Rover lay
was a cry that quickened every pulsation in the bosoms of her
crew. Many weeks had now, according to their method of cal
culation, been entirely lost in the visionary and profitless plans of
their chief. They were not of a temper to reason on the fatality
which had forced the Bristol trader from their toils; it was
enough, for their rough natures, that the rich spoil had escaped
them. Without examining into the causes of this loss, they
were disposed to visit their disappointment on the head of the
innocent officer who had been charged with the care of a vessel
that they already considered a prize. Here, then, was at length
an opportunity to repair their loss. The stranger was about to
encounter them in a part of the ocean where succour was nearly
hopeless, and where time might be afforded to profit to the utmost, by any success that the freebooters should obtain. Every
man in the ship seemed sensible of these advantages; and, as
the words sounded from mast to yard, and from yard to deck,
they were taken up in cheerful echoes from fifty mouths, which
repeated the cry until it was heard issuing from the inmost recesses of the vessel.

The Rover himself manifested unusual satisfaction at this new
prospect of a capture. He was quite aware of the necessity of
some brilliant or of some profitable exploit, to curb the rising

tempers of his men ; and long experience had taught him that
he could draw the cords of discipline the tightest in moments that
appeared the most to require the exercise of his own high courage
and consummate skill.   He walked forward, therefore, among his
people, with a countenance that was no longer buried in reserve,
speaking to several, whom he addressed by name, and of whom
he did not even disdain to ask opinions concerning the character
of the distant sail.   When a sort of implied assurance that their
recent offences were overlooked had thus been given, he summoned Wilder, the general, and one or two others of the superior
officers, to the poop, where they all disposed themselves to make
more particular and more certain observations, by the aid of a
half-dozen excellent glasses.

Many minutes were now passed in intense scrutiny.   The day
was cloudless, the wind fresh without being heavy, the sea long,
even, and far from high, and, in short, all things combined, as
far as is ever seen on the restless ocean, not only to aid their
examination, but to favour those subsequent evolutions which
each instant rendered more probable would become necessary.

" It is a ship !" said the Rover, lowering his glass, the first to
proclaim the result of the long inspection.

" It is a ship !" echoed the general, across whose weather-worn
features a ray of something like satisfaction was making an effort
to shine.

" A full-rigged ship !" continued a third, relieving his eye in
turn, and answering the grim smile of the soldier.

" There must be something to hold up all those lofty spars,"
resumed their commander.   " A hull of price is beneath. — But
you say nothing, Mr. Wilder !   You make her out——'

" A ship of size," returned our adventurer, who, though silent,
had been far from the least interested in his investigations.
" Does my glass deceive me — or——'

" Or what, sir ?"

"I see her to the heads of her courses"

"You see her as I do. It is a tall ship, on an easy bowline, with every thing set that will draw. And she is standing hither-ward. Her lower sails have lifted within five minutes."

"I thought as much. But——"

"But what, sir? There can be little doubt but she is heading north-and-by-east. Since she is so kind as to spare us the pains of a chase, we will not hurry our movements. Let her come on. How like you the manner of the stranger's advance, general?"

"Unmilitary, but enticing! There is a look of the mines about her very royals."

"And you, gentlemen, do you also see the fashion of a galleon in her upper sails?"

"'T is not unreasonable to believe it," answered one of the inferiors. "The Dons are said to run this passage often in order to escape speaking us gentlemen who sail with roving com-missions."

"Ah, your Don is a prince of the earth! There is charity in lightening his golden burden, or the man would sink under it, as did the Roman matron under the pressure of the Sabine shields. I think, by your eye, you see no such gilded beauty in the stranger, Mr. Wilder?"

"It is a heavy ship!"

"The more likely to bear a noble freight. You are new, sir, to this merry trade of ours, or you would know that size is a quality we greatly esteem. If they carry pennants, we leave them to meditate on the many 'slips which exist between the cup and the lip;' if stored with metal no more dangerous than that of Potosi, they generally sail the faster after passing a few hours in our company."

"Is not the stranger making signals?" demanded Wilder, quickly.

"Is he so alert? A good look-out must be had, when a vessel, that is merely steadied by her stay-sails, can be seen so far Vigilance is a never-failing sign of value !"

There was a pause, during which all the glasses, in imitation of Wilder's, were again raised in the direction of the stranger. Different opinions were given; some affirming and some doubting the fact of the signals. The Rover himself was silent, though his observation was keen, and long continued.

" We have wearied our eyes till sight is getting dim," he said. " I have found the use of trying fresh organs when my own have refused to serve me. Come hither, lad," he continued, address-ing a man who was executing some delicate job in seamanship on the poop, at no great distance from the spot where the group of officers had placed themselves; " come hither; tell me what you make of the sail in the south-western board."

The man proved to be Scipio, who had been chosen, for his expertness, to perform the task in question. Placing his cap on the deck, in a reverence even deeper than that which the seaman usually manifests towards his superior, he lifted the glass in one hand, while with the other he covered the eye for which at that moment he had no particular use. No sooner did the wandering instrument fall on the distant object, than he dropped it again, and fastened his look in a sort of stupid admiration on Wilder.

" Did you see the sail ?" demanded the Rover

" Masser can see him wid he naked eye."

" Ay, but what do you make of him with the glass ?"

" He 'm a ship, sir."

" True. On what course ?"

" He got he starboard tacks aboard, sir."

" Still true. Has he signals abroad ?"

" He 'm got t'ree new cloths in he maintop-gallant-royal, sir."

" His vessel is all the better for the repairs. Did you see his flags ?"

" He 'm show no flag, masser."

"I thought as much myself. Go forward, lad—stay—one often gets a true idea by seeking it where it is not thought to exist. Of what size do you take the stranger to be?"

" He'm just seven hundred and fifty tons, masser."

" How's this! The tongue of your negro, Mr. Wilder, is as exact as a carpenter's rule. The fellow speaks of the size of a vessel that is hull down, with an air as authoritative as a runner of the king's customs could pronounce on the same, after she had been submitted to the office admeasurement."

"You will have consideration for the ignorance of the black; men of his unfortunate race are seldom skilful in answering interrogatories."

"Ignorance!" repeated the Rover, glancing his eye uneasily and with a rapidity peculiar to himself, from one to the other, and from both to the rising object in the horizon? "skilful! I know not: the man has no air of doubt. You think her tonnage precisely that which you have said?"

The large dark eyes of Scipio rolled, in turn, from his new commander to his ancient master, while for a moment, his faculties appeared to be lost in confusion. But the uncertainty continued only for a moment. He no sooner read the frown that was gathering on the brow of the latter, than the air of confidence with which he had pronounced his former opinion vanished in a look of obstinacy so settled, that one might well have despaired of ever driving, or enticing him again to seem to think.

"I ask you, if the stranger may not be a dozen tons larger or smaller than what you have just named?" continued the Rover, when he found his former question was not likely to be soon answered.

" He'm just as masser wish 'em," returned Scipio.

"I wish him a thousand; he will then prove the richer prize."

"I s'pose he'm quite a t'ousand, sir."

" Or a snug ship of three hundred, if lined with gold, might do.'

" He look berry just like t'ree hundred."

" To me it seems a brig."

" I t'ink him a brig, too, masser."

" Or, possibly, after all, the stranger may prove a schooner, with many lofty and light sails."

" A schooner often carry a royal," returned the black, resolute to acquiesce in all the other said.

" Who knows it is a sail at all! Forward there! It may be well to have more opinions than one on so weighty a matter. Forward there! send the foretopman that is called Fid upon the poop. Your companions are so intelligent and so faithful, Mr. Wilder, that you are not to be surprised if I show an undue desire for their opinions."

Wilder compressed his lips, and the rest of the group manifested a good deal of amazement; but the latter had been too long accustomed to the caprice of their commander, and the former was too wise, to speak at a moment when his humour seemed at the highest. The topman, however, was not long in making his appearance, and then the chief saw fit to pursue his purpose.

" And you think it questionable whether it be a sail at all ?" he continued.

" He'm sartain nothing but a fly-away," returned the obstinate black.

" You hear what your friend the negro says, Master Fid; he thinks that yonder object, which is lifting so fast to leeward, is not a sail."

As the topman saw no sufficient reason for concealing his astonishment at this wild opinion, it was manifested with all the embellishments with which the individual in question usually delivered his sentiments. After casting a short glance in the direction of the sail, in order to assure himself there had been no deception, he turned his eyes in great disgust on Scipio, to vindicate the credit of the association at the expense of some little contempt for the ignorance of his companion.

"What the devil do you take it for, Guinea? — a church?"

"I t'ink he'm church, too," responded the acquiescent black.

"Lord help the dark-skinn'd fool. Your honour knows that conscience is d——nably overlooked in Africa, and will not judge the nigger hardly for any little blunder he may make on account of religion. But the fellow is a thorough seaman, and should know a top-gallant-sail from a weathercock. Now, look you, S'ip, for the credit of your friends, if you've no great pride on your own behalf, just tell his——"

"It is of no account," interrupted the Rover; "take the glass yourself, and pass an opinion on the sail in sight."

Fid scraped his foot, made a low bow, in acknowledgment of the compliment, and then, depositing his little tarpaulin on the deck of the poop, he very composedly, and, as he flattered himself, very understandingly, disposed of his person to take the desired view. The gaze of the topman was far longer than that of his black companion; and it is to be presumed, in consequence, much more accurate. Instead, however, of venturing any sudden opinion, when his eye was wearied, he lowered the glass, and with it his head, standing long in the attitude of one whose thoughts had received some subject for deep cogitation. During the process of thinking, the weed was diligently rolled over his tongue, and one hand was stuck a-kimbo into his side, as if he would brace all his faculties to support some extraordinary mental effort.

"I wait your opinion," resumed his attentive commander, when he thought sufficient time had been allowed to mature the opinion even of Richard Fid.

"Will your honour just tell me what day of the month this here may be, and mayhap, at the same time, the day of the week too, if it shouldn't be giving too much trouble?"

His two questions were answered.

"We had the wind at east-with-southing, the first day out, and then it chopp'd in the night, and blew great guns at north-west, where it held for the matter of a week. After which there was an Irishman's hurricane, right up and down, for a day; then we got into these here trades, which have stood as steady as a ship's chaplain over a punch-bowl, ever since——"

Here the topman closed his soliloquy, in order to agitate the tobacco again, it being impossible to conduct the process of chewing and talking at one and the same time.

"What of the stranger?" demanded the Rover, a little impatiently.

"It's no church, that's certain, your honour," said Fid, very decidedly.

"Has he signals flying?"

"He may be speaking with his flags, but it needs a better scholar than Richard Fid to know what he would say. To my eye there are three new cloths in his main-top-gallant-royal,* but no bunting abroad."

"The man is happy in having so good a sail. Mr. Wilder, do *you*, too, see the cloths in question?"

"There is certainly something which might be taken for new canvass. I believe I first mistook it, as the sun fell brightest on the sail, for the signals I named."

"Then we are not seen, and may lie quiet for awhile, though we enjoy the advantage of measuring the stranger, foot by foot— even to the new cloths in his royal!"

The Rover spoke in a manner that was strangely divided be-

---

* It has been objected to this term, that the sail is called the main-royal. The writer is old enough to remember when seamen always inserted the other word, when they wished to speak with a "full mouth." Main-sail; main-top-sail; main-top-gallant-sail, main-top-gallant-royal, were, and indeed are still, the proper appellations of these sails. "Main-royal" is, beyond dispute, the familiar name now most in use.

tween sarcasm and suspicion. He made an impatient gesture to the seamen to quit the poop. When they were alone, he turned to his silent and respectful officers, continuing, in a manner that was grave while it was conciliatory,—

" Gentlemen," he said, " our idle time is past, and fortune has at length brought us active service. Whether the ship in sight be of just seven hundred and fifty tons, is more than I can pretend to pronounce, but something there is which any seaman may know. By the squareness of her upper-yards, the symmetry with which they are trimmed, and the press of canvass she bears on the wind, I pronounce her to be a vessel of war. Do any differ from my opinion? Mr. Wilder, speak."

" I feel the truth of all your reasons, and think with you."

The shade of distrust, which had gathered over the brow of the Rover during the foregoing scene, lighted a little as he listened to the direct and frank avowal of his lieutenant.

" You believe she bears a pennant? I like this manliness of reply. Then comes another question : shall we fight her?"

To this interrogatory it was not so easy to give a decisive answer. Each officer consulted the opinions of his comrades in their eyes, until their leader saw fit to make his application still more personal.

" Now, general, this is a question peculiarly fitted for your wisdom," he resumed. " Shall we give battle to a pennant? or shall we spread our wings and fly?"

" My bullies are not drilled to the retreat. Give them any other work to do, and I will answer for their steadiness."

" But shall we adventure, without a reason ?"

" The Spaniard often sends his bullion home under the cover of a cruiser's guns," observed one of the inferiors, who rarely found pleasure in any risk that did not infer its correspondent benefit. " We may feel the stranger; if he carries more than his guns, he will betray it by his reluctance to speak; if poor, we shall find him fierce as a half-fed tiger."

"There is sense in your counsel, Brace, and it shall be regarded. Go then, gentlemen, to your several duties. We'll occupy the half-hour that must pass, before his hull shall rise, in looking to our gear, and overhauling the guns. As it is not decided to fight, let what is done be done without display. The people must see no receding from a resolution that is once taken."

They separated, each man preparing to undertake the task that more especially belonged to the situation he filled in the ship. Wilder was retiring with the rest, when a sign kept him on the poop alone with his new confederate.

"The monotony of our lives is now likely to be interrupted, Mr. Wilder," commenced the former, first glancing his eye around to make sure they were alone. "I have seen enough of your spirit and steadiness to be sure that, should accident disable me to conduct the fortunes of these people, my authority will fall into firm and able hands."

"Should such a calamity befall us, I hope it will be found that your expectations are not to be deceived."

"I have confidence, sir; and, where a brave man reposes his confidence, he has a right to hope it will not be abused. Do I speak in reason?"

"I acknowledge the justice of what you say."

"I would, Wilder, that we had known each other earlier. But what matter vain regrets? These fellows of yours are keen of sight to note those new cloths so soon!"

"'T is just the observation of people of their class. The nicer distinctions which marked the cruiser came first from yourself!"

"And then 'the seven hundred and fifty tons' of the black! It was giving an opinion to a foot."

" It is the quality of ignorance to be positive."

" Very true. Cast an eye at the stranger, and tell me how he comes on."

Wilder obeyed, glad to be relieved from a discourse that he found embarrassing. Many moments were passed before he dropped the glass, during which time not a syllable fell from the lips of his companion. When he turned, however, to deliver the result of his observations, he met an eye, that seemed to pierce his soul, fastened on his countenance. Colouring highly, as if he resented the suspicion betrayed by the act, Wilder closed his half-open lips, and continued silent.

" And the ship?" deeply demanded the Rover.

" The ship has already raised her courses; in a few more minutes we shall see the hull."

" It is a swift vessel! She is standing directly for us."

" I think not. Her head is lying more to the eastward."

" It may be well to make certain of that fact. You are right," he continued, after taking a look himself at the approaching cloud of canvass; " you are very right. As yet we are not seen. For-ward there! haul down that head stay-sail; we will steady the ship by her yards. Now let him look with all his eyes; they must be good to see these naked spars at such a distance."

Our adventurer made no reply, assenting to the truth of what the other had said by a simple inclination of his head. They then resumed the walk to and fro in their narrow limits, neither manifesting, however, any disposition to renew the discourse.

" We are in good condition for the alternative of flight or combat," the Rover at length observed, while he cast a rapid look over the preparations which had been unostentatiously in progress from the moment when the officers dispersed. " Now will I confess, Wilder, a secret pleasure in the belief that yonder audacious fool carries the boasted commission of the German who wears the crown of Britain. Should he prove more than man may dare attempt, I will flout him, though prudence shall check any further attempts; and, should he prove an equal, would it not gladden your eyes to see St. George come drooping to the water?"

"I thought that men in our pursuit left honour to silly heads, and that we seldom struck a blow that was not intended to ring on a metal more precious than iron."

"'T is the character the world gives us; but I, for one, would rather lower the pride of the minions of King George, than possess the power of unlocking his treasury! Said I well, general?" he added, as the individual he named approached; "said I well, in asserting there was glorious pleasure in making a pennant trail upon the sea?"

"We fight for victory," returned the martinet. "I am ready to engage at a minute's notice."

"Prompt and decided as a soldier. Now tell me, general, if Fortune, or Chance, or Providence, whichever of the powers you may acknowledge for a leader, were to give you the option of enjoyments, in what would you find your deepest satisfaction?"

The soldier seemed to ruminate.

"I have often thought that, were I commander of things on earth, I should, backed by a dozen of my stoutest bullies, charge at the door of that cave which was entered by the tailor's boy, him they call Aladdin."

"The genuine aspirations of a freebooter! In such a case, the magic trees would soon be disburdened of their fruit. Still it might prove an inglorious victory, since incantations and charms are the weapons of the combatants. Call you honour nothing?"

"Hum! I fought for honour half of a reasonably long life, and found myself as light at the close of all my dangers as at the beginning. Honour and I have shaken hands, unless it be the honour of coming off conqueror. I have a strong disgust of defeat, but am always ready to sell the mere honour of the victory cheap."

"Well, let it pass. The quality of the service is much the same, find the motive where you will. How now! who has dared to let yonder top-gallant-sail fly?"

The startling change in the voice of the Rover caused all within hearing of his words to tremble. Deep, anxious, and threatening displeasure was in its tones; and each man cast his eyes upwards, to see on whose devoted head the weight of the dreaded indignation of their chief was likely to fall. As there was little but naked spars and tightened ropes to obstruct the view, all became, at the same instant, apprised of the truth. Fid was standing on the head of that topmast which belonged to the particular portion of the vessel where he was stationed, and the sail in question was fluttering, with all its gear loosened, far and high in the wind. His hearing had probably been drowned by the heavy flapping of the canvass; for, instead of lending his ears to the powerful call just mentioned, he rather stood contemplating his work, than exhibiting any anxiety as to the effect it might produce on the minds of those beneath him. But a second warning came in tones too terrible to be any longer disregarded by ears even as dull as those of the offender.

"By whose order have you dared to loosen the sail?" demanded the Rover.

"By the order of King Wind, your honour. The best seaman must give in, when a squall gets the upper hand."

"Furl it! away aloft, and furl it!" shouted the excited leader. "Roll it up; and send the fellow down who has been so bold as to own any authority but my own in this ship, though it were that of a hurricane."

A dozen nimble topmen ascended to the assistance of Fid. In another minute the unruly canvass was secured, and Richard himself was on his way to the poop. During this brief interval, the brow of the Rover was dark and angry as the surface of the element on which he lived, when blackened by the tempest. Wilder, who had never before seen his new commander thus excited, began to tremble for the fate of his old comrade, and drew nigher as the latter approached, to intercede in his favour, should the circumstances seem to require such an interposition.

" And why is this ?" the still stern and angry captain demanded of the offender. " Why is it that you, whom I have had such recent reason to applaud, should dare to let fall a sail, at a moment when it is important to keep the ship naked?"

" Your honour will admit that his rations sometimes slips through the best man's fingers, and why not a bit of canvass?" deliberately returned the delinquent. " If I took a turn too many of the gasket off the yard, it is a fault I am ready to answer for."

" You say true, and dearly shall you pay the forfeit. Take him to the gangway, and let him make acquaintance with the cat."

" No new acquaintance, your honour, seeing that we have met before, and that, too, for matters which I had reason to hide my head for; whereas, here, it may be many blows, and little shame.' "

" May I intercede in behalf of the offender?" interrupted Wilder, with earnestness and haste. " He is often blundering, but rarely would he err, had he as much knowledge as good-will."

" Say nothing about it, Master Harry," returned the topman, with a peculiar glance of his eye. " The sail has been flying finely, and it is now too late to deny it; and so, I suppose, the fact must be scored on the back of Richard Fid, as you would put any other misfortune into the log."

" I would he might be pardoned. I can venture to promise, in his name, 't will be the last offence——"

"Let it be forgotten," returned the Rover, struggling to conquer his passion. "I will not disturb our harmony at such a moment, Mr. Wilder, by refusing so small a boon; but you need not be told to what evil such negligence might lead. Give me the glass again; I will see if the fluttering canvass has escaped the eye of the stranger."

The topman bestowed a stolen but exulting glance on Wilder, when the latter motioned the other hastily away, turning himself to join his commander in the examination.

# CHAPTER XXVI.

As I am an honest man, he looks pale. Art thou sick or angry?
                                        *Much ado about Nothing.*

THE approach of the strange sail was becoming rapidly more and more visible to the naked eye. The little speck of white, which had first been seen on the margin of the sea, resembling some gull floating on the summit of a wave, had gradually arisen during the last half-hour, until a tall pyramid of canvass was reared on the water. As Wilder bent his look again on this growing object, the Rover put a glass into his hands, with an expression which the other understood to say, "You may perceive that the carelessness of your dependant has betrayed us!" Still the look was one rather of regret than of reproach; nor did a single syllable of the tongue confirm the language of the eye. On the contrary, it would seem that his commander was anxious to preserve their recent amicable compact inviolate; for, when the young mariner attempted an awkward explanation of the probable causes of the blunder of Fid, he was met by a quiet gesture, which said, in a sufficiently intelligible language, that the offence was pardoned.

"Our neighbour keeps a good look-out, as you may see," observed the other. "He has tacked, and is laying boldly up across our forefoot. Well, let him come on; we shall soon get a look at his battery, and then we may form our conclusion as to the nature of the intercourse we are to hold."

"If you permit the stranger to near us, it might be difficult to throw him off the chase, should we be glad to get rid of him."

"It must be a fast-going vessel, to which the Dolphin cannot spare a top-gallant-sail."

"I know not, sir. The sail in sight is swift on the wind, and it is to be believed that she is no duller off. I have rarely known a vessel rise so rapidly as she has done since we first made her."

The youth spoke with such earnestness, as to draw the attention of his companion from the object he was studying to the countenance of the speaker.

"Mr. Wilder," he said, quickly, and with an air of decision, "you know the ship?"

"I'll not deny it. If my opinion be true, she will be found too heavy for the Dolphin, and a vessel that offers little inducement for us to attempt to carry."

"Her size?"

"You heard it from the black."

"Your followers know her also?"

"It would be difficult to deceive a topman in the cut and trim of sails, among which he has passed months—nay years."

"Ha! I understand the 'new cloths' in her top-gallant-royal! Mr. Wilder, your departure from that vessel has been recent?"

"As my arrival in this."

The Rover continued silent for several minutes. His companion made no offer to disturb his meditations; though the furtive glances he often cast in the direction of the other betrayed some little anxiety for the result of his own frank avowal.

"And her guns?" his commander at length abruptly demanded.

"She numbers four more than the Dolphin."

"The metal?"

"Is still heavier. In every particular she is a ship a size above your own."

"Doubtless she is the property of the king?"

"She is."

"She shall change masters. By Heaven, she shall be mine!"

Wilder shook his head, answering only with an incredulous smile.

"You doubt it. Come hither, and look upon that deck. Can he, whom you so lately quitted, muster fellows like these?"

The crew of the Dolphin had been chosen, by one who thoroughly understood the character of a seaman, from among all the different people of the Christian world. There was not a maritime nation in Europe which had not its representative among that band of turbulent and desperate spirits. Even the descendant of the aboriginal possessors of America had been made to abandon the habits and opinions of his progenitors, to become a wanderer on that element which had laved the shores of his native land for ages, without exciting a wish to penetrate its mysteries in the bosoms of his simple-minded ancestry. All had been fitted, by lives of wild adventure on the two elements, for their present lawless pursuits; and, directed by the mind which had known how to obtain and to continue its despotic ascendency over their efforts, they truly formed a most dangerous and (considering their numbers) a resistless crew. Their commander smiled in exultation, as he watched the evident reflection with which his companion contemplated the indifference, or fierce joy, which different individuals among them exhibited at the appearance of an approaching conflict. Even the rawest of their numbers, the luckless waisters and afterguard, were as confident of victory as those whose audacity might plead the apology of uniform and often repeated success.

"Count you these for nothing?" asked the Rover, at the elbow of his lieutenant, after allowing him time to embrace the whole of the grim band with his eye. "See! here is a Dane; ponderous and steady as the gun at which I shall shortly place him. You may cut him limb from limb, and yet he will stand like a tower, until the last stone of the foundation has been sapped. And here we have his neighbours, the Swede and the Russ, fit companions for managing the same piece; which, I'll answer, shall not be silent, while a man of them all is left to apply a match, or handle a sponge. Yonder is a square-built, athletic mariner, from one of the free towns. He prefers our liberty to that of his native city; and you shall find that the venerable Hanseatic institutions shall give way sooner than he be known to quit the spot I give him to defend. Here you see a brace of Englishmen; and, though they come from the island that I love so little, better men at need will not be often found. Feed them and flog them, and I pledge myself to their swaggering and their courage. D'ye see that thoughtful-looking, bony miscreant, that has a look of godliness in the midst of his villany? That fellow fished for herring till he got a taste of beef, when his stomach revolted at its ancient fare; and then the ambition of becoming rich got uppermost. He is a Scot, from one of the lochs of the North."

"Will he fight?"

"For money — the honour of the Macs — and his religion. He is a reasoning fellow, after all; and I like to have him on my own side in a quarrel. Ah! yonder is the boy for a charge. I once told him to cut a rope in a hurry, and he severed it above his head instead of beneath his feet, taking a flight from a lower yard into the sea, as a reward for the exploit. But, then, he always extols his presence of mind in not drowning! Now are his ideas in a hot ferment; and, if the truth could be known, I would wager a handsome venture that the sail in sight is, by some mysterious process, magnified to six in his fertile fancy."

"He must be thinking, then, of escape?"

"Far from it; he is rather plotting the means of surrounding them with the Dolphin. To your true Hibernian, escape is the last idea that gives him an uneasy moment. You 'see that pensive-looking, sallow mortal, at his elbow. That is a man who will fight with a sort of sentiment. There is a touch of chivalry in him, which might be worked into heroism, if one had but the opportunity and the inclination. As it is, he will not fail to show a spark of the true Castilian. His companion has come from the Rock of Lisbon; I should trust him unwillingly, did I not know that little opportunity of taking pay from the enemy is given here. Ah! here is a lad for a dance of a Sunday. You see him at this moment, with foot and tongue going together. That is a creature of contradictions. He wants for neither wit nor good-nature, but still he might cut your throat on an occasion. There is a strange medley of ferocity and *bonhommie* about the animal. I shall put him among the boarders; for we shall not be at blows a minute before his impatience will be for carrying every thing by a *coup-de-main.*"

"And who is the seaman at his elbow, that apparently is occupied in divesting his person of some superfluous garments?" demanded Wilder, irresistibly attracted by the manner of the Rover to pursue the subject.

"An economical Dutchman. He calculates that it is just as wise to be killed in an old jacket as in a new one; and has probably said as much to his Gascon neighbour, who is, however, resolved to die decently, if die he must. The former has happily commenced his preparations for the combat in good season, or the enemy might defeat us before he would be in readiness. Did it rest between these two worthies to decide this quarrel, the mercurial Frenchman would defeat his neighbour of Holland before the latter believed the battle had commenced; but should he let the happy moment pass, rely on it the Dutchman would give him trouble. Forget you, Wilder. that the day has been when the countrymen of that slow-moving and heavy-moulded fellow swept the narrow seas with a broom at their mast-heads?"

The Rover smiled wildly as he spoke, and what he said he uttered bitterly. To his companion, however, there appeared no such grounds of unnatural exultation in recalling the success of a foreign enemy, and he was content to assent to the truth of the historical fact with a simple inclination of his head. As if he even found pain in this tacit confession, and would gladly be rid of the mortifying reflection altogether, he rejoined, in some apparent haste,—

"You have overlooked the two tall seamen, who are making out the rig of the stranger with so much gravity of observation."

"Ay, those are men that came from a land in which we both feel some interest. The sea is not more unstable than are those rogues in their knavery. Their minds are but half made up to piracy. 'Tis a coarse word, Mr. Wilder, but I fear we earn it. But these rascals make a reservation of grace in the midst of all their villany."

"They regard the stranger as if they saw reason to distrust the wisdom of letting him approach so near."

"Ah! they are renowned calculators. I fear they have detected the four supernumerary guns you mentioned; for their vision seems supernatural in affairs which touch their interests. But you see there is brawn and sinew in the fellows; and, what is better, there are heads which teach them to turn those advantages to account."

"You think they fail in spirit?"

"Hum! It might be dangerous to try it on any point they deem material. They are no quarrellers about words, and seldom lose sight of certain musty maxims, which they pretend come from a volume that I fear you and I do not study too intently. It is not often that they strike a blow for mere chivalry; and, were they so inclined, the rogues are too much disposed to logic, to mistake, like your black, the Dolphin for a church. Still, if they see reason, in their puissant judgments, to engage, mark me, the two guns they command will do better service than all the rest of the battery. Should they think otherwise, it would occasion no surprise were I to receive a proposition to spare the powder for some more profitable adventure. Honour, forsooth! the miscreants are too well practised in polemics to mistake the point of honour in a pursuit like ours. But we chatter of trifles, when it is time to think of serious things. Mr. Wilder, we will now show our canvass."

The manner of the Rover changed as suddenly as his language. Losing the air of sarcastic levity in which he had been indulging, in a mien better suited to maintain the authority he wielded, he walked aside, while his subordinate proceeded to issue the orders necessary to enforce his commands. Nightingale sounded the usual summons, lifting his hoarse voice in the cry of " All hands make sail, ahoy !''

Until now, the people of the Dolphin had made their observations on the sail that was growing so rapidly above the waters, according to their several humours. Some had exulted in the prospect of a capture; others, more practised in the ways of their commander, had deemed the probability of their coming in collision at all with the stranger a point far from settled; while a few, more accustomed to reflection, shook their heads as the stranger drew nigher, as if they believed he was already within a distance that might be attended with too much hazard. Still, as they were ignorant alike of those secret sources of information which the chief had so frequently proved he possessed, to an extent that often seemed miraculous, the whole were content patiently to await his decision. But, when the cry above mentioned was heard, it was answered by an activity so general and so cheerful, as to prove it was entirely welcome. Order now followed order from the mouth of Wilder, in quick succession, he being, in virtue of his station, the proper executive officer for the moment.

As both lieutenant and crew appeared animated by the same spirit, it was not long before the naked spars of the Dolphin were clothed in vast volumes of snow-white canvass. Sail had fallen after sail, and yard after yard had been raised to the summit of its mast, until the vessel bowed before the breeze, rolling to and fro, but still held stationary by the position of her yards. When all was in readiness to proceed, on whichever course might be deemed necessary, Wilder ascended again to the poop, in order to announce the fact to his superior. He found the Rover attentively considering the stranger, whose hull had by this time risen out of the sea, exhibiting a long, dotted, yellow line, which the eye of every man in the ship well knew to contain the ports where the guns that marked her particular force were to be sought. Mrs. Wyllys, accompanied by Gertrude, stood nigh, thoughtful, as usual, but permitting no occurrence of the slightest moment to escape her vigilance.

" We are ready to gather way on the ship," said Wilder; " we wait merely for the course."

The Rover started, and drew closer to his subordinate. Looking him full and intently in the eye, he said,—

" You are certain that you know that vessel, Mr. Wilder?"

" Certain."

" It is a royal cruiser," said the governess with the swiftness of thought.

" It is. I have already pronounced her to be so."

" Mr. Wilder," resumed the Rover, " we will try her speed. Let the courses fall, and fill your forward sails."

The young mariner made an acknowledgment of obedience, and proceeded with alacrity to execute the wishes of his commander. There was an eagerness, and perhaps a trepidation, in the voice of Wilder, as he issued the necessary orders, that was in remarkable contrast to the deep-toned calmness which characterised the utterance of the Rover. The unusual intonations did not entirely escape the ears of some of the elder seamen ; and looks of peculiar meaning were exchanged among them, as they paused to catch his words. But obedience followed these unwonted sounds, as it had been accustomed to succeed the more imposing utterance of their own long-dreaded chief. The head-yards were swung, the sails were distended with the breeze, and the mass, which had so long been inert, began to divide the waters, as it heavily overcame the state of rest in which it had reposed. The ship soon attained its velocity; and then the contest between the two rival vessels became of engrossing interest.

By this time the stranger was within a half-league, directly under the lee of the Dolphin. Closer and more accurate observation had satisfied every eye in the latter ship of the force and character of their neighbour. The rays of a bright sun fell clear upon her broadside, while the shadow of her sails was thrown across the waters, in a direction opposite to their own. There were moments when the eye, aided by the glass, could penetrate through the open ports into the interior of the hull, catching fleeting and delusory glimpses of the movements within. A few human forms were distinctly visible in different parts of her rigging; but, in all other respects, the repose of high order and perfect discipline was discernable in all about her.

When the Rover heard the sounds of the parted waters, and saw the little jets of spray that the bows of his own gallant ship cast before her, he signed to his lieutenant to ascend to the place which he still occupied on the poop. For many minutes, his eye was on the strange sail, in close and intelligent contemplation of her powers.

" Mr. Wilder," he at length said, speaking like one whose doubts on some perplexing point were finally removed, " I have seen that cruiser before."

" It is probable; she has roamed over most of the waters of the Atlantic."

" Ay, this is not the first of our meetings! A little paint has changed her exterior, but I think I know the manner in which they have stepp'd her masts."

" They are thought to rake more than is usual "

" They are thought to do it with reason. Did you serve long aboard her?"

" Years."

" And you left her——"

" To join you."

" Tell me, Wilder, did they treat you, too, as one of an inferior order? Ha! was your merit called 'provincial?' Did they read America in all you did?"

" I left her, Captain Heidegger."

" Ay, they gave you reason. For once they have done me an act of kindness. But you were in her during the equinox of March?"

Wilder made a slight bow of assent.

" I thought as much. And you fought a stranger in the gale? Winds, ocean, and man, were all at work together."

" It is true. We knew you, and thought for a time that your hour had come."

" I like your frankness. We have sought each other's lives like men, and we shall prove the truer friends, now that amity is established between us. I will not ask you further of that adventure, Wilder; for favour, in my service, is not to be bought by treachery to that you have quitted. It is sufficient that you now sail under my flag."

" What is that flag?" demanded a mild firm voice at his elbow.

The Rover turned suddenly, and met the riveted, calm, and searching eye of the governess. The gleamings of some strangely

contradictory passions crossed his features, and then his countenance changed to that look of bland courtesy which he most
affected when addressing his captives.

"Here is a female reminding two old mariners of their duty!"
he exclaimed. "We have forgotten the civility of showing the
stranger our bunting. Let it be set, Mr. Wilder, that we omit
none of the observances of nautical etiquette."

"The ship in sight carries a naked gaft."

"No matter; we shall be foremost in courtesy. Let the colours
be shown."

Wilder opened the little locker which contained the flags most
in use, but hesitated which to select, out of a dozen that lay in
large rolls within the different compartments.

"I hardly know which of these ensigns it is your pleasure to
show," he said, in a manner that appeared sufficiently like putting
a question.

"Try him with the heavy-moulded Dutchman. The commander of so noble a ship should understand all Christian
tongues."

The lieutenant made a sign to the quarter-master on duty;
and, in another minute, the flag of the United Provinces was
waving at the peak of the Dolphin. The two officers narrowly
watched its effect on the stranger, who refused, however, to make
any answering sign to the false signal they had just exhibited.

"The stranger sees we have a hull that was never made for the
shoals of Holland. Perhaps he knows us?" said the Rover,
glancing at the same time a look of enquiry at his companion.

"I think not. Paint is too freely used in the Dolphin for even
her friends to be certain of her countenance."

"She is a coquettish ship, we will allow. Try him with the
Portuguese: let us see if Brazil diamonds have favour in his
eyes."

The colours already set were lowered, and, in their place, the

emblem of the house of Braganza was loosened to the breeze.
Still the stranger pursued his course in sullen inattention, eating
closer and closer into the wind, as it is termed in nautical language, in order to lessen the distance between him and his chase
as much as possible.

"An ally cannot move him," said the Rover. "Now let him
see the taunting *drapeau blanc*."

Wilder complied in silence. The flag of Portugal was hauled
to the deck, and the white field of France was given to the air.
The ensign had hardly fluttered in its elevated position, before a
broad, glossy blazonry rose, like some enormous bird taking
wing, from the deck of the stranger, and opened its folds in
graceful waves at his gaft. The same instant, a column of
smoke issued from his bows, and had sailed backward through
his rigging, ere the report of the gun of defiance found its way,
against the fresh breeze of the trades, to the ears of the Dolphin's
crew.

"So much for national amity!" dryly observed the Rover.
"He is mute to the Dutchman, and to the crown of Braganza;
but the very bile is stirred within him at the sight of a table-
cloth! Let him contemplate the colours he loves so little, Mr.
Wilder; when we are tired of showing them, our lockers will
furnish another."

It would seem, however, that the sight of the flag which the
Rover now chose to bear produced some such effect on his neighbour as the moleta of the nimble banderillo is known to excite
in the enraged bull. Sundry smaller sails, which could do but
little good, but which answered the purpose of appearing to wish
to quicken his speed, were instantly set aboard the stranger; and
not a brace, or a bowline, was suffered to escape without an additional pull. In short, he wore the air of the courser who re-
ceives the useless blows of the jockey when already at the top
of his speed, and when any further excitement is as fruitless as

his own additional exertions. Still there seemed but little use in these efforts. By this time, the two vessels were fairly trying their powers of sailing, and with no visible advantage in favour of either. Although the Dolphin was renowned for her speed, the stranger manifested no inferiority that the keenest scrutiny might detect. The ship of the freebooter was already bending to the breeze, and the jets of spray before her were cast still higher and farther in advance; but each impulse of the wind was equally felt by the stranger, and her movement over the heaving waters seemed to be as rapid and as graceful as that of her rival.

"Yonder ship parts the water as a swallow cuts the air," observed the chief of the freebooters to the youth, who still kept at his elbow, endeavouring to conceal an uneasiness which was increasing at each instant. "Has she a name for speed?"

"The curlew is scarcely faster. Are we not already nigh enough, for men who cruise with commissions no better than our own pleasure?"

The Rover glanced a look of impatient suspicion at the countenance of his companion; but its expression changed to a smile of haughty audacity, as he answered,—

"Let him equal the eagle in his highest and swiftest flight, he shall find us no laggards on the wing! Why this reluctance to be within a mile of a vessel of the crown?"

"Because I know her force, and the hopeless character of a contest with an enemy so superior," returned Wilder, firmly. "Captain Heidegger, you cannot fight yonder ship with success; and, unless instant use be made of the distance which still exists between us, you cannot escape her. Indeed, I know not but it is already too late to attempt the latter."

"Such, sir, is the opinion of one who over-rates the powers of his enemy, because use, and much talking, have taught him to reverence it as something more than human. Mr. Wilder, none are so daring, or so modest, as those who have long been accustomed to place their dependence on their own exertions  I have been nigher to a flag even, and yet you see I continue to keep on this mortal coil.''

" Hark ! 'T is a drum.  The stranger is going to his guns.''

The Rover listened a moment, and was able to catch the well-known beat which calls the people of a vessel of war to their quarters.  First casting a glance upwards at his sails, and then throwing a general and critical look on all and every thing which came within the influence of his command, he calmly answered,—

" We will imitate his example, Mr. Wilder.  Let the order be given.''

Until now, the crew of the Dolphin had either been occupied in such necessary duties as precede an action, or were gazing at the strange ship.  The low but continued hum of voices, sounds such as discipline permitted, had afforded the only evidence of the interest they took in the scene; but the instant the first tap on the drum was heard, each group severed, and every man repaired, with bustling activity, to his well-known station.  The stir among the crew was but of a moment's continuance ; it was succeeded by the breathing stillness which has already been noticed in our pages on a similar occasion.  The officers, however, were seen making hasty, but strict, enquiries into the conditions of their several commands; while the munitions of war, that were drawn from their places of deposit, announced a preparation more serious than ordinary.  The Rover himself had disappeared ; but it was not long before he was again seen at his elevated look-out, accoutred for the conflict that appeared to approach, and employed, as ever, in studying the properties, the force, and the evolutions of his advancing antagonist.  Those who knew him best, however, said that the question of combat was not yet decided in his mind; and many eager glances were thrown in the direction of his eye, as if to penetrate the mystery in which he chose to conceal his purpose.   He had thrown aside the sea-cap, and stood with his fair hair blowing about a brow that seemed formed to give birth to thoughts far nobler than those which apparently had occupied his life; while a species of leathern helmet lay at his feet; the garniture of which was of a nature to lend an unnatural fierceness to the countenance of its wearer.   Whenever this boarding-cap was worn, all in the ship were given to understand that the moment of serious strife was at hand; but, as yet, that never-failing evidence of the hostile intention of their leader was unnoticed.

In the mean time, each officer had examined into and reported the state of his division; and then, by a sort of implied permission on the part of their superiors, the death-like calm, which had hitherto reigned among the people, was allowed to be broken by suppressed but earnest discourse; the calculating chief permitting this departure from the usual rules of more regular cruisers, in order to come at the temper of the crew, on which so much of the success of his desperate enterprises so frequently depended.

# CHAPTER XXVII

——For he made me mad,
To see him shine so brisk, and smell so sweet,
And talk so like a waiting gentlewoman.
*King Henry IV.*

THE moment was one of high and earnest excitement. Each individual charged with a portion of the subordinate authority of the ship had examined into the state of his command, with the care which always deepens as responsibility draws nigher to the proofs of having been worthily bestowed. The voice of the harsh master had ceased to enquire into the state of those several ropes and chains that were deemed vital to the safety of the vessel; each chief of a battery had assured and re-assured himself that his artillery was ready for the most effective service; extra ammunition had already issued from its dark and secret repository; and even the hum of dialogue had ceased in the all-absorbing interest of the scene. Still the quick and ever-changing glance of the Rover could detect no reason to distrust the firmness of his people. They were grave, as are ever the bravest and steadiest in the hour of trial; but their gravity was mingled with no signs of concern. It seemed rather like the effect of desperate and concentrated resolution, such as braces the human mind to efforts which exceed the ordinary daring of martial enterprise. To this satisfactory exhibition of the humour of his crew the wary and sagacious leader saw but three exceptions; they were found in the persons of his lieutenant and his two remarkable associates.

It has been seen that the bearing of Wilder was not altogether such as became one of his rank in a moment of great trial. The keen, jealous glances of the Rover studied and re-studied his manner, without arriving at any conclusion as to its cause. The colour was as fresh on the cheeks of the youth, and his limbs were as firm, as in the hours of entire security; but the unsettled wandering of his eye, and an air of doubt and indecision which pervaded a mien that ought to display qualities so opposite, gave his commander concern. As if to find an explanation of the enigma in the deportment of the associates of Wilder, his look turned to the persons of Fid and the negro. They were both stationed at the piece nearest to the place he himself occupied, the former filling the station of captain of the gun.

The ribs of the ship itself were not firmer in their places than was the attitude of the topman, as he occasionally squinted along the massive iron tube over which he was placed in command; nor was that familiar and paternal care, which distinguishes the seaman's interest in his particular trust, wanting in his manner. Still, an air of broad and inexplicable surprise had possession of his rugged lineaments; and as his look wandered from the countenance of Wilder to their adversary, it was not difficult to discover that he marvelled to find the two in opposition. He neither commented on, nor complained, however, of an occurrence he evidently found so extraordinary, but appeared perfectly disposed to pursue the spirit of that well-known maxim of the mariner, which teaches the obedient tar "to obey orders, though he break owners." Every portion of the athletic form of the negro was motionless, except his eyes. These large, jet-black orbs, however, rolled incessantly, like the more dogmatic organs of the topman, from Wilder to the strange sail, seeming to drink in fresh draughts of astonishment at each new look.

Struck by these evident manifestations of some extraordinary and yet common sentiment between the two, the Rover profited by his own position, and the distance of the lieutenant, to address them. Leaning over the slight rail that separated the break of the poop from the quarter-deck, he said, in that familiar manner which the commander is most wont to use to his inferiors when their services are becoming of the greatest importance,—

"I hope, Master Fid, they have put you at a gun to your liking?"

"There is not a smoother bore, nor a wider mouth, in the ship, your honour, than these of 'Blazing Billy,' " returned the topman, giving the subject of his commendations an affectionate slap. "All I ask is a clean sponge and a tight wad. Guinea, score a foul anchor, in your own fashion, on a half-dozen of the shot; and, after the matter is over, they who live through it may go aboard the enemy, and see in what manner Richard Fid has planted his seed."

"You are not new in action, Master Fid?"

"Lord bless your honour! gunpowder is no more than dry tobacco in my nostrils! tho'f I will say——"

"You were going to add——"

"That sometimes I find myself shifted over, in these here affairs," returned the topman, glancing his eye first at the flag of France, and then at the distant emblem of England, "like a jib-boom rigged abaft, for a jury to the spanker. I suppose Master Harry has it all in his pocket, in black and white; but this much I will say, that if I must throw stones, I should rather see them break a neighbour's crockery, than that of my own mother. I say, Guinea, score a couple more of the shot; since, if the play is to be acted, I've a mind the 'Blazing Billy' should do something creditable for the honour of her good name."

The Rover drew back, thoughtful and silent. He caught a look from Wilder, whom he again beckoned to approach.

"Mr. Wilder," he said, in a tone of kindness, "I comprehend your feelings. All have not offended alike in yonder vessel, and you would rather your service against that haughty flag should commence with some other ship. There is little else but empty honour to be gained in the conflict — in tenderness to your feelings, I will avoid it."

"It is too late," said Wilder, with a melancholy shake of the head.

"You shall see your error. The experiment may cost us a broadside, but it shall succeed. Go, descend with our guests to a place of safety : by the time you return, the scene will have undergone a change."

Wilder eagerly disappeared in the cabin, whither Mrs. Wyllys had already withdrawn ; and, after communicating the intentions of his commander to avoid an action, he conducted them into the depths of the vessel, in order that no casualty might arrive to embitter his recollections of the hour. This grateful duty promptly and solicitously performed, our adventurer again sought the deck with the velocity of thought.

Notwithstanding his absence had seemed but a moment, the scene had indeed changed in all its hostile images. In place of the flag of France, he found the ensign of England floating at the peak of the Dolphin, and a quick and intelligible exchange of signals in active operation between the two vessels. Of all that cloud of canvass which had so lately borne down the vessel of the Rover, her top-sails alone remained distended to the yards; the remainder was hanging in festoons, and fluttering loosely before a favourable breeze. The ship itself was running directly for the stranger, who, in turn, was sullenly securing his lofty sails, like one who was disappointed in a high-prized and expected object.

"Now is yon fellow sorry to believe him a friend whom he had lately supposed an enemy," said the Rover, directing the attention of his lieutenant to the confiding manner with which their neighbour suffered himself to be deceived by his surreptitiously obtained signals. "It is a tempting offer; but I pass it, Wilder, for your sake."

The gaze of the lieutenant seemed bewildered, but he made no reply. Indeed, little time was given for deliberation or discourse. The Dolphin rolled swiftly along her briny path, and each moment dissipated the mist in which distance had enveloped the lesser objects on board the stranger. Guns, blocks, ropes, bolts, men, and even features became visible, in rapid succession, as the water that divided them was parted by the bows of the lawless ship. In a few minutes the stranger, having secured most of his lighter canvass, came sweeping up to the wind; and then, as his after-sails, squared for the purpose, took the breeze on their outer surface, the mass of his hull became stationary.

The people of the Dolphin had so far imitated the confiding credulity of the deceived cruiser of the crown, as to furl all their lofty duck, each man employed in the service trusting implicitly to the discretion and daring of the singular being whose pleasure it was to bring their ship into so hazardous a proximity to a powerful enemy — qualities that had been known to avail them in circumstances of even greater delicacy than those in which they were now placed. With this air of audacious confidence, the dreaded Rover came gliding down upon her unsuspecting neighbour, until within a few hundred feet of her weather-beam, when she, too, with a graceful curve in her course, bore up against the breeze and came to a state of rest. But Wilder, who regarded all the movements of his superior in silent amazement, was not slow in observing that the head of the Dolphin was laid a different way from that of the other, and that her progress had been arrested by the counteracting position of her head-yards; a circumstance that afforded the advantage of a quicker command of the ship, should there be need to require a sudden recourse to the guns.

The Dolphin was still drifting slowly under the influence of

19

her recent motion, when the customary hoarse and nearly unintelligible summons came over the water, demanding her appellation and character.   The Rover applied his trumpet to his lips,
with a glance directed towards his lieutenant, and returned the
name of a ship in the service of the king, that was known to be
of the size and force of his own vessel.

"Ay, ay," returned a voice from the other ship, "'twas so, I
made out your signals."

The hail was then reciprocated, and the name of the royal
cruiser given in return, followed by an invitation from her commander to visit his superior.

Thus far, no more had occurred than was usual between seamen in the same service; but the affair was rapidly arriving at
a point that most men would have found too embarrassing for
further deception.   Still the observant eye of Wilder detected no
hesitation or doubt in the manner of his chief.   The beat of the
drum was heard from the cruiser, announcing the "retreat from
quarters;" and, with perfect composure, he directed the same
signal to be given for his own people to retire from their guns.
In short, five minutes established every appearance of entire confidence and amity between two vessels which would have soon
been at deadly strife, had the true character of one been known
to the other.   In this state of the doubtful game he played, and
with the invitation still ringing in the ears of Wilder, the Rover
motioned his lieutenant to his side.

"You hear that I am desired to visit my senior in the service
of his majesty," he said, smiling ironically.   "Is it your pleasure
to be of the party?"

The start with which Wilder received this hardy proposal was
far too natural to proceed from any counterfeited emotion.

"You are not so mad as to run the risk!" he exclaimed, when
words were at command.

"If you fear for yourself, I can go alone."

"Fear!" echoed the youth, a bright flush giving an additional glow to the flashing of his kindling eyes. "It is not fear, Captain Heidegger, but prudence that tells me to keep concealed. My presence would betray the character of this ship. You forget that I am known to all in yonder cruiser."

"I had indeed forgotten that portion of the plot. Then remain while I go to play upon the credulity of his majesty's captain."

Without waiting for an answer, the Rover led the way below, signing for his companion to follow. A few moments sufficed to arrange the fair golden locks that imparted such a look of youth and vivacity to the countenance of the former. The undress, fanciful frock he wore in common was exchanged for the attire of one of his assumed rank and service, which had been made to fit his person with the nicest care, and with a coxcombical attention to the proportions of his really fine person; and in all other things was he speedily equipped for the disguise he chose to affect. No sooner were these alterations completed (and they were effected with a brevity and readiness that manifested much practice in similar artifices), than he disposed himself to proceed on the intended experiment.

"Truer and quicker eyes have been deceived," he coolly observed, turning his glance from a mirror to the countenance of his lieutenant, "than those which embellish the rugged countenance of Captain Bignall."

"You know him, then?"

"Mr. Wilder, my business imposes the necessity of knowing much that other men overlook. Now is this adventure, which, by your features, I perceive you deem so forlorn in its hopes of success, one of easy achievement. I am convinced that not an officer or man on board the Dart has ever seen the ship whose name I have chosen to usurp. She is too fresh from the stocks to incur that risk. Then there is little probability that I, in my other self, shall be compelled to acknowledge acquaintance with any of her officers; for you well know that years have passed since your late ship has been in Europe; and, by running your eye over these books, you will perceive, I am that favoured mortal, the son of a lord, and have not only grown into command, but into manhood, since her departure from home."

"These are certainly favouring circumstances, and such as I had not the sagacity to detect. But why incur the risk at all?"

"Why! Perhaps there is a deep-laid scheme to learn if the prize would repay the loss of her capture — perhaps it is only my humour. There is fearful excitement in the adventure!"

"And there is fearful danger."

"I never count the price of these enjoyments, Wilder," he added, turning to him with a look of frank and courteous confidence. "I place life and honour in your keeping; for to me it would be dishonour to desert the interests of my crew."

"The trust shall be respected," repeated our adventurer, in a tone so deep and choked as to be nearly unintelligible.

Regarding the countenance of his companion intently for an instant, the Rover smiled as if he approved of the pledge, waved his hand in adieu, and turning, was about to leave the cabin; but a third form, at that moment, caught his wandering glance. Laying a hand lightly on the shoulder of the boy, whose form was placed somewhat obtrusively in his way, he demanded, a little sternly,—

"Roderick, what means this preparation?"

"To follow my master to the boat."

"Boy, thy service is not needed."

"It is rarely wanted of late."

"Why should I add unnecessarily to the risk of lives, when no good can attend the hazard?"

"In risking your own, you risk all to me."

The answer was given in a tone so resigned, and yet so faltering, that the tremulous and nearly smothered sounds caught no ears but those for whom they were intended.

The Rover for a time replied not. His hand still kept its place on the shoulder of the boy, whose working features he read, as the eye is sometimes wont to penetrate the mysteries of the heart.

"Roderick," he said, in a milder and kinder voice, "your lot shall be mine: we will go together."

Dashing his hand hastily across his brow, the wayward chief ascended the ladder, attended by the lad, and followed by the individual in whose faith he reposed so great a trust. The step with which the Rover trod the deck was firm, and the bearing of his form as steady as if he felt no hazard in his undertaking. His look passed, with a seaman's care, from sail to sail; not a brace, yard, or bowline escaped the quick glances he cast about him, before he proceeded to the side. At length he entered a boat which he had ordered to be in waiting. A glimmering of distrust and hesitation was now, for the first time, discoverable through the decision of his features. For a moment, his foot lingered on the ladder. "Davis," he said sternly, speaking to the individual whom, by experience, he knew to be well practised in treachery, "leave the boat. Send me the gruff captain of the forecastle in his place. So bold a talker in common should know how to be silent at need."

The exchange was instantly made; for no one there was ever known to dispute a mandate that was uttered with the air of authority he then wore. A deeply intent attitude of thought succeeded; then every shadow of care vanished from his brow. A look of high and generous confidence was seated in its place, as he added,—

"Wilder, adieu! I leave you captain of my people, and master of my fate: I am certain that both trusts are reposed in worthy hands."

Without waiting for reply, as if scorning the vain ceremony of idle assurances, he descended swiftly into the boat, which at the next instant was pulling boldly towards the king's cruiser. The brief interval between the departure of the adventurers and their arrival at the hostile ship was one of intense and absorbing suspense on the part of all whom they had left behind.    The individual most interested in the event, however, betrayed none of the anxiety which so intently beset the minds of his followers. He mounted the side of his enemy amid the honours due to his imaginary rank with a self-possession and ease that might readily have been mistaken by those who believe these fancied qualities have a real existence, for the grace and dignity of lofty recollections and high birth.    His reception, by the honest veteran, whose long and hard services had received but a meagre reward in the vessel he commanded, was frank, manly, and seamanlike.    The usual greetings had no sooner passed, than the latter conducted his guest into his own apartments.

" Find such a berth, Captain Howard, as suits your inclination." said the unceremonious old seaman, seating himself as frankly as he invited his companion to imitate his example.    " A gentleman of your extraordinary merit must be reluctant to lose time in useless words, though you are so young—young for the pretty command it is your good fortune to enjoy ! "

" On the contrary, I do assure you I begin to feel myself quite an antediluvian," returned the Rover, coolly placing himself at the opposite side of the table, where he might, from time to time, look his half-disgusted companion in the eye : " would you imagine it, sir, I shall have reached the age of three-and-twenty, if I live through the day ? "

" I had given you a few more years, young gentleman ; but London can ripen the human face as speedily as the equator."

" You never said truer words, sir.    Of all cruising grounds, Heaven defend me from that of St. James's !    I do assure you,

Bignall, the service is quite sufficient to wear out the strongest constitution. There were moments when I really thought I should have died that humble, disagreeable mortal — a lieutenant!"

"Your disease would then have been a galloping consumption!" muttered the old seaman. "They have sent you out in a pretty boat at last, Captain Howard."

"She's bearable, Bignall, but frightfully small. I told my father that, if the first lord didn't speedily regenerate the service by building more comfortable vessels, the navy would get altogether into vulgar hands  Don't you find the motion excessively annoying in these single-decked ships, Bignall?"

"When a man has been tossing up and down for five-and-forty years, Captain Howard," returned his host, stroking his grey locks, for want of some other manner of suppressing his ire, "he gets to be indifferent whether his ship pitches a foot more or a foot less."

"Ah! that, I dare say, is what one calls philosophical equanimity, though it is little to my humour. But, after this cruise, I am to be posted; and then I shall make interest for a guardship in the Thames: every thing goes by interest, now-a-days, you know, Bignall?"

The honest old tar swallowed his displeasure as well as he could; and, as the most effectual means of keeping himself in a condition to do credit to his own hospitality, he hastened to change the subject.

"I hope, among other new fashions, Captain Howard," he said, "the flag of Old England continues to fly over the Admiralty. You wore the colours of Louis so long this morning, that another half-hour might have brought us to loggerheads."

"Oh! that was an excellent military ruse! I shall certainly write the particulars of that deception home."

"Do so; do so, sir; you may get knighthood for the exploit.'

"Horrible, Bignall! my lady-mother would faint at the sugges tion. Nothing so low has been in the family, I do assure you, since the time when chivalry was genteel."

"Well, well, Captain Howard, it was happy for us both that you got rid of your Gallic humour so soon; for a little more time would have drawn a broadside from me. By heavens, sir, the guns of this ship would have gone off of themselves, in another five minutes!"

"It is quite happy as it is. What do you find to amuse you (yawning) in this dull quarter of the world, Bignall?"

"Why, sir, what between his majesty's enemies, the care of my ship, and the company of my officers, I find few heavy moments."

"Ah! your officers: true, you *must* have officers on board; though, I suppose, they are a little oldish to be agreeable to *you*. Will you favour me with a sight of the list?"

The commander of the Dart did as he was requested, putting the quarter-bill of his ship into the hands of his unknown enemy, with an eye that was far too honest to condescend to bestow even a look on a being so despised.

"What a list of thorough 'mouthers! All Yarmouth, and Plymouth, and Portsmouth, and Exmouth names, I do affirm. Here are Smiths enough to do the iron-work of the whole ship. Ha! here is a fellow that might do good service in a deluge. Who may this Henry Ark be, that I find rated as your first lieutenant?"

"A youth who wants but a few drops of your blood, Captain Howard, to be one day at the head of his majesty's fleet."

"If he be then so extraordinary for his merit, Captain Bignall, may I presume on your politeness to ask him to favour us with his society. I always give my lieutenant half an hour of a morn- ing — if he happen to be bearable."

"Poor boy! God knows where he is to be found at this mo

ment. The noble fellow has embarked, of his own accord, on a most dangerous service, and I am as ignorant as yourself of his success. Remonstrance, and even entreaties, were of no avail. The admiral had great need of a suitable agent, and the good of the nation demanded the risk; then, you know, men of humble birth must earn their preferment in cruising elsewhere than at St. James's; for the brave lad is indebted to a wreck, in which he was found an infant, for the very name you find so singular."

"He is, however, still borne upon your books as first lieutenant, I see?"

"And I hope ever will be, until he shall get the ship he so well merits. Good Heaven! are you ill, Captain Howard? Boy, a tumbler of grog here."

"I thank you, sir," returned the Rover, smiling calmly, and rejecting the offered beverage, as the blood returned into his features with a violence that threatened to break through the ordinary boundaries of its currents. "It is no more than an ailing I inherit from my mother. We call it in our family, the 'De Vere ivory;' for no other reason that I could ever learn, than that one of my female ancestors was particularly startled, in a delicate situation, you know, by an elephant's tooth. I am told it has rather an amiable look, while it lasts."

"It has the look of a man who is fitter for his mother's nursery than a gale of wind. But I am glad it is so soon over."

"No one wears the same face long now-a-days, Bignall. And so this Mr. Ark is not any body, after all?"

"I know not what you call 'any body,' sir; but, if sterling courage, great professional merit, and stern loyalty, count for any thing in your estimation, Captain Howard, Henry Ark will soon be in command of a frigate."

"Perhaps, if one only knew exactly on what to found his claims," continued the Rover, with a smile so kind, and a voice so insinuating, that they half counteracted the effect of his as-

19 *

sumed manner, "a word might be dropped, in a letter home, that should do the youth no harm."

"I would to Heaven I dared but reveal the nature of the service he is on!" eagerly returned the warm-hearted old seaman, who was as quick to forget, as he was sudden to feel, disgust. "You may, however, safely say, from his general character, that it is honourable, hazardous, and has the entire good of his majesty's subjects in view. Indeed, an hour has scarcely gone by since I thought it was completely successful. Do you often set your lofty sails, Captain Howard, while the heavier canvass is rolled upon the yards? To me, a ship clothed in that style looks something like a man with his coat on, before he has cased his legs in the lower garment."

"You allude to the accident of my main-top-gallant-sail getting loose when you first made me?"

"I mean no other. We caught a glimpse of your spars with the glass; but had lost you altogether, when the flying duck met the eye of a look-out. To say the least it was remarkable, and it might have proved an awkward circumstance."

"Ah! I often do things in that way, in order to be odd. It is a sign of cleverness to be odd. But I, too, am sent into these seas on a special errand."

"Such as what?" bluntly demanded his companion, with an uneasiness about his frowning eye that he was far too simple-minded to conceal.

"To look for a ship that will certainly give me a famous lift, should I have the good luck to fall in with her. For some time, I took you for the very gentleman I was in search of; and I do assure you, too, if your signals had not been so very unexceptionable, something serious might have happened between us."

"And pray, sir, for whom did you take me?"

"For no other than that notorious knave, the Red Rover."

"The devil you did! And do you suppose, Captain Howard,

there is a pirate afloat who carries such hamper above his head as is to be found aboard the Dart? Such a set to her sails—such a step to her masts—and such a trim to her hull? I hope, for the honour of your vessel, sir, that the mistake went no further than the captain!"

"Until we got within reading distance of the signals, at least a moiety of the better opinions in my ship was dead against you, Bignall, I give you my declaration. You've really been so long from home, that the Dart is getting quite a roving look. You may not be sensible of it, but I assure you of the fact merely as a friend."

"And, perhaps, since you did me the honour to mistake my vessel for a freebooter," returned the old tar, smothering his ire in a look of facetious irony, which changed the expression of his mouth to a grim grin, "you might have conceited this honest gentleman here to be no other than Beelzebub."

As he spoke, the commander of the ship which had borne so odious an imputation directed the eyes of his companion to the form of a third individual, who entered the cabin with the freedom of a privileged person, but with a tread so light as to be inaudible. As this unexpected form met the quick impatient glance of the pretended officer of the crown, he arose involuntarily, and, for half a minute, that admirable command of muscle and nerve which had served him so well in maintaining his masquerade appeared entirely to desert him. The loss of self-possession, however, was but for a time so short as to attract no notice; and he coolly returned the salutations of an aged man, of a meek and subdued look, with that air of blandness and courtesy which he so well knew how to assume.

"This gentleman is your chaplain, sir, I presume, by his clerical attire," he said, after he had exchanged bows with the stranger.

"He is, sir, A worthy and an honest man, whom I am not

ashamed to call my friend. After a separation of thirty years, the admiral has been good enough to lend him to me for the cruise; and, though my ship is none of the largest, I believe he finds himself as comfortable in her as he would aboard the flag. This gentleman, doctor, is the *Honourable* Captain Howard, of his majesty's ship Antelope. I need not expatiate on his remark-able merit, since the command he bears at his years is a sufficient testimony on that important particular."

There was a look of bewildered surprise in the gaze of the divine, when his glance first fell upon the features of the pretended scion of nobility; but it was far less striking than had been that of the subject of his gaze, and of much shorter continuance. He bowed meekly, and with the respect which long use begets in those who are accustomed to pay deference to hereditary rank; but he did not appear to consider that the occasion required more than the customary words of salutation. The Rover turned calmly to his veteran companion, and continued the discourse.

" Captain Bignall," he said, again wearing that grace of man-ner which became him so well, " it is my duty to follow your motions' in this interview. I will now return to my ship; and if, as I begin to suspect, we are in these seas on a similar errand, we can concert at our leisure a system of co-operation, which, properly matured by your experience, may serve to bring about the common end we have in view."

Greatly mollified by this concession to his years and to his rank, the commander of the Dart pressed his hospitalities more warmly on his guest, winding up his civilities by an invitation to join in a marine feast at an hour somewhat later in the day. All the former offers were politely declined, while the latter was accepted; the invited making the invitation itself an excuse that he should return to his own vessel, in order that he might select such of his officers as he should deem most worthy of partici-pating in the promised banquet. The veteran and really meritorious Bignall, notwithstanding the ordinary sturdy blustering of his character, had served too long in indigence and comparative obscurity not to feel some of the longings of human nature for his hard-earned and protracted preferment. He consequently kept, in the midst of all his native and manly honesty, a wary eye on the means of accomplishing this material object. It is to occasion no surprise, therefore, that his parting from the supposed son of a powerful champion at court was more amicable than the meeting. The Rover was bowed from the cabin to the deck, with at least an appearance of returning good will. On reaching the latter, a hurried, suspicious, and perhaps an uneasy glance, was thrown from his restless eyes on many faces that were grouped around the gangway; but their expression became calm again, and a little supercilious withal, in order to do no discredit to the part in the comedy which it was his present humour to enact. Then, shaking the worthy and thoroughly deceived old seaman heartily by the hand, he touched his hat, with an air half-haughty, half-condescending to his inferiors. He was in the act of descending into the boat, when the chaplain was seen to whisper something, with great earnestness, in the ear of his captain. The commander hastened to recall his departing guest, desiring him, with startling gravity, to lend him his private attention for another moment. Suffering himself to be led apart by the two, the Rover stood awaiting their pleasure, with a coolness of demeanour that, under the peculiar circumstances of his case, did signal credit to his nerves.

"Captain Howard," resumed the warm-hearted Bignall, "have you a gentleman of the cloth in your vessel?"

"Two, sir," was the answer.

"Two! It is rare to find a supernumerary priest in a man of war! But, I suppose, court influence could give the fellow a bishop," muttered the other. "You are fortunate in this particular. young gentleman, since I am indebted to inclination, rather than to custom, for the society of my worthy friend here. He has, however, made a point that I should include the reverend gentleman — I should say gentle*men* — in the invitation."

"You shall have all the divinity of my ship, Bignall, on my faith."

"I believe I was particular in naming your first lieutenant."

"Oh! dead or alive, he shall surely be of your party," re-turned the Rover, with a suddenness and vehemence of utterance that occasioned both his auditors to start with surprise. "You may not find him an ark to rest your weary foot on; but, such as he is, he is entirely at your service. And now, once more, I salute you."

Bowing again, he proceeded, with his former deliberate air, over the gangway, keeping his eye riveted on the lofty gear of the Dart as he descended her side, with the sort of expression with which a *petit-maître* is apt to regard the fashion of the garments of one newly arrived from the provinces. His superior repeated his invitation with warmth, and waved his hand in a frank but temporary adieu; thus unconsciously suffering the man to escape him, whose capture would have purchased the long postponed and still distant advantages for whose possession he secretly pined with the withering longings of a hope cruelly deferred.

# CHAPTER XXVIII.

— Let them accuse me by invention; I will answer in mine honour.
*Coriolanus*.

" YES," muttered the Rover, as his boat rowed under the stern of the royal cruiser; "yes! I, and my officers, will taste of your banquet! But the viands shall be such as these hirelings of the king shall little relish! Pull with a will, my men, pull; in an hour, you shall rummage the store-rooms of that fool for your reward!"

The greedy freebooters could scarcely restrain their shouts, in order to maintain the air of moderation which policy still imposed; but they gave vent to their excitement, by redoubling their efforts to regain their own ship. In another minute, the adventurers were all in safety again under the sheltering guns of the Dolphin.

His people gathered, from the haughty eye of the Rover, as his foot once more touched the deck of his own ship, that the period of action was at hand. For an instant, he lingered on the quarter-deck, surveying, with stern joy, the sturdy materials of his command; then he abruptly entered his cabin, forgetful that he had conceded it to others, or, in the excited state of his mind, indifferent to the circumstance. A sudden and tremendous blow on the gong announced not only his presence, but his humour.

" Let the first lieutenant be told I await him," was the order that followed the appearance of the attendant he had summoned

During the short period which elapsed before his mandate could be obeyed, the Rover seemed struggling with a passion that choked him. But when the door of the cabin was opened, and Wilder stood before him, the most suspicious and closest observer might have sought in vain any evidence of the fierce feelings which agitated the inward man. With the recovery of his self-command, returned a recollection of the manner of his intrusion into a place which he had himself ordained should be privileged. It was then that he first sought the shrinking females, and hastened to relieve the terror that was too plainly to be seen in their countenances, by words of apology and explanation.

" In the hurry of an interview with a friend," he said, " I may have forgotten that I am host to even such guests as it is my happiness to entertain, though I discharge my duties so indifferently."

" Spare your civilities, sir," said Mrs. Wyllys, with dignity. " In order to make us less sensible of intrusion, be pleased to act the master here."

The Rover first saw the ladies seated ; and then, like one who appeared to think the occasion might excuse any little departure from customary forms, he signed, with a smile of high courtesy, to his lieutenant to imitate their example.

" His majesty's artisans have sent worse ships than the Dart upon the ocean, Wilder," he commenced, significantly, as if he intended that the other should supply all the meaning that his words did not express : " but his ministers might have selected a more observant individual for the command."

" Captain Bignall has the reputation of a brave and honest man."

" He should deserve it, strip him of these two qualities, and little would remain. He gives me to understand that he is especially sent into this latitude in quest of a ship that we have all heard of, either in good or in evil report ; I speak of the Red Rover !"

The involuntary start of Mrs. Wyllys, and the sudden manner in which Gertrude grasped the arm of her governess, were certainly seen by the speaker, but in no degree did his manner betray the consciousness of such an observation. His self-possession was admirably emulated by Wilder, who answered with a composure that no jealousy could have seen was assumed,—

" His cruise will be hazardous, not to say without success."

" It may prove both. And yet he has lofty expectations of the results."

" He probably labours under the common error as to the character of the man he seeks."

" In what does he mistake ? "

" In supposing that he will encounter an ordinary freebooter, — one coarse, rapacious, ignorant, and inexorable, like others of——"

" Of what, sir ? "

" I would have said, of his class ; but a mariner like him we speak of, forms the head of his own order."

" We will call him, then, by his popular name, Mr. Wilder — a rover. But is it not remarkable that so experienced a seaman should come to this little frequented sea in quest of a ship whose pursuits ought to call her into more bustling scenes ? "

" He may have traced her through the narrow passages of the islands, and followed on the course she has last been seen steering."

" He may, indeed," returned the Rover, musing. " Your thorough mariner knows how to calculate the chances of winds and currents, as the bird finds its way in air. Still a description of the ship would at least be needed, as a clue."

Wilder, notwithstanding an effort to the contrary, suffered his eyes to sink before the piercing gaze they encountered.

" Perhaps he is not without that knowledge, too," he answered.

"Perhaps not. Indeed, he gave me reason to believe he has an agent in the secrets of his enemy. Nay, he expressly avowed the same, and acknowledged that his prospects of success depended on the skill and information of that individual, who no doubt has his private means of communicating what he learns of the movements of those with whom he serves."

"Did he name him?"

"He did."

"It was——"

"Henry — Ark, *alias* Wilder."

"It is vain to attempt denial," said our adventurer, rising with an air of pride that he intended should conceal the uneasy sensation that in truth beset him; "I find you know me."

"For a false traitor, sir!"

"Captain Heidegger, you are safe, here, in using these reproachful terms."

The Rover struggled, and struggled successfully, to keep down the risings of his temper; but the effort lent to his countenance gleamings of fierce scorn.

"You will communicate that fact also to your superiors," he said, with taunting irony. "The monster of the seas, he who plunders defenceless fishermen, ravages unprotected coasts, and eludes the flag of King George, as other serpents steal into their caves at the footstep of man, is safe in speaking his mind, backed by a hundred and fifty freebooters, and in the security of his own cabin. Perhaps he knows, too, that he is breathing in the atmosphere of peaceful and peace-making woman."

But the first surprise of the subject of his scorn had passed, and he was neither to be goaded into retort, nor terrified into entreaties. Folding his arms with calmness, Wilder simply replied,—

"I have incurred this risk, in order to drive a scourge from the ocean, which had baffled all other attempts at its extermination. I knew the hazard, and shall not shrink from its penalty."

"You shall not, sir!" returned the Rover, striking the gong again with a finger that appeared to carry in its touch the weight of a giant. "Let the negro, and the topman his companion, be secured in irons; on no account permit them to communicate, by word or signal, with the other ship." When the agent of his punishments, who entered at the well-known summons, had retired, he again turned to the firm and motionless form that stood before him. "Mr. Wilder," he continued, "there is a law which binds together this community, into which you have so treacherously stolen, that would consign you and your miserable confederates to the yard-arm, the instant your true character should be known to my people. I have but to open that door, and to pronounce the nature of your treason, and to yield you to the tender mercies of the crew."

"You will not! no, you will not!" cried a voice at his elbow, which thrilled on even his iron nerves. "You have forgotten the ties which bind man to his fellows, but cruelty is not natural to your heart. By all the recollections of your earliest and happiest days; by the tenderness and pity which watched your childhood; by that holy and omniscient Being who suffers not a hair of the innocent to go unrevenged, I conjure you to pause, before you forget your own awful responsibility. No! you will not — cannot — dare not be so merciless!"

"What fate did he contemplate for me and my followers, when he entered on this insidious design?" hoarsely demanded the Rover.

"The laws of God and man are with him," continued Mrs. Wyllys, for it was she; "'t is reason that speaks in my voice; 't is mercy, which I know is pleading at your heart. The cause, the motive, sanctify his acts; while your career can find justification in the laws neither of heaven nor earth."

" This is bold language to sound in the ears of a blood seek-ing, remorseless pirate ! " said the other, looking around with a smile so proud, that it seemed to proclaim how plainly he saw that the speaker relied on the very reverse of the qualities he named,

" It is the language of truth; and ears like yours cannot be deaf to the sounds. If——"

" Lady, cease," interrupted the Rover, stretching his arm to-wards her with calmness. " My resolution was formed on the instant; and no remonstrance, nor apprehension of the conse-quence, can change it. Mr. Wilder, you are free. If you have not served me as faithfully as I once expected, you have taught me a lesson in the art of physiognomy which shall leave me a wiser man for the rest of my days."

The conscious Wilder stood self-condemned and humbled. The strugglings which stirred his inmost soul were to be read in the workings of a countenance that was no longer masked in artifice, but which expressed both shame and sorrow. The conflict lasted but a moment.

" Perhaps you know not the extent of my object, Captain Hei-degger," he said : " it embraced the forfeit of your life, and the destruction or dispersion of your crew."

" According to the established usages of that portion of the world which, having the power, oppresses the remainder, it did. Go, sir; rejoin your proper ship; I repeat, you are free."

" I cannot leave you, Captain Heidegger, without one word of justification."

" What ! can the hunted, denounced, and condemned freebooter command an explanation ? Is even his good opinion necessary to a virtuous servant of the crown ? "

" Use such terms of triumph and reproach as suit your plea-sure, sir; to me your language can convey no offence; still I would not leave you without removing part of the odium which you think I merit."

"Speak freely. Sir, you are my guest."

The most cutting revilings could not have wounded the repentant Wilder so deeply as this generous conduct, but he subdued his feelings, and continued,—

"You are not now to learn," he said, "that vulgar rumour has given a colour to your conduct and character which is not of a quality to command esteem."

"You may find leisure to deepen the tints," hastily interrupted his listener, though the tremour in his voice denoted how deeply he felt the wound given by a world that he affected to despise.

"If called upon to speak at all, my words shall be those of truth, Captain Heidegger. Is it surprising that, filled with the ardour of a service you once thought honourable yourself, I should be found willing to risk life, and if you will, even to play the hypocrite, in order to achieve an object that would not only have been rewarded, but approved, had it been successful? With such sentiments I embarked on the enterprise; but, as Heaven is my judge, your manly confidence had half disarmed me, when my foot had hardly crossed the threshold of my enterprise."

"You turned not back?"

"There might have been irresistible reasons to the contrary," resumed the defendant, glancing his eyes at the females. "I kept my faith at Newport; and, had my two followers then been released from your ship, my foot should never have entered her again."

"Young man, I am willing to believe you. I think I penetrate your motives. You have played a delicate game; instead of repining, you will one day rejoice that it has been fruitless. Go, sir — a boat shall attend you to the Dart."

"Deceive not yourself, Captain Heidegger, in believing that any generosity of yours can shut my eyes to my proper duty. The instant I am seen by the commander of the ship you name, your character will be betrayed."

"I expect it."

"Nor will my hand be idle in the struggle that must follow. I may die, here, a victim to my mistake, if you please; but, the moment I am released, I unavoidably become your enemy."

"Wilder!" exclaimed the Rover, grasping his hand with a smile that partook of the wild energy of his manner, "we should have been acquainted earlier! But regret is idle. Go; should my people learn the truth, any remonstrances of mine would be like whispers in a whirlwind."

"When I joined the Dolphin last, I did not come alone."

"Is it not enough," rejoined the Rover, recoiling a step, "that I offer you liberty and life?"

"Of what service can a being, fair, helpless, and unfortunate as this, be in a ship devoted to pursuits like those of the Dolphin?"

"Am I to be cut off for ever from communion with the best of my kind? Go, sir; leave me the image of virtue, at least, though I may be wanting in its substance."

"Captain Heidegger, once, in the warmth of your better feelings, you pronounced a pledge in favour of these females, which I hope came from the heart."

"I understand you, sir. What I then said is not, nor shall it be, forgotten. But whither would you lead your companions? Is not one vessel on the high seas as safe as another? Am I to be deprived of every means of making friends unto myself? Leave me, sir — go — you may linger until my permission to depart cannot avail you."

"I shall never desert my charge," said Wilder, firmly.

"Mr. Wilder, — or I should rather call you Lieutenant Ark, I believe," — returned the Rover, — "you may trifle with my good nature till the moment of your own security shall be past."

"Act your will on me : I die at my post, or go accompanied by those with whom I came."

"Sir, the acquaintance of which you boast is not older than my own. How know you that they prefer you for their protector? I have deceived myself, and done poor justice to my own intentions, if they have found cause for complaints, since their happiness or comfort has been in my keeping. Speak, fair one; which of us do you choose for a protector?"

"Leave me, leave me!" exclaimed Gertrude, veiling her eyes, from the insidious smile with which he approached her, as she would have avoided the glance of a basilisk. "Oh! if you have pity in your heart, let us quit your ship!"

Notwithstanding the vast self-command which the being she so ungovernably and spontaneously repelled had in common over his feelings, no effort could repress the look of deep and humiliating mortification with which he heard her. A cold and haggard smile gleamed over his features, as he murmured, in a voice which he in vain endeavoured to smother,—

"I have purchased this disgust from all of my species, and dearly must the penalty be paid!— Lady, you and your lovely ward are mistresses of your own acts. This ship, and this cabin, are at your command; or, if you elect to quit both, others will receive you."

"Safety for our sex is only to be found beneath the fostering protection of the laws," said Mrs. Wyllys. "Would to God——"

"Enough!" he interrupted, "you shall accompany your friend. The ship will not be emptier than my heart, when all have left me."

"Did you call?" asked a low voice at his elbow, in tones so plaintive and mild that they could not fail to catch his ear.

"Roderick," he hurriedly replied, "you will find occupation below. Leave us, good Roderick. For a while, leave me."

Then, as if anxious to close the scene as speedily as possible, he gave another of his signals on the gong. An order was given

to convey Fid and the black into a boat, whither he also sent the
scanty baggage of his female guests.  So soon as these brief arrangements were completed, he handed the governess with
studied courtesy, through his wondering people, to the side, and
saw her safely seated, with her ward and Wilder, in the pinnace.
The oars were manned by the two seamen, and a silent adieu
was given by a wave of his hand; after which he disappeared
from those to whom their present release seemed as imaginary
and unreal as most of the other events of the few preceding
weeks.

The threat of the interference of the crew of the Dolphin was,
however, still ringing in the ears of Wilder.  He made an impatient gesture to his attendants to ply their oars, cautiously
steering the boat on such a course as would soonest lead her from
beneath the guns of the freebooters.  While passing under the
stern of the Dolphin, a hoarse hail was sent across the waters,
and the voice of the Rover was heard speaking to the commander
of the Dart.

"I send you a party of your guests," he said; "and, among
them, all the divinity of my ship."

The passage was short; nor was time given for the liberated
to arrange their thoughts, before it became necessary to ascend
the side of the cruiser of the crown.

"Heaven help us!" exclaimed Bignall, catching a glimpse of
the sex of his visitors through a port; "Heaven help us both,
parson!  That young hare-brained fellow has sent us a brace of
petticoats aboard; and these the profane reprobate calls his divin-
ities!  One may easily guess where he has picked up such quality,
but, cheer up, doctor; we may honestly forget the cloth in five
fathom water, you know."

The facetious laugh of the old commander of the Dart betrayed
that he was more than half disposed to overlook the fancied presumption of his audacious inferior; furnishing a sort of pledge

that no undue scruples should defeat the hilarity of the moment. But when Gertrude, flushed with the excitement of the scene through which she had just passed, and beaming with a loveliness that derived so much of its character from its innocence, appeared on his deck, the veteran rubbed his eyes in an amazement which could not have been greatly surpassed, had one of that species of beings the Rover had named actually fallen at his feet from the skies.

"The heartless scoundrel!" cried the worthy tar, "to lead astray one so young and so lovely! Ha! as I live, my own lieutenant! How's this, Mr. Ark? have we fallen on the days of miracles?"

An exclamation, which came from the heart of the governess, and a low and mournful echo from the lips of the divine, interrupted the further expression of his indignation and his wonder.

"Captain Bignall," observed the former, pointing to the tottering form which was leaning on Wilder for support, "on my life, you are mistaken in the character of this lady. It is more than twenty years since we last met, but I pledge my own character for the purity and truth of hers."

"Lead me to the cabin," murmured Mrs. Wyllys. "Gertrude, my love, where are we? Lead me to some secret place."

Her request was complied with; the whole party retiring in a body from the sight of the spectators who thronged the deck. Here the agitated governess regained a portion of her self-command, and then her wandering gaze sought the meek countenance of the chaplain.

"This is a tardy and heart-rending meeting," she said, pressing the hand he gave her to her lips. "Gertrude, in this gentleman you see the divine that united me to the man who once formed the pride and happiness of my existence."

"Mourn not his loss," whispered the reverend priest, bending over her chair with the interest of a parent. "He was taken

20

from you at an early hour; but he died as all who loved him might have wished."

" And none was left to bear, in remembrance of his qualities, his name to posterity! Tell me, good Merton, is not the hand of Providence visible in this dispensation? Ought I not to humble myself before it, as a just punishment of my disobedience to an affectionate, though too obdurate, parent?"

" None may presume to pry into the mysteries of the righteous government that orders all things. Enough for us, that we learn to submit to the will of Him who rules, without questioning His justice."

" But," continued the governess, in tones so husky as to betray how powerfully she felt the temptation to forget his admonition, " would not one life have sufficed? was I to be deprived of all?"

" Madam, reflect! What has been done was done in wisdom, as I trust it was in mercy."

" You say truly. I will forget all of the sad events, but their application to myself. And you, worthy and benevolent Merton, where and how have been passed your days since the time of which we speak?"

" I am but a low and humble shepherd of a truant flock," returned the meek chaplain, with a sigh. " Many distant seas have I visited, and many strange faces, and stranger natures, has it been my lot to encounter in my pilgrimage. I am but lately returned from the East, into the hemisphere where I first drew breath; and, by permission of our superiors, I came to pass a month in the vessel of a companion, whose friendship bears even an older date than yours."

" Ay, ay, madam," returned the worthy Bignall, whose feelings had been a little disturbed by the previous scene; " it is near half a century since the parson and I were boys together, and we have been rubbing up old recollections on the cruise.

Happy am I that a lady of so commendable qualities has come to make one of our party."

" In this lady you see the daughter of the late Captain ——, and the relict of the son of our ancient commander, Rear Admiral de Lacey," hastily resumed the divine, as if he knew the well-meaning honesty of his friend was more to be trusted than his discretion.

"I knew them both; brave men and thorough seamen were the pair! The lady was welcome as your friend, Merton; but she is doubly so, as the widow and child of the gentlemen you name."

" De Lacey!" murmured a voice in the ear of the governess.

"The law gives me a title to bear that name," returned she, whom we shall still continue to call by her assumed appellation, folding her weeping pupil long and affectionately to her bosom. "The veil is unexpectedly withdrawn, my love, and concealment would now be worse than useless. My father was the captain of the flag-ship. Necessity compelled him to leave me more in the society of your young relative than he would have done, could he have foreseen the consequences. But I knew both his pride and his poverty too well, to dare to make him arbiter of my fate, after the alternative became, to my inexperienced imagination, worse even than his anger. We were privately united by this gentleman, and neither of our parents knew of the connection. Death——"

The voice of the widow became choked, and she made a sign to the chaplain, as if she would have him continue the tale.

" Mr. de Lacey and his father-in-law fell in the same battle, within a short month of the ceremony," added the subdued voice of Merton. " Even you, dearest madam, never knew the melancholy particulars of their end. I was a solitary witness of their deaths; for to me were they both consigned, amid the confusion of the battle. Their blood was mingled; and your parent, in blessing the young hero, unconsciously blessed his son."

"Oh! I deceived his noble nature, and dearly have I paid the penalty!" exclaimed the self-abased widow. "Tell me, Merton, did he ever know of my marriage?"

"He did not. Mr. de Lacey died first, and upon his bosom, for he loved him ever as a child; but other thoughts than useless explanations were uppermost in their minds."

"Gertrude," said the governess, in hollow, repentant tones, "there is no peace for our feeble sex but in submission; no happiness but in obedience."

"It is over now," whispered the weeping girl; "all over and forgotten. I am your child — your own Gertrude, the creature of your formation."

"Harry Ark!" exclaimed Bignall, clearing his throat with a hem so vigorous as to carry the sound to the outer deck, seizing the arm of his entranced lieutenant, and dragging him from the scene while he spoke. "What the devil besets the boy! You forget that, all this time, I am as ignorant of your own adventures as his majesty's prime minister is of navigation. Why do I see you, here, a visitor from a royal cruiser, when I thought you were playing the mock pirate? and how came that harum-scarum twig of nobility in possession of so goodly a company, as well as of so brave a ship?"

Wilder drew a long breath, like one that awakes from a pleasing dream, reluctantly suffering himself to be forced from a spot where he fondly felt that he could have continued, without weariness, for ever.

# CHAPTER XXIX.

Let them achieve me, and then sell my bones.

*Henry V.*

THE commander of the Dart and his bewildered lieutenant had gained the quarter-deck before either spoke again. The direction first taken by the eyes of the latter was in quest of the neighbouring ship; nor was the look entirely without that unsettled and vague expression which seems to announce a momentary aberration of the faculties. But the vessel of the Rover was in view, in all the palpable and beautiful proportions of her admirable construction. Instead of lying in a state of rest, as when he left her, her head-yards had been swung, and as the sails filled with the breeze, the stately fabric had begun to move gracefully, though with no great velocity, along the water. There was not the slightest appearance in the evolution, however, of any attempt at escape. On the contrary, the loftier and lighter sails were all furled, and men were at the moment actively employed in sending to the deck those smaller spars which were absolutely requisite in spreading the canvass that would be needed in facilitating her flight. Wilder turned from the sight with a sickening apprehension; for he well knew that these were the preparations that skilful mariners are wont to make, when bent on desperate combat.

" Ay, yonder goes your St. James's seaman, with his three topsails full, and his mizzen out, as if he had already forgotten

he is to dine with me, and that his name is to be found at one
end of the list of commanders, and mine at the other," grumbled
the displeased Bignall.  " But we shall have him coming round,
I suppose, when his appetite tells him the dinner hour.  He
might wear his colours in presence of a senior, too, and no disgrace to his nobility.  By the Lord, Harry Ark, he handles his
yards beautifully !  I warrant you, now, some honest man's son
is sent aboard his ship for a dry nurse, in the shape of a first
lieutenant, and we shall have him vapouring, all dinner time,
about 'how my ship does this,' and 'I never suffer that.'  Ha !
is it not so, sir ?   He has a thorough seaman for his first ?"

" Few men understand the profession better than the captain
of yonder vessel himself," returned Wilder.

" The devil he does !  You have been talking with him, Mr.
Ark, about these matters, and he has got some of the fashions
of the Dart.  I can see into a mystery as quick as another !"

" I do assure you, Captain Bignall, there is no safety in confiding in the ignorance of yonder extraordinary man."

" Ay, ay, I begin to overhaul his character.  The young dog
is a quiz, and has been amusing himself with a sailor of what he
calls the old school.  Am I right, sir ?  He has seen salt water
before this cruise ?"

" He is almost a native of the seas; for more than thirty years
he has passed his time on them."

" There, Harry Ark, he has done you handsomely.  Now, 1
have his own assertion for it, that he will not be three-and-twenty
until to-morrow."

" On my word, he has deceived you, sir."

" I don't know, Mr. Ark ; that is a task much easier attempted
than performed.  Threescore and four years add as much weight
to a man's head as to his heels !  I may have undervalued the
skill of the yonker, but, as to his years, there can be no great
mistake.  But where the devil is the fellow steering to ?  Has

he need of a pinafore from his lady-mother to come on board of a man-of-war to dine?"

"See! he is indeed standing from us!" exclaimed Wilder, with a rapidity and delight that would have excited the suspicions of one more observant than his commander.

"If I know the stern from the bows of a ship, what you say is truth," returned the other, with some austerity. "Hark ye, Mr. Ark, I've a mind to furnish the coxcomb a lesson in respect for his superiors, and give him a row to whet his appetite. By the Lord, I will; and he may write home an account of this manœuvre, too, in his next despatches. Fill away the after-yards, sir! fill away. Since this *honourable* youth is disposed to amuse himself with a sailing-match, he can take no offence that others are in the same humour."

The lieutenant of the watch, to whom the order was addressed, complied; and, in another minute, the Dart was also beginning to move a-head; though in a direction directly opposite to that taken by the Dolphin. The old man highly enjoyed his own decision, manifesting his satisfaction by the infinite glee and deep chuckling of his manner. He was too much occupied with the step he had just taken to revert immediately to the subject that had so recently been uppermost in his mind; nor did the thought of pursuing the discourse occur to him, until the two ships had left a broad field of water between them, as each moved, with ease and steadiness, on its proper course.

"Let him note that in his log-book, Mr. Ark," the irritable old seaman then resumed, returning to the spot which Wilder had not left during the intervening time. "Though my cook has no great relish for a frog, they who would taste of his skill must seek him. By the Lord, boy, he will have a pull of it, if he undertake to come-to on that tack. But how happens it that you got into his ship? All that part of the cruise remains untold."

"I have been wrecked, sir, since you received my last letter."

"What! has Davy Jones got possession of the red gentleman at last?"

"The misfortune occurred in a ship from Bristol, aboard which I was placed as a sort of prize-master.—He certainly continues to stand slowly to the northward!"

"Let the young coxcomb go! he will have all the better appetite for his supper. And so you were picked up by his majesty's ship the Antelope. Ay, I see into the whole affair. Give an old sea-dog his course and compass, and he will find his way to port in the darkest night. But how happened it that this Mr. Howard affected to be ignorant of your name, sir, when he saw it on the list of my officers."

"Ignorant! Did he seem ignorant? perhaps——"

"Say no more, my brave fellow, say no more," interrupted Wilder's considerate but choleric commader. "I have met with such rebuffs myself; but we are above them, sir, far above them and their impertinences together. No man need be ashamed of having earned his commission, as you and I have done, in fair weather and in foul. Zounds, boy, I have fed one of the upstarts for a week, and then had him stare at a church across the way, when I have fallen in with him in the streets of London, in a manner to make a simple man believe the puppy knew for what it had been built. Think no more of it, Harry: worse things have happened to myself, I do assure you."

"I went by an assumed name while in his ship," Wilder forced himself to add. "Even the ladies, who were the companions of my wreck, knew me by no other."

"Ah! that was prudent; and, after all, the young sprig was not pretending genteel ignorance. How now, Master Fid! you are welcome back to the Dart."

"I've taken the liberty to say as much already to myself, your honour," resumed the topman, who was busying himself near his

two officers, in a manner that seemed to invite their attention
"A wholesome craft is yonder, and boldly is she commanded,
and stoutly is she manned; but, for my part, having a character
to lose, it is more to my taste to sail in a ship that can show her
commission when properly called on for the same."

The colour on Wilder's cheeks went and came, like the flushings
of the evening sky, and his eyes were turned in every direction
but that which would have encountered the astonished gaze of
his veteran friend.

"I am not quite sure that I understand the meaning of the
lad, Mr. Ark. Every officer, from the captain to the boatswain,
in the king's fleet, that is, every man of common discretion,
carries his authority to act as such with him to sea, or he might
find himself in a situation as awkward as that of a pirate."

"That is just what I said, sir; but schooling and long use have
given your honour a better outfit in words. Guinea and I have
often talked the matter over together, and serious thoughts has
it given to us both, more than once, Captain Bignall. 'Suppose,'
says I to the black, 'suppose one of his majesty's boats should
happen to fall in with this here craft, and we should come to loggerheads and matches,' says I, 'what would the like of us two
do in such a godsend?'—'Why,' says the black, 'we would stand
to our guns on the side of Master Harry,' says he; nor did I
gainsay the same; but, saving his presence and your honour's,
I just took the liberty to add, that, in my poor opinion, it would
be much more comfortable to be killed in an honest ship than on
the deck of a buccaneer."

"A buccaneer!" exclaimed his commander, with eyes distended, and an open mouth.

"Captain Bignall," said Wilder, "I may have offended past
forgiveness, in remaining so long silent; but when you hear my
tale, there may be found some passages that shall plead my apology. The vessel in sight is the ship of the renowned Red Rover

20 *

—nay, listen, I conjure you, by all that kindness you have so long shown me, and then censure as you will."

The words of Wilder, aided as they were by an earnest and manly manner, laid a restraint on the mounting indignation of the choleric old seaman. He listened gravely and intently to the rapid but clear tale which his lieutenant hastened to recount; and, ere the latter had done, he had more than half entered into those grateful, and certainly generous, feelings which had made the youth so reluctant to betray the obnoxious character of a man who had dealt so liberally by himself. A few strong, and what might be termed professional, exclamations of surprise and admiration occasionally interrupted the narrative; but, on the whole, he curbed his impatience and his feelings, in a manner that was sufficiently remarkable, when the temperament of the individual is duly considered.

"This is wonderful indeed!" he exclaimed, as the other ended; "and a thousand pities is it that so honest a fellow should be so arrant a knave. But, Harry, we can never let him go at large after all; our loyalty and our religion forbid it. We must tack ship, and stand after him; if fair words won't bring him to reason, I see no other remedy than blows."

"I fear it is no more than our duty, sir," returned the young man, with a sigh.

"It is a matter of morals. And then the prating puppy that he sent on board me is no captain after all! Still it was impossible to deceive me as to the air and manner of a gentleman. I warrant me, some young reprobate of a good family, or he would never have acted the sprig so well. We must try to keep his name a secret, Mr. Ark, in order that no discredit should fall upon his friends. Our aristocratic columns, though they get a little cracked and defaced, are, after all, the pillars of the throne; and it does not become us to let vulgar eyes look too closely into their unsoundness."

" The individual who visited the Dart was the Rover himself."

" Ha ! the Red Rover in my ship—nay, in my very presence!" exclaimed the old tar, in honest horror. " You are now pleased, sir, to trifle with my good nature."

" I should forget a thousand obligations ere I could be so bold. On my solemn asseveration, sir, it was no other."

" This is unaccountable !—extraordinary to a miracle ! His disguise was very complete, I will confess, to deceive one so well-skilled in the human countenance. I saw nothing, sir, of his shaggy whiskers, heard nothing of his brutal voice, nor per-ceived any of those monstrous deformities which are universally acknowledged to distinguish the man."

" All of which are no more than the embellishments of vulgar rumour. I fear, sir, that the boldest and most dangerous of all our vices are often found under the most pleasing exteriors."

" But this is not even a man of inches, sir."

" His body is not large, but it contains the spirit of a giant."

" And do you believe yonder ship, Mr. Ark, to be the vessel that fought us in the equinox of March ?"

" I know it to be no other."

" Hark ye, Harry, for your sake I will deal generously by the rogue. He once escaped me by the loss of a topmast, and stress of weather; but we have here a good working breeze that a man may safely count on, and a fine regular sea. He is therefore mine, so soon as I choose to make him so;—for, after all, I do not think he has any serious intention to run."

" I fear not," returned Wilder, unconsciously betraying his wishes in the words.

" Fight he cannot, with any hopes of success ; and, as he seems to be altogether a different sort of personage from what I had supposed, we will try the merits of negotiation. Will you undertake to be the bearer of my propositions ?—or, perhaps, he might repent of his moderation."

"I pledge myself for his faith," eagerly exclaimed Wilder. "Let a gun be fired to leeward. Mind, sir, all the tokens must be amicable—a flag of truce set at our main, and I will risk every hazard to lead him back into the bosom of society."

"By George, it would at least be acting a Christian part," returned the commander, after a moment's thought; "and, though we miss knighthood below, lad, for our success, there will be better berths cleared for us aloft."

No sooner had the warm-hearted, and perhaps a little visionary, captain of the Dart, and his lieutenant, determined on this measure, than they both eagerly set about the means of ensuring its success. The helm of the ship was put a-lee; and, as her head came sweeping up into the wind, a sheet of flame flashed from her leeward bow-port, sending the customary amicable intimation across the water, that those who governed her movements would communicate with the possessors of the vessel in sight. At the same instant, a small flag, with a spotless field, was seen floating at the topmast elevation of all her spars, whilst the flag of England was lowered from the gaff. A half minute of deep inquietude succeeded these signals. Their suspense was, however, speedily terminated. A cloud of smoke issued from the vessel of the Rover, and then the smothered explosion of the answering gun came dull upon their ears. A flag, similar to their own, was seen floating as it might be like a dove fanning its wings, far above her tops; but no emblem of any sort was borne at the spar where the colours which distinguish the national character of a cruiser are usually seen.

"The fellow has the modesty to carry a naked gaff in our presence," said Bignall, pointing out the circumstance to his companion, as an augury favourable to their success. "We will stand for him until within a reasonable distance, and then you shall take to the boat."

In conformity with this determination, the Dart was brought

on the other tack, and several sails were set to quicken her speed. When at the distance of half cannon-shot, Wilder. suggested to his superior the propriety of arresting their further progress, in order to avoid the appearance of hostilities. The boat was immediately lowered into the sea, and manned; a flag of truce set in her bows; and the whole was reported ready to receive the bearer of the message.

"You may hand him this statement of our force, Mr. Ark; for, as he is a reasonable man, he will see the advantage it gives us," said the captain, after having exhausted his manifold and often repeated instructions. "I think you may promise him indemnity for the past, provided he comply with all my conditions; at all events, you will say that no influence shall be spared to get a complete white-washing for himself at least. God bless you, boy! Take care to say nothing of the damages we received in the affair of March last; for — ay — for the equinox was blowing heavy at the time, you know. Adieu! and success attend you!"

The boat shoved off from the side of the vessel as he ended, and in a few moments the listening Wilder was borne beyond the sound of further counsel.

Our adventurer had sufficient time to reflect on the extraordinary situation in which he now found himself during the row to the still distant ship. Once or twice, slight and uneasy glimmerings of distrust, concerning the prudence of the step he was taking, beset him; though a recollection of the lofty feeling of the man in whom he confided ever presented itself in sufficient season to prevent the apprehension from gaining any undue ascendency Notwithstanding the delicacy of his situation, that characteristic interest in his profession which is rarely dormant in the bosom of a thoroughbred seaman was strongly stimulated as he approached the vessel of the Rover. The perfect symmetry of her spars, the graceful heavings and settings of the whole fabric, as it rode, like a marine bird, on the long, regular swells of the trades, and the graceful inclinations of the tapering masts, as they waved across the blue canopy, which was interlaced by all the tracery of her complicated tackle, was not lost on an eye that knew no less how to prize the order of the whole than to admire the beauty of the object itself. There is a high and exquisite taste, which the seaman attains in the study of a machine that all have united to commend, which may be likened to the sensibilities that the artist acquires, by close and long contemplation of the noblest monuments of antiquity. It teaches him to detect those imperfections which would escape a less instructed eye; and it heightens the pleasure with which a ship at sea is gazed at, by enabling the mind to keep even pace with the enjoyment of the senses. It is this powerful (and to a landsman incomprehensible) charm that forms the secret tie which binds the mariner so closely to his vessel, and which often leads him to prize her qualities as one would esteem the virtues of a friend, and almost to be equally enamoured of the fair proportions of his ship and of those of his mistress. Other men may have their different inanimate subjects of admiration; but none of their feelings so thoroughly enter into the composition of the being as the affection which the mariner comes, in time, to feel for his vessel. It is his home, his theme of constant and frequently of painful interest, his tabernacle, and often his source of pride and exultation. As she gratifies or disappoints his high-wrought expectations, in her speed or in the fight, 'mid shoals and hurricanes, a character for good or luckless qualities is earned, which are as often in reality due to the skill or ignorance of those who guide her, as to any inherent properties of the fabric. Still does the ship itself, in the eyes of the seaman, bear away the laurel of success, or suffer the ignominy of defeat and misfortune; and, when the reverse arrives, the result is merely regarded as some extraordinary departure from the ordinary character of the vessel, as if the construction possessed the powers of self-command and volition.

Though not so deeply imbued with that superstitious credulity on this subject as the inferiors of his profession, Wilder was keenly awake to most of the sensibilities of a mariner. So strongly, indeed, was he alive to this feeling on the present occasion, that for a moment he forgot the critical nature of his errand, as he drew within plainer view of a vessel that, with justice, might lay claim to be a jewel of the ocean.

"Lay on your oars, lads," he said, signing to his people to arrest the progress of the boat; "lay on your oars! Did you ever see masts more beautifully in line than those, Master Fid, or sails that had a fairer fit?"

The topman, who rowed the stroke-oar of the pinnace, cast a look over his shoulder, and, stowing into one of his cheeks a lump that resembled a wad laid by the side of its gun, he was not slow to answer.

"I care not who knows it," he said, "for done by honest men or done by knaves, I told the people on the forecastle of the Dart, in the first five minutes after I got among them again, that they might be at Spithead a month, and not see hamper so light, and yet so handy, as is seen aboard that flyer. Her lower rigging is harpened in, like the waist of Nell Dale, after she has had a fresh pull upon her stay-lanyards, and there is n't a block among them all that seems bigger in its place than the eyes of the girl in her own good-looking countenance. That bit of a set that you see to her fore-brace-block was given by the hand of one Richard Fid; and the heart on her mainstay was turned in by Guinea here; and, considering he is a nigger, I call it ship-shape."

"She is beautiful in every part!" said Wilder, drawing a long breath. "Give way, my men, give way! Do you think I have come here to take the soundings of the ocean?"

The crew started at the hurried tones of their lieutenant, and in another minute the boat was at the side of the vessel. The stern and threatening glances that Wilder encountered, as his foot touched the planks, caused him to pause an instant, ere he advanced further amid the crew; but the presence of the Rover himself, who stood, with his peculiar air of high and imposing authority, on the quarter-deck, encouraged him to proceed, after permitting a delay that was too slight to attract attention. His lips were in the act of parting, when a sign from the other induced him to remain silent until they were both in the privacy of the cabin.

"Suspicion is awake among my people, Mr. Ark," commenced the Rover, when they had retired, laying a marked emphasis on the name he used. "Suspicion is stirring, though, as yet, they hardly know what to credit. The manœuvres of the two ships have not been such as they are wont to see, and voices are not wanting to whisper in their ears matter that is somewhat injurious to your interests. You have not done well, sir, in returning among us."

"I came by the order of my superior, and under the sanction of a flag."

"We are small reasoners in the legal distinctions of the world, and may mistake your rights in so novel a character; but if you bear a message, I may presume it is intended for my ears?"

"For no other. We are not alone, Captain Heidegger."

"Heed not the boy; he is deaf at my will."

"I could wish to communicate to you only, the offers that I bear."

"That mast is not more senseless than Roderick," said the other calmly, but with decision.

"Then I must speak at every hazard. The commander of yonder ship, who bears the commission of our royal master, George the Second, has ordered me to say thus much for your consideration. On the condition that you will surrender this vessel, with her stores, armament, and warlike munitions, unin-jured, he will content himself with taking ten hostages from your crew, to be decided by lot, yourself, and one other of your offi-cers, and either to receive the remainder into the service of the king, or to suffer them to disperse in pursuit of a calling more creditable, and, as it would now appear, more safe."

"This is the liberality of a prince! I should kneel and kiss the deck before one whose lips utter such sounds of mercy!"

"I repeat but the words of my superior," Wilder resumed, colouring. "For yourself, he further promises, that his interest shall be exerted to procure a pardon, on condition that you quit the seas, and renounce the name of Englishman for ever."

"The latter is done to his hands; but may I know the reason that such lenity is shown to one whose name has been so long proscribed of men?"

"Captain Bignall has heard of your generous treatment of his officer, and the delicacy that the daughter and widow of two ancient brethren in arms have received at your hands. He con-fesses that rumour has not done entire justice to your charac-ter."

A mighty effort kept down the gleam of exultation that flashed across the features of the Rover, who, however, succeeded in con-tinuing entirely calm and immovable.

"He has been deceived. sir?" he resumed, as if to encourage the other to proceed.

"That much is he willing to acknowledge. A representation of this common error to the proper authorities will have weight in procuring the promised amnesty for the past, and, as he hopes, brighter prospects for the future."

"And does he urge no other motive than his pleasure why I should make this violent change in all my habits, why I should renounce an element that has become as necessary to me as the

one I breathe, and why, in particular, I am to disclaim the vaunt-
ed privilege of calling myself a Briton?"

"He does.   This statement of a force, which you may freely
examine with your own eyes, if so disposed, must convince you
of the hopelessness of resistance, and will, he thinks, induce you
to accept his offers."

"And what is *your* opinion?" the other demanded, with a
peculiar emphasis, as he extended a hand to receive the written
statement.   "But I beg pardon," he hastily added, taking the
look of gravity from the countenance of his companion;  "I trifle
when the moment requires seriousness."

The eye of the Rover ran rapidly over the paper, resting once
or twice, with a slight exhibition of interest, on particular points
that seemed most to merit his attention.

"You find the superiority such as I had already given you
reason to believe?" demanded Wilder, when the look of the other
wandered from the paper.

"I do."

"And may I now ask your decision on the offer?"

"First, tell me what does your own heart advise?   This is but
the language of another."

"Captain Heidegger," said Wilder earnestly, "I will not
attempt to conceal that, had this message depended solely on myself, it might have been couched in different terms; but as one
who still deeply retains the recollection of your generosity, as a
man who would not willingly induce even an enemy to an act of
dishonour, I urge their acceptance.   You will excuse me, if I say,
that, in our recent intercourse, I have had reason to believe you
already realise that neither the character you could wish to earn,
nor the content that all men crave, is to be found in your present
career."

"I had not thought I entertained so close a casuist in Mr
Henry Wilder.   Have you more to urge, sir?"

"Nothing," returned the disappointed and grieved messenger

"Yes, yes, he has," said a low but eager voice at the elbow of the Rover, which rather seemed to breathe out the syllables than dare to utter them aloud; "he has not yet delivered the half of his commission, or sadly has he forgotten the sacred trust!"

"This boy is often a dreamer," interrupted the Rover, smiling with a wild and haggard look. "He sometimes gives form to his unmeaning thoughts, by clothing them in words."

"My thoughts are not unmeaning," continued Roderick, in a louder and bolder strain. "If his peace or happiness be dear to you, do not leave him. Tell him of his high and honourable name; of his youth; of that gentle and virtuous being that he once so fondly loved, and whose memory, even now, he worships. Speak to him of these, as you know how to speak; and, on my life, his ear will not be deaf, his heart cannot be callous, to your word."

"The urchin is mad!"

"I am not mad; or if maddened, it is by the crimes, the dangers, of those I love. Oh! Mr. Wilder, do not leave him  Since you have been among us, he is nearer to what I know he once was, than formerly. Take away that mistaken statement of your force; threats do but harden him. As a friend, admonish; but hope for nothing as a minister of vengeance. You know not the fearful nature of the man, or you would not attempt to stop a torrent. Now—now speak to him; for his eye is already growing kinder.'

"It is in pity, boy, at witnessing how thy reason wavers."

"Had it never swerved more than at this moment, Walter, another need not be called upon to speak between thee and me! My words would then have been regarded, my voice would then have been loud enough to be heard. Why are you dumb? a single happy syllable might now save him."

" Wilder, the child is frightened by this counting of guns and numbering of people. He fears the anger of your anointed master. Go: give him a place in your boat, and recommend him to the mercy of your superior."

" Away, away !" cried Roderick, " I shall not, will not, cannot leave you. Who is there left for me in this world but you ?"

" Yes," continued the Rover, whose forced calmness of expression changed to one of melancholy musing; " it will indeed be better that he should go. See, here is much gold; you will commend him to the care of that admirable woman who already watches one scarcely less helpless, though possibly less——"

" Guilty! speak the word boldly, Walter. I have earned the epithet, and shall not shrink to hear it spoken. Look," he said, taking the ponderous bag, which had been extended towards Wilder, and holding it above his head, in scorn, " this can I cast from me; but the tie which binds me to thee shall never be broken."

As he spoke, the lad approached an open window of the cabin; a plash upon the water was heard, and then a treasure that might have furnished a competence to moderate wishes, was lost for ever to the uses of man. The lieutenant of the Dart turned in haste to deprecate the anger of the Rover; but he could trace, in the features of the lawless chief, no other emotion than a pity which was discoverable even through his unmoved smile.

" Roderick would make but a faithless treasurer," he said. " Still, it is not too late to restore him to his friends. The loss of the gold can be repaired; but, should any serious calamity befall the boy, I might never regain a perfect peace of mind."

" Then keep him near yourself," murmured the lad, whose vehemence seemingly had expended itself. " Go, Mr. Wilder, your boat is waiting; a longer stay will be without an object."

" I fear it will !" returned our adventurer, who had not ceased, during the previous dialogue, to keep his look fastened in manly commiseration, on the countenance of the boy ; — " I greatly fear it will ! — Since I have come the messenger of another, Captain Heidegger, it is your province to supply the answer to my proposition."

The Rover took him by the arm, and led him to a position whence they might look upon the outer scene. Pointing upward at his spars, and making his companion observe the small quantity of sail he carried, he simply said, " Sir, you are a seaman, and may judge of my intentions by this. I shall neither seek nor avoid your boasted cruiser."

# CHAPTER XXX.

---- i ront to front,
bring thou this fiend ----
Within my sword's length set him; if he 'scape,
Heaven forgive him too!

*Macbeth.*

" You have brought the grateful submission of the pirate!"
exclaimed the sanguine commander of the Dart, as the foot of his
messenger touched his deck.

" I bring nothing but defiance!"

" Did you exhibit my statement? Surely, Mr. Ark, so material a document was not forgotten?"

" Nothing was forgotten that the warmest interest in his safety
could suggest, Captain Bignall. Still he refuses to hearken to
your conditions."

" Perhaps, sir, he imagines that we are defective in some of our
spars? He may hope to escape by pressing the canvass on his
own light-heeled ship?"

" Does that look like flight?" demanded Wilder, extending an
arm towards the nearly naked spars and motionless hull of their
neighbour. " The utmost I can obtain is an assurance that he
will not be the assailant."

" 'Fore George, he is a merciful youth! and one that should
be commended for moderation! He will not run his disorderly
picarooning company under the guns of a British man-of-war,
because he owes a little reverence to the flag of his master! Hark
ye, Mr. Ark, we will remember the circumstance when questioned

at the Old Bailey.   Send the people to their guns, sir, and ware the ship round, to put an end at once to this foolery, or we shall have him sending a boat aboard to examine our commissions."

"Captain Bignall," said Wilder, leading his commander still further from the ears of their inferiors, "I may lay some little claim to merit for services done under your own eyes, and in obedience to your orders   If my former conduct gives me any title to presume to counsel one of your great experience, suffer me to urge a short delay."

"Delay!   Does Henry Ark hesitate, when the enemies of his king, nay more, the enemies of man, are daring him to his duty?"

"Sir, you mistake me.   I hesitate, in order that the flag under which we sail may be free from stain, and not with any intent of avoiding the combat.   Our enemy, *my* enemy, knows that he has nothing now to expect for his past generosity, but kindness should he become our captive.   Still, Captain Bignall, I ask for time, to prepare the Dart for a conflict that will try all her powers, and to ensure a victory that will not be bought without a price."

"But, should he escape——

"On my life, he will not attempt it.   I not only know the man, but his formidable means of resistance.   A half hour will put us in the necessary condition, and do no discredit either to our spirit or to our prudence."

The veteran yielded a reluctant consent, which was not, however, accorded without much muttering concerning the disgrace a British man-of-war incurred in not running alongside the boldest pirate that floated, and blowing him out of water with a single match.   Wilder, who was accustomed to the honest professional bravados that often formed a peculiar embellishment to the really firm and manly resolution of the seamen of that age, permitted him to complain at will, while he busied himself in a manner that he knew was now of the last importance, and in a duty that properly came under his more immediate inspection.

The "order for all hands to clear ship for action" was again given, and received in the cheerful temper with which mariners are wont to welcome any of the more important changes of their exciting profession. Little remained, however, to be done; for most of the previous preparations had still been left, as at the original meeting of the two vessels. Then came the beat to quarters, and the more serious and fearful-looking preparations for certain combat. After these arrangements were completed, the crew at their guns, the sail-trimmers at the braces, and the officers in their several batteries, the after-yards were swung, and the ship was once more put in motion.

During this brief interval, the vessel of the Rover lay, at the distance of half a mile, in a state of entire rest, without betraying the smallest interest in the obvious movements of her hostile neighbour. When, however, the Dart was seen yielding to the breeze, and gradually increasing her velocity, until the water was gathering under her fore-foot in a little rolling wave of foam, the bows of the other fell off from the direction of the wind, the top-sail was filled, and, in her turn, the hull was held in command by giving to it the impetus of motion. The Dart now set again at her gaff that broad field which had been lowered during the conference, and which had floated in triumph through the hazards and struggles of a thousand combats. No answering emblem, however, was exhibited from the peak of her adversary.

In this manner the two ships "gathered way," as it is expressed in nautical language, watching each other with eyes as jealous as if they had been rival monsters of the great deep, each endeavouring to conceal from his antagonist the evolution he contemplated next. The earnest manner of Wilder had not failed to produce its influence on the straight-minded seaman who commanded the Dart, and, by this time, he was as much disposed as his lieutenant to approach the conflict leisurely, and with proper caution.

The day had hitherto been cloudless, and a vault of purer blue never canopied a waste of water, than the arch which had stretched for hours above the heads of our marine adventurers. But, as if nature frowned on their present bloody designs, a dark, threatening mass of vapour was blending the ocean with the sky, in a direction opposed to the currents of the air. These well-known and ominous signs did not escape the vigilance of those who manned the hostile ships, but the danger was deemed too remote to interrupt the higher interest of the approaching combat.

" We have a squall brewing in the west," said the experienced and wary Bignall, pointing to the frowning symptoms as he spoke ; " but we can handle the pirate, and get all snug again, before it works its way up against this breeze."

Wilder assented ; for, by this time, professional pride was swelling in his bosom also, and a generous rivalry was getting the mastery of feelings that were possibly foreign to his duty, however natural they might have been in one as open to kindness as himself.

"The Rover is even sending down all his lighter masts !" exclaimed the youth; "it would seem that he distrusts the weather."

" We will not follow his example; for he will wish they were aloft again, the moment we get him fairly under the play of our batteries. By George our King, but he has a pretty moving boat under him ! Let fall the main-course, sir; down with it, or we shall have it night before we get the rogue a-beam."

The order was obeyed; when the Dart, feeling the powerful impulse, quickened her speed, like an animated being that is freshly impelled by its apprehensions or its wishes. By this time, she had gained a position on the weather-quarter of her adversary, who had not manifested the smallest desire to prevent her attaining so material an advantage. On the contrary, while the Dolphin kept the same canvass spread, she continued to lighten her

21

top-hamper, bringing as much of the weight as possible from the towering height of her tall masts, within the greater security of the hull.     Still, the distance between them was too great, in the opinion of Bignall, to commence the contest, while the facility with which his adversary moved ahead threatened to protract the important moment to an unreasonable extent, or to reduce him to a crowd of sail that might prove embarrassing, while enveloped in the smoke, and pressed by the urgencies of the combat.

" We will touch his pride, sir, since you think him a man of spirit," said the veteran.     " Give him a weather-gun, and show him another of his master's ensigns."

The roar of the piece, and the display of three more of the fields of England, in quick succession from different parts of the Dart, failed to produce the slightest evidence even of observation aboard their seemingly insensible neighbour.     The Dolphin still kept on her way, occasionally swooping up to touch the wind, and then deviating from her course again to leeward, as the porpoise is seen to turn aside from his direction to snuff the breeze, while he lazily sports along his briny path.

" He will not be moved by any of the devices of lawful and ordinary warfare," said Wilder, when he witnessed the indifference with which their challenge had been received

" Try him with a shot."

A gun was now discharged from the side next the still receding Dolphin.     The iron messenger was seen bounding along the surface of the sea, skipping lightly from wave to wave, until it cast a little cloud of spray upon the deck of their enemy, as it boomed harmlessly past her hull.     Another, and yet another, followed, without in any manner extracting signal or notice from the Rover.

" How 's this ?" exclaimed the disappointed Bignall.     " Has he a charm for his ship, that all our shot sweep over him in rain ! Master Fid, can you do nothing for the credit of honest people and the honour of a pennant? Let us hear from your old favourite; in times past, she used to speak to better purpose."

"Ay, ay, sir," returned the accommodating Richard, who, in the sudden turns of his fortune, found himself in authority over a much-loved and long-cherished piece. "I christened the gun after Mistress Whiffle, your honour, for the same reason, that they both can do their own talking. Now, stand aside, my lads, and let clattering Kate have a word in the discourse."

Richard, who had coolly taken his sight while speaking, deliberately applied the match with his own hand, and, with a philosophy that was sufficiently to be commended in a mercenary, sent what he boldly pronounced to be "a thorough straight-goer" in the direction of his recent associates. The usual moments of suspense succeeded, and then the torn fragments which were scattered in the air announced that the shot had passed through the nettings of the Dolphin. The effect on the vessel of the Rover was nearly magical. A long stripe of cream-coloured canvass, which had been artfully extended from stem to stern, in a line with her guns, disappeared as suddenly as a bird would shut its wings, leaving in its place a broad, blood-red belt, that was bristling with the armament of the ship. At the same time, an ensign, of a similar ominous colour, rose from her poop, and, fluttering darkly and fiercely for a moment, it became fixed at the end of the gaff.

"Now I know him for the knave that he is!" cried the excited Bignall; "and, see! he has thrown away his false paint, and shows the well-known bloody side, from which he gets his name Stand to your guns, my men! the pirate is getting to be in earnest."

He was still speaking, when a sheet of bright flame glanced from out that streak of red which was so well adapted to work upon the superstitious awe of the common mariners, and was followed by the simultaneous explosion of a dozen wide-mouthed pieces of artillery. The startling change from inattention and indifference to this act of bold and decided hostility produced a strong effect on the boldest heart on board the king's cruiser. The momentary interval of suspense was passed in unchanged attitudes and looks of breathless attention; and then the rushing of the iron storm was heard hurtling through the air, as it came fearfully on. The crash that followed, mingled as it was with human groans, and succeeded by the tearing of riven plank, and the scattering of splinters, ropes, blocks, and the implements of war, proclaimed the fatal accuracy of the broadside. But the surprise and the brief confusion endured but for an instant. The English shouted, sending back a return to the deadly assault they had just received, recovering manfully and promptly from the shock it had assuredly given.

The ordinary and more regular cannonading of a naval combat succeeded. Anxious to precipitate the issue, both ships pressed nigher to each other the while, until in a few moments, the two white canopies of smoke that were wreathing about their respective masts were blended in one, marking a solitary spot of strife, in the midst of a scene of broad and bright tranquillity. The discharges of the cannon were hot, close, and incessant. While the hostile parties, however, closely imitated each other in their zeal in dealing out destruction, a peculiar difference marked the distinction in character of the two crews. Loud, cheering shouts accompanied each discharge from the lawful cruiser, while the people of the Rover did their murderous work in the silence of desperation.

The spirit and uproar of the scene soon quickened that blood in the veins of the veteran Bignall, which had begun to circulate a little slowly by time.

"The fellow has not forgotten his art!" he exclaimed, as the effects of his enemy's skill were getting to be but too manifest in the rent sails, shivered spars, and tottering masts of his own ship. "Had he but the commission of the king in his pocket, one might call him a hero!"

The emergency was too urgent to throw away the time in words. Wilder answered only by cheering his own people to their fierce and laborious task. The ships had now fallen off before the wind, and were running parallel to each other, emitting sheets of flame that were incessantly glancing through immense volumes of smoke. The spars of the respective vessels were alone visible, at brief and uncertain intervals. Many minutes had thus passed, seeming to those engaged but a moment of time, when the mariners of the Dart found that they no longer held their vessel in the quick command, so necessary to their situation. The important circumstance was instantly conveyed from the master to Wilder, and from Wilder to his superior. A hasty consultation on the cause and consequences of this unexpected event was the immediate and natural result.

"See!" cried Wilder, "the sails are already hanging against the masts like rags; the explosions of the artillery have stilled the wind."

"Hark!" answered the more experienced Bignall: "there goes the artillery of Heaven among our own guns. The squall is already upon us—port the helm, sir, and sheer the ship out of the smoke! Hard a-port with the helm, sir, at once! hard with it a-port, I say!"

But the lazy motion of the vessel did not answer to the impatience of those who directed her movements, nor did it meet the pressing exigencies of the moment. In the mean time, while Bignall and the officers whose duties kept them near his person, assisted by the sail-trimmers, were thus occupied, the people in the batteries continued their murderous employment. The roar of cannon was incessant, and nearly overwhelming, though there were instants when the ominous mutterings of the atmosphere were too distinctly audible to be mistaken. Still the eye could lend no assistance to the hearing, in determining the judgment of the mariners.   Hulls, spars, and sails were alike enveloped in the curling wreaths which wrapped heaven, air, vessels, and ocean, alike, in one white, obscure, foggy mantle.   Even the persons of the crew were merely seen at instants labouring at the guns, through brief and varying openings.

"I never knew the smoke pack so heavy on the deck of a ship before," said Bignall, with a concern that even his caution could not entirely repress.   "Keep the helm aport — jam it hard, sir ! By Heaven, Mr. Wilder  those knaves well know they are strug-gling for their lives ! "

"The fight is all our own ! " shouted the second lieutenant, from among the guns, staunching, as he spoke, the blood of a severe splinter-wound in the face, and far too intent on his own immediate occupation, to notice the signs of the weather.   "He has not answered with a single gun, for near a minute."

" 'Fore George, the rogues have enough ! " exclaimed the delighted Bignall.   "Three cheers for vic——"

"Hold, sir ! " interrupted Wilder, with sufficient decision to check his commander's premature exultation;  "on my life, our work is not so soon ended.   I think, indeed, his guns are silent; — but see ! the smoke is beginning to lift.   In a few more min-utes, if our own fire should cease, the view will be clear."

A shout from the men in the batteries interrupted his words; and then came a general cry that the pirates were sheering off. The exultation at this fancied evidence of their superiority was, however, soon and fearfully interrupted.   A bright vivid flash penetrated through the dense vapour which still hung about them in a most extraordinary manner, and was followed by a crash from the heavens, to which the simultaneous explosion of fifty pieces of artillery would have sounded feeble.

"Call the people from their guns ! " said Bignall, in those suppressed tones that are only more portentous from their forced and unnatural calmness: "call them away at once, sir, and get the canvass in!"

Wilder, startled more at the proximity and apparent weight of the squall than at words to which he had long been accustomed, delayed not to give an order that was so urgent. The men left their batteries, like athletæ retiring from the arena, some bleeding and faint, some fierce and angry, and all more or less excited by the furious scene in which they had just been actors. Many sprang to the well-known ropes, while others, as they ascended into the cloud which still hung on the vessel, became lost to the eye in her rigging.

"Shall I reef, or furl?" demanded Wilder, standing with the trumpet at his lips, ready to issue the necessary order.

"Hold, sir; another minute will give us an opening."

The lieutenant paused; for he was not slow to see that now, indeed, the veil was about to be drawn from their real situation. The smoke which had lain upon their very decks, pressed down by the superincumbent weight of the atmosphere, first began to stir, was then seen eddying among the masts; and, finally, whirled wildly away before a strong current of air. The view was, indeed, now all before them.

In place of the glorious sun, and that bright, blue canopy which had lain above them a short half-hour before, the heavens were clothed in one immense black veil. The sea reflected the portentous colour, looking dark and angrily, the waves had already lost their regular rise and fall, and were tossing to and fro, awaiting the power that was to give them direction and force. The flashes from the heavens were not in quick succession; but the few that did break upon the gloominess of the scene, came in majesty and with dazzl'ng brightness. They were accompanied by the terrific thunder of the tropics, in which it is scarcely profanation to fancy that the voice of One who made the universe is actually speaking to the creatures of his hand. On every side was the appearance of a fierce and dangerous struggle in the elements. The vessel of the Rover was running lightly before a breeze, which had already come fresh and fitful from the cloud, with her sails reduced, and her people coolly, but actively employed in repairing the damages of the fight.

Not a moment was to be lost in imitating the example of the wary freebooters. The head of the Dart was hastily, and happily, got in a direction contrary to the breeze; and as she began to follow the course taken by the Dolphin, an attempt was made to gather her torn, and nearly useless canvass to the yards. But precious minutes had been lost in the smoky canopy, that might never be regained. The sea changed its colour from a dark green to a glittering white; and then the fury of the gust was heard rushing fearfully along the water, and with a violence that could not be resisted.

"Be lively, men!" shouted Bignall himself, in the exigency in which his vessel was placed; "roll up the cloth; in with it all — leave not a rag to the squall! 'Fore George, Mr. Wilder, but this wind is not playing with us; cheer the men to their work; speak to them cheerily, sir!"

"Furl away!" shouted Wilder. "Cut, if too late; work away with knives and teeth — down, every man of you, down — down for your lives, all!"

There was an energy in the voice of the lieutenant which sounded supernatural in the ears of his people. He had so recently witnessed a calamity similar to that which again threatened him, that his feelings lent horror to the tones. A score of forms descended swiftly through an atmosphere that appeared sensible to the touch. Nor was their escape, which might be likened to the stooping of birds that dart into their nest, too earnestly pressed. Stripped of its rigging, and already tottering under numerous wounds, the lofty and overloaded spars yielded to the mighty force of the squall, tumbling in succession towards the hull, until nothing stood but the three firmer, but shorn, and nearly useless, lower masts. By far the greater number of those aloft reached the deck in time to insure their safety, though some there were too stubborn, and still too much under the sullen influence of the combat, to hearken to the words of warning. These victims of their own obstinacy were seen clinging to the broken fragments of the spars, as the Dart, in a cloud of foam, drove away from the spot where they floated, until their persons and their misery were alike swallowed in the distance.

"It is the hand of God!" hoarsely exclaimed the veteran Bignall, while his eye drank in the destruction of the wreck. "Mark me, Henry Ark; I will for ever testify that the guns of the pirate have not brought us to this condition."

Little disposed to seek the same miserable consolation as his commander, Wilder exerted himself in counteracting, as far as circumstances would allow, an injury that he felt, however, at that moment to be irreparable. Amid the howling of the gust, and the fearful crashing of the thunder, with an atmosphere now lurid with the glare of lightning, and now nearly obscured by the dark canopy of vapour, and with all the frightful evidences of the fight still recking and ghastly before their eyes, did the men of the British cruiser prove true to themselves and to their ancient reputation. The voices of Bignall and his subordinates were heard in the tempest, uttering those mandates which long experience had rendered familiar, or encouraging their people to their duty. Happily the strife of the elements was of short continuance. The squall soon swept over the spot, leaving the currents of the trade returning into their former channels, and a sea that was rather stilled than agitated, by the counteracting influence of the wind.

But, as one danger passed away from before the eyes of the mariners of the Dart, another, scarcely less to be apprehended, forced itself upon their attention. All recollection of the favours

21 *

of the past, and every feeling of gratitude, was banished from the mind of Wilder by the mountings of professional pride, and that love of glory which becomes inherent in the warrior, as he gazed on the untouched and beautiful symmetry of the Dolphin's spars, and all the perfect and unharmed order of her tackle. It seemed as if she bore a charmed fate, or that some supernatural agency had been instrumental in preserving her amid the violence of a second hurricane. But cooler thought, and more impartial reflection, compelled the internal acknowledgment, that the vigilance and wise precautions of the remarkable individual who appeared not only to govern her movements, but to control her fortunes, had their proper influence in producing the result.

Little leisure, however, was allowed to ruminate on these changes, or to deprecate the advantage of their enemy. The vessel of the Rover had already opened many broad sheets of canvass; and, as the return of the regular breeze gave her the wind, her approach was rapid and unavoidable.

"'Fore George, Mr. Ark, luck is all on the dishonest side to-day," said the veteran, when he perceived, by the direction which the Dolphin took, that the encounter was likely to be renewed. "Send the people to quarters again, and clear away the guns; we are likely to have another bout with the rogues."

"I would advise a moment's delay," Wilder earnestly observed, when he heard his commander issuing an order to his people to prepare to deliver their fire, the instant their enemy should come within a favourable position. "Let me entreat you to delay; we know not what may be his present intentions."

"None shall put foot on the deck of the Dart, without submitting to the authority of her royal master," returned the stern old tar. "Give it to him, my men! Scatter the rogues from their guns! Let them know the danger of approaching a lion, though he should be crippled!"

Wilder saw that remonstrance was too late; for a fresh broadside was hurled from the Dart, to defeat any generous intentions that the Rover might entertain. The ship of the latter received the iron storm while advancing, and immediately deviated from her course, in such a way as to prevent its repetition. Then she was seen sweeping towards the bows of the nearly helpless cruiser of the king, and a hoarse summons was heard ordering her ensign to be lowered.

"Come on, ye villains!" shouted the excited Bignall. "Come, and perform the office with your own hands!"

The graceful ship, as if sensible herself to the taunts of her enemy, sprang nigher to the wind, and shooting across the forefoot of the Dart, delivered her fire, gun after gun, with deliberate and deadly accuracy, full into that defenceless portion of her antagonist. A crush like that of meeting bodies followed, when fifty grim visages were seen entering the scene of carnage, armed with the deadly weapons of personal conflict. The shock of so close and so fatal a discharge had, for the moment, paralysed the efforts of the assailed; but no sooner did Bignall and his lieutenant see the dark forms that issued from the smoke on their own decks, than, with voices that had not even lost their authority, each summoned a band of followers, backed by whom they bravely dashed into opposite gangways of their ship, to stay the torrent. The first encounter was fierce and fatal, both parties receding a little, to wait for succour and recover breath.

"Come on, ye murderous thieves!" cried the dauntless veteran, who stood foremost in his own band, conspicuous by the grey locks that floated around his naked head, "well do ye know that Heaven is with the right!"

The grim freebooters in his front recoiled and opened; then came a sheet of flame, from the side of the Dolphin, through an empty port of her adversary, bearing in its centre a hundred deadly missiles. The sword of Bignall was flourished furiously and wildly above his head, and his voice was still heard shouting, till utterance failed him,—

"Come on, ye knaves! come on!" he cried. — "Harry — Harry Ark! O, God! — Hurrah!"

He fell like a log, and died the unwitting owner of that very commission for which he had toiled throughout a life of hardship and danger. Until now, Wilder had made good his quarter of the deck, though pressed by a band as fierce and daring as his own; but at this fearful crisis in the combat a voice was heard in the *mêlée* that thrilled on all his own nerves, seeming even to carry its fearful influence over the minds of his men.

"Make way there, make way!" it said, in tones clear, deep, and breathing with authority, "make way, and follow; no hand but mine shall lower that vaunting flag!"

"Stand to your faith, my men!" shouted Wilder, in reply. Shouts, oaths, imprecations, and groans, formed a fearful accompaniment of the rude encounter, which was, however, too violent to continue long. Wilder saw, with agony, that numbers and impetuosity were sweeping his supporters from around him. Again and again he called them to the succour with his voice, or stimulated them to daring by his example.

Friend after friend fell at his feet, until he was driven to the utmost extremity of the deck. Here he again rallied a little band, against which several furious charges were made in vain.

"Ha!" exclaimed a voice he well knew; "death to all traitors! Spit the spy as you would a dog! Charge through them, my bullies; a halbert to the hero who shall reach his heart."

"Avast, ye lubbers!" returned the staunch Richard. "Here are a white man and a nigger at your service, if you've need of a spit."

"Two more of the gang!" continued the general, aiming a blow that threatened to immolate the topman, as he spoke.

A dark, half-naked form was interposed to receive the descending blade, which fell on the staff of a half-pike, severing it as if it were a reed. Nothing daunted by the defenceless state in which he found himself, Scipio made his way to the front of Wilder, where with a body divested to the waist of every garment, and empty-handed, he fought with his brawny arms, like one who despised the cuts, thrusts, and assaults, of which his athletic frame became the helpless subject.

"Give it to 'em, right and left, Guinea," cried Fid; "here is one who will come in as a backer, as soon as he has stopped the grog of the marine."

The parries and science of the unfortunate general were at this moment set at nought by a blow from Richard, which broke down all his defences, descending through cap and skull to the jaw.

"Hold, murderers!" cried Wilder, who saw the numberless blows that were falling on the defenceless body of the still undaunted black. "Strike here! but spare an unarmed man!"

The sight of our adventurer became confused, for he saw the negro fall, dragging with him to the deck two of his assailants; and then a voice deep as the emotion which such a scene might create, uttered in the very portals of his ear,—

"Our work is done! He that strikes another blow makes an enemy of me."

## CHAPTER XXXI.

——Take him hence!
The whole world shall not save him.
*Cymbeline.*

THE recent gust had not passed more fearfully and suddenly over the ship than the scene just related; but the smiling aspect of the tranquil sky, and the bright sun of a Caribbean sea, found no parallel in the horrors that succeeded the combat. The momentary confusion which accompanied the fall of Scipio soon disappeared, and Wilder was left to gaze on the wreck of all the boasted powers of his cruiser, and on that waste of human life which had been the attendants of the struggle. The former has already been sufficiently described; but a short account of the present state of the actors may serve to elucidate the events that are to follow.

Within a few yards of the place he was permitted to occupy himself, stood the motionless form of the Rover. A second glance was necessary, however, to recognise, in the grim visage to which the boarding-cap already mentioned lent a look of artificial ferocity, the usually bland countenance of the man. As the eye of Wilder roamed over the swelling, erect, and triumphant figure, it was difficult not to fancy that even the stature had been suddenly and unaccountably increased. One hand rested on the hilt of a yatagan, which, by the crimson drops that flowed along its curved blade, had evidently done fatal service in the fray; and one foot was placed, seemingly with supernatural weight, on that national emblem which it had been his pride to lower. His eye was wandering sternly, but understandingly, over the scene, though he spoke not, nor in any other manner betrayed the deep interest he felt in the past. At his side, and nearly within the circle of his arm, stood the cowering form of the boy Roderick, unprovided with weapon, his garments sprinkled with blood, his eye contracted, wild, and fearful, and his face pallid as those in whom the tide of life had just ceased to circulate.

Here and there were to be seen the wounded captives, still sullen and unconquered in spirit, while many of their less fortunate enemies lay in their blood, around the deck, with such gleamings of ferocity on their countenances as plainly denoted that the current of their meditations was still running on vengeance. The uninjured and the slightly wounded of both bands, were already pursuing their different objects of plunder or of secretion.

But so thorough was the discipline established by the leader of the freebooters, so absolute his power, that a blow had not been struck, or blood drawn, since the moment his prohibitory mandate was heard. There had been enough of destruction, however, to satisfy the most gluttonous longings, had human life been the sole object of the assault. Wilder felt many a pang, as the marble-like features of some humble friend or faithful servitor came, one after another, under his recognition; but the shock was the greatest when his eye fell upon the rigid and still frowning countenance of his veteran commander.

" Captain Heidegger," he said, struggling to maintain the fortitude which became the moment; " the fortune of the day is yours: I ask mercy and kindness for the survivors."

" They shall be granted to those who, of right, may claim them : I hope it may be found that all are included in this promise."

The voice of the Rover was solemn and full of meaning : it appeared to convey more than the simple import of the words.

Wilder might have mused long and vainly, however, on the equivocal manner in which he had been answered, had not the approach of a body of the hostile crew, among whom he instantly recognised the most prominent of the late mutineers of the Dolphin, speedily supplied a clue to the hidden meaning of their leader.

"We claim the execution of our ancient laws!" commenced the foremost of the gang, addressing his chief with a brevity and fierceness which the late combat might have generated, if not excused.

"What would you have?"

"The lives of traitors!" was the sullen answer.

"You know the conditions of our service. If any such are in our power, let them meet their fate."

Had any doubt remained in the mind of Wilder, as to the meaning of these terrible claimants of justice, it would have vanished at the manner with which he and his two companions were immediately dragged before the lawless chief. Though the love of life was strong and active in his breast, it was not, even in that fearful moment, exhibited in a deprecating or unmanly form. Not for an instant did his mind waver, or his thoughts wander to any subterfuge that might prove unworthy of his profession, or of his former character. One anxious, enquiring look was fastened on the eye of him whose power alone could save him. He witnessed the short, severe struggle that softened the rigid muscles of the Rover's countenance; and then he saw the instant, cold, and calm composure which settled on every one of its disciplined lineaments. He knew, at once, that the feelings of the man were smothered in the duty of the chief, and more was unnecessary to teach him the hopelessness of his condition. Scorning to render his state degrading by useless remonstrances, the youth remained where his accusers had seen fit to place him —firm, motionless, and silent.

"What would ye have?" the Rover at length asked, in a voice that even his iron nerves scarce rendered deep and full-toned as common. "What ask ye?"

"Their lives!"

"I understand you: go; they are at your mercy."

Notwithstanding the horrors of the scene through which he had just passed, and that high excitement which had sustained him through the fight, the deliberate, solemn tones with which his judge delivered a sentence that he knew consigned him to a hasty and ignominious death, shook the frame of our adventurer nearly to insensibility. The blood recoiled backward to his heart, and the sickening sensation that beset his brain threatened to upset his reason. But the shock passed, on the instant, leaving him erect, and seemingly firm as ever, and certainly with no evidence of mortal weakness that human eye could discover.

"For myself nothing is demanded," he said, with admirable steadiness. "I know your self-enacted laws condemn me to a miserable fate; but for these ignorant, confiding, faithful followers, I claim, nay, beg, entreat, implore your mercy; they knew not what they did, and——"

"Speak to these!" said the Rover, pointing with an averted eye, to the fierce knot by which he was surrounded: "these are your judges, and the sole ministers of mercy."

Strong and nearly unconquerable disgust was apparent in the manner of the youth; with a mighty effort he subdued it, and, turning to the crew, continued,—

"Then even to these will I humble myself in petitions. Ye are men, and ye are mariners——"

"Away with him!" exclaimed the croaking Nightingale; "he preaches! Away with him to the yard-arm!—away!"

The shrill, long-drawn winding of the call which the callous boatswain sounded in mockery, was answered by an echo from twenty voices, in which the accents of nearly as many different people mingled in hoarse discordancy, each shouting in turn,—

"To the yard-arm! Away with the three!—away!"

Wilder made a last appeal to the Rover with his eye, but he met no look in return, the face of the other being intentionally averted. With a burning brain, he felt himself rudely transferred from the quarter-deck into the centre and less privileged portion of the ship. The violence of the passage, the hurried reeving of cords, and all the fearful preparations of a nautical execution, appeared but the business of a moment, to one who stood so near the verge of time.

"A yellow flag for punishment!" bawled the revengeful captain of the forecastle; "let the gentleman sail on his last cruise under the rogue's ensign!"

"A yellow flag! a yellow flag!" echoed twenty brawling throats. "Down with the Rover's ensign, and up with the colours of the prevôt-marshal! A yellow flag! a yellow flag!"

The hoarse laughter, and mocking merriment, with which this coarse device was received, stirred the ire of Fid, who had submitted in silence so far to the rude treatment he received, for no other reason than that he thought his superior was the best qualified to utter the little which it might be necessary to say.

"Avast, ye villains!" he hotly exclaimed, prudence and moderation losing their influence under the excitement of anger; "ye cut-throat, lubberly villains! That ye are villains, is to be proved in your teeth, by your getting your sailing orders from the devil; and that ye are lubbers, any man may see by the fashion in which ye have rove this cord about my throat. A fine jam will ye make with a turn in your whip! But ye'll all come to know how a man is to be decently hanged, ye rogues, ye will. Ye'll all come honestly by the knowledge, in your day, ye will!"

"Clear the turn and run him up!" shouted one, two, three

voices, in hurried succession; "a clear whip, and a swift run to heaven!"

Happily, a fresh burst of riotous clamour from one of the hatchways interrupted the intention; and then was heard the cry of,—

"A priest! a priest! Pipe the rogues to prayers, before they take their dance on nothing!"

The ferocious laughter, with which the freebooters received this sneering proposal, was hushed as suddenly as if One answered to their mockery from that mercy-seat whose power they so sacrilegiously braved. A deep, menacing voice was heard in their midst, saying,—

"By Heaven, if touch, or look, be laid too boldly on prisoner in this ship, he who offends had better beg the fate ye give these miserable men, than meet my anger. Stand off, I bid you, and let the chaplain approach!"

Every bold hand was instantly withdrawn, and each profane lip was closed in trembling silence, giving the terrified and horror-stricken subject of their liberties room and opportunity to advance to the scene of punishment.

"See," said the Rover, calmly, but still with authority, "you are a minister of God, and your office is sacred charity. If you have aught to smooth the dying moment to fellow-mortal, haste to impart it!"

"In what have these offended?" demanded the divine, when power was given to speak.

"No matter; it is enough that their hour is near! If you you would lift your voice in prayer, fear nothing. The unusual sounds shall be welcome even here. Ay, and these miscreants, who so boldly surround you, shall kneel, and be mute, as beings whose souls are touched by the holy rite. Scoffers shall be dumb, and unbelievers respectful, at my beck. Speak freely!"

"Scourge of the seas!" commenced the chaplain, across whose

pallid features a flash of holy excitement cast its glow, "remorseless violator of the laws of man! audacious contemner of the mandates of your God! a fearful retribution shall avenge this crime Is it not enough that you have this day consigned so many to a sudden end, but your vengeance must be glutted with more blood? Beware the hour when these things shall be visited, in almighty power, on your own devoted head!"

"Look!" said the Rover, smiling, but with an expression that was haggard, in spite of the unnatural exultation that struggled about his quivering lip; "here are the evidences of the manner in which Heaven protects the right!"

"Though its awful justice be hidden in inscrutable wisdom, for a time, deceive not thyself; the hour is at hand when it shall be seen and felt in majesty!" The voice of the chaplain became suddenly choked; for his wandering eye had fallen on the frowning countenance of Bignall, which, set in death, lay but half concealed beneath a flag which the Rover himself had cast upon the body. Then, summoning his energies, he continued in the clear and admonitory strain that befitted his sacred calling:— "They tell me you are but half lost to feeling for your kind; and, though the seeds of better principles, of better days, are smothered in your heart, that they still exist, and might be quickened into goodly——"

"Peace! You speak in vain. To your duty with these men, or be silent."

"Is their doom sealed?"

"It is."

"Who says it?" demanded a low voice at the elbow of the Rover, which, coming upon his ear at that moment, thrilled upon his most latent nerve, chasing the blood from his cheek to the secret recesses of his frame. But the weakness passed away with the surprise, and he calmly, and almost instantly, answered,—

"The law."

"The law!" repeated the governess. "Can they who set all order at defiance, who despise each human regulation, talk of law? Say it is heartless vindictive vengeance, if you will; but call it not by the sacred name of law. — I wander from my object! They have told me of this frightful scene, and I am come to offer ransom for the offenders. Name your price, and let it be worthy of the subject we redeem; a grateful parent shall freely give it all for the preserver of his child."

"If gold will purchase the lives you wish," the other interrupted, with the swiftness of thought, "it is here in hoards, and ready on the moment. What say my people? Will they take ransom?"

A brooding pause succeeded; and then, a low, ominous murmur was raised in the throng, announcing their reluctance to dispense with vengeance. The glowing eye of the Rover scanned the fierce countenances by which he was environed; his lips moved with vehemence; but, disdaining further intercession, nothing was uttered for the ear. Turning to the divine, he added, with the forced composure of his wonderful manner,—

"Forget not your sacred office—time is leaving us." He was then moving slowly aside, in imitation of the governess, who had already veiled her features from the revolting scene, when Wilder addressed him :—

"For the service you would have done me, from my soul I thank you," he said. "If you would know that I leave you in peace, give me yet one solemn assurance before I die."

"To what?"

"Promise, that they who came with me into your ship shall leave it unharmed, and speedily."

"Promise, Walter," said a solemn, smothered voice in the throng.

"I do."

"I ask no more. Now, reverend minister of God, perform

thy holy office, near my companions. Their ignorance may profit
by your service. If I quit this bright and glorious scene, with
out thought of, and gratitude to, that Being who, I humbly trust,
has made me an heritor of still greater things, I offend wittingly,
and without hope. But these may find consolation in your
prayers."

Amid an awful silence, the chaplain approached the devoted
companions of Wilder. Their comparative insignificance had
left them unobserved during most of the foregoing scene; and
material changes had occurred unheeded, in their situation. Fid
was seated on the deck, his collar unbuttoned, his neck encircled
with the cord, sustaining the head of the nearly helpless black,
which he had placed, with singular tenderness and care, in his lap.

" This man, at least, will disappoint the malice of his enemies,"
said the divine, taking the hard hand of the negro into his own;
" the termination of his wrongs and his degradation approaches;
he will soon be far beyond the reach of human injustice. Friend,
by what name is your companion known ?"

"It is little matter how you hail a dying man," returned
Richard, with a melancholy shake of the head. "He has commonly been entered on the ship's books as Scipio Africa, coming,
as he did, from the coast of Guinea; but, if you call him S'ip,
he will not be slow to understand."

" Has he known baptism ? Is he a Christian ?"

" If he be not, I don't know who the devil is !" responded
Richard, with an asperity that might be deemed a little unseasonable. " A man who serves his country, is true to his messmate, and has no skulk about him, I call a saint, so far as mere
religion goes. I say, Guinea, my hearty, give the chaplain a
gripe of the fist, if you call yourself a Christian. A Spanish
windlass would not give a stronger screw than the knuckles of
that nigger an hour ago; and, now, you see to what a giant may
be brought !"

"His latter moment is, indeed, near. Shall I offer a prayer for the health of the departing spirit?"

"I don't know, I don't know!" answered Fid, gulping his words, and uttering a hem, that was still deep and powerful, as in the brightest and happiest of his days. "When there is so little time given to a poor fellow to speak his mind in, it may be well to let him have a chance to do most of the talking. Something may come uppermost, which he would like to send to his friends in Africa; in which case we may as well be looking out for a proper messenger. Hah! what is it, boy? You see he is already trying to rowse something up out of his ideas."

"Misser Fid—he'm take a collar," said the black, struggling for utterance.

"Ay, ay," returned Richard, again clearing his throat, and looking to the right and left fiercely, seeking some object on which to wreak his vengeance. "Ay, ay, Guinea; put your mind at ease on that point, my hearty, and, for that matter, on all others. You shall have a grave as deep as the sea, and Christian burial, boy, if this here parson will stand by his work. Any small message you may have for your friends shall be logg'd, and put in the way of coming to their ears. You have had much foul weather in your time, Guinea, and some squalls have whistled about your head that might have been spared, mayhap, had your colour been a shade or two lighter. For that matter it may be that I have rode you down a little too close myself, boy, when overheated with the conceit of skin; for all which may the Lord forgive me as freely as I hope you will do the same thing!"

The negro made a fruitless effort to rise, endeavouring to grasp the hand of the other, saying, as he did so,—

"Misser Fid beg a pardon of a black man! Masser aloft forget he'm all, Misser Richard; he t'ink 'em no more."

"It will be what I call a d—d generous thing, if he does," returned Richard, whose sorrow and whose conscience had stirred up his uncouth feelings to an extraordinary degree. "There's the affair of slipping off the wreck of the smuggler has never been properly settled atween us, neither; and many other small services of like nature, for which, d'ye see, I'll just thank you while there is opportunity; for no one can say whether we shall ever be borne again on the same ship's books."

A feeble sign from his companion caused the topman to pause, while he endeavoured to construe its meaning as well as he was able. With a facility, that was in some degree owing to the character of the individual, his construction of the other's meaning was favourable to himself, as was quite evident by the manner in which he resumed,—

"Well, well, mayhap we may. I suppose they berth the people there in some such order as is done here below, in which case we may be put within hailing distance, after all. Our sailing orders are both signed; though, as you seem likely to slip your cable before these thieves are ready to run me up, you will be getting the best of the wind. I shall not say much concerning any signals it may be necessary to show, in order to make one another out aloft, taking it for granted that you will not overlook Master Harry on account of the small advantage you may have in being the first to shove off, intending myself to keep as close as possible in his wake, which will give me the twofold advantage of knowing I am on the right tack, and of falling in with you."

"These are evil words, and fatal alike to your own future peace, and to that of your unfortunate friend," interrupted the divine. "His reliance must be placed on One, different in all his attributes from your officer, to follow whom, or to consult whose frail conduct, would be the height of madness. Place your faith on another——"

"If I do, may I be——"

"Peace," said Wilder; "the black would speak to me."

Scipio had turned his looks in the direction of his officer, and was making another feeble effort towards extending his hand. As Wilder placed his own within the grasp of that of the dying negro, the latter succeeded in laying it on his lips, and then, flourishing with a convulsive movement that Herculean arm which he had so lately and so successfully brandished in defence of his master, the limb stiffened and fell, though the eyes still continued their affectionate and glaring gaze on that countenance he had so long loved, and which, in the midst of all his long-endured wrongs, had never refused to meet his look of love in kindness. A low murmur followed this scene, and then complaints succeeded, in a louder strain, till more than one voice was heard, openly muttering its discontent that vengeance should be so long delayed.

" Away with them!" shouted an ill-omened voice from the throng. "Into the sea with the carcass, and up with the living."

" Avast!" burst out of the chest of Fid, with an awfulness and depth that stayed even the daring movements of that lawless moment. " Who dare to cast a seaman into the brine, with the dying look standing in his lights, and his last words still in his messmate's ears? Ha! would ye stopper the fins of a man as ye would pin a lobster's claw? That for your fastenings and your lubberly knots together!" The excited topman snapped the lines by which his elbows had been imperfectly secured, while speaking, and immediately lashed the body of the black to his own, though his words received no interruption from a process that was executed with a seaman's dexterity. " Where was the man in your lubberly crew that could lay upon a yard with this here black, or haul upon a lee-earing, while he held the weather-line? Could any one of ye all give up his rations, in order that a sick messmate might fare the better! or work a double tide to spare the weak arm of a friend? Show me one who had as little dodge under fire, as a sound mainmast, and I will show you all

22

that is left of his better. And now sway upon your whip, and thank God that the honest end goes up, while the rogues are suffered to keep their footing for a time."

"Sway away!" echoed Nightingale, seconding his hoarse and ominous cry by the winding of his call; "away with them to heaven!"

"Hold!" exclaimed the chaplain, happily arresting the cord before it had yet done its fatal office. "For His sake, whose mercy may one day be needed by the most hardened of ye all, give but another moment of time! What mean these words! Do I read aright? 'Ark of Lynnhaven!'"

"Ay, ay," said Richard, loosening the rope a little, in order to speak with greater freedom, and transferring the last morsel of the weed from his box to his mouth, as he answered; "seeing you are an apt scholar, no wonder you make it out so easily, though written by a hand that was always better with a marling-spike than a quill."

"But whence came the words? Why do you bear those names, thus written indelibly in the skin! Patience, men! monsters; demons! Would ye deprive the dying man of even a minute of that precious time which becomes so dear to all, as life is leaving us?"

"Give yet another minute!" said a deep voice from behind.

"Whence come these words, I ask?" again the chaplain demanded.

"They are neither more nor less than the manner in which a circumstance was logged, which is now of no consequence, seeing that the cruise is nearly up with all who are chiefly concerned. The black spoke of the collar; but, then, he thought I might be staying in port, while he was drifting between heaven and earth, in search of his last moorings."

"Is there aught, here, that I should know?" interrupted the eager, tremulous voice of Mrs. Wyllys. "O, Merton! why these questions? Has my yearning been prophetic? Does nature give so mysterious a warning of its claim!"

"Hush, dearest madam! your thoughts wander from probabilities, and my faculties become confused.—'The Ark of Lynnhaven' was the name of an estate in the islands, belonging to a near and dear friend, and it was the place where I received, and whence I sent to the main the precious trust confided to my care. But——"

"Say on!" she exclaimed, rushing madly in front of Wilder, and seizing the cord which, a moment before, had been tightened nearly to his destruction, stripping it from his throat with a sort of supernatural dexterity: "it was not then the name of a ship?"

"A ship! surely not. But what mean these hopes?—these fears?"

"The collar! the collar! speak; what of that collar?"

"It means no great things, now, my lady," returned Fid, very coolly placing himself in the same condition as Wilder, by profiting by the liberty of his arms, and loosening his own neck from the halter, notwithstanding a movement made by some of the people to prevent it, which was, however, stayed by a look from their leader's eyes. "I will first cast loose this here rope; seeing that it is neither decent, nor safe, for an ignorant man, like me, to enter into such unknown navigation a-head of his officer. The collar was just the necklace of the dog, which is here to be seen on the arm of poor Guinea, who was, in most respects, a man for whose equal one might long look in vain."

"Read it," said the governess, a film passing before her own eyes; "read it," she added, motioning with a quivering hand to the divine to peruse the inscription, that was distinctly legible on the plate of brass.

"Holy Dispenser of good! what is this I see? 'Neptune, the property of Paul de Lacey!'"

A loud cry burst from the lips cf the governess; her hands were clasped one single instant upward, in that thanksgiving which oppressed her soul, and then, as recollection returned, Wilder was pressed fondly, frantically to her bosom, while her voice was heard to say, in the piercing tones of all-powerful nature,—

"My child! my child!—You will not—cannot—dare not rob a long-stricken and bereaved mother of her offspring! Give me back my son, my noble son! and I will weary Heaven with prayers in your behalf. Ye are brave, and cannot be deaf to mercy. Ye are men, who have lived in constant view of God's majesty, and will not refuse to listen to this evidence of his pleasure. Give me my child, and I yield all else. He is of a race long honoured upon the seas, and no mariner will be deaf to his claims. The widow of De Lacey, the daughter of ——, cries for mercy. Their united blood is in his veins, and it will not be spilt by you! A mother bows herself to the dust before you, to ask mercy for her offspring. Oh! give me my child! my child!"

As the words of the petitioner died upon the ear, a stillness settled on the place, that might have been likened to the holy calm which the entrance of better feelings leaves upon the soul of the sinner. The grim freebooters regarded each other in doubt; the workings of nature manifesting themselves even in their stern and hardened visages. Still, the desire for vengeance had got too firm a hold of their minds to be dispossessed at a word. The result would have been doubtful, had not one suddenly re-appeared in their midst who never ordered in vain; and who knew how to guide, to quell, or to mount and trample on their humours, as his own pleasure dictated. For half a minute, he looked around him, his eye still following the circle, which receded as he gazed, until even those longest accustomed to yield to his will began to wonder at the extraordinary aspect in which it was now exhibited. The gaze was wild and bewildered; and the face pallid as that of the petitioning mother. Three times did the lips sever, before sound issued from the caverns of his chest; then arose on the attentive ears of the breathless and listening crowd, a voice that seemed equally charged with inward emotion and high authority. With a haughty gesture of the hand, and a manner that was too well understood to be mistaken, **he** said,—

"Disperse! Ye know my justice; but ye know I will be obeyed. My pleasure shall be known to-morrow."

# CHAPTER XXXII.

——This is he;
Who hath upon him still that natural stamp:
It was wise nature's end in the donation,
To be his evidence now.
SHAKSPEARE.

THAT morrow came, and with it an entire change in the scene
and character of our tale. The Dolphin and the Dart were
sailing in amity, side by side; the latter again bearing the ensign
of England, and the former carrying a naked gaff. The injuries
of the gust and the combat had so far been repaired that, to a
common eye, each gallant vessel was again prepared equally to
encounter the hazards of the ocean or of warfare. A long, blue,
hazy streak, to the north, proclaimed the proximity of the land;
and some three or four light coasters of that region, which were
sailing nigh, announced how little of hostility existed in the present purposes of the freebooters.

What those designs were, however, still remained a secret
buried in the bosom of the Rover alone. Doubt, wonder, and
distrust were, each in its turn, to be traced in the features of his
captives, and in those of his own crew. Throughout the whole
of the long night, which had succeeded the events of the important day just past, he had been pacing the poop in brooding
silence. The little he had uttered was merely to direct the
movements of the vessels; and when any ventured, with other
design, to approach his person, a sign, that none there dared disregard, secured him the solitude he wished. Once or twice,

indeed, the boy Roderick was seen hovering at his elbow, but it was as a guardian spirit would be fancied to linger near the object of its care, unobtrusively, and, it might almost be added, invisible. When, however, the sun came burnished and glorious, out of the waters of the east, a gun was fired, to bring a coaster to the side of the Dolphin; and then it seemed that the curtain was to be raised on the closing scene of the drama. With his crew assembled on the deck beneath, and the principal personages among his captives beside him on the poop, the Rover addressed the former:—

"Years have united us by a common fortune," he said: "we have long been submissive to the same laws. If I have been prompt to punish, I have been ready to obey. You cannot charge me with injustice. But the covenant is now ended. I take back my pledge, and I return you your faiths. Nay, frown not— hesitate not—murmur not! The compact ceases, and our laws are ended. Such was the condition of the service. I give you your liberty, and little do I claim in return. That you need have no grounds of reproach, I bestow my treasure. See," he added, raising that bloody ensign with which he had so often braved the power of the nations, and exhibiting beneath it sacks of that metal which has so long governed the world; "see! This was mine: it is now yours. It shall be put in yonder coaster; there I leave you, to bestow it, yourselves, on those you may deem most worthy. Go: the land is near. Disperse, for your own sakes: nor hesitate; for, without me, well do ye know that vessel of the king would be your master. The ship is already mine; of all the rest, I claim these prisoners alone for my portion. Farewell!"

Silent amazement succeeded this unlooked-for address. There was, indeed, for a moment, some disposition to rebel; but the measures of the Rover had been too well taken for resistance. The Dart lay on their beam, with her people at their guns, matches lighted, and a heavy battery.  Unprepared, without a leader, and surprised, opposition would have been madness.  The first astonishment had scarce abated, before each freebooter rushed to secure his individual effects, and to transfer them to the deck of the coaster.  When all but the crew of a single boat had left the Dolphin, the promised gold was sent, and then the loaded craft was seen hastily seeking the shelter of some secret creek.  During this scene, the Rover had been silent as death.  He next turned to Wilder; and making a mighty but successful effort to still his feelings, he added,—

"Now must we, too, part.  I commend my wounded to your care.  They are necessarily with your surgeons  I know the trust I give you will not be abused."

"My word is the pledge of their safety," returned the young De Lacey.

"I believe you.—Lady," he added, approaching the elder of the females, with an air in which earnestness and hesitation strongly contended, "if a proscribed and guilty man may still address you, grant yet a favour."

"Name it : a mother's ear can never be deaf to him who has spared her child."

"When you petition Heaven for that child, forget not there is another being who may still profit by your prayers :—no more.— And now," he continued, looking about him like one who was determined to be equal to the pang of the moment, however difficult it might prove, and surveying, with an eye of painful regret, those naked decks which were so lately teeming with scenes of life and revelry; "and now—ay—now we part !  The boat awaits you."

Wilder soon saw his mother and Gertrude into the pinnace ; but he still lingered himself.

"And you !" he said, "what will become of you?"

"I shall shortly be— forgotten.—Adieu !"

The manner in which the Rover spoke forbade delay.  The young man hesitated, squeezed his hand, and left him.

When Wilder found himself restored to his proper vessel. of which the death of Bignall had left him in command, he immediately issued the order to fill her sails, and to steer for the nearest haven of his country.  So long as sight could read the movements of the man who remained on the decks of the Dolphin, not a look was averted from the motionless object.  She lay, with her maintop-sail to the mast, stationary as some beautiful fabric placed there by fairy power, still lovely in her proportions, and perfect in all her parts.  A human form was seen swiftly pacing her poop, and, by its side, glided one who looked like a lessened shadow of that restless figure.  At length distance swallowed these indistinct images; and then the eye was wearied, in vain, to trace the internal movements of the distant ship.  But doubt was soon ended.  Suddenly a streak of flame flashed from her decks, springing fiercely from sail to sail.  A vast cloud of smoke broke out of the hull, and the deadened roar of artillery followed.  To this succeeded, for a time, the awful, and yet attractive spectacle of a burning ship.  The whole was terminated by an immense canopy of smoke, and an explosion that caused the sails of the distant Dart to waver, as if the winds of the trades were deserting their eternal direction.  When the cloud had lifted from the ocean, an empty waste of water was seen beneath ; and none might mark the spot where that beautiful specimen of human ingenuity had so lately floated.  Some of those who ascended to the upper masts of the cruiser, and were aided by glasses, believed, indeed, that they could discern a solitary speck upon the sea; but whether it was a boat, or some fragment of the wreck, was never known.

From that time, the history of the dreaded Red Rover became lost in the fresher incidents of those eventful seas.  But the mariner, long after was known to shorten the watches of the

night, by recounting scenes of mad enterprise that were thought
to have occurred under his auspices.   Rumour did not fail to
embellish and pervert them, until the real character, and even the
name of the individual were confounded with the actors of other
atrocities.   Scenes of higher and more ennobling interest, too,
were occurring on the Western Continent, to efface the circumstances of a legend that many deemed wild and improbable.   The
British colonies of North America had revolted against the government of the crown, and a weary war was bringing the contest
to a successful issue.   Newport, the opening scene of this tale,
had been successively occupied by the arms of the king, and by
those of that monarch who had sent the chivalry of his nation
to aid in stripping his rival of her vast possessions.

The beautiful haven had sheltered hostile fleets, and the peaceful villas had often rung with the merriment of youthful soldiers.
More than twenty years after the events just related had been
added to the long record of time, when the island town witnessed
the rejoicings of another festival, the allied forces had compelled
the most enterprising leader of the British troops to yield himself and army captive to their numbers and skill.   The struggle
was believed to be over, and the worthy townsmen had, as usual,
been loud in the manifestations of their pleasure.   The rejoicings, however, ceased with the day; and, as night gathered over
the place, the little city was resuming its customary provincial
tranquillity.   A gallant frigate, which lay in the very spot where
the vessel of the Rover had first been seen, had already lowered
the gay assemblage of friendly ensigns which had been spread in
the usual order of a gala-day.   A flag of intermingled colours,
and bearing a constellation of bright and rising stars, alone was
floating at her gaff.   Just at this moment, another cruiser, but
one of less magnitude, was seen entering the roadstead, bearing
also the friendly ensign of the new States.   Headed by the tide,
and deserted by the breeze, she soon dropped an anchor, in the

pass between Connanicut and Rhode, when a boat was seen making for the inner harbour, impelled by the arms of six powerful
rowers.    As the barge approached a retired and lonely wharf, a
solitary observer of its movements was enabled to see that it contained a curtained litter, and a single female form.   Before the
curiosity, which such a sight would be apt to create in the breast
of one like the spectator mentioned, had time to exercise itself in
conjectures, the oars were tossed, the boat had touched the piles,
and, borne by the seamen, the litter, attended by the woman,
stood before him.

"Tell me, I pray you," said a voice, in whose tones grief and
resignation were singularly combined, "if Captain Henry de
Lacey, of the continental marine has a residence in this town of
Newport?"

"That has he," answered the aged man, addressed by the
female, "that has he; or as one might say, two; since yonder
frigate is no less his than the dwelling on the hill just by."

"Thou art too old to point us out the way; but if grandchild,
or idler of any sort, be near, here is silver to reward him."

"Lord help you, lady!" returned the other, casting an oblique
glance at her appearance as a sort of salvo for the term, and
pocketing the trifling piece she offered, with singular care; "Lord
help you, madam! old though I am, and something worn down
by hardships and marvellous adventures, both by sea and land,
yet will I gladly do so small an office for one of your condition.
Follow, and you shall see that your pilot is not altogether unused
to the path."

The old man turned, and was leading the way off the wharf,
even before he had completed the assurance of his boasted ability.
The seamen and the female followed, the latter walking sorrow-
fully and in silence by the side of the litter.

"If you have need of refreshment," said their guide, pointing
over his shoulder. "yonder is a well-known inn, and one much

frequented in its time by mariners. Neighbour Joram and the
Foul Anchor have had a reputation in their day, as well as the
greatest warrior in the land; and, though honest Joe is gathered
in for the general harvest, the house stands as firm as the day he
first entered it. A goodly end he made, and profitable is it to the
weak-minded sinner to keep such an example before his eyes!"

A smothered sound issued from the litter; but, though the
guide stopped to listen, it was succeeded by no other evidence of
the character of its tenant.

"The sick man is in suffering," he resumed, "but bodily pain,
and all afflictions which we suffer in the flesh, must have their
allotted time. I have lived to see seven bloody and cruel wars,
of which this, which now rages, is, I humbly trust, to be the last.
Of the wonders which I witnessed, and the bodily dangers which
I compassed in the sixth, eye hath never beheld, nor can tongue
utter, their equal!"

"Time hath dealt hardly by you, friend," meekly interrupted
the female. "This gold may add a few more comfortable days
to those that are already past."

The cripple, for their conductor was lame as well as aged,
received the offering with gratitude, apparently too much occupied in estimating its amount, to give any more of his immediate
attention to the discourse. In the deep silence that succeeded,
the party reached the door of the villa they sought.

It was now night; the short twilight of the season having disappeared while the bearers of the litter were ascending the hill.
A loud rap was given by the guide; and then he was told that
his services were no longer needed.

"I have seen much and hard service," he replied, "and well
do I know that the prudent mariner does not dismiss the pilot
until the ship is safely moored. Perhaps old Madam de Lacey
is abroad, or the captain himself may not——"

"Enough: here is one who will answer all our questions."

The portal was opened, and a man appeared on its threshold, holding a light. The appearance of the porter was not, however, of the most encouraging aspect. A certain air, which can neither be assumed nor gotten rid of, proclaimed him a son of the ocean, while a wooden limb, which served to prop a portion of his still square and athletic body, sufficiently proved he was one who had not attained the experience of his hardy calling without some bodily risk. His countenance, as he held the light above his head, to scan the persons of those without, was dogmatic, scowling, and a little fierce. He was not long, however, in recognising the cripple, of whom he unceremoniously demanded the object of what he was pleased to term " such a night squall."

" Here is a wounded mariner," returned the female, with tones so tremulous that they instantly softened the heart of the nautical Cerberus, " who is come to claim hospitality of a brother in the service, and shelter for the night  We would speak with Captain Henry de Lacey."

" Then you have struck soundings on the right coast, madam," returned the tar, " as Master Paul, here, will say in the name of his father, no less than in that of the sweet lady his mother; not forgetting old madam his grandam, who is no fresh-water fish herself, for that matter."

" That he will," said a fine manly youth of some seventeen years who wore the attire of one who was already in training for the seas, and who was looking curiously over the shoulder of the elderly seaman. " I will acquaint my father of the visit, and, Richard, do you seek out a proper berth for our guests without delay."

This order, which was given with the air of one who had been accustomed to act for himself, and to speak with authority, was instantly obeyed. The apartment selected by Richard was the ordinary parlour of the dwelling. Here, in a few moments, the litter was deposited; the bearers were then dismissed, and the female only was left, with its tenant and rude attendant, who had not hesitated to give them so frank a reception. The latter busied himself in trimming the lights, and in replenishing a bright wood fire, taking care, at the same time, that no unnecessary vacuum should occur in the discourse to render the brief interval, necessary for the appearance of his superiors, tedious. During this state of things an inner door was opened, the youth already named leading the way for the three principal personages of the mansion.

First came a middle-aged, athletic man, in the naval undress of a captain of the New States. His look was calm and his step still firm, though time and exposure were beginning to sprinkle his head with grey. He wore one arm in a sling, a proof that his service was still recent; on the other leaned a lady, in whose matronly mien, but still blooming cheek and bright eyes, were to be traced most of the ripened beauties of her sex. Behind them followed a third, a female also, whose step was less elastic, but whose person continued to exhibit the evidences of a peaceful evening to the troubled day of life. The three courteously saluted the stranger, delicately refraining from making any precipitate allusion to the motive of her visit. Their reserve seemed by no means unnecessary; for by the manifest agitation which shook the shattered frame of one who appeared as much sinking with grief as infirmity, it was too apparent that the unknown lady needed a little time to collect her energies, and to arrange her thoughts.

She wept long and bitterly, as if alone; nor did she essay to speak until further silence would have become suspicious. Then, drying her eyes, and with cheeks on which a bright hectic spot was seated, her voice was heard for the first time by her wondering hosts.

"You may deem this visit an intrusion," she said; "but one, whose will is my law, would be brought hither."

"Wherefore?" mildly asked the officer, observing that her voice was already choked

"To die!" was the whispered, husky answer.

A common start manifested the surprise of her auditors; and then the gentleman arose, and approaching the litter, he gently drew aside a curtain, exposing its hitherto unseen tenant to the examination of all in the room. There was understanding in the look that met his gaze, though death was too plainly stamped on the lineaments of the wounded man. His eye alone seemed still to belong to earth; for, while all around it appeared already to be sunk into the helplessness of the last stage of human debility, that was still bright, intelligent, and glowing—it might almost have been described as glaring.

"Is there aught in which we can contribute to your comfort, or to your wishes?" asked Captain de Lacey, after a long and solemn pause, during which all around the litter had mournfully contemplated the sad spectacle of sinking mortality.

The smile of the dying man was ghastly, though tenderness and sorrow were singularly and fearfully combined in its expression. He answered not; but his eyes wandered from face to face, until they became riveted, by a species of charm, on the countenance of the oldest of the two females. His gaze was met by a look as settled as his own; so evident was the sympathy which existed between the two, that it could not escape the observation of the spectators.

"Mother!" said the officer, with affectionate concern; "my mother! what troubles you?"

"Henry—Gertrude," answered the venerable parent, extending her arms to her offspring, as if she asked support; "my children, your doors have been opened to one who has a claim to enter them. Oh! it is in these terrible moments, when passion is asleep and our weakness most apparent, in these moments of debility and disease, that nature so strongly manifests its impres sion! I see it all in that fading countenance, in those sunken features, where so little is left but the last lingering look of family and kindred!"

"Kindred!" exclaimed Captain de Lacey. "Of what affinity is our guest?"

"A brother!" answered the lady, dropping her head on her bosom, as if she had proclaimed a degree of consanguinity which gave pain as well as pleasure.

The stranger, too much overcome himself to speak, made a joyful gesture of assent; but he never averted a gaze that seemed destined to maintain its direction so long as life should lend it intelligence.

"A brother!" repeated her son, in unfeigned astonishment. "I knew you had a brother: but I had thought him dead a boy."

"'T was so I long believed, myself; though frightful glimpses of the contrary have often beset me; but now the truth is too plain, in that fading visage and those fallen features, to be misunderstood. Poverty and misfortune divided us. I suppose we thought each other dead."

Another feeble gesture proclaimed the assent of the wounded man.

"There is no further mystery. Henry, the stranger is thy uncle—my brother—once, my pupil!"

"I could wish to see him under happier circumstances," returned the officer, with a seaman's frankness; "but, as a kinsman, he is welcome. Poverty, at least, shall no longer divide you."

"Look, Henry—Gertrude!" added the mother, veiling her own eyes as she spoke, "that face is no stranger to you. See ye not the sad ruins of one ye both fear and love?"

Wonder kept her children mute, though they looked until sight became confused, so long and intense was their examination.

Then a hollow sound which came from the chest of the stranger, caused them to start; and, when his low, but distinct enunciation reached their ears, doubt and perplexity vanished.

"Wilder," he said, with an effort in which his utmost strength appeared exerted, "I have come to ask the last office at your hands."

"Captain Heidegger!" exclaimed the officer.

"The Red Rover!" murmured the younger Mrs. de Lacey, involuntarily recoiling a pace from the litter.

"The Red Rover!" repeated her son, pressing nigher with ungovernable curiosity.

"Laid by the heels at last!" bluntly observed Fid, stumping up towards the group, without relinquishing the tongs which he had kept in constant use, as an apology for remaining in the room.

"I had long hid my repentance, and my shame, together," continued the dying man, when the momentary surprise had a little abated; "but this war drew me from my concealment. Our country needed us both. and both has she had! You have served as one who never offended might serve; but a cause so holy was not to be tarnished by a name like mine. May the little I have done for good be remembered, when the world speaks of the evil of my hands! Sister—mother—pardon."

"May that God, who forms his creatures with such fearful natures, look mercifully on all our weaknesses!" exclaimed the weeping Mrs. de Lacey, bowing to her knees, and lifting her hands and eyes to Heaven. "Oh, brother! brother! you have been trained in the holy mystery of your redemption, and need not now be told on what Rock to place your hopes of pardon!"

"Had I never forgotten those precepts, my name would still be known with honour. But—Wilder!" he added, with startling energy, "Wilder!"

All eyes were eagerly bent on the speaker. His hand was

holding a roll, on which he had been reposing, as on a pillow. With a supernatural effort, his form rose on the litter ; and, with both hands elevated above his head, he let fall before him that blazonry of intermingled stripes, with its blue field of rising stars, a glow of high exultation illumining every feature of his face, as in his day of pride.

" Wilder !" he repeated, laughing hysterically, " we have triumphed !"—He fell backward, without motion, the exulting lineaments settling in the gloom of death, as shadows obscure the smiling brightness of the sun.

**THE END.**

# GLOSSARY OF NAUTICAL TERMS

Common shipboard terms such as *tide, anchor, rudder, port,* and so forth are omitted from the following list. The tense of the verbs and the number of the nouns are reproduced as they appear in the text of *The Red Rover.* Most of the words can be found in either or both of the two standard marine dictionaries most often cited in the nineteenth century: William Falconer's *A New Universal Dictionary of the Marine* (1769) and W. H. Smyth's *The Sailor's Word-Book* (1867).

*aback*—condition of the sails when the wind strikes their front surfaces and drives them back against the masts; said also of the ship to which this has happened

*abaft*—in the stern section of a ship

*a-beam*—in a line at right angles to the ship's length, opposite to the center of her side

*aft*—in or near the hinder part or stern of a ship

*after-shroud*—the rigging (sets of ropes) leading from the top of the main mast or the mizzenmast

*after-yards*—the horizontal bars on the main and mizzenmasts

*aloft*—on or to a higher part of the ship (the deck as opposed to the hold; the rigging or masthead as opposed to the deck)

*alow*—in or into a lower part of the vessel (to the deck from the rigging; to the hold or cabin from the deck)

*athwart*—from side to side of a ship

*azimuth*—arc connecting zenith and horizon, or quadrant of a great circle of the sphere passing through these two points; in either case, used in navigational computations *backstay*—long rope fastened to the side of the ship, used to brace the mast against pressure from the wind in the sails

*beams*—horizontal transverse timbers running across a ship and supporting the deck

*bearing down on*—proceeding speedily toward

*belay*—make fast; or stop, quit

*bent*—tied, fastened

*berths*—bunks, shelves, or other sleeping places on a ship; figuratively, any resting places

*bight*—the loop in a rope

*bilboes*—shackles attached to an iron bar which, in turn, is fastened to the floor; used to confine prisoners

*blunderbusses*—short guns with large bores for firing many small balls or slugs; good for close-range combat

*boat-hook*—pole with an iron hook and spike on one end; used to push, pull, or maneuver a small boat

*boatswain*—ship's officer in charge of sails and rigging who summons crew to duty with his pipe or whistle

*bobstays*—ropes that pull downward on the bowsprit (the pole projecting forward from the bow) ; used to counteract the upward pull of ropes from the foremast

*bolts*—stout metal pins, not necessarily threaded, used to hold parts of the ship together

*bomb-ketch*—a small, sturdy, two-masted vessel carrying one or two mortars for bombarding purposes

*booms*—long poles used to extend something (such as a sail) farther or to carry a rope out over a greater distance

*bouse*—pull, haul

*bowline*—rope fastened to perpendicular edge of a square sail and used to hold the sail forward for precision when sailing close-hauled (*q.v.*)

*bowsprit*—large spar running out beyond the bow of a ship, to which lines bracing the foremast are attached

*brace-block*—a pulley attached to a brace (iron strap from which a moving part, such as the rudder, is slung) *bulkheads*—partitions dividing the hold of a ship

*bunt*—center part of a sail, deliberately made baggy to catch the wind

*carlings*—smaller timbers (about 5″ square) perpendicular to the larger cross timbers supporting the deck

*carrick-bend*—knot used to join the ends of two large ropes or hawsers

*cat-heads*—posts projecting horizontally from the sides of the bow of a ship, used to keep the anchor and anchor cable clear of the ship

*clapped a stopper on*—checked or put a check on

*clear offing*—fair weather in the visible distance seaward beyond a shore or anchorage

*clew down*—lower (a sail)

*clew-lines*—ropes in block-and-tackle assembly used to draw up sails to be furled (the *clew* is the lower corner of the sail to which these lines are attached)

*clew up*—raise (a sail)

*close-hauled*—having sails tightly set in order to steer as nearly against the wind as possible

*coasters*—vessels, or their crews, which sail along the shore

*colours*—flags or ensigns of a ship

*coming foul*—becoming entangled

*counter*—the curved part of the stern of a ship

*cross-trees*—two horizontal crosspieces that spread the upper shrouds (*q.v.*)

*Davy Jones*—spirit of the sea; deity of the ocean floor

*dead off shore*—straight out from the shore

*double-decker*—a ship with two decks above the water line

*doubled*—sailed round or passed a cape or point so that the ship's course has turned back on itself

*dry rub*—sticking along the skids or ways during a launching; figuratively, an obstacle to one's plans

*earing*—rope used to fasten upper canvas of a sail to a yard-arm (*q.v.*)

*eboarding-nettings*—network of ropes on the side of a ship to prevent enemies from entering

*fake*—one of the circles or windings of a hawser lying in a coil

*fall off*—to fail to keep in the thrust of the wind

*fid*—either a conical pin (10–20 inches long) of hardwood, used to separate the strands of a rope for splicing, or a square bar of wood or iron used to support the weight of the crossarm of a mast

*fidded*—secured and held fast to a mast with a fid (*q.v.*)

*Flemish account*—an unsatisfactory report

*fly-away*—a delusive appearance of land; a mirage

*flying-jib*—an additional jib sail set ahead of the regular jib (*q.v.*)

*for'ard*—toward the bow of a ship ("forward")

*fore-course*—the largest, and lowest, sail on the foremast

*fore-foot*—forward part of a ship where the keel and bow section meet

*foundering*—sinking

*fresh*—having a strong force; said of a hard wind

*full and by*—sailing closely in line with the wind, within six points on compass

*furled*—rolled up and tied

*gaff*—either a staff tipped with an iron hook or a spar used to extend the spread of a sail

*galleon*—a short, high-decked warship of Spanish origin; also used to denote various types of ships used by Spaniards in their trade with the New World

*gammonings*—set of ropes running from the bowsprit (*q.v.*) to the cut-water or prow (the blade which divides the water before it strikes the bow)

*garnet*—a block-and-tackle assembly swung from the main mast for hoisting light supplies aboard a ship

*gasket*—small rope used to tie a furled (*q.v.*) sail to the horizontal arm of a mast *gathering way*—beginning to feel the force of the wind on the sails

*get in at the cabin windows*—acquire responsibilities without experience; said of ship's officer commissioned without previous shipboard experience

*grapplings*—fastenings to a ship; or, the actions involved in attaching something to a ship or holding two ships together

*gripes*—ropes or canvas bands that secure a lifeboat

*halyards*—ropes or block-and-tackle assemblies used for raising and lowering sails

*hamper*—equipment which, though necessary to a ship, is occasionally cumbersome or in the way

*handspikes*—wooden bars used as levers

*harping*—forward parts of the wales (sides) of a ship that are thicker than the rest to withstand the shock of the waves

*hatch*—square or oblong opening in the deck through which cargo is loaded or unloaded

*hawse*—that part of the bow into which holes are cut for entry of the anchor cables

*head and heels*—bow and stern, front and rear

*head-lands*—high points or promontories projecting into the sea

*head sail*—general name for any sail attached to the foremast or bowsprit (*q.v.*)

*head-way*—motion ahead or forward; rate of progress

*head-yards*—horizontal spars supporting the sails on the foremast

*heave in*—pull in

*heaving-to*—bringing a ship to a stand-still by setting the sails so as to counteract each other

*helm*—lever or wheel controlling rudder; sometimes, the whole steering mechanism

*horse-bucket*—covered water pail

*hulk*—a ship or its hull; also, the hull of a disabled or dismantled ship

*in the wind's teeth*—directly into the wind

*jewel-block*—pulley assembly at extreme end of a yard (*q.v.*), through which a halyard (*q.v.*) passes

*jib*—a triangular sail stretching from a spar on the bow to the foremast

*jolly-boat*—a short, stubby, and very sturdy boat, smaller than a cutter, slung from the stern of a ship; used for ferrying supplies and personnel to and from shore

*Jonah*—person to whose presence bad luck is often attributed

*jury*—temporary, make-shift; usually combined with another word: *jury-mast, jury-rig*

*kedge*—small anchor with an iron stock

*ketch*—strongly-built two-masted vessel of 100–250 tons burden, sometimes used for coastal shipping, sometimes for naval bombardment (see *bomb-ketch*)

*kites*—the highest sails of a ship, usually set only in a light wind

*knighthead*—one of the two large timbers rising obliquely from the keel to support the bowsprit (*q.v.*)

*lanyards*—short pieces of rope fastened to anything, either to secure it or to serve as a handle for it

*larboard*—left side of a ship

*lay on your oars*—to rest

*lead*—a weight (often of the metal lead) suspended by a string to determine the depth of the water

*lee*—the sheltered side of any object; the side away from the wind

*lee-earing*—an earing (*q.v.*) on the lee (*q.v.*) side

*lee-shore*—side of an island or cape protected from the wind

*lee-swifter*—a guy line to brace a mast (or some other assembly), on the lee (*q.v.*) side of the ship

*lochs*—partially land-locked arms of the sea

*logg'd*—recorded distance travelled by a ship

*long-boat*—the largest boat on a sailing ship

*lubber*—a clumsy seaman, or an unseamanlike person

*luffed*—brought the prow of the ship more nearly into the wind; one *luffs* during the process of *tacking* (*q.v.*)

*lugger*—a small vessel, of two or three masts, with four-cornered sails

*lug-sails*—four-sided sails hung, lengthwise of a ship, from a yard-arm (*q.v.*) tipped obliquely forward

*mainsail*—the largest sail on a ship

*main-top*—the top (small platform) of the main mast

*manning*—staffing a ship or boat with the necessary crew; or, the activity of the men operating a ship

*marlingspike*—tapered iron tool used to separate the strands of a rope for splicing purposes (often spelled *marlin-spike*)

*messmate*—companion at meals; one of ten or twelve crew members who eat at the same table or sitting

*mizzen*—a sail hung from the mizzenmast (*q.v.*), or a small fore-and-aft (not transverse) sail set behind the mizzenmast

*mizzen-channels*—broad, thick planks, projecting horizontally from a ship's side abreast of the mizzenmast (*q.v.*)

*mizzenmast*—mast farthest to rear on a three-masted vessel (also spelled *mizenmast*)

*moored*—fastened or secured, docked or anchored

*moorings*—equipment for or location of fastening, securing, docking, or anchoring

*mud-hooks*—slang for *anchors*

*night-glass*—telescope with low *f*-number to increase its light-gathering power for use at night

*overhauling*—overtaking, gaining upon; or slackening a rope by pulling in opposite direction

*painter*—rope attached to bow of a boat to fasten it to ship or shore; sometimes the rope used to hold anchor securely to side of ship's bow

*picaroon*—thief, pirate; or, pirate ship or privateer

*piping*—summoning to some duty or assignment by means of a whistle

*ploughing the main*—cutting briskly through the sea

*poop*—enclosed superstructure at the stern of a ship

*press*—as much sail as the state of the wind will permit a ship to carry

*quarter-deck*—part of the upper deck that extends from the stern to the closest mast, restricted to the captain and superior officers

*quarters*—sleeping areas

*rake*—sweep with shot

*ratlin*—one of the small lines fastened horizontally on a shroud (*q.v.*), used as a step to climb into the rigging

*reckoning*—estimate made of a ship's position by any of several methods of calculation

*reefed*—reduced the extent of a sail by rolling up or tying part of it

*reeve*—pass a rope through a pulley opening

*riding by a single cable*—held by a single anchor, and thus allowed to swing about as the direction of the wind changes

*rigging*—the whole complex of ropes used to support the masts and to work the sails

*roadstead*—a safe anchorage near the shore

*schooner*—relatively small sea-going vessel, usually with two masts unless specially constructed for three or four

*scope*—length of the anchor cable on which a ship swings

*scud*—run before a gale with little or no sail

*sculls*—oars

*scuppers*—openings in a ship's side, at deck level, to allow water to run out

*shape a course*—determine or direct a ship's course

*sheer*—turn aside, alter direction, swerve to either side of a course

*sheered-off*—changed directions; moved off a previously held course *sheet*—rope or cable that regulates the angle at which a sail is set in relation to the direction of the wind

*ship-shape*—arranged properly; in good nautical form or order

*shroud*—set of ropes running to top of a mast to relieve the lateral strain on it; it is part of the ship's standing rigging

*slack*—that part of a rope or sail that hangs loose; or, a stretch of quiet water

*slaver*—a slave ship

*slip*—to allow an anchor cable to run out quickly, especially when leaving an anchorage hastily

*sloop*—small, single-masted vessel, with sail rigged lengthwise (formerly armed, at times, for naval service)

*slushed*—greased a mast with tallow or fat

*snug*—trim, neat, compact, comfortable

*spanker*—small sail, fore-and-aft (lengthwise), set near stern of a ship and swung on a boom

*spanker-boom*—the pole attached to the bottom of a spanker (*q.v.*)

*spars*—general term for all gaffs, booms, and wooden poles other than masts

*square-sails*—four-sided sails supported by spars set across a vessel

*stanchions*—upright posts supporting a deck

*starboard*—the right side of a ship

*stay-sails*—triangular sails set on a hawser or cable instead of on a mast assembly

*stow*—fill the hold with cargo; to fit up with necessities

*stretched*—sailed continuously on the same tack (*q.v.*) or in the same direction

*studding-sails*—sails set out beyond the vertical edges of the principal sail; or, in a ship rigged fore-and-aft (lengthwise) a sail behind the principal sail

*tack*—sail obliquely against the wind, first to one side of the wind and then to the other *taffrail*—a railing around the stern of a ship; or, the upper, flat part of the stern of a ship, sometimes ornamented

*tides-way*—a channel in which a tidal current runs; or, the tidal section of a river

*top-gallants*—either very high sails or tops (platforms) above the topsails

*top-hamper*—weights or encumbrances in the upper structure of a ship, *e.g.*, upper masts, sails, rigging

*trader*—a commercial vessel

*triced*—hauled up and secured with ropes; said of sails or ladders

*trimming*—adjusting a ship's balance, load, and sails

*waist*—center part of a ship

*waister*—inexperienced or aged seaman, physically unfit for work in the rigging, who works on the upper deck, usually in the waist (*q.v.*)

*warp*—move a ship by hauling on a rope attached to an anchor or fixed point ashore

*watch*—period of time for which each of the divisions of a ship's company remains on deck (four hours, except for dog-watches which are two)

*watch-coat*—heavy overcoat for cold or stormy weather at sea

*ward-room*—either the living quarters or the mess room of commissioned officers on a warship

*weather*—sail to the windward of a point

*weather-helm*—tendency in a ship under sail to turn directly into wind, requiring tiller to be set slightly windward

*weather-side*—the side of a ship toward the wind

*wedge*—raise a ship for launching by driving wooden wedge under it

*wing-and-wing*—condition of a ship sailing directly before the wind, with the foresail swung out over one side and the main sail out over the other

*yard-arm*—either end of the yard (crosspole) of a mast

*yawl*—a ship's boat, usually with four or six oars; or, a very small sailing boat

*yellow-flag*—signal of quarantine

## A NOTE ON THE EDITOR

Warren S. Walker was born in 1921 in Brooklyn, New. York. After World War II military service in Italy, he studied at the State University of New York at Albany (A.B., 1947; M.A., 1948) and at Cornell University (Ph.D., 1951). During 1961–1962 he served as Fulbright Lecturer in American Literature at Ankara University in Turkey. Now Dean of the Humanities Division at Parsons College in Fairfield, Iowa, Dr. Walker has published numerous articles in such scholarly periodicals as *American Literature, Modern Language Notes, New York Folklore Quarterly, Midwest Folklore,* and *Modern Fiction Studies.* He has edited four volumes including an edition of *The Spy* (1960) and *Twentieth-Century Short Story Explication* (1961), and is the author of *James Fenimore Cooper: An Introduction and Interpretation* (1962).